MY
SWEET
GIRL

MY
SWEET
GIRL

AMANDA JAYATISSA

BERKLEY
NEW YORK

BERKLEY
An imprint of Penguin Random House LLC
penguinrandomhouse.com

Export edition ISBN: 9780593438015

Library of Congress Cataloging-in-Publication Data

Names: Jayatissa, Amanda, author.
Title: My sweet girl / Amanda Jayatissa.
Description: First edition. | New York : Berkley, 2021.
Identifiers: LCCN 2021019902 (print) | LCCN 2021019903 (ebook) |
ISBN 9780593335086 (hardcover) | ISBN 9780593335109 (ebook)
Subjects: GSAFD: Suspense fiction.
Classification: LCC PR9440.9.J36 M9 2021 (print) | LCC PR9440.9.J36 (ebook) |
DDC 813/.6—dc23
LC record available at https://lccn.loc.gov/2021019902
LC ebook record available at https://lccn.loc.gov/2021019903

Printed in the United States of America
1st Printing

Title page art: Vines © higyou / Shutterstock
Book design by Alison Cnockaert

To my husband, CJ. Please accept this dedication as a formal apology for all the times I've been a Paloma to you.

1

THERE'S A SPECIAL PLACE in hell for incompetent customer service agents, and it's right between monsters who stick their bare feet up on airplane seats and mansplainers. Fake hair, false smiles, synthetic blazers that pool around their middles while they tell you that yes, they would love to help you, and thank you for your patience, and no, sorry for the inconvenience caused but they can't seem to find your paperwork even if it punched them square in the jaw.

I inhaled. *Be nice, Paloma. Be kind.*

My agent's name today is Bethany. Bethany, with badly dyed hair so red it looked like Elmo had a love child with Jessica Rabbit, and two buttons undone on her much-too-tight polka-dot polyester blouse. She smiled as if she had all the time in this crazy world, her gaze not wavering from the screen in front of her, refusing to meet my eye even when she knew she was royally messing up. She had a smear of livid coral lipstick on her teeth. It clashed hard against her hair.

My hands were trembling slightly, so I made sure they weren't on the table in front of me. I hate how they do that when I'm angry. I hate it when I'm angry. It makes it hard to think straight. And I needed to think straight right now. I couldn't have that cunning, two-faced soon-to-be-ex-roommate of mine getting in my head. The actual nerve of Arun.

I kept thinking back to that no-good loser's grin. The one he wore when he told me that he knew. *He knew.* I'd made it eighteen god-damned years in this country, and now this absolute moron who tears up when he talks about his mother's aloo paratha had the gall, no, the actual balls to try to ruin it for me? He definitely didn't know who he was messing with.

I mean, I would fucking kill him. Wrap my fingers around his blackmailing little throat and smother the life out of him. How dare he? I can't believe I actually felt sorry for him. *I really can't afford any more rent than this, please. You have to help me out.* He totally played his poor-little-immigrant card, and I bought it all up. I knew what it was like to depend on the charity of others. To have your life decided by someone who just woke up one morning and thought they'd throw you a line.

And how the hell does he go ahead and repay me? He snoops around through my things. Finds out my worst secret. Demands I buy his silence.

Another pang of anger ricocheted through me.

I double-checked that the letter was still in my pocket. Good. I know it didn't do much to have it with me, now that Arun had already read it, but it gave me the tiniest bit of comfort having it back in my possession.

My hands gave another shudder. I sat on them and turned my focus back to Bethany. She shouldn't see me this upset. She sure as hell couldn't find out that my shit-bag of a roommate was one step away from ruining a life I had already sacrificed so much for.

Concentrate, Paloma.

I gave her my best smile. "Technology, huh? Supposed to make our lives easier . . ."

Score. Her relief was palpable, like a deer realizing that the oncoming headlights weren't going to run it over. I wasn't one of those assholes who would embarrass her by making a scene in this deathly quiet, needlessly ostentatious bank. Fair enough that I was dressed like a bum in sweatpants and an oversized sweatshirt—it's not like I was in the best frame of mind to choose an outfit that would give bank tellers a good first impression of me, but I was making up for it by being so nice my jaw ached. *Model minority*, every part of me screamed. I wasn't here to cause any issues. Just take care of my request and I'll be on my way.

She smiled again, lipstick bleeding outside her lip line, as she keyed in something at a pace that made sloths look like Olympic sprinters. I resisted the urge to sigh out loud. Take your time, why don't you, Bethany? I mean, it's just my entire goddamned life that's riding on your inability to look through a file.

"So, there seems to be a bit of confusion here. One of your accounts, it's a joint checking account, I believe, is overdrawn." Well, so are your eyebrows, Bethany, but you don't hear me making a scene about it.

Don't be mean, Paloma. My mother's voice was always in my ear. She was right. No one ever got what they needed by being an asshole.

"There's a hold on the rest of the funds. We'd need form 38F to be filled out and countersigned by"—she hesitated a little, her eyes flickering from the screen to my face—"a Mr. and Mrs. Evans?" My parents. Great. There was a better chance of Arun and me spontaneously breaking out into a Bollywood dance number when I got home. They weren't signing anything for me anytime soon.

I arranged my face so that it showed nothing but amicability. I'm your friend, it said. I'm your sorority sister. I'm the girl next door who baked cookies and gave you pointers on how to grow your hair thick and shiny, just like mine. Whatever it took to get this done with already.

"If you check, I'm sure you'll see that access was transferred over to me a few months ago."

"Um." Bethany blinked into the screen. "I'm sorry, I'm new." Her chubby fingers were trembling slightly on the mouse.

Goddamn it, Bethany. You're killing me here.

"We've all been there, don't worry. You're doing great. But if you could please just check." I managed a little laugh. "It's just that it's a bit of an emergency right now, that's all."

I know . . . Arun's leer clawed its way back into my head. *I read the letter . . . I know what you did . . .*

I didn't care how much cash it took for him to disappear from my life. I'd give him every single cent I had. But Bethany just wasn't cutting me a break.

"If you could please give me a few minutes . . ."

"Take your time, I've nowhere to be." My heart was beating hard. I just needed my money. There had been no transfers made from my parents in the last two months, and now I was being bled dry by my double-crossing roommate.

"I'm really sorry, Ms. Evans." Bethany's coral lips started to tremble. Great. Just great. Now I'm the bitch who made this poor girl cry. I didn't want to make her life miserable. Don't get me wrong, I'm no saint. But I know what it's like to be the new girl. The girl who has no clue. Who makes everyone impatient. Hell, most of us have been a Bethany at some point in our lives. Admittedly, I've done it without a hack dye job, but still.

"I—I could try again but the system won't let me override it. I could give you a printout of the form now, if you could just get it signed?"

Fuck me. I could demand to speak to the manager, but there was no way someone who actually knew what they were doing would let me slip through the cracks. Damn my parents.

"Thank you, Bethany. You've been great."

Bethany gave me a relieved smile.

"Thank you, Ms. Evans. You've been so patient. It's my first week and it's taken me a while to find my footing." Nothing was more obvious in the world, but at least I wasn't at risk of setting off her waterworks again.

My hands gave another tremble.

"Oh, please, call me Paloma. And don't worry, you'll get the hang of it sooner than later." I mean, she would literally make customers kill themselves so they wouldn't have to deal with her again, but there was no point in telling her that, was there?

"Is there anything else I can do for you today?"

Know a way to get rid of a roommate who's trying to destroy your life?

"Not today. Thanks again."

How the hell was I supposed to shut Arun up now?

My whole body felt like it was vibrating as I stood up and put my phone in my pocket. I double-checked that the letter was still in there. Good.

I didn't have many options left. Maybe I could try reasoning with him again. Keep a closer handle on my rage this time.

I just really needed a drink first. I know, I know, it's a cliché. And Nina, my therapist, would *not* be pleased if she found out. I can hear her voice in my head right now—*You can't drink on this prescription, understand?* But I wasn't going to get shit-faced tonight. A shot or two would help me think straight, that's all. Besides, wasn't it more cliché to not do something simply because it was a cliché? And Nina's voice admonishing me at every sip was penance enough.

2

THE SHADOWS FROM THE torch Maya held under her chin made her smile look evil, like the devil mask hung in the assembly hall to ward off the evil eye.

We were all too excited to sleep, so Maya called all the girls to her bunk to tell us ghost stories. I didn't really want to listen. I'm too old to believe in ghosts. But I didn't want to be the only one in bed when everyone else was all the way on the other side of the dormitory.

Lihini grabbed my hand and squeezed it. I gave it a squeeze back. She loved ghost stories, which I didn't really understand. Why would anyone want to be afraid on purpose?

"Relax, Paloma," she mouthed. I usually got annoyed when people told me to relax. Like saying the words was enough to make me forget what was upsetting me in the first place. As though ghosts and demons would just go away if we simply relaxed. But Lihini was my best friend. I could never get angry with her. I scooted a little closer to her on the floor. There was no such thing as ghosts. It just made me feel safe to be near her.

Maya needed to hurry up. If we got caught out of our beds, we would definitely be scolded. Maybe even punished. They might even cancel the visit tomorrow.

I took a deep breath and shook my head. They would never do that. We hadn't gotten many visitors to the orphanage in a few months now. Tomorrow was important. Everyone told us so—our headmaster Perera sir, Miss Chandra, even Miss Sarah, our English teacher. We were to be on our best behaviour and make sure we knew exactly what we were supposed to do or say. Miss Chandra supervised the rehearsal today. Everything had to be perfect, and we were so excited that none of us could sleep.

Of course Maya would decide this was the best time to make it all about her. Sometimes I wondered if she even wanted to be adopted. She needed to be more responsible than this. She was twelve now, same as me. It's not like we were little children anymore.

"She walks slowly. Her feet are bare and dirty and covered in scratches. She wears a long, white dress." Maya purposely made her voice into a throaty whisper so every one of us leaned forward, barely breathing.

I knew this story. Vana-Mohini, or Mohini, as we call it. We've all heard it a million times. We've all told it a million times. But I still held tight to Maya's words.

"There's blood under her nails, and they are long and sharp, like talons." She made a sudden clawing motion, and Lihini leaped back, her hands over her mouth.

We all giggled nervously.

"And her long, black hair hangs over her face, like this." The torch flickered as Maya messed her hair over her face so just her eyes glinted through in the dim yellow light.

"Mohini walks only in the night, revealing herself to people who are all by themselves. *Help me. Help me*, she begs." Maya made her voice high and raspy now, like when the chalk slips when you're writing on a blackboard.

"Some people say Mohini's eyes are red. Red as blood. And when you look into them, you can see straight into hell. And if you stop to help her, she smiles, and before you know it—"

Maya dropped the torch and lunged forward, wrapping her hands around Lihini's throat. Lihini couldn't help it this time. Her small scream rang like an alarm through the dormitory.

I pulled Lihini away from Maya and put my arms around her. If I could have slapped Maya, I definitely would, but there wasn't time.

"*Haiyyo!* Quickly, everyone, to bed before we get caught," I hissed, getting Lihini to her feet and pushing her into her bunk.

Thankfully, the other girls followed.

We all lay very, very still for a few minutes. I could hear nervous panting echoing through the dormitory. Maya really did give everyone a shock. But thankfully none of the matrons came.

What on earth was she thinking? Getting us into trouble the night before Mr. and Mrs. Evans got here. Those were their names. Mr. and Mrs. Evans. Perera sir told us so we could memorise them. Evans—like when Miss Sarah told us about Mary Ann Evans, who went by George Eliot, who wrote *The Mill on the Floss*. I suppose I could understand why you would want to pretend to be someone else. But I could never, ever understand why someone wouldn't want to go by the name Evans. It was beautiful.

I whispered it out loud.

Mr. and Mrs. Evans. I hoped they liked us. And me. I really hoped they liked me.

"You okay, *sudhu*?" I called out to Lihini in the top bunk. She usually climbed down into mine after we offed the lights, but we had to be careful after the scream. We both knew it would be stupid to mess up anything for tomorrow.

"Ah, are you scared?" Maya sounded delighted.

"No way! Why would a made-up ghost scare her?" I spoke up for Lihini.

"Mohini is not made up. She walks around here in the orphanage also!" Maya replied, a little too loudly.

I could hear gasps from all the bunks. It gave me goose bumps too.

"It's true!" someone else said. "She's here in the orphanage."

This was really too much.

"Maya, stop scaring everyone, *men*. We need to sleep and be rested properly for tomorrow." I'm not usually such a Goody Two-shoes. Lihini always told me that I'm the exact opposite. Tomorrow was just too important, and it really, really annoyed me that Maya didn't seem to understand that.

"Okay, Miss," she giggled. I heard a few of the girls giggle as well. I ignored them and shut my eyes.

But I couldn't fall asleep.

I knew I was just wishing. And that just like ghosts, wishes were make-believe too. But I wished and wished and wished that the visit tomorrow would go well. That Mr. and Mrs. Evans would like me so much that they would want to make me their daughter.

Perera sir had told us that the Evanses were from America, but he didn't say anything else. I wondered what they would be like. Would they be tall or short? Have blond hair or brown? Would they say *what's up?* and *guys* like we saw when we were allowed to watch TV?

I don't know how long I lay there imagining them when I heard someone climb off their bunk. I knew it wasn't Lihini. I could hear her breathing from above me.

It was dark in the dormitory, so I stuck my head out to see who it was. If it was Maya trying to scare us again, I'd have no choice but to complain to Miss Chandra tomorrow morning.

But it wasn't Maya.

It was Shanika.

I should have known. We gave up trying to stop her sleepwalking ages ago.

She hadn't joined us when we were telling ghost stories. Why should she, when it seemed like she was barely alive herself?

Shanika's eyes were unfocused and she was humming softly as she floated past the beds and towards the door. She held on to the dirty plastic doll that she took with her almost everywhere. The scars covering the side of her face seemed to glow, even in the darkness.

I strained to hear the words, even though I knew what they were. We sang it almost every day at the orphanage. We didn't have an official anthem or anything, but if we did, I'm certain it would be this. It's one of my favourites, when it wasn't being sung by Shanika in the middle of the night.

> *Que sera, sera*
> *Whatever will be, will be*
> *The future's not ours to see*

I broke out in goose bumps again, though I wasn't quite sure why.

3

SAN FRANCISCO, CA

THE NEAT SHOTS OF rum did nothing to dull my anger. If anything, it just made it throb and echo inside me, so it was all I could do to even get back to my apartment, I was trembling so much.

Screw him. This was the last thing I needed. I wish I had never met him. He'd seemed so meek when he responded to my ad online. Almost fearful. I practically held his damn chai for him while he stuck the knife in my back.

My keys rattled against the door. It took me a few tries to get them in. It was the anger, not the rum. I pushed my therapist's disappointed expression out of my mind. Definitely not the rum.

It was dark inside. Had he left? Fuck. I'd asked him to stay put. But then again, I had been gone for much longer than I said I'd be. Rum always made me lose track of time.

"Arun?" I called out. I was surprised at how much my voice trembled.

"Arun, you in here?"

I fumbled with the lights in the entryway. It was a clear line of sight from the front door into the kitchen.

The asshole had fallen asleep, his head resting on the table. How the hell could he sleep at a time like this? I mean, my entire life rested in his despicable, blackmailing hands, and he decided to take a nap?

"Arun, look, I think I have an idea about how we could work this out." I didn't really, but I needed to buy as much time as I could until I figured out how to gather up enough money to have him disappear from my life.

He didn't move.

I crossed over to the kitchen. My feet felt unsteady beneath me. Focus, Paloma. You can't afford to be a drunk bitch right now.

"Arun?"

There wasn't as much light in the kitchen as there was in the living room.

"Arun? Hey?"

He didn't stir. I rapped the table with my palm, hoping to wake him, but my fingers came away wet.

What the fuck, Arun? I hoped he hadn't gone and spilled curry all over my spotless kitchen again. The last time he decided to make butter chicken, the walls were covered in a splatter of neon orange that took a round of bleach to remove.

I reached over to the wall and turned on the kitchen light.

There was a dark puddle on the table, around Arun's head.

"Arun?"

I shook him on the shoulder first, but he didn't move, so I grabbed the collar of his shirt and pulled him back on his chair.

His empty black eyes stared out. Blank, and unfocused, and definitely, surely dead.

Oh, fuck.

I stumbled backwards, grabbing on to the wall to steady myself. It was crimson when I pulled my hand away, the shape of those Thanksgiving turkeys we drew in the fall. My hand was sticky, like it was covered in glue. No sound escaped me, but I was screaming with every fiber of my being.

I needed to get it off me.

I rushed to the bathroom and yanked open the faucet. My hands shivered on their own as I held them under the cold water. Rust swirled down the drain in ribbons. Thick. Brown. Sticky.

What the fuck was happening?

Focus. I was stern with myself as I looked in the mirror.

How the hell had this happened? Healthy, blackmailing Indian boys don't just drop dead. There was blood. That meant—

My body went cold.

That meant he must have been killed.

And that meant that the killer could be in the apartment right now. Oh, fuck.

I haphazardly looked around the bathroom for anything I could use as a weapon.

Something moved behind me, I could see it in the mirror.

I whipped around.

That's when I saw her. *Mohini*. It was just for a second. A fraction of a second, but I knew. I knew she was back. Her black hair, her pale face. All these years I had spent trying to convince myself that she didn't exist, that she was a ghost from my childhood, just a product of an overactive imagination, and now here she was.

Fresh waves of fear crashed down on me. I had to get out of here. I had to get out. Or I'd be next.

I bolted to the door and just about made it to my corridor when I sensed her behind me. I was moving and frozen all at the same time.

The elevator was too far. I ran to the stairwell. I needed to leave. I needed to get as far away as possible.

I had just reached the steps when I felt her fingers around my neck. Felt her breathing in my ear. I couldn't fight her again. I let the floor open up and swallow me whole.

4

SAN FRANCISCO, CA

THE WOMAN'S BREATH WAS tuna melt and cigarettes as she leaned over me, her sparse eyebrows pulled together in annoyance. I knew her. She lived a few doors down.

"You alive?" she asked. I tried not to gag. My head was pounding.

She held her toddler to her hip. How the hell was the kid not throwing up at the smell of her breath? It was like something had crawled into her mouth and died. I tried to answer her, but the words were stuck in my throat.

I fought my way back to my senses and pushed myself into a sitting position on the floor like it was the most natural thing in the world to be found passed out on the stairway of my apartment building.

I guess my neighbor didn't seem to think so.

"I told you that I'd call 911 if I found you passed out in the hallway again. I don't need this"—she stabbed a finger in my direction—"around my child."

If constipation were a person, this is what they would look like. I remembered how she watched me drop a bag of groceries when I staggered home last week. She didn't even offer to pick up the oranges that bounced towards her.

I smiled weakly.

"I'm okay. Just not feeling too great."

Her kid was starting to fidget, and she carried a large reusable shopping bag in her other hand. She didn't have time for the irresponsible woman down the hall who drank too much and passed out in full view of her child.

Except—

The reality of what happened slapped me hard in the face.

I didn't just pass out. I had seen her. Mohini. But that couldn't be. She didn't exist. I had spent years in therapy understanding just that. Mohini was just a story we told ourselves in the orphanage. She wasn't real.

Then what the hell had I seen in my apartment last night?

Fear flooded through me, the pounding in my head getting harder and faster. My front tooth started to hurt.

Arun.

Arun was dead.

I took a deep breath and tried to steady myself. What the hell happened?

Fuck. Fuck. Fuck.

I pressed my thumb against my tooth to dull the ache.

"Anyway, the cops should be here soon. I really suggest you take a good look at yourself and think about how you could turn your life around."

Oh god, please make her stop talking.

I rubbed my face.

Wait, the cops were coming?

I pulled out my phone, thank god it was still in my pocket, and checked the time. It was 6:48 a.m. Fuck, I'd been out cold on the stairwell all night. Had I really passed out for so long?

"I'm going to wait for them downstairs. This behavior stops today, you hear me? I can't be raising my child around drunks like you."

But I wasn't drunk. I'd just seen my roommate slumped dead across the kitchen table. I wanted to cry. What the fuck was even happening?

I just needed the spinning to stop so I could think.

The texts, a voice broke through the throbbing in my head. *Delete the goddamned texts.*

I opened my inbox and found the conversation I needed right at the top.

I'm going to fucking kill u u piece of shit

I hit delete just as the sound of a door closing made me jump. It wasn't from my floor, so I peered up the stairs. It was just Mrs. Jenson being wheeled into the elevator by her caretaker, her big brown coat engulfing her tiny body and a large hat pulled low on her head. I needed to stop being so goddamned jumpy.

I took another deep breath.

And another.

"He was like this when I found him, Officer."

"No, I'd been out all evening."

"I'm Paloma. My roommate's name is Arun."

I practiced what I would tell them while I waited. It was all I could do, shivering on the stairs. I don't know how long I was sitting there before they found me. It could have been a minute or a day. I just sat there, shaking, until an officer with kind eyes reached me.

"It's my roommate," I told her. "He's been killed."

I ignored the incredulous look on her face as I pointed out my apartment to them and continued to wait on the stairs as they went inside.

And then, another officer, one whose eyes were not kind, was asking me to get up.

"Ma'am, could you please come in with us?"

I couldn't move. There was no way in hell I was going in there.

But he insisted. And he must have convinced me, because suddenly I was following him back inside my apartment.

Back to where I saw Arun's body.

And back to where I saw *her*.

Last night was starting to come into focus. Her face. The way her skin was so pale it was almost translucent. The way her eyes bored into mine. And the way Arun's lifeless eyes had stared out, leaving no doubt in my mind that he was dead.

The front door opened into the tiny living room, and I squeezed my eyes shut at the flood of light.

I had to open them.

I had to do this.

Come on, Paloma. You've dealt with worse.

One eyelid first, then the other.

My tooth throbbed as I adjusted my eyes.

There was no body at the table, no blood on the wall. Nothing.

The bottle of Dawn dish soap half-full by the sink. A browning banana on the counter. And not a single fucking splatter of blood.

This couldn't be.

I had seen him.

I had seen *her*.

I took a few steps inside. This must be a mistake.

"Are we in the right apartment?" The officer's eyes didn't seem as kind as before.

I looked around me. A neat pile of takeout menus on the coffee table. Shitty drapes held open by shoelaces because who the hell wastes cash on those fancy curtain-band things? Generic Ikea kitchen table with a faded blue stain from when a pen leaked. Yep. This was my apartment.

"I—I don't understand."

"You said your roommate was attacked?"

"Yes. I—think so. His body was right here."

"Right here in the kitchen?"

"Y-yes."

"And where is he now?"

She was looking at me like I was crazy. Maybe I am crazy. Maybe after eighteen years of carrying this terrible secret, I had finally lost my fucking mind.

I know . . . Arun's voice needled inside my head.

I looked around my apartment again. Where the actual fuck was Arun?

And if he was killed, did my secret die with him?

5

SAN FRANCISCO, CA

SO MUCH OF OUR lives is experienced in vignettes. Scenes, flip-
ping through—high point, low point, curated, cultivated, clean-cut,
and categorical. We remember what we want. Or maybe we just remember what we can. Who gives a fuck anyway?

At least, that's how I humor myself as I wait for them.

I say *them* because I have no idea who the hell exactly I'm waiting
for. Just that I've been asked to wait. They call this a waiting room.
They were very careful about mentioning that. It's a waiting room.
Not a holding room. Not an interrogation room.

I'm just waiting.

It's almost like I'm waiting for a cup of tea. Or to get my nails done.

They brought me here after the apartment. When it became clear
that Arun wasn't there. Dead or alive or hurt or maimed. He was nowhere to be found at all.

Except I know what I saw. You don't look into someone's blank, dead face and forget it in a hurry. Arun was dead and now his body was missing and everyone keeps looking at me like I'm some crazy drunk who doesn't know what she's talking about.

I shivered.

Not the kind of shivering that happens when you're cold. The type that writhes deep in your belly. The kind that has a voice. The kind that wraps its arms around you and whispers, its tongue lightly grazing your ear—*She's back . . .*

For what felt like the thousandth time, I checked to see if the letter was still in my pocket. It felt wrong to bring it with me into a police station. Like it tainted the rest of my story. But I wasn't letting it out of my sight anytime soon. I was never taking a risk like that again.

"Someone will be with you. Sit tight."

Sit tight. They said that to crazy people, didn't they. Was I crazy? Am I crazy? But this wasn't an interrogation room. I wasn't in any kind of trouble.

They had noticed the empty bottles of Captain Morgan in the recycling bin I hadn't taken out yet. They asked me if those were mine.

Ours, I told them, Nina's disappointed face floating in my mind. *And Arun had friends over that he drank with as well*. This wasn't a complete lie. I knew he had a girlfriend he was always singing Hindi songs to. Who was to say she didn't need a shot of rum to get through his tuneless rendition of "Chinna chinna aasai"?

What the fuck had happened to Arun? Someone must have moved his body. That meant someone else was in my apartment.

Someone else was *in your apartment*, the voice taunted.

I pushed the thought away.

I'll tell the police about seeing his body again. Someone has to believe me.

The door opened. Time to pull it together, Paloma. Time to put your grown-up mask back on.

I hadn't met the policeman who walked in. He looked a bit more, well, policeman-like. I guess it was the shadows under his eyes and the way he looked me up and down, like he was displeased with what he saw. I smoothed back my hair. I'd spent the night on a fucking stairwell, it's not like I looked, or smelled, even remotely presentable.

"I'm Officer Keller." His voice grated against my ears, raw and phlegmy. It made me want to clear my throat. I didn't, of course. He set a manila envelope and a yellow legal pad on the table. There was no offer to shake my hand or anything.

"I'm Paloma. Paloma Evans. Nice to meet you." My mother's training kicked in and I gave him a little smile. Not wide enough to seem happy, but appropriate. I didn't want him to think that this wild-haired, crazy woman who reeked of last night's drink is who I really am.

The soft flesh of his thighs drooped over the sides of the too-small plastic chair as he sat down. I forced myself to focus on the linoleum table in front of me.

"You married?"

I shook my head, forcing a small, coy smile to hide my disgust. What did that have to do with anything?

"Evans, huh? Where are you from?" There it was. Looked like a missing Indian boy wasn't enough to curb Officer Keller's curiosity.

"The Bay Area." I hoped my tone was enough to warn him, but I had no such luck.

"No, I mean—" The tinge of pink that spread across his face only deepened his dark circles. "You just don't look like an Evans, that's all."

Are we still living in the Dark Ages? Who the hell says shit like that? I took a deep breath.

It certainly would not do to have Officer Keller pissed off at me, so I should just give him what he wants.

"I was adopted from an orphanage when I was younger. My parents gave me their last name." I was laying it on thick, I know. I cast my eyes down and waited for it.

"Oh, I see. That makes a little more sense." He smiled. His assumption was right, after all. "So where are you originally from? India?"

My jaw ached as it tightened, but I didn't let the smile leave my face.

"Sri Lanka."

"But you said your roommate, Arun, he was from India, right?"

We were finally getting down to business.

I nodded. "Yes."

"What was his last name?"

"Kumar, I think."

"Do you have a copy of his ID? Or passport?"

"No." And I had never thought to ask. Our arrangement was convenient.

"Copy of a driver's license?"

I shook my head.

"Do you know if he was here by legal means?"

Well, I suppose he arrived here by legal means. But unless you call overstaying your tourist visa legal, well, looks like Arun might be in some shit. Damn, it's a good thing he's dead, because if he wasn't, I've really gone and messed things up for him.

"Address of his workplace?"

"He works over at the Curry Palace. It's downtown, right across the street from the other Indian place, Taj Masala, and next door to Peet's Coffee, I think. I could look up the address for you." Finally, some information I could offer. But Officer Keller shook his head.

"That's fine. We can find that out. Do you know when his next shift is?"

Damn it. I really hate being this clueless.

"I didn't really know him that well. He mostly kept to himself."

"Any friends? A girlfriend, maybe?"

"I think he had a girlfriend, but I've never met her." I'd hear them come in late at night when he thought I'd be asleep. He was super secretive about her, probably trying to hide the fact that he was dating a white girl or something.

"So, when was the last time you actually saw him?" He rubbed his eyes and stifled a yawn. Come on, Officer Keller. Wake the hell up and do your job.

"Maybe around three thirty."

"Three thirty in the afternoon?" The furrow in his brow deepened.

"Yes, last afternoon."

"Did you have any disagreements at this time?"

I swallowed. Fuck. What if they thought that I had something to do with him going missing?

"N-not exactly."

"The neighbors said they heard a disturbance last night."

"We did have a minor disagreement. He was"—it's a good thing I'm a fucking fantastic liar—"he was behind on his rent, you see." It wasn't like I could tell Officer Keller the truth. And besides, we weren't that loud. That bitch of a neighbor was probably exaggerating again. What an asshole.

"And you have no idea where he is now?"

I mean, how fucking dumb could Officer Keller even be?

I shook my head.

"Had he moved out recently?"

What?

The muscles in my face were about to spasm from maintaining a neutral expression.

"No, Officer."

Officer Keller raised his eyebrows.

"Did you have anything to drink last night?"

"I—yes. But I—"

"And what is it that you do?"

A change in direction. What was he trying to do here? Get my guard down?

"Freelance graphic design work, mostly." The millennial job description had the desired effect, because he didn't dwell on it. I don't think Officer Keller would approve much of where the bulk of my cash really comes from, now that I don't have access to my parents' accounts.

But I still gave him a little smile. Who knows? He didn't seem like he could be one of my regulars, but then again, I didn't have a clue what my regulars even looked like.

There was a truckload of questions left to go.

How many drinks did I have last night? Any recreational drugs? Was I on any medication? Who was my doctor? Could I repeat what happened over, and over, and over again until I thought I would scream?

Explanations peppered lightly with half-truths, then suddenly— "Okay, thank you for your time, Ms. Evans. We'll keep you posted on what we find."

What?

That's it?

"But what about Arun?"

"Well, we have to wait the allocated forty-eight hours to officially declare him missing, since we don't have any evidence that suggests an attack."

What the actual fuck? Did they not listen to a damn thing I said?

"What do you mean?"

"Well, there's no evidence of a struggle. We didn't see anything on your building's CCTV footage to suggest suspicious activity. We don't even have anything to prove he exists, at this point. We can't find any evidence of him in the system, and if he's in the country illegally, then there's little we could do to track him down right now anyway."

I know . . . Arun had grinned. He'd held the letter out of my reach as I lunged for it. And now he was dead and no one fucking believed me.

"Look, I know this must be confusing for you. Why don't you get some rest? We'll keep you posted if there's anything we find. You have a place you can stay for a day or two? Your parents, perhaps?"

I tried not to snort. They were the last people who could help me. But at least I could crash at their place. It'd been sitting empty since they embarked on their "world tour" two months ago. Who even calls it that? A couple of luxury resorts in Asia, ending up in Sri Lanka, where they were being honored as usual for their charity work, gag me now, and suddenly it's a fucking world tour.

"Yeah. I'll be fine."

"One last thing. There was this note. On the fridge." He pulled out a piece of paper from his manila envelope.

Buy milk, I had scribbled.

The future's not ours to see, Arun had written underneath. At least, I think it was him. It's not like I had ever seen his handwriting. We didn't have a communal shopping list. We certainly never left each other notes on the fridge.

"That's my shopping list."

"And this bit—*the future's not ours to see*. Does it mean anything to you?"

Something inside me stirred. It was subtle. A shifting. Or an unsteadiness. I couldn't really put my finger on it.

"Must've been Arun, but I have no clue what it means." I pushed my hands under my thighs as they started to shake again. "Like I said, I barely knew him."

But somebody seemed to know me a lot better than I'd like.

6

"PALOMA, FOR GOODNESS' SAKE, straighten your skirt. I can't be telling you a hundred and one times, no? *Haiyyo*, Lihini, your hair, please. Very good ah, very good. Shanika, at the back, please. Now. And for heaven's sake, put away that dirty doll *aney*. You there, stand straight. *Haiyyo*, these people will think we are raising a bunch of scarecrows here."

Lihini was trying not to laugh. I crossed my eyes and stuck my arms out like a scarecrow. She covered her mouth with her hands, but a small giggle still got out.

"You think it's funny, ah?" But Miss Chandra was smiling herself. She was too excited to get angry with us on a day like today.

"*Hari, hari*. Enough now. Band, are you ready?"

The band was made up of three girls holding a melodica, cymbals, and a little drum that was given to us last year by a rich family in Colombo. We all fought to play them, but Miss Nayana never even gave me a chance. She said I was completely tone-deaf, which I think is really, really unfair. I mean, the melodica sounds like a dying cat when Dumila plays it, and I'm the one who's tone-deaf?

But I shook my head. Lihini says that I'm always too negative. She says that being negative puts negative energy out into the world, and when this happens, nothing good can ever happen to you. I don't know if I believe her, but I don't really feel like risking it. Miss Chandra calls this being a "glass half-full kind of person," which I think is a bit silly. What does water have to do with any of this?

A long strand of Lihini's hair stuck out from one of her plaits. I tugged on it to get her attention and then tucked it into her hair band.

"Rest of you, get in line." Miss Chandra wouldn't stop until they got here. "Now. Look happy, *aney* for goodness' sake. They'll be here any minute. No one wants to see any long faces, okay?"

"No long faces here, Miss Chandra." His voice boomed out over our chatter, immediately hushing us. "Looking lovely, girls. Everyone remembers their places? Good. I know you will make me proud."

"Yes, Perera sir," we chorused, only half faking the smiles that we plastered on. The excitement buzzed around us so heavily we could almost reach out and touch it.

A blue car so shiny that you could see all our excited faces reflect off the side pulled up to the entrance gate, where we stood. You could hear the soft gasps, the straightening up, the smiles getting just a little wider. My hands felt sweaty, even though they were clasped behind my back just like Miss Chandra had asked us to. I snuck a glance over to Lihini again, but she wasn't looking at me this time.

She was staring at the car, of course, and I looked over, too, when the door swung open. I have seen foreigners before. I've seen Americans, and Germans, and Britishers, and even a couple from Japan. We have donors from charities from all over the world visit us. Not all the time, but it happens. Miss Chandra always tells us how lucky we are that Perera sir is so good at telling everyone about our home. I suppose she's right. Our home isn't much like the orphanages we read about that starved children, or beat them. We've always had a string of well-wishers. They've brought us all the Enid Blyton books, and all the Penguin Classics. They've given us art equipment, and last year, we got a brand-new swing set. The donors from Colombo even invite us to their homes for their children's birthday parties and concerts.

I've seen quite a few foreigners in my time, but none of them prepared me for her. No foreigner ever looked as beautiful as Mrs. Evans when she got out of the car that day. She was like an angel, with her soft blond hair falling on the whitest shoulders I've ever seen. She wore a simple pink shift dress—pink! my favourite colour—that ended quite a few inches above her knee. Miss Chandra would raise her eyebrows if any of us tried to wear something so short outside the orphanage, but of course, even she was bowled over by Mrs. Evans's beauty.

Mr. Evans got out from the other side and circled the car to join his wife. He smiled over to us. Of course, we had all forgotten everything Miss Chandra said about staring at people, and everyone was gawking at Mr. and Mrs. Evans like they were the first white people we had ever seen.

"Adorable little things, aren't they?" he said. His words were lazy and spilled over themselves. Miss Sarah would have our teeth if we spoke that way without pronouncing our *t*'s properly, but she just gave her widest smile to this tall man whose stubbly face reminded me of an actor in those Hollywood movies we were not allowed to watch.

"Thank you for visiting us, Mr. and Mrs. Evans." Perera sir strode up to them, his English sounding odd and stuffy next to theirs.

Seeing him pushed us back to reality. This was our cue.

"Welcome to the Little Miracles Girls' Home, Mr. and Mrs. Evans," we chanted melodically, drawing out our words so they sounded longer.

Mr. and Mrs. Evans looked how I felt on Christmas morning.

"Thank you. We're so happy to be here as well." Her voice was deeper than I would have expected from someone straight out of heaven. Much deeper than Miss Nayana's or Miss Chandra's for sure. It sounded breathtaking coming from her.

"Thank you." I tried to imitate her under my breath, wondering how my voice would sound if it were that deep. I got a sharp nudge from Lihini.

"Be quiet," she mouthed.

"The girls have prepared a welcome song," Miss Chandra said. Her cheeks were flushed maroon. She only ever gets shy when we have visitors to the orphanage. Other times she's as bossy as ever.

One of the younger girls stepped forward with a small bouquet of flowers. I know I shouldn't be jealous of a four-year-old, but when I saw Mrs. Evans step forward and plant a kiss on her chubby little cheek, I felt just a small stab of something in my chest. I ran my tongue along the chip on my front tooth hard enough for it to sting. I mustn't think bad thoughts.

It's not like it's bad for me here, at the orphanage. It's the only home I've ever known, really. My mother had me here, and then she left back to her village. I had asked Miss Chandra why, but she had only smiled and stroked my hair and said that she would tell me when I was older. I don't really know why adults say that. It's not like I would miss her less, or understand her more, just because I was older.

She had left me a picture of her, but no letter, no information, nothing. Miss Chandra told me that she was a maid in the Middle East, which actually sounds really exciting. She didn't look anything like me, and she certainly didn't look a thing like Mrs. Evans.

Good morning to you!
Hello! How do you do?
We are so very happy
To welcome you!

We sang loudly, gasping for air in between each line, trying to impress them by making them lose their hearing. The foreigners smiled down at us and clapped enthusiastically at the end, as did Perera sir and the rest of the teachers. Good. No one was in trouble today.

"Very good, children. Why don't you'll go and play now so that I can show Mr. and Mrs. Evans around our home?"

We hurried to our spots, and I couldn't help but crane my neck a little to get just one last look at her. Lihini was staring over, too, a little more obviously than I was. I grabbed her arm.

"Come on, *men*. You're going to get both of us scolded otherwise."

She nodded and followed me inside.

We quickly fell into our positions—Lihini and I were meant to sit near the windows and read one of the books from our small bookshelf, Maya and Dumila were supposed to practice with the rest of the band girls, others were supposed to color, to play with their dolls, sing. Even Snooby, the lazy orphanage dog, was supposed to lie in a corner.

Everything was carefully arranged so that the Evanses would like us a lot, so that they would want to make donations to the home, maybe even tell their friends about us. And if we were really, really lucky, they might even adopt one of us as their new daughter. Every time someone was adopted, we would get some more money from the main American charity. At least, that's what Perera sir explained to us. And it's because of this money that we could have such nice things, like a bookshelf full of books, or after-school English classes with Miss Sarah, and a Christmas play every year, he had said.

Lihini was just reaching for her copy of *Wuthering Heights* when I beat her to it.

"Too slow," I giggled, snatching it up and hugging it to my chest. Actually, the books on the shelf were supposed to belong to all of us, but Lihini loved *Wuthering Heights* so much that Miss Sarah gave her the copy for her Christmas present. I got *Little Women*, which was one of my favourites. But I was starting to like Heathcliff, even though all his anger got on my nerves sometimes. Yesterday, I was reading the scene where Heathcliff returned, transformed into a new person so he could get his revenge. I hadn't finished the chapter yet and I didn't want to start on another book until I did.

"It's my turn!" she giggled back.

"*Haiyyo*, I'll just read it for today. You can have it tomorrow." I hugged the book tighter. She's read it a million times. She wouldn't die if she didn't have it for one day.

She gave a big, drama-queen sigh and took *Oliver Twist* for herself instead.

"Guess what Miss Nayana gave me?" Lihini whispered. Must be something good if she couldn't wait. She edged closer to me and pulled open the pocket on her dress. A Chinese roll—Lihini's favorite. We only got the crumb fried pastries on very, very special occasions, so I was surprised that Lihini had managed to get one.

"No way!"

"She said it was because I've been helping in the kitchen."

"Can I get a bite?" It was a silly question. Of course Lihini would share with me. We shared everything.

"As soon as they leave, okay?"

"Shh!" one of the girls called from across the room, and I was about to tell her to shush herself when Lihini gave me a sharp look and went back to reading.

"And here is the playroom, where we also keep our little library," Perera sir was explaining as he pulled the door open.

My chest felt heavy. Their perfume, like jasmine mixed with musk, filled the room before they even stepped inside.

"Relax," Lihini mouthed.

The words made no sense on the page as I forced myself not to turn and stare at them. At her. At least, not too obviously. He was walking around the room, looking at our new desks, reading what we had written on the blackboard, checking out our small market stall with the plastic vegetables. But I felt her even before I knew she was coming towards me.

"Hi there." She crouched down so we were at eye level. No other adult had done that to talk to me.

"Hi," I said, but I couldn't hear myself, so I'm not sure she heard me also.

"What's your name?"

"P-Paloma." Why was I stuttering? I'd never stuttered before.

"And you?"

"I'm Lihini." Her voice came out crystal clear.

Mrs. Evans turned back to me. "You have a beautiful smile."

I thought my heart would explode. I had a chip in my front tooth from when I fell jumping *batta*, and I had always hated it.

"But my tooth," I whispered, feeling very, very shy.

"Well, I think it's absolutely adorable. You're such a sweet girl. And you both are so fair." We both beamed at this. It was true—both Lihini and I were fairer than the other girls. Not by a lot, but enough to be called *sudhu* by everyone. Miss Nayana used to make fun of us, saying we could both be in a Fair & Lovely advertisement.

"I like your dress," Lihini tried. Her cheeks were pink to match what Mrs. Evans was wearing.

Mrs. Evans looked down at herself like she had forgotten what she had on.

"This? Oh, thank you. Thank you so much." She peered over at me again.

"What are you reading there?"

"W-*Wuthering Heights*." I held up the book. The cover was peeling and the spine was cracked.

"Wow! That's my favorite." No way! "I would have thought . . .

How old are you, Paloma?" I love the way she pronounced my name. Puh-LOW-ma. I must remember to say it like that from now on.

"I'm twelve." My voice didn't shake as much this time, thank goodness.

"Me too!" Lihini piped in, and we both giggled again. We were both born in the orphanage, just three weeks apart, so we knew what our birthdays were. Many of the other girls didn't, so we were lucky.

"And do you read a lot, both of you?"

We nodded our heads emphatically. That's what we did, Lihini and I. We shared the same books and spent every afternoon we could reading. And when we couldn't read, we talked about what we read.

"And what books do you like to read?"

"We can show you." Lihini jumped to her feet excitedly.

"Yes, we can show you," I echoed, following her.

We each took one of Mrs. Evans's hands and led her over to our bookshelf. Most of the books were like *Wuthering Heights*—they once belonged to someone else, but now they were ours.

"These are *aaaaall* our books." Lihini gestured to the library with a flourish.

"*Aaaaall* our books." I tried to gesture also, but my arm knocked over a book from the corner of the shelf. It fell to the floor with a loud bang.

There was a burst of laughter from the other girls as I realized in horror what I had done. I covered my face with my hands, wishing the floor would open up and swallow me whole. I couldn't believe this was happening to me.

"Oopsie daisy," Mrs. Evans tried, but it was too late. I'd messed up.

The laughter died as suddenly as it started. I peered out from behind my fingers to see why.

It was Shanika, entering the room with two cups of tea balanced on a tray. Her face was red under her scars. Hang on, she wasn't supposed to be here. Whenever we had visitors, she was supposed to stay in the dormitory.

"Good afternoon, Mr. and Mrs. Evans. Would you like some tea?" Her words were memorized, but they weren't supposed to come from her. That was what Miss Chandra was to say, while she served the visitors their tea in Perera sir's office.

Lihini gasped softly. It was like watching a disaster happen in slow motion. We were all waiting for the crash.

But Mr. Evans simply smiled and said he would love to have some tea.

"Me too," said Mrs. Evans.

Shanika had tried brushing her hair over her left side, but it didn't do anything to hide her scars. The burns continued down her left arm, where they were joined by longer, deeper scars, although Mrs. Evans didn't seem to notice.

Perera sir was probably as dumbfounded as the rest of us, but he recovered the fastest.

"Shanika," he said. The friendly smile never left his face. "Isn't it time for your lesson with Miss Sarah?"

Shanika didn't say anything. She obviously knew that she was going to be in big trouble. Really, really big trouble.

"I . . ." But whatever Shanika was going to say was drowned out by Miss Chandra thudding into the room, her face puffed up and purple.

"There you are, child. I've been looking all over for you." She gave the visitors a knowing smile. "These children really keep you on your feet, I'm telling you."

The Evanses laughed politely as Miss Chandra steered Shanika out of the room.

"Now why don't we get you some cake before your English lessons?" She chatted to the scarred girl, although I couldn't help but notice how Miss Chandra's knuckles were white around Shanika's thin arm as they hurried out.

"Mr. Evans, Mrs. Evans, shall we move into my office?" Perera sir asked. He looked over at us and winked. I guess none of us were in trouble after all. Thank goodness. Perera sir was usually kind, but he had gotten more strict since his wife died last year.

"Sure," Mr. Evans said.

"Bye, sweet girl," Mrs. Evans said as she gave us one last smile and left. The room continued to smell like her, and I took a long, deep whiff.

7

SAN FRANCISCO, CA

I ROLLED OUT OF the Uber and shut the door with a little more force than necessary. Damn, I hope I don't lose a star for this.

"Sorry!" I called out, smiling as brightly as I could after dealing with the worst night of my life. He gave me a curt nod and pulled out. Asshole. I opened the app and gave him two stars.

I hadn't come by since my parents left on their trip. I was supposed to drop in and water the plants but I couldn't bring myself to do it those first few weeks. I mean, it's just another thing I've failed at. Couldn't even keep the damn plants alive while they were out saving orphans and feeding the hungry and planting trees with little plaques that bore their name. Well, our name.

And to top it all off, they'd decided to pull some bullshit Luddite move and do the whole thing without cell phones. *Technology detox,* they said, like it was one of those Instagram-influencer slimming teas that gave you diarrhea. I mean, I've never asked them to get on Snap-chat. Just to drop me a text every once in a while.

But then they sat me down and gave me a lecture about how it was important that they "moved like the natives" of the lands they visited in order to "be respectful." It would have made a little more sense if they weren't Diamond members in the Hilton Honors program, but Mom would have been outraged if I'd pointed that out.

Fuck this.

I looked around the quiet neighborhood I spent my teenage years both loving and hating. The streets weren't busy today, not that it ever really got busy in suburbia. TWENTY IS PLENTY the speed signs read, with a cartoon of a smiling snail.

I had struggled to remember which house was mine when I first moved here. Every lawn was neat, every house mimicked the other. It was like a suburban house of mirrors. So different from Sri Lanka, where you could literally direct people by saying things like "make a left at the mango tree" or "the house opposite the one with the ugly brown wall." I almost always missed my turn. Thank god for Google Maps.

I squared my shoulders and looked up the short path that led to our porch.

My heart stopped in my chest.

A woman was sitting on the porch chair. A woman with wild, black hair that hung over most of her face and dark, empty eyes. She held some flowers in her hand and stared at me, expressionless. She wore a tattered robe, which she clutched to her chest with skeletal fingers.

Fuck me. It couldn't be.

Was I imagining her again?

I took a deep breath and rubbed my face. No, this time it wasn't a ghost, or my imagination.

There was an actual woman sitting on my porch.

"Um, hello?" I ventured. I checked the number on the house. I wasn't in the wrong place.

She didn't say a thing. She just stood up and started walking towards me.

A pale face clawed its way into my mind, and I felt my whole body brace for impact, but the woman continued right past where I stood.

I watched her move silently across the street, where she entered what I could only imagine was her own home.

"H-hey?!" I called out, but she was inside by the time I found my voice.

I just stood there, on the now empty sidewalk, willing my heart to stop pounding. It took a moment or two longer than I would have liked.

What the actual fuck was that?

"Get ahold of yourself, Paloma. She must have just had the wrong house or something."

I shivered as I pulled out the remote to the garage door. That's right, I had a key to the garage, not even the front door, and was finally making my way up the driveway when my parents' neighbor, Ida, stuck her head out from behind her shed. She must have stepped out for her afternoon snoop around the neighborhood. I wasn't really in the mood.

"Paloma! My goodness!" Her voice was high-pitched and trembling, like a puppy's. God give me the strength. I know she hadn't been expecting to see me, but she needed to calm the hell down.

"I've been waiting for you to come by." Her forehead was a deep mess of wrinkles, though she had zero regard for how exhausted I obviously looked. "I've rung you a few times, you know." Of course I know, Ida. Whoever invented caller ID probably did it because of seventysomething-year-old women like you who couldn't take a fucking hint.

"Hi, Ida. Good to see you too." I gave her an appropriately tight smile, eyes downcast, and then yawned theatrically.

I wonder if she knew who that woman was. I was just about to ask her when she started speaking again.

"You know we have some things to discuss, dear. Shall I pop over now? Or would you rather pop over here? Goodness, we have so much to talk about. I have a pie in the oven, I just need to get it out. It was your mom's recipe, actually! Give me ten minutes and I'll pop right over."

If she said the word *pop* one more time . . .

Forget asking her about the woman on my porch. I just needed her to stop talking before I exploded.

"Actually, Ida, would you mind if I came over a bit later? I've had a pretty rough day." I yawned again, for good measure, and then hit the button on the remote. The roller door squeaked a little, but it still worked fine, thank god.

Ida frowned a little but nodded like one of those bobbleheads everyone used to keep on their dashboards. Her oversprayed, grey hair-helmet did not move, but the loose skin around her jaw flapped around like an angry bat.

"Of course, dear. I'll see you later. Why don't you come over for dinner tonight? Or even tomorrow? I'll make chicken potpie. It's still your favorite, I hope?"

"I'll give you a call. Thanks, Ida."

I smiled politely as I backed into the garage as fast as I could, then watched as the door rolled back. It took a little longer than I would have liked, and Ida kept looking concerned and waving, but I didn't move until it was all the way down. Call me paranoid, I don't care. The last thing I needed was some serial killer psychopath rolling in through the door after me and hiding out at my parents' empty house.

The future's not ours to see. The words scraped at my insides. Nails on a chalkboard. A hammer hitting the butt of a screwdriver. My jaw went numb. I rubbed my thumb over my perfect ceramic front teeth.

I was trudging through old boxes and dusty gym equipment when a handlebar snagged on the front pocket of my hoodie. I untangled the bicycle and shoved it away. I hated that damn thing, and you would, too, if yours were the only parents in your elite, snobby private school who made you ride a bike back and forth because it was better for the fucking environment. I mean, don't get me wrong, it's great that my mom threw awareness parties about global warming and Dad made donations to countless charities in my name for every birthday or special occasion, but they drove a Range Rover for fuck's sake.

I pushed my way into the kitchen. It looked exactly the same. Why wouldn't it, after all?

I could hear the security alarm beeping away—each beep louder than the last. I crossed over as fast as I could and keyed in the code. The date of their anniversary, the same as always.

I tried not to feel too guilty about the shriveled-up pots of basil and mint on the window ledge. It made the entire kitchen stink of death. I know I promised to water them, but Mom would understand. They always understood, eventually. It was what defined this family. At least, that's what I told myself. They understood my panic attacks when I moved here. My nightmares. My insistence that a ghost from Sri Lanka had followed me to the US because I couldn't cope with my guilt, even though they didn't know back then why exactly I felt so guilty. And they would eventually understand why I did what I did eighteen years ago. I had to believe that.

I pushed away the annoying voices that kept taunting me since our argument. I kept thinking they would come around, but then they left on their trip. I wish they hadn't gone. That they had just stayed back, just this once when I asked them to, so we could have worked it all out. *We gave them our word, Paloma. And who are we, at the end of the day, if we can't keep to our word?* It didn't seem like the best time to tell them that I gave zero fucks about their word. That I needed them.

And now the dregs of our disagreement settled into the deepest parts of me, the way dust settled into crevices, and who knows when I'll be able to get rid of them?

I pulled out the dead plants and dumped them, dirt and all, into the trash. There was a bottle of Mom's homemade all-purpose cleaner next to the trash can under the sink—rubbing alcohol, water, lemon essential oil, and a "secret ingredient" she wouldn't even tell me about. It was so potent, it could get rid of even the worst of stains—grease, blood, you name it.

My stomach made a rumbling sound, but first things first. I sat down at the kitchen counter and pulled out my phone.

Breathe, Paloma, I told myself.

I pulled up Arun's number and hit dial.

And couldn't get a fucking signal.

Goddamn this suburban hell.

I went to the opposite end of the kitchen, where I knew the reception would be better.

"Hullo. You've reached Arun. Please leave me a message and I will call you back. Thank you." Hearing his voice made me want to reach through the phone and strangle him. But of course he didn't pick up. There was nothing left to strangle. He was dead. I don't know what I was expecting by calling him up.

I hung up and googled the Curry Palace. There were two, but I recognized a logo from the plastic bags Arun would bring back leftovers in.

It took about six rings for someone to pick up.

"Hullo, Curry Palace." Same accent as Arun's but the voice was too deep to be his.

"Hi, I've been trying to reach Arun. Did he come into work today?" Obviously he didn't. I just had to make sure.

"Who's speaking please?"

Who the hell did this dipshit think he was? I'm trying to reach my roommate, not the goddamned president.

"Um, I'm his roommate. Just trying to get ahold of him."

"Arun Patel or Arun Mukerjee?"

"I—Patel?" I thought his last name was Kumar.

"He's scheduled to come in at six."

"Oh, I see. Thanks." I hung up.

A face popped into my mind for just a second. Long, dark hair. Pale skin. Empty eyes.

Fuck me, it's been eighteen years. It cost my parents thousands of dollars in therapy for me to get over it. It would have killed them to realize it had all been in vain.

It was the stress. It had to be. It's not every day that you were black-mailed about your worst secret and then saw your dead roommate's body in your kitchen. It probably fucked with my head. Nina would probably call it a coping mechanism.

My parents' kitchen was worlds apart from my grimy, poorly lit bathroom, and the whole idea of Mohini seemed laughable in the eye-wateringly bright afternoon sun. Nina was right, after all, Mohini *was* a coping mechanism. My nightmares of her dwindled away with ther-apy and pills that helped me sleep better at night.

But if I imagined Mohini, then who or what the fuck had been in my apartment?

I went over to the front door and made sure it was locked. The windows as well. Maybe it's not the worst thing that I stay here for a few days, strange lady on my porch and all.

I looked around the kitchen. The utilities were on a standing auto-matic payment, so the fridge was still running.

I rummaged through a few of the cupboards. Weetabix. Four jumbo boxes of Weetabix. Damn, Dad. How did a man who only ate

Weetabix for breakfast every single day of his life decide he wanted to eat curry for all three meals? I'm sure they don't have Weetabix, or anything remotely similar, back in Sri Lanka. I would have reminded him to pack a couple of boxes for his trip if he was actually talking to me. He was doing the whole *I'm not mad, just disappointed* thing at the time. It fucking sucked.

The spice rack was still labeled and arranged alphabetically. Of course Mom wouldn't have it any other way. She had all the exotic blends—pepper from Pondicherry, black salt from Cyprus, not that she really ever used them. I made sure not to mess anything up. It used to drive her crazy when I would rummage through, adding chili flakes on everything when I first got here. Not that she was a great cook. I mean, she mostly used the electric burner on the stovetop rather than actual fire, that's how haphazard she was in the kitchen. And even though she loved to serve canapés with hints of spice at her book club meetings, anything but salt or pepper would leave both her and Dad tag-teaming the bathroom the moment her guests left.

I'd have to get some groceries if I was going to stay.

I pulled out my phone again and clicked on my banking app, bracing myself. I'd been getting a few random gigs lately, but this is the Bay Area. Twelve bucks for avocado toast, right? But I exhaled when I saw my balance. Looks like my last few customers had come through, those sick sons of bitches. I wasn't as broke as I had thought.

It's your lucky day, Bethany from the bank. I won't have to deal with you again just yet.

I threw away a few old phone messages stuck to the fridge door so I could use the magnets. I didn't have my toothbrush or any clean underwear, but I always kept their postcards with me. They hadn't gotten too scuffed up from being stashed in my purse.

Namaste from New Delhi! they had written. *We'll be back soon, Paloma. We can talk then* from the Maldives. *Wish you were here, sweet girl!* from Sri Lanka. That was probably Mom. She could be cheery even when the world was ending. It hurt to swallow. The card had an elephant on it, with coconut trees in the background.

I wish we'd spoken before they left. But then, I wish a lot of things. That I had what it took to make them happy. That I didn't disappoint them every step of the way. That I had been what they expected when they brought me back eighteen years ago and gave me this perfectly wonderful life that never felt like it was mine to begin with.

I turned the cards over so that I could see only the pictures and stuck them up. At least the postcards still came. The Sri Lankan postal service was bullshit and everything took ages to get here, but at least they came.

I guess I couldn't stay holed up in the kitchen forever. I made my way upstairs. It's funny how you never notice the smell of a place when you live there, but it punches you right in the gut when you visit. The carpet cleaner Mom likes, those Jo Malone candles Dad buys her for every single special occasion, and laundry, and packed lunches, and happier times.

There was a new picture on our staircase gallery—an eight-by-ten professionally taken close-up of Mom. I know most children say their mothers are beautiful, even when they are obviously not. It was a matter of principle, I suppose, even if your mom looked like the Wicked Witch of the West. But it's not just me who thought my mother was the most breathtaking being on the planet. Straight-up Glinda, the Good Witch of the North. Strangers in the street would stop and stare at her, that's how lovely she was. Blond hair. Blue eyes. The all-American wet dream. And she only got more beautiful as she got older, like her genes aged in reverse. How the fuck is that even possible? And she wasn't just beautiful. Just like Glinda, she was good. She was kind and generous and spent countless hours volunteering her time and money towards various projects. Villages in India had potable water because of her.

Schools in Mexico had libraries. Orphans in Africa got fed, even though she always referred to Africa like it was a country, and never could remember the orphans' names. I suppose I was a project too. Probably her least successful one.

I never knew why she hated having her picture taken. The poor women in her charity circle had to practically wrestle her to pose for this portrait when she received their annual award—the Angel in the Bay. Cheesy as fuck, but fitting for someone who did as much fundraising as she did. Gorgeous *and* philanthropic. A devoted wife. An exemplary mother. The kind of woman who could be featured in one of those magazine articles about *Women Who Did It All*. She'd have been a Stepford Wife, if they weren't fucking robots. If only she had a perfect child too. It was all too fitting that they would adopt a daughter from an exotic island—the charity circle wouldn't shut up about it.

Dad got the photograph blown up despite Mom's protests about her nose being too large and her chin starting to look saggy. To him, she was perfect. If he could have worshipped the ground she walked on, he would have willingly done it. Us mere mortals could only ever dream of being loved the way my mother was. She smiled self-consciously down at me as I hesitated on the landing that led to the bedrooms.

I suppose I could just take the master. It's the bigger room, and it's not like anyone is using it right now. But I swatted the thought away. Too weird. I opened the door to my old room, and, of course, it was preserved like a shrine to my teenage angst.

The posters of Green Day and Fall Out Boy looked slightly puffed up from all the layers underneath them. Posters I had never taken down but simply tacked over. Posters of the Sri Lankan cricket team and Bollywood actor Shah Rukh Khan, which were then covered by posters of NSYNC and the Backstreet Boys, which were hastily covered up by more-alternative bands.

I still remember when Christina Hannigan came over in eighth grade. "You actually *like* cricket?" she asked, equal parts of disdain and glee dripping from her strawberry milkshake Lip Smacker–pink lips. Her mom was friends with mine and they kept insisting we hang out even though Christina got everyone in my homeroom to make sniffing sounds and say they smelled curry whenever I walked in. I begged Dad to take me to Hot Topic the very next weekend so I could redecorate, and I told the kids in homeroom that I saw Christina changing before gym and that she definitely, 100 percent, used her brother's old socks to stuff her bra.

All my old clothes were donated to the Salvation Army and various charity drives years ago, so my wardrobe and drawers were bare. Fuck, I was going to need some clothes and my phone charger at some point.

I emptied out my pockets. What I wouldn't do for a drink right now. I know my parents kept a steady supply of Glenfiddich in a cabinet in the kitchen. I shouldn't though. I should text Nina about today, not that I knew what the fuck I was supposed to say.

Hey, Nina, my asshole roommate's dead, right after he tried to blackmail me. But his body wasn't there when the cops came, and they don't seem to care too much. Oh, and remember the ghost I made up when I was twelve? Yeah, I saw her last night. Wanna hang?

No way.

She'd up my dose and call me crazy, just like everyone else.

I sat down on my bed. I needed to make sense of all this bullshit first. If only I knew where to start.

Maybe a small glass of scotch won't hurt?

8

THE DOOR TO THE Curry Palace was sticky and cold. I hesitated outside for a minute, wondering whether I should just turn the hell around and go back home. I really should be getting some sleep and settling into my parents' without rushing downtown. I hadn't even showered since yesterday. And if I was being completely honest, I didn't really know what the hell I was doing here. I just knew that I couldn't keep calling the restaurant without it seeming dodgy as fuck, and if I was looking to make sense of whatever the hell happened to Arun, this was as good a place to start as any.

So there I was, hoping for the best. Ideally, that last night had just been a very bad dream and that he would still show up to work, but infinitely more likely, that someone could at least tell me more about him. More than the fact that he really fucking loved Bollywood movies and sticking his nose where it didn't belong, because that was about as much as I knew.

I pushed my way inside. It wasn't a complete dump. I saw a few families seated at the small Formica tables, but it was mostly the college-student types. You know, the ones who insist on their curries being extra spicy and then gush out tears and sweat and snot as they chug down cups of chai and fan themselves, proudly reassuring everyone that this is the way they like it. Talk about having a BDSM relationship with your food.

I was greeted by an eager girl who accessorized her hostess uniform with those chunky sneakers that looked like space boots. She had her black hair up in a messy half bun that was more trendy than disheveled, and if I wasn't so preoccupied with my dead roommate, I might have asked her how the hell she managed to get her South Asian hair to behave like that.

"Welcome to the Curry Palace," she chirped. "Do you have a reservation?"

I wondered if I should sit down and order something. Maybe they would be chattier about Arun if they felt I was a paying customer. But my stomach turned at the thought of food.

"Actually, I'm trying to find Arun." I was too fucking tired to come up with a lie, and I mean, I had to try something.

"Patel or Mukerjee?"

"Patel." I needed to start somewhere. Fifty-fifty odds, right?

Her grin didn't waver. Good for her.

"Patel, huh? The cops already came by looking for him today. He in some kind of trouble or something?" She gave a little laugh.

Nosy bitch.

I gave her my best smile and moved in a bit closer.

"No, I'm his roommate," I said, like it was supposed to make sense. "I just—well, I was wondering if I could talk to one of his friends or something? I'm trying to figure out what happened to him."

"His roommate, huh? Hang on a bit."

She ducked inside the restaurant and went in towards what I assumed was the kitchen. I just stood there stupidly, wondering how long she would be, whether this was all a fucking mistake, whether I should just go back to my parents', when she returned with a man who had clearly eaten way too much naan and curry in his day and eyed me like I was a fly in his mango chutney.

"You're Arun's roommate?" he asked, his impressive mustache curling down.

"Y-yes. I was wondering if—"

"You tell him he's fired."

What the actual fuck? How could you fire someone who's dead?

"I—I'm sorry, I actually came here to—"

"What do these kids take me for? A bloody fool?" His voice was thunderous and his Indian accent was even thicker than Arun's. "I have had it up to here, you hear me?" He held his hand up to his head, like this was supposed to mean something to me.

"You tell that good-for-nothing *madharchod* that I never want to see his face here again. And if he comes here asking for his last salary, I don't care who the hell he sends, I will stick my foot so far up his—"

"Pa," the girl from earlier interjected, laying a hand on his arm. She looked towards the diners. A few of them had noticed the commotion and were staring our way.

"You tell Arun never to sight this place again, you hear?" He dropped his voice but didn't look any happier. "I'm fed up of helping these fellows without visas, then having them run off the moment they get a better chance somewhere, leaving me understaffed and desperate. No care about the risk I take. No care about what it does to my business when the police come sniffing around here."

I didn't need this shit. I didn't need this stupid old man treating me like I was to blame by association. I sure as fuck didn't need a restaurant full of people staring at me like I was the one who was guilty of something.

I flashed an apologetic grin and shrugged in the direction of the diners. I'm just a poor girl getting her ass handed to her.

"Sorry for wasting your time. I'm just trying to figure out what happened to him myself."

"You tell him I said to go fu—"

"Pa!" The girl took my arm and led me towards the door. "As you can tell, it looks like he's run off, and my dad's pretty pissed. This is the third guy to leave without notice this month."

It's probably because your dad's an asshole.

"The cops said he's gone missing," she continued, her voice low, "but that's pretty typical for someone in his situation. And it freaks the rest of our staff out when the cops come, you know?" Well, whose fault was it that your dad hired undocumented workers and then treated them like shit?

"Sure." I smiled. "I understand. If he does turn up, let him know that I'm looking for him, okay?"

I mean, unless the asshole rose from the dead, I knew it would never happen. I just wish someone would believe me so we could focus on the more important thing here—who the hell killed Arun, and why?

9

SAN FRANCISCO, CA

I ZIPPED UP MY jacket as I walked away from the Curry Palace, slowing down to pull out my phone. I had to text Nina. I couldn't put it off forever.

Hi, something happened

"Hey!" someone called out from behind me.

What the actual fuck was this?

I turned around, gripping my keys in my hand and tensing up.

"Hey!"

It was a waiter. Just what I fucking needed. Another reason for that asshole owner to be pissed at me.

"I'm Arun's friend. Just a minute!"

Fucking finally. A person in this godforsaken town who could verify that Arun was an actual living, breathing person.

I looked him up and down. He was in a white kurta top and waistcoat, a small smudge of orange butter masala bleeding down his sleeve. There was something familiar about him.

"Do you know where he is?" He was panting a little.

"Sorry, no." I gave a polite smile. I couldn't very well tell this stranger that I had yanked Arun's dead body off my kitchen table, could I? "That's why I came here. To see if he showed up to his shift."

"That's really weird. I thought he'd tell me if he was taking off. But then again, he probably thought it would be easier this way."

"Have you heard from his girlfriend at all? Do you know how to get in touch with her?"

"He has a girlfriend?"

I tried not to roll my eyes. He clearly didn't know anything. I was about to turn away.

"You're Arun's roommate, right? He told me about you!"

I swallowed, making sure the smile hadn't slipped off my face.

"About me?"

Fuck. Fuck. Fuck. Had he told him about the letter?

"*Lankaven ne?*" This caught me by surprise. From Sri Lanka, right?

"Yes," I replied cautiously. I hadn't spoken Sinhala in many years.

"*Mama Saman. Mehe nam kiyanne Sam kiyala,*" he continued. I'm Saman. But they call me Sam over here. Figures.

That was probably what was familiar, then. The accent.

"I'm Paloma."

"*Sinhala bari de?*" Can't speak Sinhala? No shit, Sherlock.

I shook my head, switching my expression to be adequately sheepish. The few Sri Lankans I've met here are incredibly, inexplicably easy to offend. They think I'm putting it on. Trying to sound "posh." Their words, not mine. Like not knowing how to speak Sinhalese somehow made you cooler. But you try speaking a language you haven't used in eighteen or so years and tell me how you get on with it. It's not like I have anyone in the Bay Area I can speak to, and my parents thought I was joking when I suggested they learn, and enrolled me in French instead.

You already know how to speak Sri Lankan, Paloma, why don't you try something new? Mom had explained, and she seemed so excited about the idea of it that I didn't have the heart to tell her that Sri Lankan wasn't an actual language.

"Nice meeting you, Saman. If you do hear anything, please let me know. I'd better get going." I wasn't going to leave a number. I know this type—just wants to be around the drama of a missing person, relishing in the gossip.

"*Inna, inna ithing.*" Wait, wait, will you?

I must have paused, because Saman had scribbled his number on a slip from his order pad and stuck it out to me.

"Keep my number. In case you need to talk. About Arun, or, well, anything. He told me so much about you."

It could have been what brand of shampoo I used or what I ate for breakfast each morning, knowing Arun, but something about the way he said it made the ground tilt around me. Had Arun actually said anything? Or was this guy just being weird?

I must have hesitated.

"It's okay, *nangi.*" *Nangi.* Little sister. How Sri Lankan could someone even get? His brown cheeks, covered in stubble though they were, had turned red. The paper hovered between us. "I'm new here. Arun was one of my few friends. It'll be nice to have someone to talk to. *Apeyma kenek neh?*" Someone who's one of us.

The air outside grew thicker, suffocating me. I didn't want to seem rude. Maybe this was a typical Sri Lankan guy's way of trying to be friendly. Or asking me out. It didn't mean that Arun told him anything important. It didn't mean that Arun told him about what he found out. I took the number and stuffed it into my pocket. It really was the easiest way to get this creep off my back. I'd just throw it out later.

Why did they always assume that every brown person wanted to be their friend? Like having excess melanin automatically qualified you to be a part of some special club that ate only spicy food and bitched about not having a bidet-shower next to the toilet. I really should just toss it in the trash. I took a deep breath and continued to walk away, deleting the text I had been typing to Nina.

10

RATMALANA, SRI LANKA

"COME ON, YOU KNOW you can't wish for more wishes, that's cheating." Lihini's voice was really soft, almost a whisper, but that was okay because she was so close to my ear.

"You didn't say that, no? It's the smartest wish. *Haiyyo*, stop pulling the sheet!" I made sure my voice was low also.

"*Aney*, you stop pulling the sheet!"

"Okay, okay, so. Keep it down or we'll get caught."

Lihini had climbed down from her bunk and gotten into my bed, like we did most nights. We chat and joke until one of us falls asleep.

"Don't you think Mrs. Evans smelled divine?" I asked, snuggling down under the sheet.

"Tuck your hair in, *aney*. Don't let it hang out the side of the bed." It always bugs her when my braid did that. I have no clue why.

"Okay, okay. But didn't she smell divine?"

"Divine?"

"It means lovely, no? Miss Sarah taught us last week, remember?"

"You always remember all the good words."

"I have to remember words. It's the only way I can become an actress when I get older." I wriggled my eyebrows at her.

"Being an actress is more than just remembering words, you know."

"But I can do different faces. And accents. I've even been practicing my dance moves."

"Dance moves?" She sounded shocked, but I knew what she wanted.

"I can't remember them all, okay. But you know that bit that Shah Rukh Khan does on top of that train? *Chaiya chaiya chaiya chaiya?* Remember?"

"Shh!"

"Well, I can do that, look!"

I sat up on the bed and started shaking my shoulders and chest like I had seen when Miss Nayana was watching TV the other day.

"Isn't that the boy's part?"

"Miss Nayana caught me looking before it got to the girl's dance."

"*Haiyyo.*"

"What to do?" I shrugged.

"I'll keep an eye out the next time she's watching TV, okay, *sudhu?* Maybe you can see it then."

"Thanks. So, have you decided yet?"

"What?" She always tried to avoid me.

"You know what. What you want to be when you get older, *men.*"

Lihini sighed.

"*Aney,* you know I haven't decided yet, no?"

"That's not good, *sudhu.* Everyone needs a plan. Or a direction." That was what Miss Sarah said. Everyone needs direction in life. A goal to work towards. Something we must try and reach no matter what. The day she told us that was when I decided to be an actress. I've been practicing ever since, even though Maya made fun of me the other day when I imitated an Indian accent.

"I know."

I was about to lecture her further, but we were interrupted by a soft humming sound outside. I could see Lihini raise her eyebrows in the dim, silvery light that came in through the window.

"Y-you think it's her?" I asked, holding my breath. My body was starting to go rigid.

"Maya said she saw her, you know. All in white. Miss Chandra told her not to tell any of us because we'll get scared. But she told me anyway." Lihini's eyes were like saucers.

"She saw her? All lies! Come on, you know Maya. She'll do anything for a bit of attention."

"It wasn't a lie, *men*. You should have seen her. She was shaking like a mouse."

"But I thought you can't see ghosts. Aren't they invisible?" At least, that's what they said in books, right?

"Not always, *sudhu*. They reveal themselves sometimes. When they want to put a curse on you."

"So you think Mohini put a curse on Maya?" I had to ask.

"Shhh, *aney*. You want to get us caught? I didn't say she cursed Maya, just that Maya saw her."

"Where did she see her, then?" I crossed my arms and rubbed them. I'd gotten goose bumps.

"Along the small corridor. You know, near Perera sir's office. I mean, it makes sense that she would like to be near him. Mohini wants to attack men, no?" She was speaking a little louder now, and I knew I should ask her to be more quiet, but I couldn't help it now also.

"Sin for him, no? Bad enough his wife died, now there's a ghost following him?"

"*Haiyyo*, you're giving me the chills." She always did this—brought it up and then said she was scared.

We heard the humming again. It sounded like music. I felt Lihini jump slightly next to me.

"Let's go see," I said.

"What? Are you mad?"

But I had already climbed off the bed and was creeping towards the window. I knew she thought I was being reckless, but I also knew she would follow me. She'd never let me go alone. What if I got cursed too?

I was right. I could hear her sigh as she swung herself off the bed and joined me. The moon was full, so it didn't take much effort to see into the garden.

It wasn't Mohini. I felt Lihini exhale next to me. I exhaled, too, even though I hadn't realized that I was holding my breath. Shanika was sitting by herself on the swing set in the corner of the playground. She was in the dark, her white nightgown trailing in the dirt at her feet. She was holding on to her plastic doll, cradling it in her arms, rocking it back and forth as the swing creaked. Her singing drifted in more clearly through the open window. You could barely see her scars in the moonlight, and with her long hair flowing softly down her back, she almost looked divine herself.

"It kind of annoys me that she won't shut up with that song," Lihini whispered. "I really like it and she keeps ruining it for me."

I shivered again.

"I hope she doesn't get punished for what she did during the visit," I said, but that was a lie. It really bugged me that Shanika was always given special treatment when the rest of us would get in trouble for the slightest mistake.

"Well, I wouldn't be surprised if she did. Perera sir told us also how important it is that we behave. I thought I would faint when I saw her come in."

"She's getting desperate. That's what it is. She turns fourteen in a few months. After that, it's game over for her."

"It'll be game over for us soon, too, you know. We only have two years left."

I didn't say anything. I knew she was right. Most foreigners who adopt want younger children. They say it's easier for them to get used to new cultures, learn new languages, and "fit in." After all, Miss Chandra explained, once a foreign family adopts you, you have to learn their ways and try to be more like them. The younger you are, the easier it is to get used to. The cutoff age set by the Sri Lankan government was fourteen, but it was hard enough to be considered after you turned ten. Lihini and I celebrated our birthdays every year feeling a bit sad. It's not like we hated being here, but we all wanted a home of our own. A family.

And anyways, we were only allowed to stay at the home until we turned fifteen. After that, it was on to St. Margaret's Home for Girls. And no one, not a single one of us, thought about that without our hearts racing with fear. I even felt faintish whenever I thought about it. Sister Cynthia, who ran the convent, wasn't like Perera sir or Miss Chandra. She was evil. She had seven canes in her office, and if you hadn't memorized the day's Bible verse, she would make you choose the cane she would hit your knuckles with.

We met her once a month, when she came to the orphanage to run religion classes. Even Maya's knees would tremble when she saw her. And Shanika would burst into tears and we'd have to practically drag her to the lesson.

"Okay, fine. I mean, I do feel sorry for Shanika. It must be hard looking in the mirror every day. Knowing that your father would do that to you."

We weren't sure. I mean, they never tell us anything. But Dumila had heard Miss Nayana tell Miss Sarah that Shanika's father had doused her in kerosene and tried to set fire to her when she was a baby. He had been angry, she had said, with Shanika's mother. I couldn't understand why he would do that to Shanika if he was angry with his wife though. "You think that's why she did what she did?" We both understood I wasn't talking about the tea. I meant what happened last December. We hated talking about it, but we couldn't stop ourselves at the same time.

"I don't know why she did it. But I do know that Miss Chandra said it was a sin. *Papayak*," she said. Lihini lowered her voice even further. "That people who try to suicide themselves will be reborn as dogs!" She stopped for dramatic effect, I suppose, but I was too busy staring out the window at Shanika.

"And also," she continued, "it's her fault that the Child Protection people didn't leave us alone for months. Remember, we were all scared that they would close the home? I had never seen Perera sir so upset. And now all the box cutters from the handcraft cupboard have been locked away, like we are small children."

I winced a little at this. I hated thinking about it. How Shanika had snuck into the handcraft cupboard after our Christmas concert last December, and cut herself all along her arms. I didn't even know you could kill yourself that way. I thought you had to stab your heart, or drink rat poison. Maya had seen them carry her away, and she said Shanika looked like a wild beast had clawed her.

"Just, be nice to her, okay, *sudhu*? Sin for her, no? What if she has another breakdown?"

We all remembered when she randomly started screaming and crying and tearing at her hair one night, not long after she returned from hospital. Miss Chandra said she was possessed. Perera sir even had to give her a special injection for her to calm down. Miss Chandra gives her a special medicine now, not an injection, but I don't think it helps her much. It just makes her act like she's in another world or something.

Lihini rolled her eyes. "I'm always nice to everyone." She stuck her tongue out at me and I poked her in the ribs.

It was true. She was nice to everyone. To strange girls, and to the smaller girls, and to the orphanage dog Snooby, but most importantly to me.

"Come on *aney*, let's get back to bed before Miss Chandra catches us and we get into trouble."

We clambered back in, and Lihini grabbed my braid, making sure it didn't hang out towards the floor.

11

SAN FRANCISCO, CA

I PACED THE LANDING outside my parents' room, clutching the envelope, and wearing just a towel. I'd showered, but I had nothing to put on.

I needed to go in there. I could borrow some of Mom's clothes, and put the goddamned letter back where it belonged. It couldn't stay out here in the real world, where my secret risked being exposed once again. It looked so innocent, crumpled now by my constant handling. I never should have taken it with me. I should have just left it with the rest of my paperwork.

A misplaced feeling of dread rattled around inside my head like a loose quarter. The wet towel clung to me. I was sweating, even though I'd just had a cold shower.

I opened the window on the landing and spent a moment enjoying the cool breeze that made its way in. The street was quiet below, nothing new there. A couple of neighbors pottering about their yards, and an aging lady in far-too-tight spandex jogging, breathing heavily through ridiculous puffed-up blowfish cheeks. There was a girl with bubblegum-pink hair walking three dogs. Edgier than average for this neighborhood, true, but not strange for the Bay Area. Apart from that, everything looked exactly the same as it did when I was growing up here.

One of those new electric cars that looked like a spaceship pulled into the driveway across from ours. A tall man with sandy-brown hair and a USC sweatshirt got out and started unbuckling a child from the car seat in the back. Fucking babies everywhere these days. The woman, his wife, I'm assuming, the same one who was on my porch, was slower to get out, and seemed unsteady on her feet as she squinted angrily into the morning sun. I was too freaked out yesterday to get a good look at her, so I took my chance now. She was probably Indian—she was brown, anyway, and her long black hair continued to hang down like tangled curtains. The husband bounded up the stairs, laughing at something with the baby, but she just stood there for a few moments, glancing towards our house. There was something unsettling about the way her hair fell over, covering most of her face.

The man came back without the baby, took her elbow, and guided her indoors. It didn't look like she wanted to follow him. Her face was impassive, but there was something odd about the way she moved— almost like a child learning to walk. She was wearing one of those wristbands they give you at the hospital. Or, you know, the mental asylum.

She looked straight up towards my window as he led her away, and I stepped back clumsily before she could notice me staring. Why the hell was she on my parents' porch yesterday?

Fuck, I needed to stop procrastinating and get this over with already.

I know it's a bit cliché, okay? Completely fucking nineties-Hallmark-movie cliché. I know. I know that I'm being silly about it, that I should air the place out, and that I'm a grown-ass woman who should just get on with her shit without whining about her separation anxiety and abandonment issues all the damn time. But knowing doesn't change the fact that it's still pretty fucking hard, okay?

The door stuck just a little, like it always did. The bed was made perfectly. Mom would have done it before she left, of course. She could never come home to an unmade bed. At least six coordinated throw pillows were piled on top of the quilt. They would both ceremoniously move these cushions over to the little ottoman at the foot of the bed every night. The dresser was cluttered with an extra tube of mascara, a little container of pressed powder, a half-full bottle of Anaïs Anaïs. She would have taken a brand-new bottle with her on the trip, I supposed. She'd never used any other perfume.

I remember sitting on this bed for hours, watching her brush her hair, put on her lipstick, careful not to smudge her mascara as she applied it with a delicate little flick. She was always invited to parties, to charity events, to museum openings and cocktails and fundraisers. Everyone wanted a piece of her. Who could blame them?

I could never measure up. No matter how hard I tried. I mean, it's genetics, right? I just considered myself lucky for being a part of this family. No matter what fucked-up things I had to go through to get here in the first place.

I was, definitely, 100 percent lucky. I knew it, they knew it, everyone else knew it. Strangers at the grocery store would come and tell me that my mom was an angel for giving me a better life. For saving me and bringing me to America.

Focus, Paloma.

This room used to be my safe space. So many nights, when the nightmares wouldn't stop, when I would be so afraid that I would bite down on my bottom lip and the sharp edge of my front tooth would draw blood, I would sneak in here in the middle of the night and sleep on the floor at the foot of the bed. It used to freak Dad out when I did that, but I really couldn't stay away. I needed them so I could feel safe again.

But now this room was just a reminder of all the ways I disappointed them. I was on my own, once again.

I pulled open the closet door and tried not to breathe in the mothball-and-dryer-sheet smell that burst out. I needed something to change into. Nothing fancy. Just something I could throw on till I went back to my apartment for my things. A simple T-shirt and sweats would do it.

But the idea was laughable. Elizabeth Evans would never be caught dead in sweatpants. I don't think she even owned a T-shirt. Hell, she'd put lipstick on to take out the trash and could never understand a woman who didn't do the same. *There's just no harm in looking your best*, she'd tell me as she battled with getting the tangles out of my hair while I nodded and pretended like it was totally cool that she was ripping out my scalp.

I surveyed the collection of linen shift dresses and printed peasant blouses. Some of them still had the tags on. She would regularly donate her previous season's wardrobe to women in need. I asked her once why she thought women in need wanted her clothes. If they were actually in need, wouldn't they prefer food, or money instead?

Because everyone does better when they're well dressed, Paloma, she had replied, like I should've already known this, while we drove to whatever designer boutique for her to replenish the stock of clothes she had just given away.

There was a time I would try on clothes along with her, convinced I could find something that made me look as elegant as she did. No dress ever could. I just looked like I was trying to be someone I wasn't, which wasn't altogether false.

She hated it when I did this. When I hovered over her, asking to try on the same thing. She was a big fan of what the ladies in her book club called "ethnic wear." She'd accessorize her linen with bright necklaces and trinkets that looked like they came from exotic places but were probably made in China, as besotted sales assistants would bring her clothes up to the changing room.

She'd insist that I just *hadn't found my style yet*. A style that played up my features, but didn't *overdo it*. I still don't think I understand what she meant, but then, I did find my style, and it turns out she hated ripped jeans even more than me wearing her tribal wrap dresses.

I pulled over the little stool from her dressing table and stood on it, reaching into the dark top shelf. There was a light but it had burnt out ages ago. There wasn't anything of real importance up there anyway, so why would she bother to replace it? My fingers felt dust bunnies, god I hoped they were just dust bunnies, and was that a bottle of air freshener? My heart beat faster. Was it gone?

I gave it one last swipe with my arm, and my fingers finally made contact with a cardboard box. There we go. I inhaled.

I pulled it off the shelf, taking care not to drop it. The brown Office-Max box was just like I remembered.

I took it over to the bed and sat down, making sure I didn't mess up any of the pillows.

The box was covered in a thick layer of dust, which was to be expected, I suppose. I pulled off the lid. I'd never gone through the contents in detail, though Mom told me what was in there as she walked me through how I could find these documents if I ever needed them. She was so paranoid about "documentation," as she called it. I knew she would have put the letter there after we read it. And I was right. The envelope had been on top. I grabbed it as soon as I saw it. I don't even know why the hell I took it. Like keeping it with me would change that they knew, somehow.

But even though I hung on to the letter, I had only ever read it that one time. The time that Dad had handed it over to me, silently, his lips pressed together and his eyes not meeting mine. I only read it once, but I think I had it memorized—

Dear Mr. and Mrs. Evans,

I don't know if you remember me, but my name is Chandra Nanayakkara, and I was the chief matron at Little Miracles Girls' Home in Sri Lanka. I have wanted, many times over the last eighteen years, to reach out to you. To let you know of the terrible truth surrounding the adoption of Paloma. But it is only now, that you are finally returning to Sri Lanka, that I have found the courage to let you know what truly happened.

I shuddered. I couldn't bear to look through everything now either. I just stuffed the envelope back on top, and shut the lid down tight.

I took a deep breath and weighed out my options.

Arun had read my letter, and now he's dead. He had been threatening to take me to the authorities. Murder in my apartment aside, was it really such a terrible thing to have happened? As long as he didn't tell anyone, my secret was safe. I mean, the two people who mattered the most already found out and hated me. What was the worst that could happen now?

It was a game I have been playing my whole life—what was the worst that could happen?

What was the worst that could happen if I had another drink?

What was the worst that could happen if Christina Hannigan's horrible mom told mine that I swapped out her shampoo for Nair the time Mom forced me to go to her sleepover?

What was the worst that could happen if someone found out my secret?

One of the first things I did when I moved to the US and learned about the internet was go online and research my options. I'd even double-checked after my last conversation with Arun. I knew that there was an agreement between the United States and Sri Lanka that was signed in 1999 that allowed for extradition. I also knew that extradition wouldn't be barred because of a lapse of time, which meant that I could always be sent back if I was found guilty. It hadn't changed in eighteen years.

But what was I guilty of? It's not like I could describe it in a few words—narrow it down to a simple Google search. All I know is that I had kept it a secret from everyone. And it stayed that way until Miss Chandra's fucking letter.

First my parents read it. Obviously they did. The damn thing was addressed to them. But taking it from their box of documents and keeping it with me—that was my mistake.

I still couldn't believe Arun had it in him to nose around and actually find it. What a shit.

My hands shook a little. It's almost a shame he was dead. I'd have liked to teach him a lesson.

My phone beeped—Nina. It's almost like she knew.

> Just wanted to check in—you never booked your
> appointment for this month.

Fuck, that's right. I'd been so busy trying not to think about her as I snuck in a glass or two of Dad's scotch that I forgot I was supposed to schedule our meeting.

Fantastic. Now I needed to figure out a way to tiptoe around all this bullshit without her knowing how upset I was.

I looked at Mom's clothes again, and pulled my towel closer around my body. Who the hell was I kidding? I'd just run the clothes I'd been wearing through the laundry. I could chill out for an hour or two in a towel. Mom's clothes would never fit me right anyway.

12

THE WORST THING ABOUT the religion lesson with Sister Cynthia was that it wasn't scheduled for a particular day of the month. She would just show up at our classroom and we would have the day's lesson, which usually ended with one of us getting caned and the rest in tears.

Miss Sarah once let us watch *The Sound of Music* as a special treat, but imagining Sister Cynthia sing was impossible. Imagining her as anything but an evil skeleton was inconceivable.

Bony. I guess that was the best word to describe her. She looked like a heap of bones wrapped up in a bedsheet. The flesh on her cheeks and neck sagged down like cobwebbed, brown curtains, and her wimple dragged far back on her forehead without a trace of hair, making her look more like a skull than a face.

But she wasn't scary because of the way she looked. She was scary because of the way she made us feel.

Like when we happily skipped into our sewing lesson the next day and found her sitting at the front of the room, where Miss Nayana usually sat.

It was like someone knocked all the air out of us.

"Hello there, girls." Her voice was high-pitched and soft, like a little child's. Too high to come from a skeleton. It made the small hairs on my arms stand up. It was worse somehow than if she shouted at us.

"To your seats now. Let's not waste time."

We quickly shuffled to our chairs and sat down, not meeting her eye. None of us wanted any reason to get into trouble.

Sister Cynthia twirled a cane in her hand. I'd never seen her without it. Her thin fingers wrapped around the stick, the way ivy wrapped around the gutters outside our playroom. Was this one of the seven canes she kept in her office?

And where was Lihini? She must be late because she was helping Miss Chandra clear up breakfast. I kept peering out the door for her, but she wasn't anywhere to be seen. She'd get punished for sure today. She needed to get here soon.

"Now let's see, we have some unfinished business from last month," Sister Cynthia went on. She hadn't noticed me look for Lihini.

"Dumila, where are you?"

Dumila was meek when she lifted her hand.

"Here, Sister."

"Good. Now I trust you had time to reflect on your actions from last month?"

Dumila's cheeks were as red as a tomato.

"Yes, Sister."

"And you have your lines, do you?"

Dumila had a newspaper clipping of Chaminda Vaas, the Sri Lankan bowler, that she kept in her notebook. It was one of her most prized possessions. She said she was his biggest fan, which we all argued with, but she did talk about him nonstop. Sister Cynthia had found the clipping the last time she was here and made Dumila stand at the front of the class while she scolded her, calling her names like *harlot*, though none of us knew what it meant and Miss Sarah wouldn't tell us afterwards either. Then she asked her to write *I will not have impure thoughts* five hundred times, saying a prayer between each line. She told her that God will know if she didn't. And every messy letter and every spelling mistake will get her caned three times each.

"Come to the front of class, then?"

Dumila rose slowly and walked up, clutching a sheaf of papers to her chest.

Sister Cynthia smiled. The rims outlining her teeth were grey, like her gums were rotten. It wasn't a friendly smile, and Dumila looked like she was going to faint.

"What did you write?"

"I—I will, I will not have i-impure thoughts."

"And how many times did you write it?"

"F-f-f-five hundred times, Sister."

"And did you ask God to have mercy on your soul between every time? So you won't burn in the eternal fire?"

"Y-y-yes, Sister."

"Show me."

"S-Sister?"

"Show me how you prayed to God."

Dumila knelt down slowly, and we all held our breath because she looked like she was about to fall over. She clasped her hands in front of her.

"D-d-dear God. Please f-forgive me for the wrong thing I d-did. Please have m-mercy on my soul and save me from the fires of hell." I was surprised she could speak. Her forehead was glistening with sweat.

"Very good. Now stand up."

Dumila rose to her feet.

"Did you check that you had five hundred lines exactly?"

"Yes, Sister."

"And have they been written neatly, with no errors?" She twirled her cane then, and Dumila went white.

"Y-y-yes, Sister."

Sister Cynthia reached out and grabbed Dumila's ear. Dumila winced but didn't say anything, though we could see the skeletal fingers tugging hard.

"Are you absolutely sure, Dumila?"

"Y-yes, Sister. I promise."

And we knew she wasn't lying. Dumila had spent hours on those lines. She had even asked Miss Sarah to check if they were okay. Five hundred lines wasn't easy, but there was no way she was silly enough to risk the cane. She had used her neatest handwriting, erasing and rewriting everything until it was perfect and her fingers had dark red marks on them from holding the pencil.

"Are those your lines, in your hands?"

"Y-y-yes, Sister."

Sister Cynthia let go of Dumila's ear.

"Then tear it up please."

"S-Sister?" Dumila was confused. So was I.

"You heard me. Tear up the papers."

"Y-you don't want to see them?"

Sister Cynthia smiled again with satisfaction in her eyes.

"No. God knows everything, and he knows if you have written them properly. Tear them up please."

Dumila blinked hard, and slowly but surely tore up her hard work.

"Bin is over there." Sister Cynthia pointed with her cane. "Now take your seat. We don't have time to waste. Today's story is from the first book of Kings, chapter three. Maya, if you would be kind enough to read."

Maya took Dumila's place at the front of the classroom and was midway through the reading when Lihini dashed into the classroom.

"Sorry, Miss Nayana!" she called out cheerfully. "There were so many dishes today and I—" The deathly silence gave away that something was wrong, or maybe it was our terrified faces.

Lihini froze, too, finally realising that it wasn't Miss Nayana in the class.

"Hello, Lihini." Sister Cynthia spoke softly, pleasantly, like she had just bumped into Lihini while out for a walk. We all knew that this was the worst.

"I'm sorry, Sister Cynthia. I didn't realise I was late and there was a lot of washing up today."

"I see. So you have an excuse. Very good. Let's see if God will believe your excuses when you are trying to get into heaven."

Lihini kept her head down.

Sister Cynthia paused and looked Lihini over. Her sparse eyebrows rose and my heart sank.

We usually wore a jumble of donated clothes and were allowed whatever fit us and was comfortable. Neither Miss Chandra nor Perera sir ever scolded us for what we wore, unless we were leaving the orphanage or having a visit. But Sister Cynthia was very particular about our clothes, especially about our shirts having sleeves and the length of our skirts. She said we were tempting the devil by showing off too much, and that as young ladies it was our responsibility to dress so that we were fit to enter the kingdom of God.

She had once caned Shanika for her skirt ending three inches above her knees, and Lihini's skirt today was at least two inches shorter than that.

"Look at your skirt."

Lihini glanced at it, suddenly realising her mistake as well.

"I'm sorry, Sister. I washed my clothes yesterday and they haven't been put to dry yet." We didn't even know that Sister Cynthia was coming today, so how were we supposed to dress especially for her? I'm sure she did this on purpose.

"Come here," Sister Cynthia said simply.

Lihini slowly walked to the front while Maya shrank back to the corner. I could see her shaking and I wished there was something I could do.

"Tell me, child. Have you not heard anything I have told you about sinning?"

"No, Sister. I mean, yes, Sister. I've heard."

"And even still, even still here you are. Dressed like a prostitute."

We all gasped. We definitely knew what that word meant, even though we probably weren't supposed to.

Lihini's bottom lip was trembling and her eyes were filling with tears. I felt so sorry for her. I wished there was something I could do but I knew I would only make it worse if I said something.

"I'm sorry, Sister Cynthia."

"No point apologising to me. There's a higher power you need to beg forgiveness from." She lifted up her cane and Lihini winced.

"But I do suppose I should give you something to help you remember."

Lihini took a deep breath and held out her hand. When Sister Cynthia caned Shanika, she couldn't even hold her teacup for three days.

"And what is this?" Sister Cynthia smiled.

"My hand, Sister."

"And why would I want your hand?"

Lihini looked helpless.

"For you to cane, Sister."

Sister Cynthia smiled again and I thought I was going to vomit. All of us in the classroom were holding our breath, our eyes wide in fear.

"Turn around first. Let everyone here see the way a prostitute dresses."

Lihini hesitated.

"Turn around," Sister Cynthia said, her voice going even higher.

Lihini turned in a circle, slowly, like the ballerina in a music box.

"Stop," Sister Cynthia ordered when her back was to the classroom.

Lihini stopped. I couldn't see her face but my heart was breaking for her.

"Now lift your dress."

Lihini's head snapped towards Sister Cynthia to make sure she heard her. We all weren't sure we heard her.

"Lift. Your. Dress."

Lihini just stood there.

"You seem to want to show the world everything you have, so lift your dress. Now."

Lihini's hands could barely grip the sides of the pink cotton fabric, but she inched it up just a little bit.

I couldn't breathe.

"Higher."

Her face was towards the wall again, but the back of her neck was red. If she lifted it any further, then we would see her panties.

"More."

"Sister, I—" Lihini sounded like she was crying.

"Do it." Sister Cynthia swung the cane through the air. It made a whooshing sound and Lihini jumped.

She edged up her dress until her white panties could be seen by the whole class.

"Is this what you like? To show off your private parts to everyone?" And with that, Sister Cynthia caned the backs of her legs.

She did it fast, the cane cutting through the air. She only did it once. We all gasped. I could see the red welt forming on the back of Lihini's thighs.

Lihini didn't cry out though. She didn't make a sound.

When Sister Cynthia made her return to her seat, I could see her face was soaked with tears.

I tried to make eye contact with her to tell her how sorry I was for her, but she didn't look at me.

"None of this will be tolerated when you girls join me at St. Margaret's, do you hear? I'm just training you now so you know what to expect. I will make well-behaved young ladies of you yet."

There was a small sob from my right, and I looked to see if it was Lihini. But she was staring determinedly at her notebook.

The sob came from further down. It was Shanika, who had covered her face with her hands.

There was no way I could go live at St. Margaret's when I turned fifteen. There was no way I could deal with Sister Cynthia every day. I'd burn everything to the ground if they tried.

13

I DREW A LINE with my fingernail over the cushion of the pristine white couch and then ran my thumb over the mark to erase it. It disappeared with a satisfying softness.

How the hell did Nina manage to keep her couch so clean when she had different clients sit on it all day? I had asked her once, but she just smiled. She could be infuriating like that. Don't get me wrong. Nina is great. Just in a smug-kindergarten-teacher-who-vaped-in-the-playground-after-the-kids-went-home kind of way. She might be cool, but she did spend most of the day telling people what to do.

"Paloma?" Nina uncrossed and recrossed her legs. Her white socks framed her pale, thin ankles, and she tapped her pen against the armrest of her chair.

Damn it, I'd drifted off again. She gets annoyed when I do that. Says I should be trying to focus more on the present. On the conversations that I'm really having, instead of the ones I reimagine in my head. I really needed to get my shit together. What was her question again?

"Paloma, I asked what made you so sure that Arun was dead?"

Oh yes, this is why I zoned out.

Because I saw his damn body, I wanted to scream, but I didn't. Of course I didn't. I couldn't scream at Nina. I needed her on my side. That's why I couldn't tell her everything. Not what Arun found. Not how he used it against me. And certainly, definitely not that there's the teensiest, tiniest part of me that's fucking relieved he's gone.

"I know what I saw, Nina." I kept my voice even. "I didn't imagine it." *I don't do that anymore.* I didn't say it, but Nina knew.

She kept her voice level with mine.

"I'm not saying you imagined anything. I'm just asking if you were absolutely certain, that's all."

"I'm certain."

"So, you saw Arun's body in the kitchen, and you called the police right away?"

"Um, not exactly."

Nina did this super-annoying thing where she didn't say anything and just waited for me to elaborate. She did it on purpose because she knew the awkward silence would force me to keep talking. God, I hated it when she did that.

I didn't really want to tell her about what I saw next. We've spent so long deconstructing this idea of why I couldn't get an old Sri Lankan folktale out of my mind. Why a made-up ghost followed me all the way to the Bay Area and plagued my nightmares since I was twelve years old.

I couldn't tell her that I'd seen Mohini again, after so many years. We'd worked so hard for me to understand that I'd just made the whole thing up to deal with my guilt of leaving. I get that now. I didn't quite know what the hell I saw in my apartment, but I did know that it would just upset her. And I didn't want her to be upset. Nina was one of the few friends I had.

I know you probably think it's strange that I consider my therapist a friend. I don't think even Nina likes it so much. She got all uncomfortable when I mentioned it once. But I do think of her as a friend. I mean, you would tell your friend when you're mad at your parents for leaving you, wouldn't you? You would bitch to your friend about the assholes you met on a daily basis, and you would tell your friend about some fucked-up ghost you thought you saw when you were a kid, right? Of course, a friend doesn't charge you a hundred and sixty dollars an hour that you have to co-pay for because your private insurance plan is crap, but a real friend would cancel the rest of her afternoon when you told her you saw your roommate slumped dead across your kitchen table. So, yeah, Nina was a friend. Probably one of my only friends.

"I freaked out, obviously. I rushed out of the apartment. And I think I passed out."

I couldn't read Nina's expression. Her next question seemed innocent enough.

"Have you been taking your meds?" she asked, looking inside a pristine white file. Mine, obviously. She kept all her pristine white files inside a pristine white filing cabinet, in a corner of her pristine white office. When I say *pristine*, I mean surgical-level clean. When I say *white*, I mean eyeball-searing, detergent-commercial white. She even asked her clients to take their shoes off so they wouldn't mess up the spotless shag carpet. And it always smelled like freshly laundered sheets. She probably had an air freshener tucked behind the couch or something, because there was never any laundry in sight.

"Of course." There is absolutely no way I would have gotten through the last two days without my meds.

"And you haven't been drinking?"

"Nope."

"Not even now that you're back at your parents'?" Was this bitch psychic?

"Are you serious, Nina? No."

I know, I know. Lying to my therapist was a bad idea. Lying to my friend was even worse. But I knew that the moment I mentioned it, Nina would get all upset with me, and give me a lecture, and threaten to stop my meds, and to be honest, I couldn't deal with that right now.

I know I fucked up by drinking that night. I fucked up and I needed to calm down, and being here in this soothing white office was just what I needed. Just being around Nina made me feel better. To think about things rationally and realize that I should cut down on the drinking. I just had a rough day, that's all. I was under stress. I had seen a dead body, for fuck's sake. Not even worth the $2.67 per minute to mention it.

Thankfully, she relented and changed the subject. This was a trick of hers also—switch the subject so I would get comfortable and then, *bam!* She gets me to dissect some cryptic part of my life, or so she thought anyway.

"And how are you otherwise? Have you been making progress with your website?"

Uh-oh. I knew where this was going.

"Yes," I said, matter-of-factly, hoping she would move on. But unicorns would sooner appear in Nina's office and fart rainbows before I ever got to be so lucky.

"So I take it that you've been venturing outside the scope of your little *side business*?"

Fuck you, Nina. I knew I shouldn't have ever mentioned it to you. That you would always use it against me. Damn, for someone who keeps yapping about respecting professional boundaries, she's really one hypocritical bitch.

I crossed my arms and then quickly uncrossed them. No point in coming across as defensive, even though there's nothing I hate more than someone who just won't take a hint and leave me alone. And yes,

I know that's the whole point of a therapist, but my head hurt and hints of the scotch I gulped to calm myself before I came over here still swirled around in my stomach and I just wasn't in the mood, okay?

"Nina"—I made sure I was smiling—"I know you don't think it's a good idea, but really, I'm being safe. I swear. And it's just for a little while. Until I get my graphic design thing going."

"Paloma, look, I'm not judging you. I never have. But I just want to make sure you know the risks, that's all. I don't know if you need the stress that no doubt comes from—"

"Nina, come on, you know how careful I am. I'm as risk averse as an insurance assessor on Adderall." I gave a little laugh but her face remained deadpan.

"It is a risk, Paloma. The type of people who are into this sort of thing. You are taking a risk."

"It's just business, Nina. Only until I get my freelance thing off the ground."

"Paloma, call it what you want, but you sell your used underwear on the internet to whoever bids on it. That is not a healthy business. Or a safe one."

"Of course it's safe! I use a different name, and a PO Box and everything. We've been through this."

"I don't think it's particularly safe, Paloma. You told me at our last session that you had a stalker."

Fuck. With everything that has been happening with Arun I had almost forgotten about Mr. Williams. His name curdled in my mind, bringing on fresh waves of disgust and panic.

Mr. Williams. That was all I knew about him. His name. But he has my phone number and even tracked down my address. He rang the buzzer once, but I told him to fuck right off and leave me alone. I couldn't make out his face from the fuzzy black-and-white video, so I wouldn't be able to recognize him if I ever did see him, and that freaked me out more than anything. He could be anywhere. Following me on BART. Watching me.

I shuddered.

I knew it wasn't Nina's fault, but I was pissed that she brought him up.

"Look, he's just a loser who can't take a hint. I can handle it. Please relax."

A tinge of pink had crept into her cheeks. She took a deep breath, the same thing she's always telling me to do. I know she means well.

Hell, it's not like I *wanted* to build a career around selling my worn underwear to people who contact me online. I even thought it was a joke, at first, when some random dude mentioned it on a questionable subreddit. I'd just been poking around there for fun, one night when I couldn't sleep and had run out of Ambien. A little more poking around, and the types of things people were willing to pay for really bowled me over. Underwear was the easiest for me—a couple of naughty selfies with my head strategically out of the frame, lacy panties bought by the pack from Target, and a PO Box under a different name were all I needed. The underwear were a couple of bucks. I sold them for $120 to $150 a pop. Even with the bulk-buying packages I offer, you've got to admit that it's really good margins. Some of the perverts got a little creative with their requests—one wanted me to ride a bike while wearing them, another wanted a note describing how I wore them just for him. A few requests for Polaroids of me feeling myself up through them. The world was full of sick fucks, and *I'm* to blame for figuring out a way to monetize them? Please. This was easy cash, and it's nice to get something easily for once in my life. Minimal effort, maximum rewards. With only the slight threat of a psycho stalker wanting a little more than just my undies finding out who I am and where I live.

I know it isn't the most stand-up-citizen thing to do. I never said I was a Girl Scout. But since the cash from my parents stopped, I've been broker than a tooth fairy at an old folks' home, and desperate times call for desperate measures, right?

"I don't mean to lecture you. I apologize. I worry about you, that's all."

And just like that, I wasn't mad at her anymore. Of course she was just worried. Of course she was only concerned about me. It made me feel warm inside. At least someone cared.

"So." She had her change-the-subject voice on. "How does it feel being back at your parents'?"

"It's, well, it's different. Without them there, I mean. Like I shouldn't even be staying in their home in the first place."

"Why do you think you feel that way?"

I hadn't told Nina about the letter. Just that my parents left on their three-month trip and they'd be mostly incommunicado while they did god knows what in South Asia. She didn't know how Mom cried for a whole week straight and Dad could barely look at me before he left. But truth be told, even before that, the large family house where I had my own room for the first time in my life felt, well, it wasn't mine. I just lived there. But whatever, it was a fucking palace compared to where I came from, so who the hell am I to complain?

"It's just strange being there alone, that's all."

"Is there anyone who could stay with you for a day or two while you settle in?"

I took a deep breath. She knew the answer was no. Why the hell would she even ask?

She must have read my mind, though, because she went on.

"It's just that, well, I'm not sure it's a good idea for you to be alone right now. What about your neighbor, you used to be pretty close to her, right? Ida?" I swear to god, this woman was relentless.

"No, Nina. Just because my mom used to dump me off there when I was a *teenager*"—I stressed the word—"that doesn't mean we get to hang out now. It's not like, you know, it's not like we were friends or anything." I made sure I was smiling when I said it. Not even the tiniest bit of revulsion etched on my face. I didn't want Nina to be mad at me.

"I know. But we did speak about you putting yourself out there since Fern moved out . . . and everything . . ." Her voice trailed off into a question mark. It was another trick she used to get me to open up, but I wasn't falling for it today.

I stayed quiet.

"Look, I know Fern really hurt you when she stole the diamond earrings your parents gifted you," Nina continued. Her grey eyes bored into me, sharp and precise. I swallowed and shifted my gaze to her snow-white rug. "But you can't give up on people altogether. It doesn't have to be hanging out with Ida. Maybe joining a group. Socializing a little more . . . ?"

Fuck you, Nina. What the hell do you expect me to do? Join a goddamned knitting circle? Just so I can hear a bunch of people whine about their weight gain or cheating husbands, or god help me, their bratty little children and how their lives are so fucking complete now even though they haven't slept in weeks and stink of dirty diapers. How the fuck am I supposed to connect with people who didn't have to claw their way into their new lives? Who threw away everything and everyone important to them to get to where they were today? Except where was I, really? An unemployed thirty-year-old who sold her panties to perverts and just found her blackmailing snake of a roommate bleeding out on the kitchen table?

"I've been trying. You know how it is in the city. Everyone's nice. But that's it. It's not like you can just go up to someone and ask them to be your best friend, you know."

Silence.

"I did meet someone interesting," I tried. Anything to keep her from harping on.

"Oh?"

"Another Sri Lankan, believe it or not. He was one of Arun's friends. A waiter, at the restaurant where he worked." Now that I said it out loud, I knew I had made a mistake. Nina was going to make a big deal about this, and I was going to have to bite my tongue, and she was going to pick up on it and give me a lecture about holding back, and I was going to leave here upset.

"One of Arun's friends." Another one of Nina's annoying habits was repeating what I said back to me.

"Yeah. It was weird, he kept talking to me in Sinhalese, which I haven't spoken in years, of course. But I could still understand it. Pretty cool, huh?"

"That is cool."

"He gave me his number." I thought I saw a hint of a smile. Fuck. I need to stop digging this hole deeper.

"Will you call him?"

"I don't know." Was that the best way to say *hell no*?

"You don't know?"

"Yeah." Come on, Nina. Drop this.

But I knew what she was thinking. And she was my friend. And I didn't want her to stop being my friend. And no one wants to be friends with someone who's picky and antisocial and sells their underwear on the internet.

I was going to regret these next few words, I just knew it.

"Okay, fine. I'll text him, okay?"

Maybe I could see if he knew anything more about Arun. Or about me.

Nina's lips curved into a smile but her brow furrowed. The slight wrinkle looked out of place on her smooth forehead. She tucked a rogue strand of hair behind her ear. I guess she didn't use enough hairspray today, even though her bob was always immaculate. I'd come to expect no less. It didn't stop me from being incredibly jealous of women with perfect hair though. My own hair resembled a lion's mane on a good day. Black and coarse and irritatingly poufy. Christina fucking Hannigan used to sing the intro to *The Lion King* whenever she saw me after gym class. Okay, shit, I was drifting off again.

"I don't want to nag you, you know." She smiled. God, I was glad to have her in my life. "I just want to make sure you're okay. I know all this must be tough for you—"

"Seeing my roommate's dead body?" I mean, it would be tough for anyone though. Not just me.

To be honest, I'm kind of surprised she hasn't asked me more about Arun. I expected Nina to be more shocked when I told her, but she seemed pretty nonchalant about the whole thing. Almost like she was expecting it. One thing I got to hand to Nina. It took a lot to weird her out.

"We can let the police deal with that." Pretty dismissive, Nina. Too bad the police gave even less of a shit than she did. "I'm just worried that this whole ordeal might have opened up some old feelings for you?"

"Old feelings? Like what?"

"Like, things that happened back in Sri Lanka?" How did she always know?

"Sri Lanka was a lifetime ago," I said, recrossing my arms and fighting the urge to rub my thumb against my front teeth. I suddenly couldn't care less if I seemed defensive. "And no amount of dead Indian boys will open up that can of worms for me. Whatever happened to Arun is not my fault." That much is true, right?

"What happened in Sri Lanka was not your fault, either, Paloma. You know that, don't you?"

94

I swallowed. Miss Chandra's letter burned in my mind.

"Of course." I mean, there's no point in disagreeing with Nina.

So why was she looking at me like I was some sort of goddamned math equation? Fuck her.

"Nina, I'm fine. Really. Mohini"—I took a deep breath—"was a dumb story the girls in the orphanage made up. I mean, I'm not twelve anymore, for god's sake. I've just . . . well, fuck, you know more than anyone how stressed out I've been lately."

She looked at me again.

Damn it. I hadn't said her name out loud in a while. Definitely not to Nina.

"I wasn't talking about Mohini, Paloma."

"I know, Nina. Like I said, I'm not in the best headspace lately. This whole business with Arun has left me rattled. But I'm okay. I promise."

I just need to figure out what happened that night so I can let this go and move on with my life.

The future's not ours to see. The words flashed in my mind, but then they were gone.

Nina gave me a little nod. She believed me.

"So, we'll keep your prescription as it is for now, then. Just remember what I said about the drinking, okay? I'm serious. You know the reaction from mixing the two will never lead you anywhere good. I'm talking memory loss, hallucinations, drowsiness. More than a few people have ended up in the ER."

Hallucinations. I thought back to the woman in my apartment. She didn't need to tell me twice.

"Yes, Nina." I'm sure I sounded grumpy.

I needed to move on from this bullshit. And the first step was to go back to my apartment for clean clothes, my laptop, and more underwear. I couldn't have this be bad for business. Not right now, anyway. My future sessions with Nina weren't going to pay for themselves.

14

RATMALANA, SRI LANKA

"WE'RE GOING TO GET in trouble *haiyyo*."

I know we are best friends, but it was times like these that I really wanted to smack her.

"We'll only get caught if you don't relax, okay?" I hoped I didn't sound too bossy. She always says she hates it when I get bossy. But I don't think I'm bossy. I just get annoyed when she's being a scaredy-cat like this. I mean, I wasn't asking her to come in search of Mohini or anything like that, no?

It was a Tuesday afternoon and Miss Chandra had taken some of the younger girls to the dentist. Tuesdays were Miss Nayana's off days, and Perera sir usually spent his afternoons reading in the verandah that wrapped around the building. This left the coast clear for us. That is, unless Lihini ruined it by chickening out.

Besides, like I kept telling her, what was the worst that could happen? Miss Chandra and Miss Nayana and even Perera sir were nothing like Sister Cynthia. They never treated us the way she did. If Perera sir was upset with us, we were called to his office and given a stern talking-to. It wasn't fun, but no one ever got caned. And anyways, Lihini should probably take her mind off last week's caning incident.

Checking behind my shoulder, I pushed the door open. A quick look around showed that it was empty. Of course it was.

"We really shouldn't be back here."

I sighed.

"Look, if you want to go, you should go."

I knew she never would.

Not checking to see whether she left, I crept into the dark room. Grey tufts of dust hovered around, and I held my handkerchief up to my mouth. Didn't look like anyone has been here since we visited last. I knew we'd never get caught.

Neither of us onned the light, but the curtain glowed red and made us both look like aliens. Or demons.

"Oooooh!" I mimicked a ghost's cry and watched as Lihini rolled her eyes at me.

"Come on, *sudhu*, you know you want to see it as much as I do."

"Fine." She walked over to the filing cabinet at the back of the room and opened the second drawer. "I just don't want to take a hundred years in here, that's all. If we get caught, they'll send us to St. Margaret's for sure."

I felt a sharp prick on my calf and swatted a mosquito dead. She had a point. The blood smeared on my palm and I wiped it on the hem of my dress.

"Is it there?"

"It's here. Who else will take it, *aney*?" She held out the two cardboard file covers. One faded pink and the other faded yellow.

I went over to the small table at the back of the room, making sure I didn't step on or trip over anything. This was a storage room, we guessed. We never saw anyone come in, but the green plastic chair that Maya broke last year was left here, along with other odd bits of furniture, a few garbage bags of donated clothes that weren't sorted, and of course, the filing cabinet.

We'd wandered in here by mistake a few months ago when we were looking for a better reading spot. Since then, we tried to come back whenever we could. Lihini and I had read about Aladdin's Cave of Wonders. To us, this was even better than that.

She sat across the table and handed me the pink file. I held it up to my nose, inhaling the camphor and ageing paper. One of my favourite smells. Slowly, I took out the three pieces of paper in the file.

The first, I had read a million times, and it mattered the least to me. A birth certificate, oversized, yellowing, the Sinhala typesetting already starting to smudge. Father's name: unknown. Mother's name: Kusuma Manike. Race: Sinhalese. It went on. All details I knew.

I lingered on the second document. It also wasn't what I was here for, but it still made my heart hurt to look at it. The Sinhala handwriting was messy and hardly legible. I didn't bother reading it closely. I knew what it said. It was what my mother signed when she left me. That she was handing me over to the girls' home. That she couldn't be responsible for me. That she didn't want me. That she thought it was best.

I blinked hard as I put the paper down. I snuck a look over at Lihini to see if she had noticed, but she was studying her own file.

The third item wasn't paper, but a card. A photograph. It was small. Smaller than my hand. And it was brown and white. A picture of her. Of Kusuma Manike. Of my mother.

She looked so serious in the picture. Almost angry. Her hair was in a long plait, like mine, but it frizzed around her face like a cloud. Her face was thin and long, and she wore round earrings. I looked at her ears, the line of her nose, the way her lips lay in a straight line.

"I definitely look like her," I told Lihini.

She looked up at me, studying my face. I knew what she was about to say. We went over this every time.

"Yes, you do, *sudhu*."

It was a lie. I was fair. My cheeks were round. My chin was sharp and my front tooth was chipped. My hair was straight, and while it was a little messy, it was nowhere as frizzy as hers. I looked more like Lihini than I did my own mother. The thought made me feel a little empty. Like I would always be missing something.

I stood up from the table, making it jerk.

"Be careful!"

But I grabbed the photo and went to the other corner of the room.

"*Sudhu*, what are you doing?" Her voice was sharp and urgent. For all the times we'd snuck in here, I'd never done this before.

I knew where I was going though. I had spotted it the last time. A small hand mirror, lying on a shelf. I grabbed it and rubbed it on my skirt, trying to clean the glass.

"You shouldn't take that!"

"Stop worrying all the time, Lihini!"

I held the mirror up, trying to compare my face against the one I just saw. The features that were so fresh in my mind a second ago were now blurred. It wasn't working.

I tried to hold the photo next to my face, but the mirror was too small. I needed more distance. I tried to balance it against a pile of tools that were on the shelf, wedging it between a hammer and a screwdriver to keep it upright.

"Paloma, do you know who that belonged to?"

Did it look like I cared? I needed to see. I needed to make sure I was actually hers. If I couldn't have her, could I at least have this?

The mirror kept sliding around, so I pushed the hammer in a little further. Not perfect. But at least I could try to—

The crash was loud and sudden.

Lihini rushed to my side.

Oh gosh. The mirror had slid right off the shelf and onto the ground.

"That's seven years of bad luck," I said. My throat felt tight.

"It might be a little more than that."

"Why? We could just sweep the glass under the table over there. No one comes in here anyway. I'm sure no one will know it's us."

"It's not that." Her eyes were wide and she was breathing hard.

"Then what?"

"The mirror. I've seen it before. It belonged to her."

"To who?" She really frustrated me sometimes.

"To *Mrs. Perera.*"

Perera sir's dead wife.

My body went cold. I took a deep breath and crossed myself, the way Miss Sarah did sometimes.

"We need to clean this up before Miss Chandra finds out." Lihini's voice was urgent, but I stood rooted on the spot.

"Come on, *sudhu.*" She crouched down and started picking up the shards of glass. "Help me, will you?"

I was going to have bad luck for seven years. Why should I bother picking up the glass? I took a step back. I needed to sit down.

"Paloma! *Haiyyo* what's wrong with—oww!" Lihini's cry was soft, but it echoed through the empty room, bouncing off the unused furniture and boxes. She held up her hand. A trail of blood dripped down her palm and fell to the floor with a ripe splat.

15

SAN FRANCISCO, CA

I WAS OUTSIDE MY apartment building, but I couldn't bring myself to go in. She was suddenly everywhere—the woman who brushed past me in a hurry, the man whistling something as he walked by, scrolling on his phone. It wasn't the same song. It couldn't be. But I could feel her, like a spiderweb I had walked into, clinging to my skin, refusing to be brushed off, strangling me.

Inhale, Paloma.

It isn't real. None of this is real.

Just go inside and get your things. You can do this. You've escaped her before, you can do it again.

And so, even though it felt like I was moving in slow motion, even though my legs felt heavy and my chest hurt when I took a deep breath, I put one foot in front of the other and made my way inside.

There was one thing that drove me forward—one thing more important than my toothbrush or clean clothes or my laptop or fresh packs of lacy underwear. And that's my mail.

My mailbox was on the ground floor, and that was the first step. I just had to make it there first.

And I was in luck.

I had the usual supermarket deals and cheap Wi-Fi promotions, but nestled in the middle of them was a lifeline. A rectangular card bearing the photograph of a leopard. I couldn't tell if it was Mom or Dad who had written this one. The writing had gotten smudged, but I could still make out *Love to our sweet girl!* I felt lighter as I tucked the postcard into the pocket of my hoodie. I swear sometimes these postcards were the only thing keeping me going.

I took the stairs up. It took longer, but it gave me more time to prepare myself. The stairwell was pretty dark, so I turned on the flashlight on my phone and tried my best not to think about the last time I was there. It smelled like a fucking porta potty in here, so that did a pretty good job of distracting me. Silver goddamned linings.

My hands shook as I unlocked the door, but once I got inside, it was all business. I wasn't good at many things, but one thing I managed to excel at was shutting my mind down and focusing on whatever the fuck needed to get done.

I turned on all the lights and strode over to the curtains in the living room, tugging them open.

Bathed in light, my apartment revealed itself to be exactly what it was—small, overpriced, clean, and devoid of any fucking demons unless you counted the bitch in the apartment next door.

I glanced at my empty kitchen, just once, to make sure, and then kept my back firmly turned away from it. There was no blood anywhere, not even where I touched the wall on my way to the bathroom. Did blood clean away from wall paint so easily? I know that baking soda usually does the trick, but I'd have to google it later.

Grabbing a large duffel bag from the hallway closet, I went into my room and started to pack.

I wasn't like my mom. I never coordinated outfits into color-coded packing cubes and used those ridiculous miniature plastic bottles for my toiletries that would barely last one shower, let alone an entire trip, but even Mom would have a meltdown if she saw the way I yanked random pieces of clothing out from various corners of my room and stuffed them in my bag. Tank tops, sweaters, an extra pair of jeans. Thank god my homeless-person vibe didn't take much coordination.

A cold breeze found its way into the room.

I must have left my window open the last time I was here, because hydrangea petals from Mrs. Jenson's balcony upstairs swept over my comforter. I stuck my head out the window and peered up. Her care-taker sometimes came out to the fire escape to have a smoke. I wonder if she saw anything that night.

But the fire escape was empty, and I shut the window, making sure it was latched.

I grabbed some new packages of underwear, my laptop, camera, and the notebook where I wrote down my client requests—the last one wanted me wearing cotton panties, size small, preferably with a heart or bow print on them, with ribbons at the waist. And he made it very, very clear that I had to be *hairless* when wearing them. He didn't want a Polaroid.

I rolled my eyes just thinking about it. This thinly veiled pedo's request wasn't even the creepiest one I'd got. The world was full of sick assholes, and here I was, afraid of a ghost from when I was twelve years old.

Que sera, sera
Whatever will be, will be

I couldn't help the words drifting into my mind much more than I could stop the memory of her wrapping her fingers around my neck, breathing into my ear. Arun's empty eyes staring right past me as blood continued to leak down the back of his skull.

Breathe, Paloma. None of this shit is real.

I kept a bottle of Captain Morgan hidden under the sink for emergencies. It was emptier than I remembered, but hey, if being in an apartment where you saw your dead roommate wasn't an emergency, I don't know what was.

I took a little swig and nudged open Arun's bedroom door. I hadn't been inside since he moved in, not even when the police went in to check if he was in there, so I had no way of knowing whether anything was out of place.

The room was empty. Not just empty of a person. Empty of everything. The stripped-down mattress that came with the ratty box bed stood near the radiator, but there was nothing else. No clothes, no bedsheets, not a thing to suggest that an actual human being, let alone an extorting asshole, had lived here for a couple of months except for the stale smell of Axe aftershave that lingered on the cheap carpet.

What the actual hell? Did the police take his things as evidence or something? But they wouldn't do that, would they?

No wonder Officer Keller thought I was batshit crazy. It didn't look like Arun existed at all.

The closet was empty. I got on my knees and looked under the bed. I don't know what I was expecting—a box, perhaps, or a file full of secrets. A USB drive full of clues. I guess I'd been watching too much TV.

Just dust bunnies. Not even a stray sock. Nothing, absolutely not a fucking thing to suggest that I had a roommate to begin with.

But I did have a roommate.

He found out my secret and blackmailed me.

And then he died.

I took another sip of Captain Morgan to steady myself.

I just wish there was a way I could retrace my steps that night. Or at least see if anyone else entered my apartment.

Hang on.

There was something. A speck of dust floating just out of my reach. It was something Officer Keller had said.

We didn't see anything on your building's CCTV footage to suggest suspicious activity.

I stood right up and set down my bottle. CCTV footage. Of course. I was such a fucking idiot for not thinking of this sooner. I mean, how the hell would Officer Keller know who was suspicious and who wasn't? The moron could barely comprehend what I was telling him.

16

SAN FRANCISCO, CA

I KNOCKED FIRMLY ON Jason Wong's office door, holding a cup of coffee and a blueberry muffin that I had run across the street to buy. I wasn't sure if he even drank coffee, but there were a few things I picked up from my mom over my teenage years—one of the most important being that people rarely said no to you if they felt they owed you something.

Being a building superintendent has got to be one of the shittier jobs in the world. Not the worst, of course, that was reserved for pedicurists and preschool teachers, but it sure couldn't be fun being the go-to person when a toilet needed unclogging. I'm sure he'd appreciate a kind gesture, even if it did come with a string or two attached. I hadn't been best buds with Mr. Wong, but I wasn't exactly a bitch to him, like Mrs. Jenson upstairs was, either.

"Come in," he called out.

I set my duffel bag out in the hallway—no way in hell I was going back to my apartment again if I could help it—and pushed my way inside.

The office was nondescript. Just a grey little box and a hard fluorescent light that gave Mr. Wong some of the worst under-eye shadows I've ever seen. No pictures on the wall, no knickknacks on the desk, no plants, no windows, no soul. A bit like Jason Wong himself.

"Paloma Evans, 17D, right?" he asked.

Maybe under normal circumstances I would be weirded out that he remembered me, but then again, not many tenants brought a team of police officers into the building before you could have your first cup of coffee for the morning.

"Yep, that's me." I smiled. "I just wanted to apologize, for the other day, you know."

"Apologize?" He looked surprised. I guess everyone really did treat him like shit.

"Yeah, I know it must have been a shock to you. Police coming into the building so early in the morning. Causing all that disturbance. I just wanted to say sorry." My cheeks felt artificially plumped up as I kept smiling.

"Oh, okay. I mean, it's not me you should apologize to. It's Miss Fabien. She was the one whose child you woke up when, you know." He rubbed his head, his elbow sticking up in the air. His hair poked out in greasy clumps, and the armpit of his white T-shirt was yellow. I handed the coffee and muffin over to him instead of setting it on the table just so he would put his arm back down. My smile stayed put and I made sure not to wrinkle my nose. And I definitely resisted the urge to let him know that adding half a cup of borax to his laundry would get rid of his disgusting pit stains.

Miss Fabien, huh? Guess the bitch neighbor with the bratty kid had a name.

"I just, I'm so confused, you know." I pulled out a chair that was next to his desk and sat down, ignoring that he looked uncomfortable.

He didn't say anything, though, so I continued, leaning forward slightly.

"That night was such a blur to me. I think I might have been sick. I really wish there was a way for me to figure out what happened." I leaned forward a little further, hoping he would take the bait.

"You want to see the CCTV footage, don't you?"

"If it's not too much trouble."

"Sure. I have it all ready anyway. Since the cops reviewed it and everything."

So it looked like the police did take me seriously, even though they didn't give a shit when we spoke.

"They didn't find anything out of the ordinary though. And neither will you."

I couldn't quite read his expression. He turned on an ancient desktop computer and sat there, staring at the start-up screen, waiting patiently. I could see the old Windows hourglass reflected in his glasses. He tapped his finger against the mouse. You would have thought he had all the time in the world.

My tooth gave another small throb but I ignored it and smiled at Wong instead. "Technology, huh? Supposed to make our lives easier . . ."

But I guess Jason Wong gave zero fucks about making small talk.

"The computer is slow," he said simply. I don't need you to be a fucking narrator, Wong, just show me the goddamned footage.

After an adequately torturous length of time, he found the file we were looking for.

"This is what I showed the cops." He opened up the video and made it full screen, although it was so grainy and pixelated that it hardly did any good. The CCTV camera was located about seven feet away from my apartment, and angled away from my door towards the elevator. You couldn't really see anyone entering or leaving through my front door, per se, but you couldn't reach the elevator without passing by the camera. The stairs were closer to my door, so there wasn't a clear line of sight if you weren't standing right in the middle of the corridor.

The corridor was very dimly lit, and this translated to barely more than dark outlines of people as they walked by to the elevator or stairwell.

He dragged the cursor back and forth a little, stopping a bit to make sure of the time.

Three thirty-five p.m. showed me storm towards the elevator and punch the button repeatedly. Figures. I had just argued with Arun and was heading over to the bank. I was pissed as hell.

The doors finally opened and I got on.

Mr. Wong hit the fast-forward button and we watched the video whiz by.

No other movement. No one entered or left.

It was a small, quiet building, so this wasn't strange. Mostly retirees and a few single moms who were getting priced out of anywhere decent in the city but weren't able to take the plunge to move out of the Bay Area.

I came back at 10:16 p.m., and stumbled as I stepped off the elevator. My stomach twisted as I remembered the drinks I chugged to gather up the courage to confront Arun. I really thought I'd come back earlier than that. And more sober than that.

"Had a couple?" Mr. Wong asked.

Fuck you, Wong. Why the hell does everyone think I'm some sort of raging alcoholic? You would want some goddamned liquid courage, too, if the roommate you tried to help out betrayed you and then wound up dead.

I wasn't able to say anything, though, because the fast-forwarded video showed me rush out of my apartment a few minutes later, at 10:22 p.m.

"Hey, just a sec."

"Sorry?" said Mr. Wong, hitting pause.

"Could you rewind, just a little?"

He gave me a look, but he did what I asked.

The video showed me run out of my apartment, like I was being chased by a, well, you know. But there was no one after me. At least in the few feet that were visible, I was alone. You could just see a very blurry, potentially drunk me rush towards the stairs, where there was barely any visibility anyway, and disappear. No Mohini, obviously, but no one else chasing me either.

Mr. Wong hit the fast-forward button again, and the video ran ahead until 5:47 a.m., when Fabien, my condescending bitch neighbor with the toddler and terrible breath, left her apartment. You couldn't really see her surprise, or was it revulsion, of seeing me in the stairwell from the angle of the camera, but I'm sure that didn't stop her from filling Jason Wong, or the police, in on how she felt.

The police showed up at 6:23 a.m.

"That can't be right. Isn't there anything else?"

"This is all we have."

Are you kidding me, Jason Wong?

I made sure my voice was even. My smile definitely could not slip here.

"And the other floors?"

He raised an eyebrow.

"You want the other floors?"

"Well, if that's okay."

"Look, Miss Evans, I'm sure you had a bad night. But the police have reviewed all the footage and they haven't noted anything strange."

"But that can't be all. Someone was in my apartment that night.

Someone—" I stopped myself. I couldn't tell Jason Wong about Arun's body. He thought I was some sort of degenerate as it is. The last thing I needed was for him to think I was hallucinating too.

"It's my roommate, you see. He's missing." I mean, he technically *was* missing, alive or dead. "And the video doesn't show him leave."

I know the CCTV recordings were fuzzy as fuck but surely, someone couldn't move a body without even a part of it being recorded?

But Mr. Wong's lips turned into a downward U.

"Ms. Evans, you know you are not allowed to have a roommate, right? We make it clear in our contract that we don't allow subletting. Anyone who wanted to share an apartment has to go through a credit check and have references. I told the police as much when they woke me up before dawn."

I could have slapped myself.

Of course I fucking knew that. It was why Arun and I barely had an agreement and he paid me in cash for everything. Well, that, and the fact that he technically didn't even have a credit score. It was why I told him to always use the stairs, never the elevator. And keep to himself. He seemed happy enough to comply. There weren't many places he could rent this easily in the city.

"As far as I know, Miss Evans, you never even had a roommate. And I would appreciate it if you didn't worry the other residents so much every time you went on a bender. Your neighbor told me she only called the police because she was afraid you were hurt."

Well, fuck you, too, Jason Wong.

"Could I please just see the other floors?"

"I'll tell you what. I'll email you a link to all the footage. That'll be easier, right? But trust me, I can tell you right now that there really isn't anything to see. Mrs. Jenson's caretaker took her out a little before the police came, but no one else really came or left the building between your, um, episode and Miss Fabien finding you. Well, except—"

He looked down and frowned, then rubbed his head again.

"Except?"

"Look, you'd probably had some sort of accident. That's fine. But it would be great if you could return that mop and cleaning supplies. Those items are for the common areas, not personal use."

Huh? What was Jason Wong going on about now?

"That's not possible."

"What do you mean, that's not possible? The cleaning equipment is for the janitor's use only. Not for tenants. We need it back or I'll have to take it out of your deposit."

"No, I mean—" It took every ounce of my energy to keep my voice light and calm. "I never took your mop. Or any cleaning products."

Jason Wong's eyes narrowed.

"Here." He fiddled with the video again. It was the floor above mine. Same camera angle, except it showed part of the utility closet. It was 11:05 p.m.

A woman opened the door of the utility closet and pulled out a mop and a bunch of cleaning solutions. A woman wearing sweatpants and a hoodie, just like I'd been wearing that night. Like I was even wearing right now. You couldn't see her face, but she had black hair that streamed out from under her hood, which was pulled up.

Wong shifted his gaze back to me, his face resting smugly as if to say, *I told you so.*

I had to hand it to Wong, that did look a fuck load like me, but surely, I didn't get into the janitor's closet that night?

I held my thumb up to my tooth, and my hands gave a small tremble as Nina's voice wriggled its way into my mind—*You can't drink with these, okay?*

"I—I'm sorry about that. Really. I could Venmo you the cost? I'll make sure—"

But something else on his screen caught my attention. He'd switched back to my floor, and was clicking through something, but the video was still running on fast-forward. A man stepped out of the elevator.

"What's that?" My voice squeaked.

Wong gave the screen an unhurried look.

"That's later on in the day." The time stamp said 10:05 a.m. I would have been at the station by then.

"Could you play that again?"

He did not look happy, but he clicked through for me to see a man walk out of the elevator, disappear towards my apartment door, and then return to the elevator exactly two minutes later. There was nothing distinct about him—he wore an ascot cap pulled low over his face, along with a jacket of sorts. Definitely better dressed than the men you found sneaking away from these apartments in the early hours of the morning.

Surely, that couldn't be Mr. Williams? Could it? I could hear Nina's voice in my ear: *You told me at our last session that you had a stalker. Was it really him?*

I started to feel sick. Call me dense, but I never thought he would actually make it into my building. And he was here the morning after Arun died? What kind of ridiculous coincidence is that? The few sips of Captain Morgan I'd taken earlier were starting to rise in my throat.

I clumsily took down Jason Wong's details and gave him my email address. I don't care that the police went through it already, I needed to see the CCTV recordings again. There was no way, no way in hell, that I had just been hallucinating that evening.

No way.

Right?

17

I GOT THE HELL out of his suffocating hole of an office as fast as I could. I thought visiting Wong would give me answers, but it left me more confused than ever. How had Mr. Williams actually made it inside my building? I mean, security here was pretty much nonexistent. I guess I'd never considered that he would be this determined.

And why the fuck would I need a mop and bleach?

Well, apart from the fucking obvious.

I was seriously losing my shit here.

I pushed the main door open, almost crashing into Mrs. Jenson and her caretaker as they were coming inside. Mrs. Jenson didn't look great, but maybe that's just the way old people looked, especially those who were confined to a wheelchair and probably just a few weeks away from kicking the proverbial bucket. She was engulfed in her huge brown coat as usual and had a billowy floral scarf wrapped around her head.

"Oh! You!" she called out.

I really wasn't in the mood to hang around chatting with senile women. I needed to get as far away from this cursed building as I could, but a quick thought had me swallow my irritation and call out instead.

"Hi, Mrs. Jenson. How are you?"

"At my age, dear, it's a good thing just to wake up." I guess she had a point. Her voice rasped like she'd smoked one too many cigarettes in her day.

"I was just wondering—the other day, you know, when the police came. I was wondering if you heard anything? Or maybe saw anyone strange in the building?"

"You know, I'm glad you brought it up. It really isn't becoming of a young lady to scream at her beau like you do."

Wait. What?

"I'm sorry?"

"Your beau, dear. We can hear you upstairs, you know, arguing all the time. I know you are from a place where people are very, well, what's the word, *hot-blooded*, you know. But that's no excuse to take it out on your man. It simply doesn't do for a lady to behave that way."

Hot-blooded? What the actual fuck was this stupid old fossil on about? I only ever argued with Arun once.

"I—I'm sorry." I tried to sound haughty but I was too upset. Besides, she still hadn't answered my question. "He's actually just my roommate, but, well . . ." I trailed off. What the hell was I supposed to say to this?

I looked at her caretaker. She was blond and seemed afraid the wheelchair would run her over.

"Did it disturb you also?" Surely, someone in their right mind would know if Mrs. Jenson was making this shit up because she was irritable.

"Of course you couldn't disturb her, dearie, she's new. My old caretaker up and quit the day after all that nonsense." Her eyes narrowed as if a new idea just came into her mind. "I suppose I have you to thank for that. Keeping us up at all hours with your lovers' spats."

Oh, hell no.

I wanted to reach out and slap this doddering prune, but I took a deep breath instead.

Be nice, Paloma.

"It's getting quite chilly out here, Mrs. Jenson. Why don't we get you inside?"

She just shrugged and allowed herself to be wheeled away. But I still couldn't shake off the unease that was slowly working its way through me.

I walked around as if I were in a dream, not a clue where the hell I was going, until I finally collapsed onto a bench at the bus stop.

I was shaking so hard I could barely get my phone out of my pocket. I tried to take deep breaths, just like Nina had told me to, but it wasn't working. What the fuck was happening to me?

Whatever will be, will be

Get ahold of yourself, Paloma.

18

RATMALANA, SRI LANKA

IT'S ONLY PERERA SIR'S office. I had to try not to be so scared.

The air smelled like old books and dust as I took a deep breath. I hoped it would make me relax. Books usually did. But my heart just wouldn't slow down. It felt like raindrops on the *takaran* roof we had in the bathroom, that time I got caught in there during a monsoon shower. Loud, hard bangs that I could feel all the way to my fingertips.

We only get called into Perera sir's office for two reasons—either we've been very good, or we've been very bad. And I know that I definitely hadn't come first in class or won any awards, so I had an idea what it could be. I didn't think anyone saw us sneak into the storeroom, but someone must have told. The curse was probably working.

I know we are too old to believe in curses, but we couldn't help it. I've noticed Lihini, looking over her shoulder, checking behind the curtains and under the bed when she thinks I won't notice. She was convinced that she was cursed also, after she cut her hand on the mirror. She had bandaged it up, told everyone she cut it when she tripped in the back garden, and kept muttering prayers to herself. I don't know what's wrong with her. I broke the mirror. If there was a curse, I was definitely a goner. I could feel it, a presence all around me, following me, watching me. The small hairs on the back of my neck had started standing up at odd times. I could feel a cold breeze even during hot afternoons.

Lihini even snuck some limes from the kitchen yesterday and said we should cut them to ward off evil, like we saw a medicine man do to Shanika after she, well, you know. But neither of us could remember the chants he said, and we didn't have his fancy knife.

But a voice of reason broke through all my worrying—we were both in the room that day, so why did Perera sir call only me?

I had taken some extra biscuits from the tin that Miss Nayana kept in the kitchen, but she did say I could have some because I had helped her clean the whole playroom and arrange all the crayons. Or maybe it was because I knocked that book over when Mr. and Mrs. Evans came. It had been two weeks now since their visit, and no one said anything about it so far. I thought it would be okay. Maybe I was wrong.

Perera sir wasn't here yet, and this made me worry some more. Miss Chandra had told me to come to his office, sit down, and not touch anything. I couldn't stay still though. Listening for footsteps, I slowly slid off the chair. Perera sir's office wasn't very large, but it was full of the most wonderful things. He had a globe on his desk, for starters. I carefully twirled it around on its stand, looking at the way the different countries swung by. Italy, Switzerland, Australia . . . all places I could only dream about, outlined like pieces of a jigsaw puzzle.

We usually only left the orphanage to go to school in the old white van that Perera sir's nephew drove. Our school was just down the lane. When I was too small to go to school, I could even hear the children singing and playing on a quiet morning. About three times a year, Miss Chandra and Miss Nayana took us to the Mount Lavinia beach. I mean, it's amazing when we go and we do have the best time, but sometimes I wonder if I could just jump in and keep swimming until I reach India, or maybe even Cambodia. Of course, I wasn't really sure if I could even swim. I've read about it, but we've never been to a swimming pool or a lake like the children in the books we read. That reminded me—

The books in Perera sir's office were far nicer than the ones we had in our library. They were still old, or at least older than what we had, but they were clothbound and had the title stamped across the covers in gold and silver. And the smell! I moved closer to the bookcase, past the small door right behind the desk that Perera sir always kept locked, so I could reach over and sniff them. Divine! I saw my reflection in the small glass panels on the door—*haiyyo*, my hair was such a mess. Good thing I noticed before Perera sir came. I tried the doorknob, just out of curiosity. Locked as always. The girls said Perera sir would lock naughty children in there, but he's never done it as long as I could remember.

I looked through his desk too. Not much, not disarranging anything. Miss Nayana says that curiosity killed the cat, but then again, she also says that cats have nine lives, so I don't see any harm in looking around.

I found a first aid box in his top drawer. Bingo. I could take some vitamin C tablets for Lihini and me. Those sour white tablets were the best and we loved how it made our faces scrunch up. But when I opened the box, all I saw were a bunch of injections in their packets.

I shut the box quickly. These must be the special injections that Perera sir gave Shanika to calm her down when she tried to suicide herself.

I heard his footsteps before he entered, and I jumped back into my seat, my heart beginning to pound again. I studied his face carefully as he sat across from me behind his desk, but he looked the same as always. His hair was perfectly parted to one side, his little mustache was trimmed perfectly, and his white shirt was tucked neatly. Miss Sarah had explained the saying "not a hair out of place" to us a while back, and I had asked her if I could use Perera sir as an example. She'd laughed and said she couldn't think of a better one.

"Well, Paloma, how are you today?"

How was I? Ready to faint.

"I'm very well, thank you, sir. And you?" Thank goodness Miss Chandra had drilled it into me.

"Well. I'm well. Thank you. Good to see Miss Chandra is teaching you your manners."

I wish he would just tell me why I was here. Tell me what my punishment is and let me go. He was nothing like Sister Cynthia. I'm sure his punishment wouldn't be bad. The waiting was killing me. I ran my tongue over my chipped tooth like I always did when I was nervous.

"So, as you remember, Mr. and Mrs. Evans visited us a few weeks back."

So that was it, then. My heart sank. It was the dropped book. I didn't think he would have remembered. But I guess what everyone has been saying is true—since Mrs. Perera died last year, Perera sir isn't the same. He gets angry more easily, and Dumila said she even heard him yelling at someone a few days ago. We've never heard Perera sir yell, so that's really, really bad. And he had arranged the day so beautifully during the visit and I went and ruined it by dropping that stupid book. How could I have been so silly?

"Y-yes, sir."

"You know, Paloma, the Evanses are a very important family." The Evanses. I loved how it sounded. It had such a nice ring to it. But now the Evanses hated me. And Perera sir hated me. It's the curse. I'm sure of it. I broke a mirror and now my luck will be bad for seven years. Or maybe even forever, who knew?

I forced myself to keep listening to Perera sir, trying not to get distracted.

"They are good friends with Mr. Whittaker, you know him, don't you? He's the head of the charity that funds Little Miracles. Every year, it's his blessings that provide for our food, books, expenses." Perera sir made a sweeping gesture with his hand and I gulped. I wondered what my punishment would be. I've only ever gotten into serious trouble once before, when Maya told Miss Chandra that I poured turpentine on the old orphanage cat, Panchi.

"So that's why, Paloma, it's so important that we try to impress Mr. Whittaker. To show him that his efforts are not being wasted. I depend heavily on you girls to let him know that."

I nodded, even though I felt like I was about to vomit.

"I know that many of you girls hope to be adopted when we have visitors, even though that is not always why they come. While it saddens me a little, because I do think of you all as my family"—his mustache twitched a bit here—"I know that I have to let you go if there's a better life for you. I know you want it also, which is why these visits can bring about so much excitement and nervousness."

I braced myself. He was going to start scolding me at any moment. Would he stop me from attending English classes? Or take away my books? Maybe I could hide just one book before he took them away. I could sneak it under my mattress. Or ask Lihini to hide it for me. I wonder if he would send me to St. Margaret's to live with Sister Cynthia. Surely I didn't deserve that?

"Paloma, you did very well at the last visit. Very well, indeed. So well, that Mr. and Mrs. Evans would like to welcome you into their family. Paloma, they would like to adopt you."

I counted eight beats of my heart. Then I took a deep breath.

He must be joking. There was no way.

"Me?" I asked. My goodness, I sounded so stupid.

"Yes, you. They initially thought they wanted someone younger, which is why they spent so much time with the smaller girls. But after Mrs. Evans saw you reading her favourite book in the playroom, well, she said you shared a connection."

If miracles did exist—if fairies and pots of gold at the ends of rainbows and geese that laid golden eggs were all given to me, if every wish I had ever wished for decided to come true all at once, I still couldn't believe this. This. This was pure magic. I thought back to Mrs. Evans and the way her golden hair shone in the sunlight. She truly was an angel. And she had flown down from heaven and chosen me, her sweet girl.

"Paloma, are you okay?"

I nodded my head. My legs felt weak even though I was sitting down. I was about to burst out crying. I couldn't explain why.

"I just—I just can't believe it," I finally managed. My voice shook. It felt hard to speak. Or to breathe.

"Well, take it in. This is big news. The Evanses have been trying to adopt for quite a while and have finally been cleared by the NCPA, that's the National Child Protection Authority. We are lucky they decided to visit our home after getting their approvals. They have gone back to California for now, to make all the necessary arrangements while your paperwork gets cleared from this end. But it shouldn't take too long, thanks to Mr. Whittaker's connections."

He kept talking more about forms I had to sign and interviews I needed to have with the NCPA, but I couldn't listen. California! That was in America! America, like we saw on TV! America, where beautiful, light-haired women roller-skated on the beach, and they drank milkshakes, and ate burgers and french fries, and went shopping and got these big, beautiful cardboard bags with shop names printed on them in fancy letters. America, where movies were made. Where everyone wore tennis shoes, not rubber slippers like we did, and denim jackets and denim jeans.

"Paloma, do you understand? You need to keep this to yourself for now, okay? We'll call an assembly tomorrow to announce the news."

"I can't tell anyone?"

"Just for today, it'll be our little secret, okay?" He winked at me. "News like this, well, you know how some of the girls might get upset." He meant Shanika, of course. We're always having to tiptoe around her now.

"It'll be a hard adjustment when you leave too. For your friends to get used to you being gone."

Oh my goodness! Lihini! How could I have forgotten? How could I live without her, all the way in a faraway country? She would be heartbroken if I left her. A memory flashed into my mind of Lihini crying, the way she cried that time Beth died in *Little Women*. And that wasn't even real. Oh gosh. Suddenly, America didn't feel so exciting after all.

"Perera sir?"

"Yes?"

"Will they—will Mr. and Mrs. Evans be adopting only me? Wouldn't they like someone else also?"

"Why, Paloma, are you scared to go?"

"No. No, sir, I just thought—"

But I couldn't finish.

Perera sir smiled, but it was without his usual twinkle.

"No, Paloma, it's just you."

19

I PUT THE BOTTLE of scotch back in my dad's liquor cabinet and dumped my mug into the sink, running the tap so the remainder of last night's drink rinsed off. I've always taken Dad's scotch in a coffee mug. He had been so mad at me the time he found me drinking from one of his lowball tumblers from Tiffany's. I think that upset him more than the fact that I was sneaking his scotch at fifteen. God, I must have been a difficult kid.

I eyed the six glasses with their diamond-point edging, laid out next to the matching $500 ice bucket. I suppose I could just drink from them now. He'd never find out.

Somehow it felt preposterous.

More preposterous than the drink I needed last night after watching the hour hand of the clock above my bed slowly circle its way around more than three times while I tried to stop myself from imagining Mohini snaking her fingers around my neck.

It's not real, I kept telling myself. She's not real. But things that don't feel real during the day have a way of sliding into bed with you at night, caressing you until you're too numb to move, choking you down until you can't breathe.

And there was that image of me, taking the mop out of the janitor's closet. Surely, I had to remember that? I know I liked to stress clean, but I had passed out in the stairwell for fuck's sake. I wasn't about to go Marie Kondo my apartment when I'd just seen my roommate's dead body there. Right?

Fuck, I need to shake myself out of this bullshit.

I could smell my breath, rancid and sour. Whatever was left of the drink churned around in my stomach. I needed some actual coffee in my mug.

My phone had died and I'd left my charger in the kitchen last night, so I plugged it in while I waited for my coffee to brew.

I felt my heart beat a little faster as the phone turned on, but there was nothing serious I had missed. Of course there were no calls from the police. I don't know what the hell I was expecting anyway.

I loaded up my email. There was one from Mr. Williams, right on top. My thumb shook a little as I tapped on it.

Miss Evans,

> *There's really no point in going to such lengths to avoid me. We will meet sooner or later. It is certainly in your best interest to return my calls.*

That fucker. Who does he think he is, trying to force my hand like this? I'll see you in hell first, asshole. I hit delete.

I had two emails from some of my more normal clients—*Sweaty and Wet;)* read one subject line, *Pink Floral Panties???* read the other, but those were fine, I'd deal with them when things settled down a bit. I also had two voice mails.

That's weird. Who the hell leaves voice mails anymore? Doesn't everyone just text?

I hesitated for a second but then took a deep breath and tapped the notification.

I listened to the first few seconds, my breathing slowing down. The first one was only Ida. I suppose it's impressive that she even had a cell phone to start with.

> *Hello, dear. Glad you're back home and hope you are settling in. Just wanted to check in with you. Let me know if tomorrow at ten a.m. is a good time for you to come over? There's someone I'd like you to meet. As you know, we do have a few things to chat about. Anyway, I'll see you at ten tomorrow at my place. This is Ida, by the way.*

Someone she'd like me to meet? Hell, no. Dealing with random strangers at my parents' dinner parties was bad enough, but I'll be damned if I let myself be cornered into an old lady's matchmaking scheme.

I tapped on the icon to listen to the second voice mail.

It was Ida, again.

> *Hello again, dear. It's Ida. I can't remember if I told you, but could we meet at ten a.m. tomorrow, at my place? There's someone I'd like you to meet. Hope that's all right with you? See you soon.*

Wow, Ida really was getting old.

I looked through my texts. Nothing unread, but I realized with a jolt that I had, in fact, followed through on my promise to Nina and messaged Sam. We were supposed to meet this evening. What the actual fuck was drunk me thinking?

It's not that I didn't want to meet him. I should. I needed to. I had to know if Arun had told him anything. It was the way he said it—*I've heard so much about you.* It started up the humming again. The same humming I felt when I saw the note that was left on my fridge.

Even though Arun found out about what I did, how could he have found out about the song? He must have had contact with someone from Sri Lanka. Or did someone else leave me that note on the fridge? Perhaps the same person who killed Arun, and this was his way of telling me I was next? Or maybe I was just being a paranoid lunatic.

Fuck me, there was only one way to find out. And we'd already set up a time and place to meet in the city.

I just can't believe that I don't remember messaging him. I guess this is what Nina meant. Drinking on my meds wasn't the best idea.

I turned my laptop on and logged on to my Facebook account, keying in Arun Patel in the search bar. There were fucking hundreds of them. Arun Mukerjee was no better. And every single goddamned one of them forced me to think of Arun's vacant eyes after I pulled his head back in my kitchen.

I tried searching for Sam and then Saman. I didn't have his last name, and it was an even more useless exercise than searching for Arun, so I let it go.

But I did go on my own profile to check what Sam would see if he figured out who I was. Not that he would have much luck, I'm sure. I was always cautious about my privacy online. I only used my initial, P. Evans, and lord knows there were enough Evanses around to give me at least a little anonymity.

My last post was about a month ago. A video of a puppy dancing around on his hind legs with his dinner bowl in his mouth. Nothing too heavy, nothing too political. Good. A few weeks before that, someone had tagged me in a flyer about some club opening. I didn't go, obviously, but at least it made it look like I had some sort of social life going on. I looked good, albeit a little blurry, in my profile picture too—a candid of me holding a giant ice cream cone and laughing, my new, perfect teeth on full display. The shot was grainy enough, edited to look "vintage" so my features weren't super clear. It was taken by my ex-roommate Fern, before the whole diamond-earring debacle. It's almost a shame she left. She sure could take a mean photo.

On autopilot, I clicked on my newsfeed and scrolled through, only half glancing at the bland memes and news articles people shared to make themselves look funny, or concerned about the environment, or politically inclined. I stopped when I saw a post by Christina Hannigan, who made my life in private school absolute hell—she was holding a fat pink baby, her hair still falling in perfect, blond, artfully messy waves, casually tucked behind one ear to reveal a perfect pearl Chanel earring. How tacky. She was fucking glowing though. I visited her profile and scrolled through carefully. I didn't want to accidentally "like" something and have her know I was stalking her.

She'd posted something about the benefits of a vegan diet. She'd captioned it *I just really care what I put into my body.* I saw the boys you dated in high school, Christina. You most certainly do not.

Christina married a wealthy finance-bro type. You know what I mean, the kind that has an Armani suit in every shade of charcoal and takes helicopter rides up to Napa Valley. He looked like a goblin decided to procreate with a scarecrow, but whatever, they seemed pretty happy. Her profile was full of pictures of her baby, who was unfortunately taking after his dad. Ah, well. Karma is a bitch, or something like that anyway. You couldn't even see the scar on her chin anymore from when I punched her and it split open. Of course, her parents flew her to LA to meet with the best plastic surgeons, and she was given a BMW convertible so she would "feel safe getting to school and back," while I was suspended for a week and had my phone privileges taken away. Like, who the hell was I going to call anyway? And she was the one who got Adam Green, the class creep, to tell everyone that I'd let him go to third base with me and that I smelled like onions and garlic down there.

My hands were shaking again, so I closed my laptop and went over to the fridge. I was careful not to look at the postcards, even though I had already stuck on the one with the leopard that I picked up yesterday when I went back to my apartment.

The kitchen window looked into the street, and the lacy white curtains were open. The girl with short, neon-pink hair was walking Ida's dog. Damn, I knew Ida was old, but she really must be getting on if she needed someone else to help walk her dog. She loved that terrier like it was a child of her own. Of course, she never had a child of her own, so maybe Ida did have more common sense than I gave her credit for.

I noticed the woman across the street suddenly, and almost dropped my coffee mug. She was standing at the top of my driveway, staring straight at the house. That's all she did—just stood there, swaying slightly. Her hair was even wilder than before, like it hadn't been brushed in days, and she wore the same white robe she had on earlier. It hung open over a T-shirt that had a picture of a cross on it.

I was rooted to the spot. I wanted to go out there, to ask her what the fuck she wanted, but I couldn't make myself move. I don't know if she could see me through the window, but she suddenly cocked her head to one side and smiled.

And then she put something in my mailbox.

I could hear the blood pounding in my ears as she turned around and walked back to her house.

I'm not sure how long I stood there, willing myself to calm down. It's nothing, I said to myself. She's just a neighbor. She just put something in your mailbox. Just because she's brown and her hair is disheveled doesn't mean she's someone from your past that's out to get you.

When I finally felt like I could be steady on my feet, I walked slowly down my driveway. I looked over at her house, but there was no movement from inside. If she was standing by a window, watching me, I'd never know.

It's like pulling off a Band-Aid, Paloma, just do it quickly and get it over with.

I yanked open the door to the mailbox and reached inside, bracing myself.

It was a package wrapped in brown paper. I ripped it open.

An aged copy of *Wuthering Heights*.

I flipped to the first page even though my hands shuddered enough that I could barely hold the book.

I saw what I knew would be there—*To our sweet Paloma, from your new mom & dad.*

The book they gave me when I first moved here. *A welcome present*, they said.

How the hell did the nut job across the street get her hands on this?

I rushed back inside and locked the door, making sure I had activated the alarm. I can't remember if I did it last night. Fuck, I needed to be more careful when I was drinking. I hugged the book to my chest and took deep breaths.

Calm down, Paloma. There must be some explanation for this. No need to jump to any conclusions.

I took another deep breath and looked at the time. Shit, it was well after noon. I should shower, and start getting ready for my meeting with Sam. I thought about the effort of shaving my legs and drying my hair. I mean, I know it isn't a date or anything, that I'm just meeting him to make sure that Arun didn't go shoot his mouth off. But there was no way I was going to meet him looking like shit. If my mother taught me anything, it was that it's far easier to get what you want when you look like the best possible version of yourself.

Nothing wrong with being well presented, she would say, and judging from the amount of free stuff she would get, it's true. She was pure sugar. I could never be that sweet. Especially not with men.

Maybe I should just cancel with Sam. It did seem like a lot of effort right now.

If only Arun's face didn't claw its way into my mind every time I shut my eyes.

Fuck, if I don't figure out what the hell is going on sooner than later, I will seriously lose my shit.

20

RATMALANA, SRI LANKA

I HAVE NEVER BEEN very good at running. Not terrible, of course. I wasn't a slowpoke like Dumila, who huffed and puffed after just one round of run and catches. But I was never fast enough to be picked first. Actually, I have never been picked first for anything my whole life. The only reason I even got cast as Mary in the Christmas play was because I had begged and begged Miss Sarah, and even then, it was the angel Gabriel who got more lines. So I really, really couldn't understand how Mr. and Mrs. Evans chose me.

She had said it was because I liked *Wuthering Heights*. Thank goodness I hadn't finished the chapter I was on the day before. *Wuthering Heights*—how fitting. Mrs. Evans was going to be my Catherine. She was going to save me.

But was that all? Surely they wouldn't just invite me into their family based on a book? I considered myself, weighing out the pros and cons like Lihini always kept saying I should. I was fairer than most of the girls, like a *suddha*, a foreigner, myself. At least according to everyone else. Maybe that was one of the reasons why they would like me?

I mean, Miss Nayana says it'll be easy for me to find a husband one day because I'm so fair, but that wouldn't be why the Evanses would choose me to be their child, right? Could people's lives really change like that, just because of how fair or dark they are?

Besides, Lihini is as fair as I am, and they still picked me. Me, with my ugly, chipped tooth that she *had* said was adorable, for some amazing reason. I made up my mind, right then and there—I was going to be Mrs. Evans's sweet girl. I was going to be as sweet as they came. I was going to be worthy of her love, or both of their love, and not just because of the lightness of my skin.

All day long, the news fluttered around like a crow inside my belly. How could I tell Lihini? How could I leave her behind? Would she hate me? Lihini and I have been best friends from the day she was born. Miss Chandra said our mothers were from the same background, whatever that meant, and that when they stayed at the orphanage in the weeks before we were born, that they became friends too. So actually, we were friends since before we were born. So when I tell her the news, she'll be happy for me, right? I really, really hope she'll be happy for me. I just need to find a way to tell her so she won't hate me.

And then, there was another part of me, a part that made the crow flap its wings even harder. A part that imagined what life would be like in California. A part that kept popping pictures into my mind, of Mrs. Evans making me breakfast, of Mr. Evans dropping me off to my new school. Thank goodness I'm so good at my English classes. I didn't think anyone there would know how to speak Sinhala.

"What's wrong, *sudhu*?" Lihini asked. She didn't know that I had been at Perera sir's office this morning, or she would have asked me immediately what it was for.

"Nothing." I shrugged, trying my best to look like my heart wasn't about to explode. "Why?"

"You've been staring at the same page for fifteen minutes."

Haiyyo.

"I'm just thinking, that's all."

"Is it about"—she dropped her voice even though there really wasn't anyone around—"the curse?"

I snorted. The curse was the furthest thing from my mind right now. The curse couldn't be real. I wasn't unlucky. I was the exact opposite of unlucky. My dreams had come true.

We were at the playground, under the ambarella tree that grew in the corner. It shaded us from the hot April sun—the hottest April yet, Miss Nayana said. This was one of our favorite spots. Most of the other girls were off fighting about whose turn it was next on the swings, and we would lean our backs against the bark of the big tree and read without anyone to trouble us.

Lihini got a small smile on her face. "Is it about a boy, then?"

"A boy?" *Haiyyo*, Lihini, seriously? I loved her, but she was such a romantic. Always imagining hearts and flowers and cupid's bows to fly out of somewhere.

"Well?" She wriggled her eyebrows at me.

"*Aney*, you're mad? The only boy we even see is that Upul, and he's such a creep. He never leaves us alone."

"You mean he never leaves you alone." Lihini's smile grew wider. "If he wasn't Perera sir's nephew, I'm sure he'd be in trouble by now."

I thought of the way he licked his lips as he stared at me in the rearview mirror when he drove us to school. This wasn't the first time someone had mentioned him either. Maya keeps saying that Upul couldn't take his eyes off me. She sounded jealous when she said it. Goodness knows why. She was more than welcome to him if she wanted.

"You're just imagining things, Lihini. He's just being—oh, I don't know." My cheeks felt hot. I really didn't want to keep talking about this. Why was Lihini so crazy about boys?

"*Haiyyo*, Paloma, don't you understand? That's the way these boys give you attention. He's probably just shy."

"Isn't he in his twenties? That's way too old to be shy, if you ask me."

I leaned back against the tree and focused on the page again. I was reading *Anne of Green Gables* now, which Miss Sarah said was more suitable than *Wuthering Heights*. It irritated me a little when she said that, but Anne was divine. Upul was no Gilbert Blythe though. Not even the annoying Gilbert at the beginning of the story, when he pulled on Anne's hair and called her "carrots." I guess it didn't matter anyway, now that I was leaving.

I thought about Mrs. Evans for the millionth time.

"Kindred spirits," I whispered.

"Huh?"

"Oh, no, it was nothing. Just something in the book."

"Is it good? *Aiyyo*, I knew I should have picked that one first."

"You can have it as soon as I'm done, no? I'll be fast, I pro—" But I couldn't finish what I was trying to say.

My book was snatched from my hands and thrown away as Shanika hurled herself at me, scratching at my face, pulling at my hair. I threw my hands out and tried to push her away, screaming over her own shrieks.

"How could you? You stole it from me! You stole it from me!" She was half sobbing, never easing up on her attack.

"Shanika!" Lihini had jumped to her feet and was trying to pull her away, but Shanika was strong and pushed her off.

"Ow! Miss Chandra! Miss Chandra!" Lihini was screaming, too, and the girls in the playground started noticing and gathered around.

"Get. Off. Me." My hands were now acting by themselves. Slapping back. I couldn't focus. Everything felt red.

"I need this!" There were tears on her face.

"Girls! Girls! What is the meaning of this?!" Miss Chandra's voice boomed out over the screaming and the sobbing, harder than any slap we could give each other. Miss Nayana was right behind her.

But Shanika didn't stop. "You stole it from me. You don't understand. You stole it from me," she kept screaming.

"What, Shanika? What did she steal? Was it the book? You can have it, okay? Just stop." Lihini was trying to reason with her. Anything to get her to stop. I saw Upul and the gardener run onto the playground. They would be able to wrench her off.

"She took my place. She stole Mr. and Mrs. Evans. They were meant to be my parents, but she took them. You don't understand. I can't go and live with Sister Cynthia. I can't. I need this."

Lihini pulled Shanika's hair back and slapped her across the face. It echoed out like a gunshot.

Shanika stopped attacking me and hunched over, in shock. Upul grabbed her from behind and pulled her away. I bent over, too, breathing hard. My face felt like it was on fire, and I wasn't sure if it was just from her scratches.

"Miss Chandra, her face!" Miss Nayana exclaimed. She sounded worried. If Shanika had given me a scar, I would kill her.

"Let's see." Miss Chandra took my face in her rough hands and inspected my wounds. "Not too bad, thank god."

"Will it heal before—?"

"Yes, yes, looks like she just needs some ice." Miss Nayana looked relieved.

"You should know better," Miss Chandra continued. "It will ruin the whole image of the orphanage if we hand you over looking like a street brawler! Inside now, everyone."

Lihini didn't meet my eye, so I watched as Upul and the gardener half dragged, half carried a sobbing Shanika inside. Her hair was messed up over her face, and her clothes were dirty. She'd picked up that stupid doll again. Her blouse had gotten untucked from the loose skirt she was wearing. I could have sworn I saw Upul push his hand inside the material as he pulled her away. He saw me looking and gave me a cheeky grin. I felt sick.

"Did you see that?" I asked Lihini in horror.

But she wasn't looking at Upul and Shanika.

"Is it true? Are Mr. and Mrs. Evans adopting you?"

It felt like there were at least five crows inside me now, and they were pecking at my insides. How much longer was I supposed to keep this from her, anyway? She's my best friend. I wanted to tell her that. I wanted to tell her that I wasn't abandoning her. That I would convince them to adopt her too. That we would come back for her. That I was excited to go but terrified of leaving her. That I couldn't imagine spending even a day without her. That this was killing me.

"Yes," was all that would come out.

I couldn't leave it like this. I had to say something to make her feel better.

"You don't understand. I don't even want to go."

The crows flapped harder. Lihini looked away, her face changed. It had gotten darker. Different. Her eyes grew sad. The air stood still. I couldn't breathe.

But when she finally looked back at me, it was with her usual, warm smile. When she wrapped her arms around me, it was with her usual love.

"*Sudhu*, you mustn't say that! I can't believe this. This is the best news ever."

The crows calmed down. Lihini had set them free.

21

I'D ARRIVED AT HEIGHTS fifteen minutes early, so I spent the next ten minutes sitting on a bench two blocks away, near the BART station, scrolling through my Facebook feed. I hoped Sam didn't spot me on his way in. Tons of tech bros mulled around, all plain grey T-shirts and leather bomber jackets, smartphones in their hands and egos out on display, ignoring the homeless woman standing on the corner of Sixteenth and Mission with the GOD IS A WOMAN, AND SHE'S DEFINITELY MENOPAUSAL sign. I hate what is happening to this city.

Still, it wasn't terrible to get out of the house. I took a deep breath. It fucking stank, but I tried to ignore that. It felt good to distract myself from everything that had been happening over the last few days.

The setting sun gave everything a golden sheen. It was Instagram heaven. I thought about posting a picture of the skyline but decided against it. Too cheesy.

I flipped my phone camera on to selfie mode and discreetly checked out my hair and makeup. Everything looked natural, not like I was trying too hard. Good. No one needed to know that I spent almost two hours showering, shaving, drying, curling, and layering on the concealer to look like I just rolled out of bed oozing natural radiance. Same with what I was wearing. A white T-shirt and jeans, both just tight enough to show some curves, but not enough to make me look desperate. No jewelry except my usual diamond earrings. White, basic-bitch Converse. Not ideal, but I hadn't thought to grab a fancier pair at my apartment. The frilly red thong I had on was a literal pain in my ass, but hey, a girl's got to do what a girl's got to do. *I like the way red looks against your caramel skin*, the email had said. *Make sure you get nice and sweaty for me while you wear them. Think of me while it rides up.* Sick fuck. Nothing pisses me off more than my skin being perpetually compared to food—caramel, honey, mocha, syrup. I mean, get more creative if you're trying to commodify me, asshole. But whatever, repeat clients are good for business. I made a mental note to buy more underwear while I stayed at my parents'. I was shorter in supply than I had initially thought.

I flipped all my hair over my shoulder. Nope, that looked weird. I pushed it back again. Okay, better. It wasn't like I was interested in Sam, let's get that clear. I was just here to see what he knows about me. But if anyone was rejecting the other based on looks, it had to be me, that's all.

"Hi, I'm Paloma," I said, not too loudly, practicing my smile in the phone camera. My teeth looked fucking perfect. "Table for two, please."

The homeless woman shuffled down the block and stood across the street from my bench. She was staring right at me. I tried a tentative smile, but her gaze didn't waver. Her large green jacket looked too big, too heavy for the mild fall. I looked away. I didn't want to stare back. Even still, I could feel her eyes on me, watching me, judging me. I snuck a glance up again.

"You know what you did!" Her voice was hoarse and loud. Nails on a chalkboard.

I looked around quickly. Everyone around me hurried by—no one gave me, or her, a second glance. Thank god.

I shuddered and stood up. Early or not, it was time for me to go. It's not like I was guilty of anything, I just couldn't deal with all of this. The image of me sneaking a mop and bucket wriggled its way into my mind, but I shoved it firmly away.

Focus, Paloma.

I hadn't been to Heights before. Hadn't even heard about it until Sam recommended it, so naturally, I thought it would be a nice, midrange establishment fit for a good Sri Lankan boy. I was surprised to see that it was a trendy rooftop bar. The kind that had a signature wall covered in monstera leaves and served overpriced cocktails in mason jars with reusable bamboo straws.

Sam was waiting for me at the entrance when I got there. I wished he wasn't so I could've ducked into the bathroom to do another quick hair and makeup check. It was windy on the walk over.

"I was surprised you texted. You didn't look like you wanted to talk to me so much the other day." His accent twanged, as sharp as ever, but at least he wasn't speaking in Sinhala. It still punched me right in the face, though—I was suddenly twelve again, and fighting to get away.

Damn, get ahold of yourself, Paloma. Don't let your imagination make you lose control again.

"I was having a rough day." I smiled. Nothing too suggestive, I hoped, but I didn't want to seem unfriendly.

"Of course. Of course. It was rude of me. I apologize. I was just so happy to see another Sri Lankan. You understand, no?" I actually couldn't imagine anything worse.

"Sure, of course," I conceded. "Shall we go inside?"

"Yes, yes, of course." He did the quintessential Sri Lankan head nod that confused all Americans. I remembered how I had to train myself not to do it anymore because it pissed my mom off so much. *Are you saying yes or no, Paloma? No one understands when you shake your head like a cow.* Thank god I managed to kick the habit early on.

He opened the door to the rooftop and held it so I could step out before him, then circled around me to lead the way to our corner table. Not that this was a date, but damn, this was way more than I had come to expect from the usual men I'd meet for a drink. The last jackass picked me up in his mother's beat-up station wagon and handed me a cup of stale coffee before getting straight to the point and asking me for a hand job in my apartment parking lot. He didn't even offer to return the favor afterwards.

I snuck a quick once-over on Sam. His long-sleeved, printed shirt was a little loud and stood out sharply in a sea of grey, but at least he didn't have one of those ridiculous lumberjack beards, or worse, a man bun. He pulled a stool up for me and waited until I clambered on before he sat down himself. What kind of serial killer was he?

A waitress with Amy Winehouse hair and winged eyeliner set down two menus elaborately calligraphed on tiny blackboards.

"And where are you both from?" I wanted to reach over and rip off her overly volumized beehive. Why does everybody assume that I'm not from here? I know I'm brown, but isn't San Francisco supposed to be a fucking melting pot of cultures? Isn't that what it says on every damn blog post about the place? *San Francisco—the poster child for cultural diversity.* So what was it about me that screamed out, Hey, I'm an immigrant?

"The Bay Area." I gave her my sweetest smile.

"Sri Lanka," Sam replied. I wanted to fucking punch him.

"Ooh, how exotic." She ignored me completely. Sam beamed.

"You know where that is?" he asked, doing a piss-poor job of masking the glee in his voice.

"Of course, hon. Isn't it in India?"

My jaw hurt as I held a polite smile. Sam didn't seem fazed as he launched into the usual explanation—not India, but a small island, just underneath, famous for its tea, blah blah blah.

Finally, after his goddamned geography lesson, I managed to order a glass of red wine. I needed some form of lubricant to get me through this but didn't want to risk another evening of scotch. Damn shame, because Sam looked like the kind of guy who wouldn't let me pay either.

"So, how long have you been here for? In the US, I mean." Was the whole *Coming to America* bullshit all this guy could talk about? It was called the land of the goddamned free, so why did I always feel like I was in some sort of a cage—an animal, always required to parade around?

"A long time, probably around eighteen years." I didn't like reminding myself that I just crossed over to my thirties.

"Wow, so you're a full-fledged American."

Thankfully, our drinks showed up, and I could take a large gulp of wine.

"So, Sam, what about you?" I was desperate to talk about anything other than myself, even if it meant hearing his life story.

"Well, you saw, no? I'm a waiter, just like Arun was. Is. Sorry. Sorry." He closed his eyes for a second. It was painful. For me, I mean. I gave zero fucks about his melodramatic bullshit. I was just here to see if he knew anything that could put me at risk.

I arranged my phone and coaster so they were both parallel to the edge of the table, and let him continue.

"I'm so sorry. I'm just very worried about him, that's all. I have never really had someone close to me disappear like this before."

His lip trembled.

Fuck.

I had to stop this before I killed someone.

I positioned my face into a kind but firm smile.

Arun hadn't disappeared. Arun was dead. But there was no point in telling him that. God knows how he would react.

I pushed the image of me going into the janitor's closet out of my mind for the millionth time.

"Sam, when we met the other day, you said he mentioned me. Anything in particular?"

Sam looked at me knowingly.

I gulped.

"That you were Sri Lankan, of course. I asked him if he knew where you were from. I mean, it's a small place. We probably have a friend in common somewhere."

My heart beat a fraction harder.

"I doubt it. I left when I was very young."

"But you know Sri Lanka. Surely our paths would have crossed, no?"

If I could have reached across the table and shoved him over the railing of the rooftop, I gladly would have. I took a deep breath. Why the fuck am I doing this? I should just leave.

And then Arun's slimy grin slid into my mind, and I knew I had to stick this out for at least one drink.

"I don't know if Arun told you, Sam, but I was adopted." This should be enough elbow room for him to bring up whatever Arun might have said. Sam didn't seem like the kind of guy to try and extort me, unlike his jackass friend. Then again, I never thought Arun would have it in him either.

But the dumbstruck look on Sam's face was enough for me to gather that this had never been brought up before. Great.

I cast my eyes down—classic damsel. Hopefully now he'll take the hint and shut up.

"No, he never said . . ."

"It's still a little hard for me to talk about." I could tell that this news was making his curiosity spin out of control, but Sam ate up my act like it was a steaming plate of rice and curry.

He held his hands up like he was surrendering.

"You're absolutely right. What was I thinking? I was just excited to meet a Sri Lankan after so long so I was just being nosy. *Haiyyo.* You know the way we are, no? Anyway, enough of me being annoying. I told myself I would enjoy this evening, get to know a new friend, and that is what we will do."

Sri Lankans are so dramatic. They're dramatic even when they are trying not to be dramatic. It's ridiculous.

I took another sip of wine.

"So, are you working at the restaurant full-time?" Small talk was good, right? Keeps the focus off me, and maybe he would slip up and tell me something of value.

"No, not full-time. I've just been there a couple of months. It's only till I graduate. My parents thought it'd be good for me to work a bit. You know how Lankan parents are, no?" No, of course I don't know, you insensitive moron. I never had them.

"You're in college, then?"

"I'm getting my master's at San Jose State. I left Sri Lanka midway through my degree." He looked a little hesitant. "You've heard about the ragging that happens at our local universities, no? I think they probably call it *hazing* over here."

I nodded, even though I had no clue what he was talking about. I gave zero fucks about the trials of spoiled Sri Lankan boys.

"Well, after I got here, it took me a while to finish my undergrad because I changed my major, twice. My father was so angry with me. He really wanted me to stick it out with my local degree and take over the family business. But instead, I came here. Thankfully, I got a scholarship."

His parents are definitely still sending him cash though, because how the hell could he afford twenty-dollar drinks at Heights working at the Curry Palace? Lucky shit. I thought back to when my parents would give me a monthly allowance. They had me work for it, even though it wasn't the usual mundane chores most kids my age were stuck with. My mom had me help out with her charity events—doing readings and talking about life back in Sri Lanka. All the book club ladies wanted to know what it was *really* like. Was it terrible? There was no internet, or air-conditioning, and did we even wear shoes? *Of course it must have been terrible for you, poor thing.* I made extra cash when I told them that we had hand-me-down clothes, and that I had never eaten McDonald's until I came to the US, like that ever even mattered to me.

Those were simpler times.

My phone started to vibrate. It was Mr. Williams. I froze for a second. First he showed up at my apartment and now the nonstop emails and calls. A part of me wanted to pick up and tell him to back the fuck off, but of course I'd never do that. I hit the button to silence my phone and gave Sam an apologetic smile, hoping he hadn't noticed my hands tremble.

"And you're returning to Sri Lanka after you're done?" I asked. "Or chasing the great, white, American dream?"

He smiled. "It's great here, but I would like to go back someday I think. I miss home. I can't tell you how happy I am to meet another Lankan." Something inside me grated, but I shrugged it off.

"So what about you? What do you do, Paloma?"

I get paid a fair bit of money to send naughty Polaroids and pairs of my used underwear to people who can't get laid in real life. It's al-most like a community service, if you think about it. But I doubt Sam's the kind of guy who would see it that way.

"I mostly do freelance graphic design work." My phone buzzed again. I eyed it, but resisted the urge to pick it up. It wasn't him. The subject line of the email I received flashed across the screen—*I want you to sit on my face* . . . I exhaled in relief. It was just one of my regu-lars, Big Pete. He sends me pictures of his junk with every request. *A little (or big!) something for you!* he would add, like I should be thank-ful to get an unsolicited dick pic in my inbox every week. I could assure him that he was certainly not worthy of his preferred name, but hey, he paid on time and ordered in bulk, so I'd call him whatever the fuck he wanted. He was due another package soon. I made a mental note to slip him an extra Polaroid next time. He might be a pervert, but at least he knew his boundaries.

Sam must have seen me glance at my phone.

"I don't really mind if you pick it up. You know we aren't as sensi-tive about cell phones the way Americans are. If you have a call, then you have a call. It could be work. It could be your mother."

I stuffed the phone in my jacket pocket.

A woman with long black hair walked by me, her elbow managing to smack into my back.

"Excuse me," I called out, giving her my best smile. Bitch. She didn't even hear me. The bar felt loud and cramped. We were on a rooftop, why the hell was it so hard to breathe?

"I need to go to the ladies' room. Excuse me." I slid off the stool and touched my jacket pocket again to make sure my phone hadn't fallen out. Fern used to say that I was emotionally attached to my phone, but she said a lot of shit that barely made sense. I can't help it that I'm care-ful with my things. She was the one obsessed with my emotional attach-ments, which was kind of ironic if you thought about it.

It wasn't like I would ever pee in a public restroom. I just needed a moment. I washed my hands and wiped them carefully. I fluffed out my hair—it hadn't gotten too frizzy, thankfully. The soft brown highlights I had my colorist painstakingly put in had started going brassy, but it cost a fucking arm and a leg, so I should probably hold off until I get some steady work. I hoped the color didn't make me look too fake. I fucking hated pretenders.

Damn, the lighting in the bathroom made my skin look fantastic.

I took a deep breath, just like Nina had told me. Sam didn't know anything. He seemed friendly, and nice, and apart from being as Sri Lankan as they got, nothing else seemed particularly wrong with him.

That's a fucking relief.

"Hi." I smiled into the mirror. "I'm Paloma." I heard someone flush at the last stall.

Fuck.

I'm not just some crazy girl talking to myself. I just want to see what others see. So many people go through life having no idea what they really look like. Who they really are. You know that psychologists have said that if you were to see a clone of yourself walking down the street, the chances are that you wouldn't recognize them? That's how little we really know about who we are and what we look like to everyone else. Think about it.

I pulled out my lipstick and started touching up as a very skinny, very blond, very, very drunk girl swayed her way up to the counter next to mine. Her eyes glazed over a little as she pawed at her hair. She hadn't washed her hands and didn't seem to have any intention to.

Our eyes met briefly in the mirror. I gave her a polite smile.

"Love your shoes," I said. I didn't. It was just something to say to a drunk girl in the bathroom.

"Oh Em Gee! Aarthi!"

"Sorry?"

"You biatch! I haven't seen you since college! How are you?"

She was facing me now, not looking at me through the mirror.

"Sorry, I don't think you have the right person."

"Fuck off, how drunk do you think I am?"

Bitch was pretty fucking plastered. But she wouldn't leave me alone.

"We partied together at the Alpha Delta Pi cultural night. You rocked up in a sari and showed me how to put one on. I can't believe you don't remember!" She let out a loud belch and swayed a little.

"That was definitely not me, I promise." The smile hadn't left my face, but this conversation needed to end. I stuck the lipstick back in my purse and checked my phone.

"You definitely look like her." Drunk Blondie shrugged. "You sure you don't have a twin, or sister?"

"You know, I think I just have one of those faces." Yeah, right. What I had was a tan and the terrible luck of being a brown person in a place where everyone thought we looked the same because our skin was the color of goddamned caramel.

I braced myself and smiled even wider. "You have a nice night now."

I pushed open the bathroom door with my elbow and let it bang shut. Another stupid fucking white person. Find someone with brown skin and black hair and figure they all come from India, and they all know to drape a fucking sari and make curry and dance the goddamn *bhangra*. It wasn't just this drunk bitch in the bathroom—I was so often being mistaken for some other brown chick, whether or not they looked anything like me.

I stalked back to the table and downed my glass of wine without even sitting down.

"You okay?" Sam asked. He was just a little too cheery. Like he had made up his mind to stop moping about his missing friend and enjoy the evening. Sri Lankans were great at that—avoiding anything uncomfortable. Well, good. I'm more than happy to avoid all this bullshit.

"Want to get out of here? I know a place where the drinks are a third the price."

22

RATMALANA, SRI LANKA

I WANTED TO GO back to the dormitory, but Miss Chandra made me wait overnight in the sickroom with a *sili-sili* bag of ice on my face. And she gave me this superlong lecture about how I should take better care of myself now that I was getting adopted, and that my part was very important because of the big donation the home would get once the adoption went through.

It was really, really annoying because she wouldn't shut up for ages, and also because the sickroom was in a completely different wing, next door to where her own room was, so she could see if I was reading instead of sleeping like she told me to. And I missed Lihini. We didn't really get a chance to speak after what happened with Shanika, and the sick feeling in my stomach stayed. She must be so upset, thinking I was just going to leave her at the orphanage, and that she was alone from the first night itself.

Miss Chandra kept me late the next morning, too, so I must have missed Lihini in the dining room. Then, straight after that, Perera sir called an assembly. I didn't think he was going to make the announcement so early in the day. But Shanika's attack on me yesterday probably pushed him to do it. She ruined everything. No wonder no one wanted her. She was a walking curse.

Miss Nayana asked me to sit right in front, but I kept turning around, trying to see if I could spot Lihini in our usual place at the back. Us older girls got the last row. We said it was because we were the tallest, but really, it was the best row because we could whisper a little and no one would catch us. I couldn't find Lihini anywhere.

Perera sir stood at the front of the hall. A bead of sweat slid from the side of his forehead and down his cheek as he fanned himself with his notebook. I wished I had a notebook to do the same.

"Good morning, girls. It's so nice to see all your smiling faces. The news I have for you today was supposed to be a surprise, but I hear that good news can sometimes spread too quickly." He looked over at me and winked, which made me smile. I couldn't sleep the whole night in the sickroom. I just kept tossing and turning, imagining what I would do to Shanika if I got the chance. I wish I slapped her back a little harder, or said a few mean things to her. Lihini got a good slap in, even though she was lucky that Miss Chandra or Miss Nayana didn't see. She always knew to act at the right time like that. I always thought about what I should do long after everything was over.

But the way Perera sir explained it now, you would think it wasn't a big deal at all. I thought back to what Lihini said about having good thoughts. I know I should let this go. I just wish my ears didn't get all hot whenever I thought about Shanika.

"You girls behaved in an exemplary manner during the recent visits we have had. This good behaviour has led to an increase in the donations given to the school, so we will be able to buy more books for your library, and also pay for a music teacher to visit you girls after school." Everyone started clapping.

"And also"—Perera sir smiled—"one of our very own is being adopted by a family in America." There were cheers now too. Everyone was happy for me. I couldn't believe it. After what happened with Shanika, I thought they would all hate me. But they were clapping and smiling and there was even a wolf whistle.

"Paloma, could you please join me?"

I stood up, even though my knees were shaking. I was already in front, just a few meters from Perera sir, so I just turned around slowly to face the room. Everyone was smiling and clapping. This was unreal. I finally saw Lihini at the back. She was smiling at me too. I made sure I didn't smile. She mustn't know that I'm so excited about this. It'll break her heart.

Shanika was at the back as well. To my surprise, she was clapping, though her face was as serious as mine. Gosh, she must hate me. I wonder if Perera sir had to give her one of those injections again, to calm her down.

"Paloma, you have been a part of our home since you were born. We are very happy and proud that you are moving on to a bigger, and brighter future. This is a wonderful step for all of us at the orphanage. As you know, we haven't had an adoption here in quite some time. We get a lot of good publicity for our little home when something like this goes through, so we thank you for impressing Mr. and Mrs. Evans enough for them to make you their own. As you move to America, remember to love your new family as you love your family back here. Remember to treat your new parents with the same love and respect that you have given Miss Chandra, Miss Nayana, and myself. And remember to never forget your Sri Lankan values. America is an exciting place, but it is very different from here. You must take care to not lose yourself and your roots."

I nodded. I could feel sweat starting to drip down my back.

"Tell your new friends in America about us, about the Little Miracles Home, and about what we do here. I'm sure that, in time, you will be able to show us your gratitude for taking care of you for the first twelve years of your life by helping us raise even more funds in the future. I know you won't let me or your family here down."

I was hot. Too hot. I nodded again, and Perera sir took both of my hands in his.

"I wish you all the best for a wonderful future, Paloma. Make us proud."

A slight breeze drifted into the assembly hall over the applause, blowing in the rattan blind we used to cut the glare. The relief of the cool wind made me look toward the window for just a second, and when I looked back, my eyes searching for Lihini, she was gone. She must have snuck outside.

I'll go find her right after this assembly ends. I'll go find her and tell her that things will be okay. How was I supposed to know that things would never really be okay again?

That's when we heard it, clear as a bell, cutting through the wishes and claps and whistles like a razor.

A scream.

Lihini's scream.

23

RATMALANA, SRI LANKA

I WAS THE FIRST out.

"Lihini!" I called out, my eyes taking a moment to adjust to the bright morning light after being in the gloomy assembly hall.

She was at the end of the garden, hugging herself, rocking back and forth, seated right there in the dirt.

"Lihini, what happened?" I grabbed her shoulders and forced her to look at me, though her eyes wouldn't really connect with mine. She looked helpless, like an abandoned little kitten.

"Lihini." Perera sir's voice boomed over mine. "Come now, child. What's all this?"

A small crowd had gathered around her now as she shook and shivered even though it was a really hot day.

Miss Chandra bustled over, pushing the girls aside and kneeling next to Lihini. She stroked her forehead and checked for a fever, speaking to her in the soothing voice she used when any of us were sick.

"Tell me, *baba*, what is wrong?"

Finally, Lihini looked up. She was still shaking. When she spoke, her voice trembled so much I wasn't sure I heard her right.

"I s-saw her."

"Who, child? Who did you see?"

Lihini looked straight at me, her eyes wide. "*Her.*"

What? She couldn't be serious. I looked around the garden. Apart from the girls, and teachers, and Perera sir, and even Upul and the gardener, there really was no one else.

"What do you mean, Lihini?" Perera sir asked.

"I saw the ghost. I saw Mohini."

The gasp that went through the group of girls could have been louder than Lihini's scream.

"What?" asked Maya.

"Noooo!"

"I told you ghosts were real."

"No, no, *aney*, I'm scared."

"Ooooh!"

Two claps cut through the air. Perera sir looked angry.

"Come, girls, this is more than enough. Miss Chandra, please take Lihini to the sickroom. It's clear she's very upset that her friend is leaving."

By now, Miss Nayana and Miss Sarah had joined the group as well, and they started talking to the girls, assuring them that it was nothing, that Lihini was just upset.

Miss Chandra had wrapped her fat arm around Lihini and pulled her to her feet. She kept rubbing her head and speaking to her softly.

"Come, child, let's go to the sickroom. You can have some tea and lie down for a bit. It's this heat, I tell you. We are all feeling faintish these days."

But Lihini's eyes searched me out as she left.

"I didn't imagine her," she whispered.

I felt a hand on my shoulder. Perera sir.

"Let her go, Paloma." His voice was soft, not angry anymore. "She's going through a hard time. Let's give her some space to recover, okay? Come, let's have some ice cream."

We were all given ice cream to celebrate my good news, and I was given an extra cone because, well, I was such a big part of the news, I guess.

We didn't get ice cream very often, usually only when people gave us *dhanes* during a birthday or Christmas. Vanilla was my favorite. I always liked it more than chocolate, even though everyone made fun of me because they said that's the most boring flavor. But not today. No one said a thing today as Miss Nayana handed me the pale yellow cone and I licked at it halfheartedly, making sure that I didn't drip anything onto my dress.

The whispers were still going on about Lihini, though, until Miss Chandra came back from the sickroom and told everyone that they wouldn't get any more ice cream for the whole year if she caught us talking about Mohini ever again.

And so the attention finally switched from Lihini to why we were having ice cream in the first place.

"You must all try to be like Paloma and read more," Miss Sarah told the girls. "Mrs. Evans especially chose Paloma because she saw her reading her very favourite book. See how a book could change your life?"

The little girls nodded and started to crowd around me. "*Akki, akki*, when are you going? How far away is America? Will you send us stickers?" The questions kept coming.

"*Hari, hari.* Of course. What stickers do you want?"

"I want one of Sanath Jayasuriya."

"Can I get one of the whole Sri Lanka cricket team?"

I giggled a little at this and messed up their hair.

"I don't think they play cricket in America."

The gasp that followed made me laugh. I guess they'd already forgotten about Lihini.

"No cricket? But how?"

"You must teach them. You can take my ball."

"I'll tell you what," I finally said. "When I go, you can have my sticker box. Okay, no?"

"Really?"

"Really, Paloma *akki*? Really?"

"Promise?"

"Yes, yes, I promise. I've had Jayasuriya for years, no? And most of the other cricketers as well. You can have them, but you have to promise to share, okay?"

"You will still send us letters, right? And photos also?"

"Of course. Of course I will."

One of the younger girls spoke next, her eyes brimming with tears. "You won't forget us, no?"

I pulled her into a big hug.

"You mustn't cry, okay? Then I'll start to cry. And very soon everyone will be crying. And Miss Chandra won't know what to do. Okay?"

"Why would you cry? Aren't you happy to go?"

I was happy to go. But I couldn't let them think I was abandoning them. I didn't want them to feel bad.

"I'm sad to leave you all." I hoped they would believe me. It wasn't a complete lie. Just not a whole truth. Mostly, I was relieved that I wouldn't be stuck here with no other choice but to leave to St. Margaret's in a few years. Like Shanika. I know I should be sad for her—that it would be horrid if I was in her place. But every time I thought back to how she attacked me, I started to feel a twisting deep inside. Like I was glad she was stuck here. How dare she accuse me of stealing her place? It wasn't my fault that I got chosen. Anyways, who would even want to adopt her? She's the weirdest girl here.

The whole day was similar. Girls saying they were excited for me, asking me not to forget them, asking to sign in my autograph book. No one seemed that interested in my autograph book before, so this was really, really awesome.

Remember the girl in the city
Remember the girl in the town
Remember the girl who spoiled your book

Writing upside down, Maya wrote, upside down, right on the middle page. Of course she wanted to do something to ruin my book. I slowly pulled off the sparkly pink ribbon from the end of her plait while she was concentrating on her ice cream cone, and threw it away in the dustbin. I felt a lot better after that. It was her favourite ribbon.

The sun was starting to set when I finally managed to disentangle myself from the girls and sneak back into the garden. I sat on the swing, enjoying the peace and quiet. I barely had a moment to myself since I heard the news. And I was worried about Lihini. Was she okay? What did she really see? Surely, it couldn't have been Mohini, right? Miss Sarah said we had overactive imaginations. I don't really know what that means, but this might be it. Maybe she just imagined everything. Maybe Perera sir was right, that she was just upset because I was leaving.

I noticed Upul washing the van in the driveway. He looked over at me and smiled. I looked away and jumped off the swing. It was time to stop being such a drama queen.

I thought Lihini would still be in the sickroom, so I was surprised when I saw her, reading under the tree as usual.

"*Sudhu*, are you okay?" I couldn't keep the surprise out of my voice.

"Yeah. Miss Chandra said I could leave if I was feeling better since I didn't have a fever or anything. She said a few prayers and made me learn a *gatha* to chant if I'm ever scared."

"What happened, so?"

But Lihini shook her head.

"Miss Chandra said I imagined it."

Did she, then? Her bottom lip was trembling.

"Did you have your ice cream?" I asked instead.

"No. I didn't feel like ice cream."

"In vain, *haiyyo*. It was really good," I lied.

She just shrugged.

"Lihini, I'm sorry, you know."

She finally looked at me directly.

"About what?"

"About going. You know that, right?"

"Why are you sorry?"

"I'm sorry to leave you. You must feel terrible."

"No, *sudhu*. I'm happy for you, really."

She didn't look very happy. I shook my head.

"This is me. You don't need to pretend. You know that, right?"

Her lips pressed together slightly.

"What makes you think I'm pretending?"

"I didn't say you were. I said you didn't have to."

"Well, I'm not. I'm not pretending. Or lying."

"*Aney, sudhu*, I didn't mean it like that, so."

"Why is everyone telling me how I'm supposed to be feeling? I know what I saw, you know."

"So you think you actually saw her? Mohini?"

"What do you mean I think I saw her? So you don't believe me either?" Her voice rose slightly.

"No, I mean, look, I know you're upset. It's okay to be upset. I know it must be hard for you that I'm leaving."

When Lihini stood up, it took me by surprise.

"As hard as it must be for you to imagine, Paloma, everything is not about you."

I was shocked. She never spoke to me that way.

"Oh, and also, could I have *my* book back, please?"

"Your book?"

"Yes, my *Wuthering Heights*. It's mine, remember? I've been looking all over for it. You never gave it back to me."

And with that, she stalked off back inside.

What on earth was she on about? Did she actually see a ghost or was she just upset like Perera sir said? And why was she suddenly bringing up the book? We had always shared everything before. I had left it on the bookshelf. Same as always.

I was about to follow her inside to say sorry. I didn't mean to doubt her. I knew she must be upset about the adoption.

But then Miss Chandra called me into Perera sir's room, where they had me sign some papers so I could apply for a passport.

"What's a passport?" I asked.

"It allows you to fly on a plane."

"On a plane?!"

"Yes, of course, child. How else did you think you would go to America?"

"I—I . . ." I had actually not thought about it. I would get to go on a plane? On a real-life plane? This was unbelievable! I was actually a little relieved that I was to go by plane and not boat. We weren't allowed to watch *Titanic*, but we all knew it was about a very big boat that everyone said wouldn't sink but then it hit an iceberg and Jack died, leaving Rose all alone. We even had a small poster of the *Titanic* in our dormitory, and Maya would sing "My Heart Will Go On" every single day on the swings even though she sounded terrible.

"Would I be going on the plane to America all by myself?"

"No, child. Mr. and Mrs. Evans will come and pick you up as soon as everything is ready. It will take about a month, we think, now that they have gotten all the approvals. They need to do a background check on you also."

"On me?" My heart beat faster. What if, well, what if they found something out about me that wasn't good? Like that I got a really bad mark on my science exam? Or that sometimes, Lihini and I skipped morning prayers at school and hid in an empty classroom so that we could read instead?

"Nothing to worry about. Your mother already transferred guardianship to us when you were born. They will double-check the document, that's all."

"And my father?"

Miss Chandra just pursed up her lips like she did when we asked too many questions. "He was never in the picture, Paloma. Nothing to worry about that."

"But—"

"Now, we need to make a list of things you might need for your trip," she said, interrupting me firmly. "Mr. and Mrs. Evans have already sent across an allowance for you to get new traveling clothes, and a suitcase, and whatever else you might need. So let's take a look at what you have, and we can go into Colombo next week for shopping, okay?"

I was going shopping in Colombo? We rarely get to go to Colombo. A rich family invited all the girls to their house in Colombo for their daughter's birthday last year. I remember there being a lot of traffic, and a lot of buildings, and more people than I had ever seen in one place. There was a big security checkpoint, and I was worried seeing the army uncles with their guns. What if one of them accidentally shot us? I remember Dumila had saluted them, and some of the other girls giggled.

"Why were they there?" I asked Miss Chandra.

"To keep us safe from the terrorists, child. You know this."

I did know this. I remembered the big bomb blast a few years ago at the twin towers and how that was all we could talk about for weeks. But we were in Ratmalana, away from any real danger—at least that was what Perera sir told us at assembly. He had to call a special assembly because some of the younger girls wouldn't stop crying when they heard of the bomb. I never cried, but I saw a newspaper a few days later—women climbing down ladders in their underskirts as black smoke leaked out of the building like snakes slithering after them. I had bad dreams the rest of the week about being trapped in a building I couldn't escape.

But I had to push these terrible thoughts from my mind. I was going shopping in Colombo. I had an allowance. I could buy a new dress and a suitcase. This was amazing. No. Divine.

I was thinking about what kind of dress Miss Chandra would let me buy as I walked back to the dormitory. I wished I could get a short, pink one like Mrs. Evans was wearing, but then I remembered Sister Cynthia and shuddered. I wonder if Miss Chandra would let me take Lihini when we went shopping. Or would that upset Lihini some more?

I needed to sit down and catch my breath. All these new things were happening so soon. The sun was just setting, so the whole room was purple and orange, and a little darker than it usually was. It was empty, of course. The girls were probably having their wash and helping to set up for dinner.

I reached my bed and was about to throw myself on it, but there was something on my pillow.

A book. *Wuthering Heights*.

That was strange. Maybe it was Lihini's way of saying sorry. We usually weren't allowed books in the dormitory and had to sneak them in if we wanted to read in the night by torchlight.

I picked up the book, but something felt wrong. It was heavier somehow.

My hand felt sticky, and the book was wet.

I felt my heart start to race.

I opened it.

It took a moment for me to realise, but the book was drenched in blood.

24

MY PILLOW FELT WET and crusty on my cheek. I rolled over onto my back and instantly felt like throwing up. Everything swayed, even though I was still lying down.

I heard buzzing. That must be what had woken me up.

It felt like I had my ass handed to me by a five-hunderd-pound gorilla. Eyes still partially closed, I reached out to my dresser for my phone, but my fingers couldn't feel it.

Fuck. Fuck. Fuck. I sat up in bed. If I had lost my phone . . . Nope, there it was. Just a few inches to the right of where I normally keep it. Obviously, that was the source of the buzzing sound. I'd set an alarm for this morning. My battery was at 3 percent. Definitely needed a charge. Notifications lit up on the screen. Two emails from clients, and a text from Sam.

> Had a great time. Message when you wake up. BTW, you brought back leftover Chinese food and some OJ. You wanted me to remind you. Such a responsible drunk x

I had to admit, even I impressed myself sometimes.

But why the hell did I set an alarm for so early? It wasn't like I had to be anywhere. I was just rolling around to go back to sleep when it hit me—Ida. Fuck. She wanted me to come over at ten.

I considered just not going, but then she'd probably come knocking on my door anyway. Goddamned jobless old women with nothing better to do with their time.

If only my head didn't hurt so much. What did I get up to yesterday? I felt myself under the covers. I was still wearing the same clothes as last night, thank god. I didn't want Sam to think I was some sort of booty call. I mean, he wouldn't be the worst person I've fucked. He just seemed like the kind of guy who would appreciate a bit of a chase, that's all.

Bits and pieces from last night floated around in my head. Shots from a bottle of cheap tequila we'd picked up at a corner store. Getting some delicious gas station Chinese food. That stupid blond bitch in the bathroom. Mohini walking past the bathroom door while Arun lay unconscious in the kitchen.

Fuck me. That wasn't from yesterday. I took a deep breath and held it.

Finally, when the throbbing reduced, I pulled myself out of bed and went to the bathroom. I should probably try and get some work done today, after I finished off at Ida's. My site wasn't going to build itself, and no one's going to believe I'm a freelance graphic designer without a professional website. I took a nice, long shower, making sure the water was scalding. I inhaled the steam that built around me, and let the pressure massage my shoulders, thinking back to the cold buckets of water I had to pour on myself to bathe back in the orphanage.

I was so impressed when I first got here that I used to take hour-long showers twice a day. Mom and Dad never said anything about it either. I think they were just thankful that I stopped slathering coconut oil on my hair every chance I got. I remember how Mom got upset with me when they took away the bottle I brought from Sri Lanka and I snuck into the kitchen and used the cooking oil instead. *It's just so greasy and gross*, she said, and bought me some expensive conditioner. She even convinced me to leave my hair down and stop pulling it back in a supertight braid. I wasn't popular in high school, but what little semblance I had of a social life, I owe it all to her.

I often think back to the Elizabeth Evans I saw at the orphanage. She probably had no idea what she was getting into. It was right on brand for her and Dad to want to change the life of an orphan from a tiny little island that no one had heard of. I just don't think they anticipated resistance in the form of coconut grease.

Of course, this was well before coconut oil became a huge beauty fad and then Mom would tell all the women in her charity circle that my black hair was beautiful because of the way we would take care of it "back in Asia." And suddenly, everyone didn't seem to think that coconut oil stank anymore either.

I had nicked my leg while shaving, and a single dribble of blood made its way down my calf and onto the tile. I quickly wiped it away with some tissue and all-purpose cleaner. The last thing I needed was for it to solidify into the grout. Now that would be a bitch to clean.

The steam from my shower had made the mirror fog up. I wiped it away.

"Hello, I'm Paloma," I said, more out of habit than anything, watching the way my face fell into an easy smile. Well, I guess you couldn't really call it an easy smile if it cost your parents a few thousand dollars. One of the first things we did when I arrived here was visit a dentist to get my front tooth fixed. *You're an Evans now*, Dad said. *And an Evans would certainly not have a chipped tooth.* My new teeth were perfect, just like them.

The water from the shower continued to drip down from the head even after I'd turned it off. It echoed softly through the bathroom while I toweled myself off and dried my hair. The dark circles under my eyes made me look like a straight-up crack addict, so I dabbed on two different shades of concealer that made me look ashy anyway. Damn all these makeup companies who don't have a fucking clue that brown girls aren't just one shade of "tan" and make it near impossible to find makeup that actually works.

Finally, I pulled on my jeans. I put my worn clothes in the hamper and tucked the red thong in a ziplock bag. I didn't see my shoes from yesterday. I wondered if I'd left them in the garage.

I went down to the kitchen and checked the fridge. Yep, it was definitely the tequila that made the Chinese food taste so good. I poked at the congealed bits of oil sticking to the rubbery chicken before tossing it out and pulling out a coffee pod. Thank god my parents had fancy taste in coffee. I'm sure Ida would have something for me to eat.

A fly buzzed around the kitchen. Why the hell were there so many goddamned flies in here? I opened the window to let it out.

I peeked outside, down the driveway, but it was empty. I hadn't seen the woman across the street since yesterday.

I should really go grocery shopping. I had some packages to toss in the mail anyway, so I reckoned I would just head downtown.

I addressed the envelopes, replied to a few customer emails, and checked the time. Seven minutes past ten. I hesitated. I knew I should go over, but there were no words for me to describe how desperately I just wanted to go back to bed. I chugged back my second cup of coffee and peered out the kitchen window again. The street was relatively empty, but there was a blue Toyota Camry parked outside Ida's that I had never seen before.

And was that someone at her front door?

I craned my neck but I couldn't see more than a sliver of a man in a sports jacket and chinos ringing the doorbell. A sudden sense of dread settled over me, even though I wasn't really sure why. I suppose I should just go to Ida's and get this over with.

My shoes were still nowhere to be found, so I rummaged around the coat closet and found a pair of flip-flops I could wear.

Stepping out of the living room screen door, I made my way through my backyard to Ida's backyard. I was already halfway there before I even noticed I was going that way instead of up her driveway. Force of habit, I supposed, even though it's been many, many years since Ida babysat me.

The sunlight that beamed down felt like it was scorching my corneas. It did nothing to help my headache. I seriously hoped this wouldn't take too long. Fucking chinos and sports jackets were definitely not my type anyway. If it was one of her matchmaking schemes, shouldn't she have set up tea or something, like she did the last time?

Anyway, no time to change my mind now. I was already at her back door.

"Ida?" I normally just let myself in, but I figured it wouldn't be the worst thing to set some boundaries. Who knows? Maybe it would even send her a message to back off a little.

I heard the sound of a car door close and an engine starting up.

"Ida?" I was about to knock again, when something caught my eye.

Right there, lined up neatly against the wall, next to Ida's gardening basket, was a pair of white Converse sneakers.

Hang on. Those couldn't possibly be mine. But then, they couldn't be Ida's either. Not unless she'd inexplicably decided to switch from the old-lady orthopedic shoes she's worn since I've known her. I was suddenly more aware of my heartbeat than I was before.

I reached down and checked the inner side of the left shoe. The Chinese food and tequila from the night before rose up to my mouth.

A purple patch, like a bruise screaming out against the clean white canvas. A purple patch from when I dropped a jar of grape jelly a few weeks back and a large chunk of it splattered on my white Converse All Stars.

That was so fucking weird. How much did I drink last night? I must have accidentally tried to come in through Ida's back door instead of mine yesterday. I mean, our houses did look identical. I'd have been out-of-my-mind drunk, though, to get my own house mixed up like that.

I stuck my feet into my sneakers and tossed my flip-flops back into my parents' yard.

The screen door slid right open when I tried it. Ida should be a little more concerned about her safety, shouldn't she? But then again, who was I to lecture her? I've been so drunk every night since I got back home that I haven't even been turning the security system on before going to bed.

"Ida?" I stepped inside.

I was immediately jumped on by Ida's snow-white Tibetan terrier.

"Hi, Snowy," I said, scratching behind his ears the way he liked. Damn, the little tyke must be getting on now. This was the second terrier Ida had since I moved to the US, brought in to replace the identical one who died about nine or ten years ago.

Ida's house, just like my parents', had not changed. It smelled exactly the same, for one. Talcum powder, tea, and old wood. It was pungent and distinct. I tried not to breathe too heavily. The random hand-painted plates hanging from the walls and lacy tablecloths and doilies draped over poufy floral chairs were all untouched.

And of course, the dolls. I thought they were beautiful when I was a kid, but they looked pretty creepy now. Ceramic, hand-painted faces with synthetic curls and frilly, yellowing dresses. They lined every shelf. A few were even on the flowery sofa, seated upright. It was straight out of a goddamned horror movie.

I'd forgotten how much time I spent in here as a kid, when my mom would leave for days at a time for her charity work. I mean, how would the orphaned kids in Africa eat if she and her friends didn't organize luncheons to which they could wear their Louboutins and sip on glasses of Dom Perignon? I used to do my homework on Ida's kitchen table as she brought me cookies and milk. She wasn't terrible. Just someone who didn't have kids of her own and got a little too invested in her neighbors' exotic new adopted child, I suppose.

She even had a few pictures of me on the wall. I remember when most of those went up. After my middle school graduation. When I won third place at a design competition at school. She'd never taken them down.

The layout of Ida's house was the same as mine, so it didn't take me too long to realize that I was alone, except for Snowy.

That was weird.

Why the hell would Ida drag me here so early that I couldn't even nurse my damn hangover, and then just not show? And what happened to the guy I saw ringing the doorbell?

I was wondering whether to head back home when I heard keys in the door.

"Hi, Ida, I let myself in. I hope that's—"

But it wasn't Ida. It was the woman I'd seen yesterday, the one with the fluorescent pink hair who was walking the dogs. She looked as surprised to see me as I was to see her.

"Oh, hi," she said hesitantly. She looked down and pushed her thick nerd glasses up the bridge of her nose. "Is Ida here? I'm here to take Snowy for his walk." She pronounced his name Es-novi, so I reckoned she was probably Latina. She wore about a bottle of liquid eyeliner, and boy, had she caked on her foundation. Her arms were covered with a web of poorly done, nondescript tattoos.

She probably took me staring at her tats as suspicion, because she rushed to explain, "Ida leaves her spare key for me under the gnome with the red hat. Is she not here?"

"Doesn't seem like it."

"Oh. That's strange."

"Tell me about it." I peered out the window to the street outside. The Toyota Camry was gone. So was the man in the sports jacket. I mean, it's not like Ida was too old to go places. She was probably out grocery shopping, or getting her hair dyed, or whatever the hell it was that old people did when they invited people over and forgot about it.

I just shrugged and started to pull out my phone to see if Ida had left me another voice mail or something.

"I'm Gloria, by the way." She said it Gl-OH-riah, not Glow-ria.

"I'm Paloma. Sorry, I'm just, well, Ida told me to be here at ten, so I'm a little confused."

Be nice, Paloma. Be a sweet girl. My mom's training kicked in, and I gave her a smile. She blushed and looked down again, her bright pink bangs flopping down over her face. I wish I had the balls to dye my hair pink, but my parents would have had joint aneurisms or something.

"Pah-lo-ma." She pronounced it the same way I did when I spoke to myself. "It's pretty."

"Thanks. Let me just give Ida a call."

We both moved towards the kitchen while I checked my phone, no new messages, and then tried Ida's number. Straight to voice mail.

"I can't seem to get through," I said, watching her scratch behind Snowy's ears. He seemed pretty apathetic about his walk. Poor dude was old. He probably just needed to chill, not get dragged around the block once a day.

"Well—" She hesitated.

"What?"

"No." She still refused to meet my eye. "I'm sure she just went out. Forgot Snowy. That's all."

It was the way she said it though. Damn, some people just couldn't lie for shit.

"Gloria." I pronounced her name the same way she said it, and smiled sweetly. I wanted her to know I wasn't like the pretentious suburban housewives who lived on this block and judged her because of her septum piercing or the *Para siempre* tattoo on her forearm. "It's fine, you can tell me."

"I—it's just that Miss Ida, well, she's been a little forgetful lately. She's been taking medicine for it too."

I thought back to the two voice mails she left me. Could Ida just be getting old, or was it something else?

It was suddenly a little hard to swallow. Here I was, bitching about Ida asking me over, when maybe she wanted to talk to me about her health? Maybe she needed me to help out with something, and all I've been is a massive asshole.

"Do you think we should call someone?" Who the fuck do you even call in these situations?

"Call someone?"

"Yes, call. Like a friend or something. She must have friends, right?"

Gloria looked a little helpless. I mean, how the fuck could she know, anyway? She just walked Ida's dog.

"I—I'm not too sure. We could, I don't know, maybe we should check with the neighbors? Maybe someone saw something?"

But what the fuck were we to do? Ring every damn doorbell on this street and ask if they've seen an old woman wander off? Seemed like an overreaction, even for me.

I looked around the neat kitchen that hadn't changed since she re-modeled it fifteen years ago.

"Maybe we'll give it a bit of time. She probably forgot and went out, that's all."

Gloria nodded.

A small whiteboard on the fridge caught my eye.

12th—Bus to San Diego 7 a.m.

"What day is it?" I asked.

Gloria checked her phone.

"The twelfth."

I pointed to the fridge.

"San Diego?" Gloria asked. "Why would she go to San Diego?"

"She has a sister there," I remembered. "Strange she didn't tell you, she usually doesn't shut up about her." I regretted it as soon as the words left my mouth. Gloria blushed. It must suck, feeling like the help all the time.

Fuck, I really hope Ida wasn't getting Alzheimer's or something terrible like that.

"She didn't mention anything to you at all? What about Snowy?"

"Well, she travels every month or so, and I usually take care of Snowy then. Maybe she forgot to tell me?"

Damn it, all that coffee I had drunk this morning had strung me out like a tightrope. And I really needed to pee.

"Mind if I use the bathroom?" That was dumb to ask. Why the hell would I need her permission in Ida's house?

"Sure. But the bathroom down here is being redone. You'll have to go upstairs. It's the second door on the—"

"I know where it is." I smiled again. Who the hell did this bitch think she was? I walked by the downstairs bathroom, trying the door-knob anyway. It was locked.

I snuck a quick peek around Ida's bedroom. Enough lace and dolls to be a pedophile's fun house, but no sign of anything amiss. Neat, orderly, and straight-up creepy. Just like it always was.

The cabinet in the bathroom was packed with various bottles of vitamins and medications. That was to be expected. I mean, Ida was old. But one of the bottles was left directly on the sink counter, next to a glass of water. The label said Razadyne, so I pulled out my phone and googled it.

> Razadyne is used to treat mild to moderate confusion (de-
> mentia) related to Alzheimer's disease. It does not cure Al-
> zheimer's disease, but it may improve . . .

Fuck, so it was true.

"I guess I'll head home, then," I told Gloria after I came down-stairs. "If you do end up speaking to her, please ask her to give me a ring."

I shot a small smile towards her, but pulled out my phone and quickly punched a reminder to myself for later on today—Check in on Ida.

"Sure. I'll lock up after I take Snowy out." She was just grabbing his leash from the counter when a small white card caught my eye.

Maybe it was that the thick white card looked out of place among the sunny blue kitchen tiles. But it was the name that grabbed my attention—*Mr. S. Williams*. Black ink on white board.

He had been here.

He had been to see Ida.

Oh my fucking god.

He was still trying to find me.

"You okay?" Gloria asked.

"Did you see anyone else as you were walking in?" There was an edge to my voice, but I couldn't make it go away. He could be fucking anywhere right now.

Beads of sweat had started forming on my upper lip.

She frowned slightly.

"Nothing unusual."

"Are you absolutely sure? You didn't see a man leave here?"

I was being rude. I didn't care.

"No. Are you sure you're okay? You're shaking."

"Yes, just, I must have eaten something bad. I'll see you later."

How the fuck did I let this happen? He'd followed me all the way here. He'd spoken, or at least tried to speak, to Ida.

My body went cold.

I could feel the gas station Chinese food churning inside me.

It was all I could do to rush back home and dart into the bathroom downstairs. The remnants from last night were not going to stay in my body for a moment longer. I managed to stick my head in the toilet just in time as I heaved out the entire contents of my stomach.

I was such a fucking dipshit. Of course he would track me down here. Had he given her his card himself, or slid it through her mailbox or something? Fuck, I hope it was that. That it was just his card, and not him. That he wasn't planning on tormenting her like he was me.

What the fuck am I even doing? I'm a grown-ass woman. I should be ashamed of myself. Dealing with creeps from god knows where. Not remembering the shit I get up to. First that damn mop and bucket at my apartment, now my shoes at Ida's. This is pitiful. Disgusting.

I pushed myself off the floor, unable to shake the sense of dread. I turned on the faucet and splashed some cold water on my face. I wasn't allowed to use the decorative hand towels we kept in the downstairs bathroom, so I ran my hands over my jeans. I took a deep breath in. A slow breath out. I looked in the mirror at myself. "Hi, I'm Paloma," I tried, but I sounded different. Scared. My head throbbed. I pulled the mirrored cabinet open to check whether we had any Advil. When I swung it back shut, I saw another face, just over my shoulder.

25

THE FACE IN THE mirror smiled at me. I couldn't breathe.

"HOLY FUCK!" The pill bottle in my hand clattered into the sink.

"*Haiyyo*, I'm so sorry!" Sam cried out, trying to grab my arm.

"WHAT THE FUCK ARE YOU DOING HERE?"

"Sorry. Sorry, I'm so, so sorry. *Aney.* Your front door was unlocked. I tried calling for you but I don't think you heard me. I—I think the tap was on. The door was open—"

"Fuck, do you Sri Lankans have no sense of fucking boundaries?" I put my hand on my chest. It hurt from the way my heart was hammering against it.

"Oh my gosh. I really didn't mean to scare you. I'm so, so sorry."

I pulled my arm away and stalked into the kitchen, collapsing onto a chair. I didn't care that I was being rude, my legs felt like they couldn't hold me up a moment longer. I glared at Sam when he followed me and squatted down next to me, peering over with concern.

"How do you even know where I live, anyway? This is some next-level stalker shit."

Sam kept running his hands through his hair agitatedly. It made me want to reach out and slap him.

"You don't remember? I called you an Uber last night on my phone. I told you that I'd come in and check on you if I didn't hear from you today. You—you seemed like that tequila hit you quite hard."

Okay, I must have been pretty wasted if even he noticed that I was drunk. And I had actually agreed to let him come by and check on me? What kind of bullshit did drunk me get up to?

"So I messaged you, and well, you didn't reply. You didn't pick up when I called either, so . . ."

I know social etiquette was pretty nonexistent for Sri Lankans, but this guy took the fucking cake.

I sat there awhile and let Sam get me a glass of juice. I could tell he was feeling pretty bad—he had that neglected puppy look about him, kind of like Ida's dog Snowy had. He sat with me, quietly, for once, until I calmed down some.

"I really am sorry. I'll get out of your hair." He started getting up. Just what I needed, to be made to feel bad about something that wasn't my goddamned fault at all.

"Wait." I spoke before I could stop myself. "Want to come with me to run some errands?"

I didn't know what was going on with me today, but I figured it wouldn't fucking kill me to throw the guy a bone every once in a while, right? And there was a small part of me, just the smallest, teensiest part, that didn't exactly want him to leave. The part that couldn't forget Mr. Williams's card at Ida's house. Or the way Mohini always found her way back to me. Or that I couldn't seem to stop drinking, even though I know it seriously fucked me up.

Sam, of course, was predictably ridiculous about the whole thing. He practically bounded up and pulled out his car keys, insisting that he would drive me, and did I have a grocery list, because he couldn't help but notice that my fridge was pretty empty? Don't make me regret this, asshole.

Once he calmed down, though, as all puppies do, I suppose, he really was quite tolerable. He quickly switched the music from Sinhala love songs to normal, terrible English pop hits as I got into his ancient Datsun, and didn't bring up Sri Lanka even once during our drive into town. You got to give credit where credit was due—at least he picked up on things.

"So, um, you called me my Uber yesterday?"

"Yep, well, we both got on, but your place was further away."

So he wouldn't have known what on earth I got up to when I made it home. I didn't know if that was a good thing or a bad thing.

"You were a little, well, you know what we call it, right? *Vedhila.*" Hit. Or smashed. I guess he had a point.

"It's been a rough few days."

"Arun?"

I nodded. I hadn't thought about him all morning while I was at Ida's. It felt disloyal, somehow. Like if I could easily push a dead body out of my mind, how was I any different from the cops or Nina? Was I just accepting that I'm as crazy as they seem to think I am?

But it was explanation enough for Sam, I guess. He didn't press further on anything, and I was in no hurry to discuss my spiraling mental state with a guy who had clearly seen me flatline on tequila.

"A lot of packages you got there," he remarked as he helped me grab them from his back seat once we pulled up to the post office. He had a large duffel bag there, along with a dirty-looking cricket bat. You can take the Lankan out of Sri Lanka—

"I can't even remember the last time I actually posted a letter, even back home. It really is a dying art, no?"

185

"My parents send me postcards. It takes ages to get here and they get lost sometimes. Old-fashioned letters are a pain in the ass, if you ask me. This is just work."

"But isn't most of your work online? With your social media marketing stuff?"

Who was this guy, a fucking detective? I ran my thumb over my tooth.

"Well, some customers have some very specific requests, and I try my best to comply. You got to do what you got to do to make rent, right?"

He laughed a little at this. "I hear that." His eyebrows squashed together when he laughed. Like a mix of a frown and a guffaw. It wasn't unpleasant.

We ended up at a small pizza place on the north side of town—Giovanni's. It used to be a Mexican restaurant when I was in high school, but the sombreros that hung on the walls were now replaced by arty, black-and-white pictures of Italy, and the whole place looked fresh and new. The pizza wasn't bad either. We split a Hawaiian, which was about as un-Italian as it got, but I was surprised to see Sam didn't pick out the bits of pineapple. There's nothing I hate more than people who let good pineapple go to waste. I mean, he did douse every slice in Tabasco sauce, but I was willing to let that go.

"You got Tabasco on your sleeve," I said, wiping off the red smear near his wrist with a napkin.

"Thanks, *amma*." Mom. Fucking seriously?

But he grinned and I felt my edge fading away. What was it about this moron? Did I secretly miss Sri Lanka or something? Or was it that I cared so little about what he thought that I didn't have to overanalyze everything I said? I'm starting to piss myself off. Besides, I shouldn't be out enjoying myself. I should be worried about my dead roommate and potentially missing senile neighbor.

"You know, I really didn't mean to freak you out today."

"I know," I relented. There was nothing I could do right now about Ida. I was probably overreacting anyway. She was probably in San Diego, sipping sherry with her sister as we speak.

"And I know I have boundary issues. My last girlfriend, she was American, she used to say so too. I just thought . . ."

"You thought it would be okay because I'm Sri Lankan?"

"You said it! Finally."

"What?"

"That you're Sri Lankan."

"That's not what I meant."

"I don't get it. Are you ashamed of it or something?"

"Ashamed?"

"Yeah. You seem to hate it whenever I talk about it."

"I don't hate it."

"Then what?"

"There's just, a lot that happened back there that I would like to leave behind."

"Like what?"

"I don't really talk about it. Especially not on dates."

Fuck. Slip of the tongue. Not what I meant.

But Sam looked like God himself descended down on this pizza place and made it rain hundred-dollar bills.

"We are on a date!" he proclaimed.

"Shush. Don't ruin it."

He didn't stop smiling though. It was actually a little cute. Just a little.

"I must apologize, then, my game is usually a lot better when I have the chance to preplan my dates."

"Oh?"

"Yeah, I do all kinds of romantic stuff. Candlelit dinners, picnics under the stars, carving our initials onto a tree with a hunting knife, you know?"

"Well, if you actually think that bringing a knife on a date is a good idea, then we have bigger problems."

26

RATMALANA, SRI LANKA

"WHO DO YOU THINK did it?" Lihini asked, pulling my braid off the side of the bed and stroking my hair. She had found me, terrified and crying in the dormitory before anyone else came. She sniffed the book and pointed out that it wasn't blood, just red paint, and helped me scoop the ruined book into a *sili-sili* bag, and bundle all my sheets into the laundry room. We had to ask Miss Nayana for new sheets, but Lihini smoothly told her that one of the younger girls must have had an accident. It was so amazing how she always knew the right thing to say at the right time. She could make up a story or talk around the truth in the blink of an eye. I don't know what I would do without her. Now we lay in bed together, whispering as always. Her, on the inner corner next to the wall, and me on the outer side.

"It couldn't have been one of the little girls," I said. I had thought of nothing else since it happened. "No way."

"Maybe it's the curse. Maybe Mohini did it." Oh goodness, not this again.

"Maybe," I said carefully. I didn't want to commit to anything. It was the best I could do to say sorry. I had to let her know that I believed her. Or at least that I pretended to believe her. That I didn't just think she was making all of this up for attention or something. Even though, well, ghosts aren't real, right?

"But why would Mohini destroy the book?"

"It's the curse." Her eyes were wide. I should change the subject.

"You know, it could be *her*." I pulled my hair over my face and made the hunched-over pose that Shanika usually made.

"Who? Shanika?" Lihini looked thoughtful and sat up in bed. "I don't think she really has it in her."

"She had it in her to try and scratch my eyes out, no?"

"Fair point. Did you see her much today?" She pulled a pillow across her lap.

"No. Maybe it was her, then. She's nuts, anyway. Totally *pissu*." She was. *Pissu* didn't cut it. She was completely bananas and I felt angry every time I thought about her.

A beat of silence passed. I had more important things to worry about than Shanika.

"*Sudhu*, I tried to find you before assembly. I wanted to say sorry. About earlier."

Lihini gave me a small smile.

"Forget it, *sudhu*."

"So how was the sickroom visit anyway? Did you get some toffees at least?" We only got toffees if Miss Chandra was in a good mood, but it never stopped us from trying. Besides, I should try to keep Lihini's mind off this Mohini nonsense. I didn't care if she existed or not, but I really, really wanted her to stop talking about it.

Lihini shook her head. "I think she was going to, but Perera sir came to talk to me, so then she must've forgotten."

"Perera sir came to see you?" I'd never heard of him visiting the sickroom before. That was usually left to Miss Chandra. He must have been pretty worried about her.

"Yeah, he said he had come especially to see me. To see how I was doing."

"Ah, that's good, right?"

"I guess so. He kept telling me not to scare the other girls. He said to think about the little ones and how it would give them nightmares."

"Well, he isn't wrong."

"I know what I saw, *sudhu*." No point in making her upset. Especially now that I was leaving.

"Yes, yes. No, I believe you. I was just thinking about how scared the small girls must be."

She narrowed her eyes a little, but dropped it.

"He also wanted to see if I was okay with you going."

"And?"

"What do you mean, *and*?"

"And what did you tell him, so?"

Lihini shifted around again, hugging the pillow a little more tightly.

"I told him I was happy for you. And I am. He said he'll speak to another couple for me also, to see if they would be interested."

"Really?" I sat up in bed. "That would be amazing. Imagine if another family from America adopts you, and we can live close by to each other, and go to school together, and keep being best friends?"

Lihini smiled. She looked very tired.

"That would be amazing. Now lay back down before we get in trouble."

I dropped my head back on the pillow and reached for her hand. She had to know. She had to know how it was tearing me up to leave her here. How it would kill me if she never got adopted. If she had to go live at St. Margaret's home with that horrible Sister Cynthia. What would she do when she got older? Maybe I could find her then, and ask Mr. and Mrs. Evans if she could live with us in America.

"*Sudhu*," she murmured, just as I was drifting off. "*Sudhu*, I did see her though. You believe me, right?"

"Shh," I replied. "Let's just sleep now. We'll talk about it in the morning."

We fell asleep with our arms wrapped around each other like we used to when we were little. I could feel her breathing near my ear. It made me feel so safe. She really was my best friend. The only family I'd ever known. How I wished what Perera sir said would come true, and we could both go to America together. I dreamed of the both of us holding hands as we went to our new American school, wearing jeans and tennis shoes with our hair in ponytails like I saw on TV. It was such a happy dream that I groaned a little as I felt someone sit on the edge of the bed, waking me up.

I heard the singing first. Sleep clouding my mind, I almost thought it was a ghost. But as my eyes adjusted to the darkness, I realized it was Shanika.

> *Que sera, sera*
> *Whatever will be, will be*

I wasn't awake enough to shout out. I felt locked inside my own body as she leaned in close, her hair an undone mess covering most of her face.

> *Que sera, sera*

She smelled terrible—like vomit and sour breath and rotten food. Her nightdress was pulled away from her shoulder, and her scars almost glowed in the moonlight. And when she spoke, all tune and melody gone, every hair on my body stood up straight, and I didn't even have the breath to scream.

"When you die, can I have your skin?" she asked calmly, tracing a finger over my face, before getting up and walking out of the room, leaving me so afraid that I couldn't move.

27

I WAS LATER THAN I intended getting back from dinner with Sam. I didn't even try to discreetly check my phone the whole time I was there. It was weird. The pizza was good. Giovanni's was quiet. Sam had only mentioned Sri Lanka a couple of times. It really wasn't such a bad evening. Pleasant, even.

Did I want to talk to him about the fact that I saw his friend's dead body in my kitchen? A part of me longed to—if anything, so I could be certain that Arun hadn't told Sam my secret, or better yet, convince myself that I wasn't losing my mind. But this was the first little pocket of normal that I'd had in a while, whether it was real or not, and I kind of didn't want to mess it up just yet.

When we finally pulled up in front of my parents' house, Sam was telling me about some asshole professor who automatically assumed that he would be good at accounting because he was brown.

"I mean, I don't mind it. Let him think I'm the Usain Bolt of numbers. He'll be in for a surprise soon enough."

"The Usain Bolt of numbers? Really?"

"What? It's a good analogy, no?"

"Sure."

"Are you always like this?" The smile hadn't left his face.

"Like what, exactly?"

"Such a . . . you know—*pandithaya*?" A know-it-all. Or smart-ass.

"*Pandithaya*? You're one to talk." Too much melody in my tone. I was starting to sound Sri Lankan again. I should get out of the car.

But I stayed in my seat and turned the music up instead. The street was empty, and most houses hadn't turned on their lights yet. I hadn't left a porch light on, of course. I let myself drown in the inky darkness for just a minute. A cat crossed the street and disappeared into the night. At least, I hoped it was a cat, it was hard to tell.

The blue Camry I had seen parked outside of Ida's hadn't returned. I don't know why I instinctively looked for it. Maybe because this was a neighborhood of BMWs and Audis and Teslas, and the conservative car seemed rather out of place. I thought back to Sports Jacket and Chinos, who rang Ida's doorbell earlier today—could that have been Mr. Williams? How dare he use Ida to get to me.

Thinking of him triggered everything else I was worried about, of course.

"Do you have any news about Arun?" I asked. I guess I had to bring him up sometime or other.

"No." Sam frowned. "You know, it's so strange. He was never like this. He was such a, what's the word, an oversharer, you know?"

"What do you mean?"

"Oh, you know, always talking. Couldn't shut him up. You know how it is with Indians, no? They are so much more open with things."

Like things they found out about their roommates' past?

"So he didn't say anything . . . particular before he . . . ?"

"Nope. One day we were taking our break by the dumpster behind Peet's, and the next day he's just gone."

So Arun wouldn't have had the time to tell him anything anyway. Under normal circumstances, this would have left me relieved. But once again Arun's blank, dead face pierced my mind. I took a deep breath. Maybe it wouldn't kill me to open up to someone every once in a while.

"Sam, I—I need to tell you something. About Arun."

He turned to face me.

"What is it?"

"I—I probably should have said something to you sooner, but I was, well—you have to promise me you won't think I'm losing it, okay?"

He gave me a smile. "I already think you're a little nuts, but it's what I like about you."

I rolled my eyes. Don't make me regret this, asshole.

But I had to tell someone before it drove me over the edge.

"I don't think Arun is okay."

"Don't think he's okay? You mean he's in trouble?"

"I mean he's dead."

"Dead?" His eyes widened and he sat up. "What makes you say that?"

"I—I saw him."

"Oh my god. You saw him dead? Did you call the police?"

"Yes," I lied. I mean, the police eventually came, right? Me not calling them was just a technicality.

"And? Did they do an autopsy? Do you have any details? Oh my god."

"W-well, no. The body was, well, it was gone when they got there."

"What do you mean the body was gone? How could it just disappear? Do you think someone moved it?"

The same questions that had been running through my mind. It was a small consolation to think someone else thought the same way I did.

"I don't know. The police came and there was nothing, and then they kept questioning me about how much I had drunk and Arun's visa and it was like they didn't care at all that—"

"Had you—?"

"Had I what?"

"Been drinking?"

What the actual fuck, Sam. And here I was, thinking you were a nice guy, not some asshole who jumped to conclusions.

"What does that have to do with anything?"

Sam ran a hand through his hair.

"No, no. I didn't mean it like that, so."

"No, tell me, Sam. What did you mean?" There was an edge in my voice. I needed to tone it down.

"I mean, I saw you the other day. Don't get me wrong, I love that you like to cut loose. You're like no other girl I've ever met, never mind that you're Sri Lankan. But even I get a little confused sometimes when I've been drinking. It's normal, you know?"

I stayed quiet.

"Hey, look, it's not that I don't believe you, really. It's just, you know, even the other day, it seemed like you freaked out easily. You even mumbled something about Mohini, which was a real blast from the past. I don't think I've heard that ghost story since I was a kid."

Was he right? Nina seemed to think I was imagining everything, and she knew me better than almost anyone else. I thought back to my shoes outside Ida's, and the mop I had taken out of the utility closet again. It fucking killed me to say it, but Sam did have a point—it was easy to get confused after a drink or two.

And I had imagined Mohini that night at my apartment. So what was stopping me from imagining Arun's body too? I had wished him dead, after all.

The anger I had felt towards Sam deflated like a balloon. I was left with just my rubbery facade now.

"What are the police saying?" Sam's voice cut through my thoughts.

"Well, they can't really take him seriously as a missing person because he isn't documented, you know. As far as they're concerned, he barely existed at all."

"Do you think that maybe he did that? That he decided it was time to leave? I have a lot of friends who are undocumented. None of them stay put for very long."

"Maybe."

We sat in silence again. It felt comfortable, somehow. It was a new feeling. I didn't hate it.

My phone beeped. Check in on Ida.

The fragile sense of comfort evaporated, and something inside me felt heavy again.

"I better get going. I need to check in on my neighbor."

"Ah, I see. Are they okay?"

I'd already told Sam about Arun. Describing another potentially missing person seemed like too much for one night. Even for my level of crazy.

"It's a long story."

I truly hoped Ida was okay. I'd just ring the doorbell and check if she got back. Maybe it was all just a mistake. Maybe she was really visiting her sister in San Diego and had just forgotten about our meeting this morning. Why the hell did I always assume the absolute worst?

"I'll see you around?"

"Sure."

I stuffed my groceries in the fridge and watched through the kitchen window as Sam pulled away.

I went out through my backyard and into Ida's again. Her screen door had been locked so I couldn't get in. That was probably Gloria. There were no lights turned on inside.

Goose bumps broke out on my arms, so I went back indoors and pulled on a sweater. Making sure I locked the front door behind me, I let myself out on the sidewalk. The same darkness that I was enjoying from the warmth of Sam's car suddenly seemed deep and empty. I felt it again. The hardening in the pit of my stomach.

I glanced down the empty street to make sure I was alone. What if Mr. Williams just parked his car somewhere else and was lying in wait for me in the shadows? Would he do something like that? Corner me somewhere that he knew I'd have no choice but to talk to him?

Something rustled from across the sidewalk as I walked up Ida's drive. It was probably the cat again. I peered into the darkness once more, but couldn't really see anything. The back of my neck prickled.

The blackened windows of the houses were empty eyes staring out at me. Or was someone actually watching me from the house across the street? A woman's face—I noticed, with a start.

She stood at the window as we both surveyed each other, but she stepped away a few moments later. My heart hammered against my ribs. Damn, she really freaked the fuck out of me. What was her problem, anyway?

I had not thought about the copy of *Wuthering Heights* that she had left in my mailbox since yesterday. What was she doing with it in the first place? Mom wouldn't have loaned it to her, would she? It was so special to me. Sure, they'd given me far more expensive presents—I instinctively rubbed my earrings—but I treasured this book. It was the first sign that we belonged together. That bitch across the street had no right to take it.

I hurried up Ida's driveway, longing to be indoors again. I rang the doorbell and shivered on her porch, but there weren't any lights turned on inside, so I knew it was no use. I tried knocking, too, just for luck. Nothing. Of course.

I should just go home. Go back home and call the police and report Ida missing.

But how the hell could I report another missing person in less than a week? I know the SFPD already thinks I'm a couple of fries short of a Happy Meal, but even I know that seems shady as fuck.

I looked across the street again, but no one was watching me this time.

Maybe I'll just let myself in. It's not like Ida would mind me going inside. Hell, I practically lived there when I was a teenager. I'll just have a little poke around to see if there's anything else I can learn about her whereabouts.

Pulling the key out from under the gnome was easy enough. I let myself in, shutting the unforgiving night firmly behind me. I made sure the door was locked before turning on the lights, shuddering at the thought that Mr. Williams could have been in here earlier.

"Hello?" I called out, more for the reassurance of hearing some noise than anything else. I wasn't expecting someone to call back. I pushed away the feeling that there was something waiting for me in the shadows and made my way inside.

"Snowy?" I called out.

But the house was silent. I guess Gloria had taken him with her.

The dolls smiled at me from their shelves and tabletops. It was creepier than usual in an empty house.

My younger self grinned down at me as I wandered around. The picture was taken when I came in third at my eighth-grade spelling bee. I can't remember Ida coming, but that was probably because I was more focused on Christina Hannigan and her gang sitting at the back like they usually did. They'd poured butter chicken gravy from the local Indian place into my backpack earlier that day, and for once they were right—I did stink of curry. But Ida must have been there. How else could she have the photo of me holding up a ridiculous bronze medal, looking like I'd won gold at the Olympics because I finally wasn't failing English and it made me fucking euphoric that I eventually did something my parents could be proud of? They'd been so proud, in fact, that they had invited all the kids from my class over for pizza right after the spelling bee. I had spent the rest of the evening hiding from Christina in my own home, and Mom was *not* happy.

I didn't know what the hell I was trying to prove by being here. What the fuck was I even looking for? I was no detective.

Call the police.

That was Nina in my head. I don't even have control over my own fucking imaginary voices.

I knew I should call the police, no matter how sketch it would seem for me to be reporting a second disappearance. I didn't *have* to speak to that waste-of-space, human ham Officer Keller, who clearly thought I was a nut bag. Maybe I could call a different department. The station here wouldn't be the same as the one in the city, obviously. Maybe they wouldn't make the connection.

I took out my phone to google the number, but I set it down again. I just wanted to make sure there was nothing I was missing first.

I wondered if I could find a number for Ida's sister. That way I could just check if she'd really gone to San Diego and confirm that all my paranoia was for nothing. That I was here working my drunken ass into a panic while she was happily gossiping away and overspraying her shiny, grey helmet head somewhere else.

I looked around the kitchen for a number or a phone book, but there was nothing. The counter was organized, the dishwasher and the sink emptied, and all Ida's mail was neatly stacked on the table. The little white card with Mr. Williams's name on it wasn't there either. I wondered if Gloria had moved it or tidied up. It's not like I paid much attention to anything when I was here earlier.

I moved to the little vintage writing desk Ida had tucked into the corner of the living room. There was nothing on the table itself, but I knew there was a hidden drawer underneath. Ida was old. She probably wrote down everyone's phone numbers in a notebook or diary or something.

The drawer was mostly empty. No notebook.

Just a folder. I pulled it out. It had *Evans* printed on the cover.

What the—?

I flipped it open and leafed through. Financial statements, deeds to property, a few sealed envelopes.

My parents' names were on most of them. Did they give her all of this for safekeeping before they left on their trip? It wasn't the craziest idea. I knew they trusted Ida, and it wasn't like I was on the best of terms with them before they left. It still felt like a fucking punch to the gut. They would trust anyone else rather than me.

Something Ida had said in her voice mail came back to me, and I pulled out my phone, hitting 1 to enter my mailbox.

Hello, dear. Glad you are back home and hope you are settling in. Just wanted to check in with you. Let me know if tomorrow at ten a.m. is a good time for you to come over? There's someone I'd like you to meet. As you know, we do have a few things to chat about. Anyway, I'll see you at ten tomorrow at my place. This is Ida, by the way.

What did she want to chat to me about?

I know . . . Arun's jeer rang in my head. How the hell was this happening?

I was suddenly really thirsty. I wondered if Ida had anything strong around here. She usually chugged down sherry like it was grape juice, so there was a good chance.

It didn't take me long before I found a bottle tucked away behind a box of oatmeal. Thank god. I poured a healthy two fingers into a tea-cup and gulped it down. It tasted like cough syrup, but it would do. I topped up the teacup again. Ida had random notes and pictures stuck to her fridge, I noticed, while waiting for the sherry to take some of this edge off.

There was a grocery list—eggs, bread, tomato soup, butter, laundry detergent, toilet paper. There was a picture of my parents, probably a year or so ago. It was covered by a laundry receipt, so I nudged the magnet out of the way. They were both holding oversized wine-glasses and were a little pink in the face. I think this was from when they drove up to Napa to celebrate Dad's birthday. They had asked me to come at first, but they changed their minds when they remembered I shouldn't be around all the wine tasting that was bound to happen. Pictures of Snowy. Lots of pictures of Snowy. The newspaper clipping that came out a few weeks before they left detailing Mom's charity work with the same picture that hung in our house. I turned away from the fridge. Why the fuck were you so obsessed with us, Ida?

I thought back to the lacquered wisp of a woman. The way she would comb and braid my long hair, even though Mom always asked her not to. Always one braid, never two. The way her fingers deftly tugged and pulled, like little spiders, as she hummed to herself. The way those same spotted fingers played with her expensive necklaces when she was tired. I remembered my favorite one—a large emerald, surrounded by a row of dazzling diamonds. She let me try it on some-times, and the weight of it around my neck always felt like a noose. And now she was gone. Why did I even care? I was just being sentimen-tal since I moved back home, that was all.

I suddenly couldn't take it anymore. All this not knowing was driving me up the wall. The folder with my name on it. Ida randomly disappearing. The locked downstairs bathroom. Grabbing the letter opener I saw in Ida's desk drawer, I made my way over to the bathroom door. I was going to get an answer for something today. I didn't care what.

I jammed the letter opener between the door and the lock. It didn't quite work, I mean, I'm not Harriet the goddamned Spy. I wrenched it in again, shaking hard.

Damn it.

I tried the doorknob.

To my surprise it swung open—slamming against the bathroom wall and bouncing back at me. I felt slightly off balance as I peered inside.

Did I manage to unlock it, or was it not locked in the first place? I should have really tried the knob again before I decided to jam a letter opener in there.

The small bathroom, the same as the one at my parents', was empty. It was clean and smelled of the same nauseating potpourri and disinfectant as the rest of the house. The seat of the toilet and its cover were missing, but the same lacy towels and carpets were still in there. Not a remodel per se, but maybe Ida just didn't want people using the toilet without a seat.

I sat on the side of the tub and took a few more sips of sherry. The porcelain was cold and felt like a relief. I don't know what the fuck was going on with me. I was setting the cup down when it slipped and some sherry splashed on the tile. The puddle of bright amber liquid that swelled on the clean floor reminded me of the way Arun's blood pooled on the kitchen table.

Fuck.

I got down on my knees to wipe it up, moving the rug under the sink out of the way so it wouldn't get stained.

I heard a clatter.

A black rectangle had skidded over the tile.

What the hell? Was that a cell phone?

I picked it up.

Yep, definitely an older smartphone.

My hands trembled a little as I tried to turn it on.

The battery and charger icon lit up on the screen for a second, indicating it was dead.

My heart was starting to race.

Was this Ida's phone? Why the fuck was it lying forgotten on the floor of her bathroom if she was visiting her sister in San Diego?

This wasn't right.

I reached for the cup of sherry and took another chug.

I had to call the police. Fuck. I'd left my phone in the kitchen.

I was just stumbling out of the bathroom when I saw her again, just outside the living room window. Mohini walked by the front of the house, her black hair trailing down her back. Her white dress glowing in the moonlight.

I struggled to breathe.

I wanted to lock myself in the bathroom and never come out.

But there was a part of me that needed to see her too.

To see her again so I know I'm not hallucinating.

That I hadn't imagined her the other day.

That she had found me.

After all these years, she had found me.

My legs felt like they were unable to support my weight as I inched my way closer to the window. I was shaking. But I was transfixed.

It felt like a hundred years and a millisecond rolled into one. I was ten feet away. Then six. Then two. And then I was at the window, my nose almost touching it, my breath fogging up the glass.

The street was dark and empty.

And then she was in front of me again. Staring in. Her face inches away from mine, separated by the glass. Her eyes looking straight into mine.

I screamed and shuffled backwards.

I thought I was going to faint.

Except it wasn't Mohini. It was the woman from across the street.

She was wearing the same white robe that I mistook for a dress, and her hair was loose across her face like always.

We just stood there for god knows how long. And then she turned and scurried back into her house.

"Hey! Hey!" I darted to the door and called after her.

But she was gone.

I grabbed my phone off the kitchen counter and made sure I still had Ida's phone with me before I locked up and got the hell out of there.

I could barely put the keys under the gnome, I was trembling so hard.

What the fuck was she doing?

Why the hell wouldn't she leave me alone?

28

THE PASSPORT OFFICE WAS the most crowded building I had ever been to. People packed themselves into tight lines, pressing up against someone in front of them. They definitely didn't have a teacher like Miss Chandra growing up or they would surely have been punished. Maybe they thought cramming themselves together would make the line move faster. It didn't. It took us nearly the whole day to apply for my passport, and I wouldn't even get it till next week. But the angry-looking man behind the counter told Miss Chandra that she wouldn't need to bring me to pick it up because I was a child.

"*Hari, hari. Eelangata?*" Okay, okay. Next? He waved us to the side before Miss Chandra could even pick up the slip of paper.

"*Hari, hari. Eelangata,*" I practiced, imitating his rushed way of speaking. People in Colombo offices spoke differently than we did in the orphanage. Of course, it would be even more different in America. I managed to watch some American news channels on TV. The way they spoke English was so different from the way Miss Sarah spoke it.

The words were longer somehow, and more stretched out. They rolled their *r* sounds and pronounced their *t*'s like *d*'s.

"More at four thirty," the blond woman said.

"*Morr ad fourr thirrdy*," I repeated. I must practice so Mr. and Mrs. Evans would understand me easily.

I wanted to show Lihini my American accent, but I stopped myself. She still didn't seem completely okay. I found her sneaking off to the storeroom the other day.

"What are you doing?" I asked. That was our thing. I'd never done it alone. I didn't think she would either.

"I had to check something," she said. That was all. She had to check something? And she wouldn't tell me what. She'd never been like this before.

Then I found her sitting in a corner of the playroom with Maya and the other girls, whispering to them about Mohini again. Maya seemed to be enjoying it, and was saying that she knew the home had been haunted all along, but the others seemed scared out of their minds. It was no wonder that one of the younger girls wet the bed that night.

I tried not to let my frustration with Lihini show. She was just trying to get attention because I was leaving. I knew that. But she really should be more responsible.

"What?" she asked me, her arms crossed over her chest when I lifted the crying girl out of bed and rocked her gently.

"Nothing." I bounced the toddler on my chest. "She's just had a nightmare, that's all."

"Or maybe she saw Mohini," Maya cried out from her bunk. If I could have reached up there and slapped her, I would have.

"Stop it, you're scaring the little ones."

"Don't you see? It's the curse! She's after us!" Lihini's eyes were wide and glassy, but I didn't care.

"Stop it," I hissed at her. "Get back to bed before we all get into trouble."

But it wasn't like I had a lot of time to worry about Lihini and the curse. The last two weeks were a whirlwind. Miss Chandra took me to a huge building in Colombo called House of Fashions, where she let me choose a new pink dress, new socks with bows on the side, and even new underwear! It was the first time I had completely new clothes. We usually got bags of dresses given to us around Christmastime from Mr. Whittaker's charity.

And even though Miss Chandra said absolutely no way to the dress covered in sequins that I liked, I didn't mind because I was so dazzled by everything in this huge building. Miss Chandra even bought me a new pair of shoes. My school shoes fit just fine and I told her that we could paste the broken buckle on the left foot with superglue like I always did, but she said no, that Mr. and Mrs. Evans would like me to be well dressed when I traveled. The new shoes were brown and had pink flowers stamped into the leather. They were really, really pretty, but a little too big. Miss Chandra said that was best because this way they would fit me for longer.

Of course, the best part of this whole thing was having my picture taken. Not many of us had pictures of ourselves. Once, someone had taken a few pictures of the Christmas concert, but I wasn't in any of them. Besides, the photos were all kept with Miss Chandra and Perera sir, who showed them to donors and charities who gave us things.

So when I found out that I was having my picture taken for my passport, I was really excited. The photographer uncle at the studio asked me to sit on a box, and then he got me to get off and put another cushion on the box because he said I was too short. Then he switched these lights on, which were really, really bright and made my eyes tear a little, but I managed not to let any spill out. He kept asking me to do certain things, move my head a little to the left, then he said it was too much and to move it a bit to the right, then to keep my chin down. He kept telling me not to smile, and that was hard because I was so happy. Finally, with a flash so bright that I saw spots for an hour afterwards, he took my picture.

I couldn't believe that the girl in the little stamp-sized photo was me. Even though the photographer uncle kept saying that I must not smile, my lips were slightly parted. Just enough to show the chip on my tooth. The best part about this? Miss Chandra said that we had an extra copy so I could keep it! I showed the picture to Lihini, and Maya saw it, she's such a nosey parker, and she took it and passed it around the playroom. But everyone thought the photograph was just as marvelous as I did.

"You look like a film star," Dumila said.

"She does!" said one of the others.

Shanika watched me pass around the photo from the corner of the room. She hadn't spoken to me at all since that night, but I did catch her staring at me often. I know she was just sad that I was chosen and not her, but it wasn't like I had any power over what the Evanses wanted, right? And it wasn't like the orphanage was a bad place or anything. We had everything here. We had clothes and comfortable beds and went to school and never had to ask for more food like Oliver Twist. She had at least a year, maybe even longer, until she went to St. Margaret's. I don't get why she had to be so horrible and ruin these days for me. In any case, I kept up my act—that I was a little happy to go, but that I mostly didn't want to.

I wondered if Shanika noticed that I had started to hide some of her things. It wasn't much. Her toothbrush. Her maths notebook. A few coloured pencils from her pencil case. Not enough for it to be a big deal. Just enough for her to get scolded for being forgetful. If she wasn't getting scolded for ruining *Wuthering Heights*, at least she was getting told off for something.

Miss Nayana had to finally threaten to take away the photo to get us to settle down.

The other annoying thing about getting ready to leave, apart from Shanika, was that I had to see Upul more often. I usually enjoyed the school holidays because we hardly saw him unless Miss Chandra took us somewhere, but now I had to see him almost every day.

He would lean over the steering wheel, one of his bony arms with these weird circle scars slung over the open window of the van, as he sang along to Sinhala love songs on the radio. When I was sure he was focused on driving, I snuck a look or two at him. He had bushy, wiry black hair that he kept slicking back, and a few pimples on his chin. He was no Shah Rukh Khan, that's for sure. Not even close.

Luckily, I was never alone with him. Miss Chandra sat in the front seat of the van, and I sat at the back, by myself. I hated driving long distances, it always made me feel a little sick. And the traffic from Colombo, where the shops and the passport office were, kept us on the roads for hours at a time. One time, Miss Chandra and I both fell asleep in the traffic. It was a hot afternoon, and I guess my dress must have slipped up a little bit while I slept. I woke up to Upul staring at me through the rearview mirror, right towards my lap. I quickly sat up and straightened my dress, so I don't know if he saw anything, but he gave me a smile and raised his eyebrows. I vowed to never fall asleep in the van again. He did keep staring at me through the mirror though—often at my chest. I don't know why he did. I was not like Shanika or Dumila, I really didn't have much going on in that area.

One time, he met my eyes, and he licked his lips, slowly. I thought I would vomit right then and there. I thought about telling Miss Chandra, but I guess it was also my fault for letting my dress go up like that.

Miss Chandra was always telling us that we have to behave like ladies, and she wouldn't be happy to hear about it for sure.

And today, after the passport office, Miss Chandra asked Upul to stop at the pharmacy.

"Wait a little, okay, Paloma? I have to get some cough syrup."

It was my first time being left alone with Upul, and I suddenly felt frozen.

I crossed my arms over my chest, made sure my dress was tugged down over my knees, and looked firmly out of the window, refusing to meet his gaze. I could feel his eyes, crawling over me like a pair of slimy bugs.

"So, you're going to America, no? *Sha*, how posh." Even his voice was slimy. I kept staring out the window.

"Are you going to become an American now? Like those girls on TV? Wearing bikinis?" If I don't answer him, he'll stop talking, right?

"I'd like to see you in a bikini. I'm sure you'll look very sexy, ah." My cheeks were turning red. *Haiyyo*, I hoped he couldn't see. I dug my fingers into my sides so I wouldn't cry. He waited a few moments before he went on, sounding angrier now.

"Hey, hey, why don't you look at me? Why do you have to be so proud? No one likes a proud bitch, you know. Not even in America. You'll just do sex and become a whore there anyway, so no point keeping such a big head."

Every part of me was trembling. How much longer was Miss Chandra going to be? It felt like she was gone forever. I took a deep breath to calm myself. Thankfully, I could see her leaving the building and crossing the road to get back to us. Upul must have seen her, too, because when he spoke again, it was faster and in a lower voice.

"No point looking so innocent, ah. I know you like to show me your panties from the back seat."

I gulped. So he had seen. I wished I could have closed my eyes and died, right then and there. Instead, I shut them so tightly my cheeks hurt and pressed my forehead against the glass. I heard Miss Chandra get in, and pretended to be asleep. The van ride took forever, and I was shivering the whole time, which was strange because I was sweating from my armpits. I only opened my eyes when we got back to the home. I jumped out of the van as soon as I felt it stop and I tried to quickly rush away, but Miss Chandra stopped me.

"What do we say, Paloma?"

"S-sorry?"

"Upul has been nice enough to drive us around the whole day. What do we tell him?"

"Thank you, Upul," I mumbled, still refusing to meet his eyes. It was worse than any curse put on me.

"You're welcome." Slime and vomit and every disgusting thing in the world slid off his words and down my throat.

29

SAN FRANCISCO, CA

I RUSHED BACK FROM Ida's without looking behind me. I felt safer once I made it home. I barely pulled the door shut as I went straight over to the kitchen, yanked off my sweater, and got myself a drink. Scotch this time. No more of that sherry crap. It only took a couple of gulps for it to take effect. I relished in the numbness that crept over my cheeks.

I knew I should call the police, but I needed a second to calm down. It's not like fifteen minutes would matter to Ida. The police probably would refuse to investigate shit till she'd been gone forty-eight hours anyway. I turned on the TV and collapsed onto the couch. *Friday the 13th* was on, but I flicked right past till I found some nondescript, basic rom-com featuring a cast of interchangeable white characters who managed to afford apartments and wardrobes way above their pay grade. Just the kind of unrealistic, mind-numbing bullshit I needed.

My hands weren't shaking as much, thank goodness. I pulled one of Mom's decorative knitted throws that I wasn't really supposed to use over me, relishing in the sinking feeling I always got after a good, strong drink. My eyelids felt nice and heavy and my breathing was finally slowing down. I could feel myself drift off to sleep.

And suddenly, I was awake again, though I'm not entirely sure why. Maybe I heard something? I rubbed my eyes. The sherry-scotch fog weighed me down, and my lips felt crusty. The movie was still running, a typical montage of the leading lady trying on various outfits. I looked around for the remote to turn down the volume, but couldn't find it. The security alarm beeped, an annoying soft ding that drilled right into my skull, reminding me that I hadn't turned it on again.

I thought I heard something, so I stood up clumsily and made my way to the kitchen.

The white lace curtains that hung over the kitchen sink blew in, ghosts themselves. The Bay Area winds—always howling, always wild. The lights were turned off on every house down the street except the one across from mine. The porch was empty, of course, but the swing chair they had up there was swaying back and forth. It was probably the wind. Or someone had just gotten off.

I reached over and shut the window. I didn't remember opening it.

I looked around the kitchen. Everything else was as it was supposed to be. My overpriced groceries were still where I left them. The dishwasher was still full of clean cups and dishes that I was always a little too buzzed to put away. I got myself a glass of water and leaned against the counter when I felt something poke my hip.

Oh yes, the phone from Ida's bathroom.

I checked the charging port. Looked like it took the same type of cord that my parents used. They usually kept a box of spare chargers in the garage. I mean, they kept spares of everything—batteries, cables, deodorant, detergent.

I opened the door that led to the garage. Dad had one of those arms installed that forced the door to shut automatically, so I stuck Mom's marble mortar and pestle on the floor to keep it open. The last thing I wanted was to be locked in the fucking garage tonight.

The light flickered as I surveyed the plastic storage boxes Mom had labeled. I don't know why the fuck they were prepared for the goddamned apocalypse or something, but it was a hoarder's dream. Toiletries, stationery, canned goods, electronics . . . there we go. I opened the lid and rummaged through. All the cords were neatly clipped into perfect coils. Damn, even their storage was perfect. I compared the charging port on the phone to the wire heads and just found a match when—

Bam.

The garage door shut.

What the actual fuck?

I jumped to my feet.

Leaving the boxes as they were, I edged closer to the door.

My shaking hand fumbled with the knob. My palms were sweaty, so it slipped on the brass.

Fuck this, Paloma. Get ahold of yourself.

I rubbed my hands against my jeans and tried again.

The door opened without protest.

I stubbed my toe against the mortar on the floor. I guess it couldn't hold the weight of the door, and the whole thing had swung shut.

I took a deep breath.

Seeing that woman spying on me outside Ida's house had made me jumpy. That's all this was.

I went back into the kitchen and plugged Ida's phone in to charge.

I let it sit a minute and then turned it on. The lock screen image was one of Snowy, so it was definitely Ida's phone. But why the hell would it be on the floor in her bathroom? Could she have just dropped it and forgotten about it? It didn't seem improbable, especially if her Alzheimer's was setting in.

There were a few notifications but I couldn't access them because there was a password to get in. I couldn't get into her contacts either. I tried the usual 1234 and various combinations that I figured would work, but it looked like my luck for the night had run out. Damn it, Ida. The one time you decide not to be a typical old lady and it's to come up with a creative password?

I rubbed my eyes and groaned.

That's when I noticed how quiet it was.

I'd left the TV on earlier, hadn't I?

I inched my way back to the living room. The TV was certainly turned off, and the remote was on the coffee table, where it would normally be.

What the hell was happening?

Was there someone in the house?

I was fed up with this bullshit, and there was only one way to find out. Trembling like I was about to disintegrate, I mustered up every ounce of strength I could, grabbed one of Dad's golf clubs from the closet near our front door, and checked every single room. I don't know how much good a Callaway nine iron would be against a murderer, but I had to do something.

Everything downstairs was normal. Every room upstairs as well. I left my parents' room for last, but was already much calmer by the time I got there. This was just my nerves. I was just shook up because of my strange neighbor.

I pushed the door open and turned on the light.

The decorative pillows that were typically arranged methodically on the bed were piled up on the ottoman.

The covers were pulled out. There was a clear indentation of a head on the pillow.

And a Tiffany tumbler with Dad's scotch lay on the side table.

30

RATMALANA, SRI LANKA

THE TRIP BACK FROM the passport office followed me around like a raincloud. No matter what I did, I couldn't shake off the feeling. Even when I was distracted enough to forget what he said, or the way he licked his lips at me, or the way his eyes made me feel naked, even when I was talking to the other girls, or trying to read, or go about my business, that horrible feeling was always there. The girls, of course, had no idea and crowded all around me, asking for details of the trip to Colombo.

"Was the building big?"

"How many people?"

"What's a passport?"

Then I had to complete my tasks, like mopping the dormitory and the playroom, and arranging all the books that the girls pulled out during the day. I hadn't been able to finish all my responsibilities properly these days with all the trips to Colombo. Miss Chandra said it was okay, but I didn't want Lihini to be stuck doing them because of me.

She always ends up doing my unfinished work. It was bad enough that I was leaving her. I even tried to squeeze in some of Lihini's tasks when I could, although she was recently asked to clean Perera sir's office, and she wouldn't let me because it was such a big responsibility she was trusted with. I'm glad she's helping Perera sir. Maybe if she showed him how helpful she could be, he would try harder to find her a family.

Lihini hasn't been talking to me much these days. To be fair, I've been really busy also, but I do miss her. She doesn't crawl into my bed at night as much now, and yesterday she said she was too tired, although I heard her moving around in the top bunk a lot. I know she's upset that I'm leaving soon. Maybe she's trying to get used to not having me around. It made my heart hurt.

She was still talking to everyone about how she saw Mohini though. I wished she would stop. Dumila cries in her sleep every night, and now some of the other girls only walked around in groups because they were so afraid.

I heard Lihini asking Miss Nayana questions also, about anyone who might have died before at the orphanage. Maybe a mother while giving birth? Whether anyone had any "unfinished business." Thankfully Miss Nayana had the sense to ask her to be quiet. I couldn't believe how insensitive she was being.

The only person we know who had died was Mrs. Perera, and thankfully Lihini seemed to have some sense because she didn't bring it up. I thought back to what I remember about Mr. Perera's wife. We hardly ever saw her, and if we did it was from a distance. She had always been a bit odd, from what I recall. Maya told me that Mrs. Perera's brother had died during a bomb blast. That she had never been the same since. I guess this was true. She looked so sad, the few times I did see her. And she stopped eating, and her beautiful black hair started falling out. She was nothing but skin and bones, at the end. They had wanted to take her away to Angoda, that's where people with mental problems went, but she died before that. It was really, really sad, and Perera sir was obviously heartbroken.

Thinking about Mrs. Perera pushed Upul from my mind for a few minutes, but the horrible feeling returned as soon as I let it. I wish I'd told him, well, I wish I'd told him something. No, I wish I'd told him to fuck off. I'm not really sure what that means, but I know it's a bad word and Maya uses it sometimes when none of the teachers are around.

I was so busy with all my tasks that I didn't have time to have my wash before dinner, which Miss Chandra excused, luckily. She was kinder to me these days. Maybe she was worried about missing me also?

It felt nice to step into the night when I finally made my way outside to the bathroom. It was a small room made of concrete and was a few meters away from our dormitory. This was great for days like today because it meant I could take long washes in the night without worrying about the noise disturbing anyone. I onned the light on the outer wall as I went in, glad that the bathroom was empty. I hoped the water would wash off the disgusting feeling that Upul left.

I filled the large bucket from the tap, undoing my braid and combing out my hair. I wonder if they use coconut oil on their hair in America. Miss Nayana says that if you stop putting oil in your hair, it starts to fall out. Maybe I should take a bottle with me, just to be safe. I wonder if Mrs. Evans ever puts oil in her hair.

I used a smaller bucket to pour water on myself. The water was really cold, and I shivered slightly. The good thing about washing in the afternoon is that the *takaran* roof would get hot, so it kept you nice and warm. Now, in the dark, the single bulb that hung in the middle of the bathroom only gave a dim light and no heat at all. My shadows were long and scary on the wall. I tried not to think about Upul as I soaped myself. I got my menses last year, so Miss Nayana told me that means I'm a woman now. And that being a woman means that men look at you differently. Was this all that Upul was doing? Lihini does say that that is the way boys show you that they like you—by teasing you.

But Upul wasn't just teasing me, was he? I thought back to the way he kept staring at me, the cruel things he said, and it made my skin crawl all over again. I doused myself angrily with more icy water, even though it wouldn't wash away the sick feeling in my stomach.

I know you like to show me your panties from the back seat. What if he told Miss Chandra that I did it purposely? My heart dropped. What if Sister Cynthia got to know? Would she cane me in front of everyone? Would they tell Mr. and Mrs. Evans? Oh my goodness, what if they cancelled the adoption because they thought I was a bad girl? Miss Nayana said that no one liked bad girls and that they will never get married. But surely, Mrs. Evans will understand that it was just an accident. That it was hot, and I had fallen asleep. I splashed another bucket over my head. I needed to stop overreacting.

I put soap on my hair with more force than usual. It took some effort, pushing my hands through the tangled mess. Thick, black strands wrapped around my fingers, refusing to glide off. Suds slid into my eyes, sharp and burning. For the first time since this afternoon, I felt better. I was just pouring some water onto my face when I heard the footsteps outside.

Footsteps at this time of the evening? That was odd.

"Anyone there?" I called out. The gardener would have gone home by now, and the girls should be in bed. I suppose it could be Miss Chandra or Miss Nayana coming to check on me? But that didn't seem right.

Footsteps again. And someone whistled a tune. None of the teachers ever whistled.

My body went cold. Could it be Upul? He didn't stay at the home like Miss Chandra, Miss Nayana, and Perera sir did. So he should be home by now too. But what if he didn't leave? What if he stayed behind, waiting for me?

I wanted to check outside, but I didn't want to open the door. What if he forced his way into the bathroom? There was a small window high up near the top of the wall. Maybe I could see through that?

I pushed the now empty bucket near the wall and turned it over as quietly as I could. I stepped onto it lightly, hoping it could take my weight without sliding around, and tried peering out. It was dusty with thick cobwebs along the grille. I couldn't really see much, but it didn't look like anyone was there. I was just climbing off the bucket when it happened. The light flickered once, twice, and then went off completely.

I let out a small scream, covering my mouth with my hands, but immediately scolded myself. The bulb would have gone out, that's all. No need to be such a drama queen.

I stepped down from the bucket carefully, reaching for the towel and drying myself as fast as I could. I pulled on my nightdress and opened the door with a burst. The garden looked clear, but I rushed back into the main building anyway. I knew I was being a scaredy-cat, but I couldn't help it. What if Upul was waiting for me in the darkness? What if, well, what if it was something else? Something like the ghost Lihini kept talking about? Was this a part of the curse? Gosh, I was such a chicken. I used every bit of my concentration to push Mohini out of my mind and focused on getting back inside as soon as I could.

Most of the lights were offed inside as well, but I knew my way around without a problem. Keeping my eyes fixed in front of me, I climbed the stairs to the dormitory. I only realized that I had been holding my breath when I stepped inside and released it. I leaned against the door, trying to breathe deeply, trying to calm down. See, nothing happened. The bulb would have burnt out. Miss Nayana showed us how that happened the other day, and also how to change the light when it happens. The whistling was probably nothing. Maybe the gardener was in later than usual. Maybe Perera sir had stepped outside. When I finally felt like my heart wasn't going to explode, I made my way over to the bed. The girls were fast asleep, I could tell by the gentle snores. I wondered if Lihini was asleep as well, or just pretending again.

I always check my bed properly after the *Wuthering Heights* incident, just in case. There hadn't been any repeats, thank goodness. Anyways, there wasn't any strange smell tonight, so I knew there was nothing to worry about.

But then I noticed something on my pillow. I could barely make it out in the moonlight. It was about the size of a stamp. My photograph. I picked it up and ran my fingers over it. It was dark so I couldn't see it clearly, but something felt different. I brought it close to my face and gasped. Someone had scratched out my eyes in the photo.

31

SAN FRANCISCO, CA

I BARELY GOT ANY sleep, obviously, but the fresh morning air
brought about a small sense of calm. Nina taught me this exercise
when it felt like things were spiraling out of control. The first step was
to make a list of things you could put into action right away. They
didn't have to be big things. Usually my life went like—Step one: Get
out of bed. Step two: Brush teeth. Step three: Work on graphic design
website. Step four: Do ten minutes of breathing exercises.

The first step on today's list was essential if I was to get through
this. Whatever *this* was.

Step one: Stop drinking. Even though my mind kept wandering
towards the bottles of amber liquid that Dad kept in steady supply.

Because even I'm not deluded enough to believe that all this alcohol
wasn't making my brain do somersaults. I had to keep a clear mind if
I was ever going to figure out what happened to Arun. And possibly to
Ida. Nina would be so proud of me, but, well, it wasn't like I could
tell her.

Fern, my old roommate, was around the last time I quit. It's true she was a royal pain in my ass, but she told me that I just needed something to replace the urge—something that would keep me distracted. I had suggested amping up my Tinder profile, but she kept insisting that the replacement shouldn't be "damaging" to my body. I mean, I'm all for a little bit of kink every once in a while, but what the hell kind of sex was she having?

Because she was into all this hippie-dippie, dance-naked-under-the-full-moon-and-burn-sage-to-clear-out-negativity bullshit, she encouraged me to drink green juice.

I complained, of course. Protested that it tasted like pickled sewage and made my poop turn green. But the bitch did have a point. I was still irritable as hell without a shot of rum in me, but every time I got the urge to visit the corner store, I would just head over to the juice bar instead. It smelled hot and sticky in there, like the fruit was half an hour away from rotting, but the older gentleman who ran the place said in a totally noncreepy way that I had a bright smile, and they gave me an extra shot of wheatgrass from time to time.

My skin started to look good. I lost some of the bloat that was slowly building up around my lower tummy. And miraculously, I was able to focus on some of my design work. I even tried some of the deep-breathing meditation techniques Fern was always trying to make me do. I always just ended up dozing off, but at least it got her off my back for a while.

My grocery run yesterday consisted of the basics—pasta, pesto, and soda—so I didn't have most of the vegetables or greens I needed to make juice myself. I googled the closest cold-pressed juice spot. Surprisingly, the nearest one was downtown, which was kind of strange. You'd think the trendy pseudo-hippie moms who owned Himalayan rock salt lamps and went for hot-yoga classes in my neighborhood would be lining up if a juice bar opened up around this block, but no such luck.

I pulled on a hoodie and stuck my headphones in. I guess a walk wasn't the worst thing for me right now either. Getting out of my parents' home felt like a relief.

I kept a close eye on the opposite house as I walked by, but there was no real movement that I could see. The neighbor was probably sleeping off all the crazy. I shook my head and laughed to myself a little. I couldn't believe how much she was able to scare me last night. Obviously she had some sort of problem and couldn't stop spying on me, but to think she was Mohini was beyond ridiculous. Even for me. She freaked me out enough that I didn't even grab the folder I found in Ida's desk. I would have liked to get a better look at those documents, and if I'm being honest, it makes me kind of nervous that Ida had them to begin with.

I kept flicking through the copy of *Wuthering Heights* that crazy-neighbor had left in the mailbox, hoping it would give me some sort of clue, but there was nothing. No highlighted words, no notes in the margins, nothing.

And then there was my parents' bed. That had to be me, right? It was the only explanation. I could understand someone breaking in to rob the place, but who the hell would come inside to take a fucking nap? No, it had to be me, after a few of the drinks I was explicitly told not to take.

I tried not to think about it too much.

I checked the mailbox at the top of the driveway, just in case. No books, just a few odd bits and bobs of junk mail that were in there for god knows how long, and a postcard.

It was a picture of a coconut tree–dotted beach. Yellow sand, bright blue waves. I knew where this was, of course. My heart felt full as I turned it over. *Can't wait to see you soon, my sweet girl.*

How did they know it would reach me at their place? They probably wanted to surprise me when I was watering the plants or something. My heart hurt. My head, too, just a bit.

But still, it felt good to know that they thought about me, despite it all.

The walk downtown wasn't unpleasant. The weather had cooled off this past week, even though I was too preoccupied to really notice. It was what Dad would call crisp. The leaves were that beautiful rust color that I could never get over since I moved here. I lengthened my step a little to stamp down on a fallen leaf and smiled at the satisfying crunch.

The juice bar was a little too warm when I finally made it inside.

"Green Goddess smoothie, please. Large." Yes, that's right. I was a fucking walking cliché. All I needed was a crop top, oversized hoops, and those ridiculous high-waisted mom jeans that made my ass look like the back of a Camaro to fit right in. I couldn't help it though. I fucking loved green smoothies.

The young boy behind the counter gave me a toothy smile.

"Name, please?"

"I'm Paloma." I gave a friendly smile right back. It was nice to do something normal, for once. No second-guessing. No worrying about dead roommates or potential break-ins or creepy neighbors.

I was on my phone, scrolling through Facebook profiles of various Aruns again, when someone stopped right in front of me.

"Paloma?" Fern's smile was wide but it didn't quite make it all the way up to her eyes. Her hair was ablaze with her latest botched dye job—purple and maroon this time, and her crocheted halter top was right on brand.

"Oh, hi, Fern. How are you?" *Smile, Paloma.* Mom's voice echoed in my mind as I arranged my face so I didn't look like I'd rather be anywhere else in the world right now. Fuck, what were the odds?

"I'm good. I'm actually getting my chiropractor certification at the center around the corner. This is where I come to get my juice."

Of course it fucking was. Undesirable coincidences seem to be a bit of a theme for me.

"Oh, okay." I mean, what the fuck else was I supposed to say anyway? It's not like we kept in touch after I kicked her out.

"This is out of the way for you, isn't it?"

"Just in the neighborhood." I wasn't in the mood to explain to her that I'd moved into my parents'. She'd fucking love to pull that apart, wouldn't she? Analyze what I'm doing there and give me advice and tell me that she'll support me no matter what. I already had a fucking therapist, so no, thank you, Fern.

"Hey, so, I've actually tried to get in touch with you. I just wanted—"

"Green Goddess smoothie, large, for Paloma!" Saved in the nick of time.

I guess I'll have to find out what you want some other time, Fern. And thank god for that.

I gave her a little smile and walked up to the counter.

"Enjoy your smoothie!" the boy said.

"Thanks, I will." I stuck a five-dollar bill in the tip jar. It was more than I should tip for juice, and definitely more than I could afford right now, but hell, if I could reach behind the counter and kiss this kid without being arrested, I would.

"It was nice seeing you, Fern," I said, walking by her and out into the street.

"Hey, Paloma, wait." Did she seriously follow me out? Bitch couldn't take a hint even if it hit her on the head with one of her healing crystals.

I kept walking but she caught up to me and grabbed my elbow.

"Hey, look, I just wanted to know how you were doing, that's all."

I looked at her like it was the most obvious thing in the world.

"I'm fine, Fern. As you can see." I gave her the sort of patronizing smile my mother used to give homeless people.

"I've tried calling you. Look, I just wanted to say, well, it's okay. You know. It's okay. I forgive you for what happened. I understand."

I was in no mood to do this.

"Okay, Fern. Thank you, I guess. You take care now." I just wanted to get away.

"Look, I get it, okay. You don't like getting close to anyone. It scares you. You're worried you'll let me down like you did with your friend in the orphanage. But you don't have to be scared."

The smile never left my face, but my words came out in a hiss.

"You have no fucking clue what you are talking about, Fern. You're a lying, thieving bitch and I just want you out of my life."

"You know that's a lie, Paloma." She looked pointedly at my ears. "We were friends. *Good* friends. But you don't feel like you deserve to have friends, Paloma, and so you self-sabotage. With me, with your parents—"

"Don't you dare bring them up!" My voice came out louder and some passersby turned to see what the commotion was. I took a deep breath. "You don't know what you are talking about. I can't help it that you're obsessed with me. Please, just leave me alone."

When I walked off this time, she didn't follow me, but I heard her loud and clear through the buzzing traffic.

"Nice earrings, Paloma. Guess you didn't lose them like you thought."

I didn't look back as I stomped my way home. Who the hell did she think she was, cornering me like that? Thank god she was out of my life. All that prying, all that poking, getting me to talk about my feelings. I'd only mentioned Lihini to her once. And even then I never told her the whole story.

But then she got this bright idea that we should try to trace at least some of the other girls from the orphanage and pushed me to talk to my parents about visiting Sri Lanka again, and so I knew she had to go. I hid my earrings under the soles of a pair of running shoes she never wore, cried out frantically that they were missing, and was outraged when I "discovered" them in her room. She was devastated when I asked her to get out. I was upset about it, too, of course. It was nice having her around.

But I didn't work so hard to move on from my old life just to have her meddle in it now.

I took a chug of my green juice, but that shit tasted disgusting. I dumped the cup into the trash, turned the volume up on my music, and walked back home.

It was a warm afternoon, and the whole neighborhood looked sleepy. This would change as the sun dipped further into the horizon, and the young moms in Lululemon would roll their expensive strollers without fear of sunburns as their husbands drove off in their Teslas or whatever save-the-environment car was popular to some hipster bar that sold overpriced, handcrafted, artisan beer on tap. The grass was already starting to brown on the neatly maintained front lawns, exposed and inviting and unfenced.

I crossed the street to step out of the sun, my feet moving on their own, too preoccupied about Fern and her never-ending prying to notice that I absentmindedly wandered up the wrong driveway. It was only when I saw the lady with the long hair sitting on the porch that I jerked back into reality.

I didn't think she noticed me, thank god. Her eyes were glazed over and she was clutching a small, pink blanket around her. Her lips were moving slightly, too, like she was mumbling something to someone, or maybe it was to herself. My legs felt glued to her driveway. I was transfixed. Then she looked over at me. And as our eyes met I couldn't help but shudder. Her face remained impassive, but she stood up slowly and walked into the house.

I CHECKED IDA'S PHONE again. There was a notification for a missed call, but as usual, I couldn't get into it.

I had reached step two on my list: Call the police about Ida.

Pushing away the memory of my sneakers outside Ida's back door, I dialed the number Officer Keller had given me in case Arun turned up or I thought of any other helpful information. His words, not mine.

"Keller here," he answered, sounding gruff.

"Officer Keller, hi, it's Paloma Evans."

"Who?"

"Paloma Evans. We met the other day because of my roommate's disappearance." I carefully avoided the word *murder*.

He was still silent.

"The woman from Sri Lanka?" I tried.

"Oh, yes. Undocumented Indian roommate. I remember now." Of course you fucking did, Keller. I know he couldn't see me, but I strained to keep a polite smile plastered on my face. *You can hear rudeness through the phone, Paloma.* "Did he turn up, then?"

"Um, no he didn't yet. I was—"

"Well, I wouldn't worry much about it if I were you, most of these kids do tend to disappear when their visa runs out." Arun's blank face stared back at me. Sure thing, Keller.

I could hear noises in the background. Someone was asking him something and he replied with a muffled yes.

"There's something else." I took a deep breath. I couldn't chicken out now. "My neighbor. She—she's missing." I resisted the urge to add *as well*.

"Your neighbor, huh? Is she from India also?"

I wanted to fucking punch him.

"No. She's an older lady. White. Maybe around—" Fuck, how old was Ida? "Around seventy-five or eighty, I reckon."

There was a rustling on the phone, like maybe he was also doing something else while speaking to me.

"And she's been missing for how long?"

"Since yesterday morning. A little over a day now. There's a note on her fridge that said she was going to San Diego, but she'd made plans with me, and—and well, it's not like her to just take off like that."

There was a slight pause.

"I'm just, well, I'm just worried that something might have happened to her. Or something."

Officer Keller's voice was patient when he spoke to me next. He asked me for Ida's details and I gave him what little information I had. I couldn't even remember her sister's name, let alone anything useful.

"Look, Miss Evans, she hasn't been missing forty-eight hours, and she seems to have left some indication of where she would be. I'll call this in, and I'm sorry to say it, once again, but I don't think there's much to be done at this point."

"I don't think you understand, Officer—" But he cut me off again.

"Miss Evans, I'm on patrol right now. Give me a call in a few days if she still hasn't turned up and we'll see what we can do, okay?"

"Sure. Thank you for your time." Not. On patrol right now? On a fucking doughnut run was more like it. What a useless excuse for a cop. Of all the policemen on the force, of course I'd get stuck with this guy.

He clearly didn't give a shit. Or didn't believe me.

But what if—there was the little voice in my head that sounded like Nina—what if there was nothing to believe? Even Sam said it, didn't he? I absolutely zombied out when I was drunk. Maybe . . .

But there was no fucking way I imagined Arun that night. There's something about a dead body that you couldn't just imagine. The weight of his head as I pulled it back. The smell of his blood on my fingers. He was murdered and there was a killer on the loose and thanks to this moron Keller, who looked like he was doing an impersonation of a thumb half the fucking time, no one believed me.

I was absentmindedly pacing the house again and had made my way to the kitchen.

I stared out the window, not really looking at anything. But when I focused my eyes, I noticed the woman across the street was walking up and down her porch. Not stepping out into the yard. Just going in circles, cradling that disgusting old blanket in her arms again.

Fuck, that was creepy.

I took a deep breath. I was seriously losing my mind here. I needed to calm the fuck down. I needed to do something, but I couldn't think of anything left.

I grabbed my laptop and a soda from the fridge and sat down. It was no fucking green juice, but at least it wasn't scotch, right?

Jason Wong had finally emailed me the CCTV footage, so I guess his lack of personal hygiene didn't make him a complete dipshit.

I immediately pulled up the video to where the man in the hat walked out of the elevator. I stopped it at every frame, leaning close to the screen and trying to make sense of his pixelated face. Was it actually Mr. Williams? Or was I just being paranoid? It didn't stop my hands from starting to shake a little. I needed to move on. Staring at this blurry man on my computer won't help me in the least.

I pulled the video back and watched myself run down the corridor over and over and over again, but it didn't look like anyone was chasing me. Of course, if they stayed close to the wall and knew exactly what path to take, like Arun did, they wouldn't ever be picked up by the cameras. It was one of the reasons why we both thought it was a good idea for him to sublet. My parents had left on their dumb trip and I needed the money, even though I had told myself that I'd never share my apartment again after what happened with Fern. But something about Arun made me feel, well, I felt sorry for him, I guess. I thought I was doing him a favor. Look how that turned out.

I opened up my browser and typed in the words slowly, deliberately making sure I spelled it correctly.

Little Miracles Girls Home Sri Lanka

It was my first time doing it. The first time that I let myself. I had researched the laws, the rules, the consequences, just never the home. Never the girls. I thought about them all the time. I wondered what they might look like, grown up. I would never know. So I never looked. It wouldn't ever accomplish anything, I told myself. But the truth is that it was just too hard. I never looked at the box in my parents' bedroom, I never googled the home, I never even asked my parents for any information. I'd shoved my curiosity away with my guilt and my ghosts and my secrets.

Except there was another, very different letter. It came about two years after I left Sri Lanka. My parents kept it at the very bottom of the box, beneath everything else. The letter from the agency that Dad had to read to me because I never could bring myself to even look at it. The letter that I had thought about, almost every day since, every time I looked in the mirror or someone asked me where I grew up.

> We regret to inform you that the Little Miracles Girls'
> Home in Sri Lanka has ceased to exist. The orphanage
> was unfortunately burnt down by a fire. The residents of
> the home have been transferred to alternate homes, as per
> the state protocols in Sri Lanka. Regrettably, we were

informed that, despite the authorities' best efforts, one of
the girls lost her life in the fire.

One of the girls lost her life. I knew then, even before he said it out loud. I knew when I left. I knew when I abandoned her. It was me. I had killed her.

I'm so sorry, Paloma, Dad had said, his own eyes drowning in the tears he was trying to hold back. *Lihini is . . .* He had paused there, chin trembling, and I knew, I knew in my bones what came next. *She's no more.*

No more.

No more, like we'd run out of milk. No more, like a fucking domestic violence campaign. No more.

But she wasn't "no more," because of the fire. She was "no more" from the moment I left.

The search had loaded.

Facebook pages for different girls' homes. But it wouldn't be them. Facebook didn't exist back then. Hell, computers didn't exist for orphanages in Ratmalana back then. No, they wouldn't have a Facebook page. They wouldn't even have a regular website. I clicked through about three pages of results.

The Little Miracles Girls Home Sri Lanka Fire, I tried.

Nothing. Well, not nothing. Pages and pages of well-crafted, PR company–managed orphanages.

Volunteer in an orphanage in Sri Lanka
Donate to St. Mary's Girls Home, Sri Lanka
Child Protection Authority, Sri Lanka

But not what I was looking for.

The house was completely dark around me, and the glow of the monitor blinded me from seeing anything else. Someone could be in here with me, and I'd never see them.

I thought I felt something on the back of my neck.

Was there someone else in here?

A shiver ripped through me.

A pale face. Long hair. White dress.

Fuck it, Paloma. Get a grip on yourself.

Mohini doesn't exist. She never did. I don't care what you think you saw. She doesn't exist.

I closed the laptop and stood up, willing myself to be more fearless, and pissed off that my hands shook, betraying me. Two strides and I turned the kitchen lights on. One glance and I was able to confirm that I was starting to lose it. Obviously my kitchen was empty.

I sighed. This wasn't going anywhere. I might as well get to bed. I snuck a glance out my window again, but she wasn't there.

The yawn that erupted out of me was sudden. I needed to get some sleep.

I made sure all the windows were locked and that the alarm was turned on. I even left a light on downstairs.

A whole day without a drink. It's pretty rare that I felt proud of myself, and I wished there was someone I could call. I took a nice, long shower and wore my favorite old flannel pajamas. I'd left a lamp on in my bedroom so it wasn't completely dark when I went back in there.

I was just about to climb into bed when I noticed something on my pillow.

It was a small piece of card. About the size of a postcard. I must have brought one up from my collection on the fridge or something. But there was no writing on it.

I turned it over.

It wasn't a postcard.

It was a photograph of me.

A photograph of me smiling, holding up a bronze medal.

A photograph of me smiling, holding up a bronze medal, with my eyes scratched out.

A pounding that started in my head crashed down to my ears, and everything felt woozy again.

I went back downstairs and poured myself a stiff drink. I would need it, now that I knew, beyond any doubt, that my past had finally caught up to me.

32

RATMALANA, SRI LANKA

WE WERE WOKEN EVERY morning by a bell that rings through the orphanage. But I must have slept through it because I was tossing and turning all night after I found the photo on my pillow.

When I finally woke up, the girls had all gone for breakfast. Lihini had gone too. She didn't wake me like she normally did when I over-slept.

But that was okay. I took a moment to think about who did this.

It was Shanika. I knew it. She was the only one who was jealous of me going. She was the one who attacked me. She probably thought she could scare me. That this was some sort of revenge.

Well, two could play at that game.

I got out of bed and quickly got dressed. I knew exactly what I was looking for. We weren't allowed any toys or books in the dining room, so Shanika would have left it in the playroom during breakfast. I hur-ried there while the rest of the girls ate.

I was right. The doll was left seated on a chair, like it was another person. It once had eyes that would open and close automatically as you laid it down or picked it up, but now its eyelids were stuck in a half-closed position. Its hair was matted, and it wore a fraying dress that was once pink but now an ugly greyish colour.

I picked it up with my thumb and index finger. There was no one around; the corridor was quiet. The girls would say their morning prayers and then start to eat. That meant I'd have some time.

Goodness, it was filthy. I don't think Shanika ever washed it. Typical.

I gripped the doll tightly as I crossed over through the building, making sure that Perera sir didn't hear me.

Anyways, I shouldn't have to worry. The doll wasn't Shanika's, not technically. Technically all the toys belonged to the orphanage and we were all supposed to take turns playing with them. I couldn't help it that Shanika had just decided that this doll was supposed to be hers, and just *took* it without sharing with anyone.

I didn't feel bad about what I was going to do. I knew it was Shanika who destroyed *Wuthering Heights*, and who scratched the eyes out of my photograph. It was definitely Shanika.

I got to the back garden, behind the kitchen. It was empty. Good.

The bottle of lamp oil was where it always was under the sink. I unscrewed it carefully, inhaling the sharp smell. I had to make sure I didn't get any on my hands.

I went to the very corner of the garden, right up next to the back wall, and left the doll on the ground. Looking behind me again, just to make sure, I poured a little bit of the lamp oil on it, making sure the dress was soaked.

I wondered how long it would take. Miss Nayana said things that are synthetic burn more easily, and the doll's hair was made from cheap plastic.

I lit the match from the box I had taken along with the lamp oil.

Maybe this would teach her, I told myself as I dropped the match onto the ugly, dirty doll.

I needn't have worried. The flames caught on quick, licking at the plastic hungrily for only a few moments, until the doll started to get misshapen, and then started to melt away.

The smell was disgusting, and made my eyes water.

That should teach her a lesson. That should show her to stop messing with me.

IT WAS ONE OF the hottest days in April yet. The sun beat down on us like beams of fire, making our clothes stick to our backs and our skin break out in rashes. It was too hot to be outside, but Lihini sat under our tree, book in hand, even though I could see the sweat drip down her nose as I went to join her.

"*If you look the right way, you can see that the whole world is a garden,*" I recited.

"Huh?"

"*The Secret Garden.*" I nodded towards her book. "I read it last week, remember?" I was reading a lot of other books now that we didn't have *Wuthering Heights* anymore.

"Oh." She looked like she only just noticed the book she was holding.

"You okay?" I asked, sitting down, not with my back against the tree like I usually did, but across from her. Goodness gracious, it was hot out here.

She shut the book and tried to fan herself with it, even though it was too thick to really stir up any air.

"It's an oven, no? What was I thinking, I don't know. Coming outside today." She smiled, but it was only her lips that curved. Her eyes still looked like they were far, far away.

"Shall we go inside, so?"

"No. No. Don't worry *aney*." But I did worry. I had hardly seen Lihini these days. Most of my time had been filled with forms and applications and packing and new clothes, and the few times I had been free, I was never able to find her. She never climbed into my bed at night anymore, either, and one time I climbed up the ladder to the top bunk to ask her why, but she wasn't in bed. I thought she must have spent the night in the sickroom or something, but then I heard her giggling from Maya's bed, which made my chest hurt a little.

I guessed she was trying to make new friends so that she wouldn't be so lonely when I left. She definitely seemed to be more friendly with Maya these days. I heard them planning to lay a trap for Mohini the other day. It felt like someone was reaching into my chest and squeezing my heart whenever I thought about that.

"How's the book?" I asked instead.

"Good."

"Got to the part with the key yet?"

"What?"

"The key. You know, to the garden?"

"Oh. No. Not yet. Don't tell me what happens."

"Sorry."

The air was heavy and still between us. This was strange. We always had so much to talk about. Miss Nayana always said we were like two gossiping *achchi ammas* who didn't know better. One time, we even lay in bed talking until the sun came up. But that felt so long ago now.

"So, did you—" I started, just as Lihini said, "Here, I was—"

We both paused.

"You first," I said.

"No, you go."

"Just tell, will you?"

Lihini's lips curled up into a small smile.

"What a spoiled brat, no?"

"Who?" I asked.

"Mary."

"She gets better. Her parents seemed awful too." At least we weren't talking about ghosts for once, thank goodness.

"At least she had them."

"Had. They died."

She shrugged. I knew what she was thinking. Mary's parents died. They couldn't help it. At least they didn't give her away because they didn't want her. I don't know what's worse—knowing your parents are dead, or knowing that they are out there somewhere, but they don't want anything to do with you. We didn't let ourselves think about it often. But that didn't mean these thoughts didn't exist, like little shadows, hiding in the backs of our minds.

"Anyways, she makes friends, and she gets better. That's all I'll say. Don't worry *haiyyo*, I won't spoil it for you."

"So she wasn't alone for too long?"

"Nope."

"Lucky her." The fingers around my heart squeezed again.

Snooby trotted outside the main building and wandered towards us.

"Shoo!" I drew my knees up to my chest. I finally had some time alone with Lihini and I didn't want anyone ruining it, not even the dog.

"Sin, *aney*." Lihini reached over and petted him. Snooby whimpered a little and lay down next to her. Great. Just great.

We sat there in silence. I didn't feel like opening up my book.

"I think I saw her again, you know."

"Who?" I already knew who. I was just hoping she wouldn't say it.

"You know. Mohini. I think she's trying to tell me something."

I started to feel my blood thumping in my ears.

"Tell you something?"

"Yes. I think—I think maybe she wants my help. That's usually why ghosts come back, right?"

"Help for what?"

"You don't believe me. Why should I tell you?"

My ears were pulsing now. I could feel myself getting sweaty in my armpits. I had to change the subject.

"Someone stole my passport picture and scratched my eyes out."

"And you think, what? That it was me?"

Huh? What was she on about?

"No, are you mad? I'm just saying—have you seen what Shanika has been up to lately? She's always wandering around in the night. Even more than usual."

"Shanika is always strange."

"Yeah, she is." I felt a little smug. I even thought about telling Lihini what I had done this morning. How Shanika won't be bothering me anymore.

"Maybe it wasn't Shanika at all. Maybe it was the ghost. Maybe it was Mohini."

Why was she always taking everyone else's side but mine? First Maya, now Shanika. I bit my tongue, hard, the chipped bit cutting into the soft flesh. But I didn't say anything.

There was a sound from the other end of the garden, and for the first time in my life, I was half grateful to see Upul dragging a sack of coconuts from the van into the kitchen. It wasn't much, but at least it distracted Lihini.

"He's such a creep," I said.

"Don't be so mean." Why did everything have to be such an argument?

"But he is."

She didn't say anything, but I saw her press her lips together tightly, the way Miss Chandra did when she was annoyed about something. I guess this irritated me the most.

"What?" There was an edge to my voice now.

"I heard that Perera sir beats him. Maybe he's just looking for love too."

"Perera sir beats him? That's ridiculous. Isn't he his nephew?"

"Not closely related, I think. And you know those scars he has on his arms? I heard that's from Perera sir also. From his cigarettes."

"Who told you this?"

"Maya did."

"*Haiyyo*, why do you always believe what she says? She just loves to gossip, no?"

"Doesn't make it any less true."

"But Perera sir would never—"

"How would you know?"

"I know!" Why was she being so defensive?

"Oh please, you don't know anything!"

"What?"

"You. Don't. Know. Anything." How dare she?

Snooby got up from where he was lying down and barked once.

"I know that you are being a bitch," I spat. I'd only heard the word being used once, when Miss Nayana said it to Miss Sarah about Miss Chandra and they both burst into a fit of giggles. I knew what it meant. It meant female dog, but not in a cute way. I guessed Lihini knew what it meant also, because she looked like I had slapped her.

But just for a moment. She reached out and I thought she was going to hit me. Instead, she yanked my book out of my hands and threw it in the dirt.

"God, you're just like Mary, no wonder you like her so much. Spoiled rotten. You have everything. Everyone wants you. The Evanses,

Upul, everyone picks you. And all you do is complain. You are such a spoiled brat." She practically spat at me. Her hands were shaking as she balled them into fists.

Snooby barked again.

"I don't complain about the Evanses." Okay, maybe I did complain about Upul, but he was horrible! Why couldn't Lihini see that?

"Why would you? You just get whatever you want, don't you? You just reach out and take it." Her voice was shaking as it rose louder, and her eyes got glassy. She was trembling now.

"I—I don't just take what I want, Lihini. I can't help it that they picked me, you know. I never tricked anyone. And you said it was okay. You said Perera sir would find you a family also."

"You don't even believe me." Her words sliced into me. "You say you're my best friend and you don't even believe me when I say I've seen her."

Here she was, talking about that stupid ghost again.

"Come on, *sudhu*. You know it's not like that. You know—"

But she just stood up and reached out for Snooby and I couldn't keep going. What could I say anyway? That I believed her ridiculous story? Because I didn't.

Tears were running down her face freely now, as they were on mine.

"You're so lucky, Paloma. You're the luckiest girl in the whole wide world, and all you do is complain about leaving, and about Upul, and about Shanika. It's like you don't even care about us anymore. About me. I thought you were my friend."

"You *are* my friend," I insisted. She had to see that, surely?

"You were never my friend. You only care about yourself. You might not believe me now, but I'll prove it to you that I'm right. I'll prove it to all of you."

And with that, she turned around and stomped back to the main building, leaving me under the tree with the dog. He stared after her awhile, and then looked at me sadly. I couldn't bear it.

"Go away. Shoo!"

He didn't budge.

I pushed him, gently, with my foot.

"Go away, Snooby. Now!"

Still nothing.

You were never my friend. You only care about yourself.

"Get out, Snooby."

He just blinked up at me.

I couldn't take it anymore.

I kicked his side. It wasn't even that hard.

He yelped and darted away.

Dust clung to my sticky face as I tried to calm myself. My hands started to throb. I unclenched my fists. I had dug my fingers so hard into my palms that pink crescents winked up from the whites of my hands.

The luckiest girl in the whole wide world, she said. Was I really that lucky? I didn't feel so lucky right now, crying under the ambarella tree. But maybe she was right. I thought about Mr. and Mrs. Evans. The way he smiled as if he had never known what it was like to be sad, the way she looked at me when she saw I was reading *Wuthering Heights*. Lihini was right. I was the luckiest girl in the whole wide world.

33

SAN FRANCISCO, CA

I GAVE UP EVEN attempting to sleep, but the quarter bottle of scotch must have knocked me out cold.

I guess I had opened a window because I felt the breeze tickle my face. I was glad it did. Droplets of sweat ran down my temples and into my hair, sticky and wet like honey. Or blood. My sheets twisted over me as I wrestled against them, trying to break free, trying to get some relief from these demons clawing at me, pulling me deeper into my bed, drowning me like quicksand.

A gust blew in again, its cool fingers a soft caress, giving me just a moment of relief.

I knew I wasn't alone even before I saw her.

I heard her humming first. It was soft, melodic, as welcome as the breeze. The tune rose and fell, and I let it wash over me. Goose bumps broke out over my arms as I recognized the words.

"*Que sera, sera. Whatever will be, will be.*" Of course the words followed. She was never satisfied with just humming. She had to sing.

Her pale, gaunt face. The wild, black hair. Nothing had changed in eighteen years.

"How?" I choked out. "How did you find me?"

"I've never left you. I'm always here," she rasped back. Not the song anymore, but the music was still there.

"Please," I pleaded. "Please leave me alone."

She smiled again. Her eyes were inky pools that sucked me in.

"You know why I'm here. Why I can never leave," she said. "It's because of what you did."

"What I did?"

"You know what you did."

She was holding something in her hand. I could see the moonlight bounce off the sharp metal. A box cutter.

"*Que sera, sera*," she started to sing.

The tune was haunting me now. It hung heavily between us, perfumed and rotten, like fruit going bad.

She pushed up the silver blade one section at a time, extending it up almost completely. It glinted, silver and bright and long and sharp.

"*The future's not ours to see.*" She stopped then, and licked her lips. "Now your turn."

"*Que sera, sera,*" I whispered as she stuck her tongue out almost to her chin and licked the blade, slowly, forcefully, splitting her tongue in half, her black eyes never leaving mine.

I sat straight up in bed. My chest hurt and I couldn't breathe.

"*Que sera, sera,*" I heard, but it was an echo. Water in cupped hands left over from my dream. But through all of that—the note on my fridge. Had Arun written it? Even if he read the letter, how would he know the song? Who else could have known the song?

I pulled myself out of the twisted blankets and stumbled over to the bathroom, turning on the faucet to the coldest it would go. The water felt like millions of needles stabbing at my skin, but I relished the ache. I looked in the mirror. My face was pale.

Just like hers, something in the back of my mind sneered.

No, I told myself firmly. Not like hers. Never, ever like hers.

I scraped my sweaty hair off my face and tied it back in a knot. I pushed my thumb hard against my fake front tooth, letting the ache bring me back to earth.

I glared at my reflection. Now was not the time to lose my shit.

"I'm Paloma," I said out loud. My voice bounced off the porcelain in the empty bathroom with a resounding boom. Fuck, yes.

"I'm Paloma, and I'm here, and I'll be damned if I let anyone fuck with me now."

FIRST THINGS FIRST. I had to know what the fuck was up with that woman across the street. I've had fucking enough of her sneaking around and creeping me out. Giving me all this fucking anxiety that I really didn't need right now, and worst of all, making me second-guess myself. The fact that she looked like, well, I couldn't really bring myself to even say it. She looked like she might have more to do with what was going on than I first cared to admit.

I mean, how could I have been so dumb? The copy of *Wuthering Heights*. She was definitely trying to mess with me.

You catch more flies with honey than vinegar, my mother used to say, and she was right. I watched the way she always got what she wanted. It came naturally to her, and not just because she was always the most beautiful woman in the room. Not all beautiful people had what she had—this inherent knowledge to always say and do the right thing. To get everyone to like her.

It didn't come easily to me. I had to work at it. But if I learned one thing from Mom, it's that it was usually worth it being the sweet girl.

I didn't think I had much to go on when it came to looks, not like she does anyway, but I did have the exotic card to play, no matter how much it pained me. I know I'm not supposed to do it that way. I know that we (and I use the term *we* to mean all of us who have been dealt the shitty hand of having too much melanin in this Clorox-white world) have been through too much, fought too much for our rights, been eroticized and disregarded, for me to use the exotic-brown-girl stereotype to my advantage. I get it. It cheapens our cause. I hate that I have to do it. But fuck you, this is the hand I've been dealt and now you want me not to play the only trump card I've got?

The catch is that you can't play the exotic card with other foreigners, obviously.

I had to play the "nice" card with my strange South Asian neighbor, and I wasn't sure if it would work, but I'll be damned if I didn't give it my best shot. And then maybe I could figure out if she has anything to do with the fucked-up shit that's been going on and get on with my life without her blank stares freaking me out and giving me nightmares. I know it doesn't solve any of my important problems, but it'll solve something, I hope, and I'll take whatever I can get right now.

So when I rang her doorbell with one hand, balancing a store-bought cherry pie that I had transferred onto one of Mom's baking dishes in the other, I did it with a flickering sense of optimism. I made sure I was smiling my best, most unassuming, friendly-neighbor smile and waited.

I could hear laughter from inside, and light, unnecessarily fast footsteps followed by slower, heavier ones. Someone was chasing that baby around. Babies couldn't run though, right? Was it a toddler, then?

I was wondering whether to ring the bell again when the door was yanked open. It wasn't her.

"Hello?" a man with sandy-brown hair called out. He looked a little confused to see me. It was eleven a.m. on a Tuesday. I didn't expect him to be at home. This neighborhood was far too nice for a husband who was at home on a weekday morning. Maybe he worked for one of those new-age startups that let you connect in remotely? I made a conscious effort not to groan. The only thing worse than a hipster is a wannabe yuppie hipster.

I had worn my impress-*her* outfit—a cheerful yellow skirt, and a roomy white T-shirt. Friendly, gal next door, and most importantly, nonthreatening. I definitely wasn't in my impress-*him* outfit, which leaned more towards the low-cut, tank top side of my wardrobe, so this was certainly a deviation from my plan.

"Hi! I'm Paloma. Evans," I added for good measure, in case he didn't spend most of his time spying on me like his psycho wife did. "I'm just staying at my parents' across the street. Just thought I'd come around and say hi, since we haven't had a chance to meet yet." Women use the word *just* far more than men do, an article I read recently said. They feel it makes them appear less imposing, and that's exactly what I was going for. Less imposing. Least imposing. Totally approachable. Not at all like I want to bitch-slap your wife all the way to a mental asylum.

He leaned against the doorframe, oblivious to the stamping and squealing coming from inside. He had a geometric pattern of circles and triangles tattooed on his inner arm. The discipline it took for me not to roll my eyes was giving me a headache.

"Paloma. Hi. That's nice of you to come by. I'm Gavin." He spoke cautiously, with strong undertones of *why the fuck are you here*.

"Nice to meet you, Gavin." I made sure my smile didn't drop. I probably looked psychotic. "Is your wife at home? I'd love to say hello."

He frowned a little and looked over his shoulder. "She's home, but she's been a little under the weather lately, let me check. Oh god,

Gulliver, put that down!" Who the hell names their child Gulliver? Goddamned hipsters, man. They'll never give that little shit a chance.

"Gulliver, come on, buddy." He sighed. His eyes were red rimmed and he was unshaven.

"Give me a minute. Why don't you just come in?"

I stepped inside a living room almost identical to my parents' and Ida's. Well, identical except this one looked like it had been hit by a hurricane of plastic toys, crayons, bottles, and god knows what else.

"Sorry it's such a mess. We still haven't fully settled in after the move. You know how it is with a kid."

No, Gavin. I do not know, and have absolutely no intention of ever finding out. I thought about my little apartment back in the city and how I died a little every time Arun left an unwashed dish in the sink. No chance I was ever going to let my home look like the Teletubbies took a massive dump all over it.

"Honey, are you there?" he called out. "Paloma Evans from across the street is here. And she's brought pie." He gave me a small smile like there was some secret joke between us that I was supposed to understand. Maybe there was. Maybe under different circumstances I'd giggle back, and he'd casually keep his left hand in his pocket so I wouldn't see his wedding ring, and we'd think of plausible reasons to exchange phone numbers or fuck in a bathroom somewhere. But today wasn't that day.

I stepped into the living room, my knuckles white around Mom's baking dish.

"Appy's not been feeling so great. I think she might be coming down with something. Terrible flu going around, I hear."

I didn't come all the way over here to talk about the goddamned flu, Gavin.

"Oh really?"

"Yeah, it's been going around Gulliver's playgroup. He had it too. It's why I'm home today actually. I wanted to give her a break."

So you're not a self-indulgent millennial, Gavin. That's a relief. Even though you were enough of an asshat to name your child Gulliver.

I was saved from having to come up with a mild remark that cajoled him about his generous attitude as a modern dad by the sound of a crash from the kitchen.

"Uh-oh," Gulliver warbled.

"Two secs." Gavin rushed over to the kitchen to deal with the little monster, and I tried to see if there was a picture or something of his wife. Why wasn't she coming out? She wasn't ill enough to stop spying on me, so why was she avoiding me now?

No pictures up on the walls. A few boxes stacked up in the corners of the room. I guess they really hadn't settled in yet.

A tangle of brightly colored, paisley-printed, ethnic-looking scarves that hung on the coatrack was the only evidence that an adult, probably South Asian, woman lived here to begin with.

I was still holding on to the pie, and nudged a few toys off the coffee table so I could set it down. There was some mail that spilled off to the floor and I took a quick look at who it was addressed to—Aparna Burch. Aparna. Appy. Of course she changed her name. Most of us do. Make it easier to pronounce. More accessible. Altered so no one else felt uncomfortable about who she was, even though it's pretty damn uncomfortable to be called a name that isn't yours.

I remember asking my parents if I could change mine. A new life would warrant a new name, right? Too bad for me, they loved Paloma. *Why would you want to change something so beautiful and exotic?* they asked. I tried explaining to them that it wasn't even a typical Sri Lankan name. That my mother must have picked it up from somewhere. That I could pick a different, more cultural-sounding name if they liked. But they just chuckled and Dad tousled my hair and said I was being silly.

I wonder if my neighbor had a different name before Aparna.

"Sorry about that." Gavin reappeared, running his hand through his hair, deliberately messing it up. What a tool.

"So, your wife—I guess I'll meet her another day, then?" I made sure my disappointment showed. Maybe he'd catch on and feel bad.

"Yeah." He was preoccupied again, peering into the kitchen.

"I saw her from a distance the other day. She looked super familiar." I made sure I was smiling and nonchalant when I said it. "Where's she from anyway?"

"Um, Michigan," Gavin said. "Before that she—"

"Daddyyyyy," Gulliver screamed, running up to him and wrapping his chubby arms around his knees. He had something splattered all over himself. Carrots, maybe, or pumpkin. It was orange, and he left quite a few blobs of it on his dad's expensive-looking jeans. Why? Why would anyone put themselves through this fresh hell?

He smiled at me apologetically and swept the toddler into his arms.

"Looks like it's time to give someone his lunch."

Fuck me, this wasn't helping.

"Before that she?" I encouraged, ignoring the fact that he really needed to get back to this hyperactive menace.

"Um, she grew up in Chicago, though I wouldn't mention it to her. Had a bit of a rough childhood. Anyway, I'm so sorry about all of this," he went on, not letting me slide in any more questions. "I'm sure Appy will reach out to you once she feels better."

"Sure, yes."

He walked me to the door and hesitated a little.

"You know, she really misses your mom. They got quite close before your parents left on their trip."

I tried to put my hands into my pockets to hide the sudden tremble, but the damn skirt didn't have any, so I kept them behind my back like a child.

"Oh, I see."

"Your dad and I used to hit a round of golf on the weekends. What a guy. And Appy and your mom used to hang out all the time. I think your mom had even loaned her a copy of her favorite book. Appy told me she wanted to return it to you. Did she ever get around to it?"

"Um, yes. I think she did."

"Good. Good."

One thing you can say about my mother is that she never wasted time. One brown girl out of the picture, a new one swiftly takes her place. And she even gave her the book. My book. The copy of *Wuthering Heights* that was a welcome present to my new life from my new family. I guess it didn't mean as much to them as it did to me after all. And this strange, creepy woman just went and left it in my mailbox? What if it got ruined?

I smiled and turned to leave even though my heart was pounding.

Be nice, Paloma. Stay calm. Even though I felt like screaming until I exploded.

"Also, Paloma—?" he added as I was starting to walk away.

"Yeah?"

He shoved his hands deep into his pockets and didn't meet my eye.

"Look, I'm sorry to even bring this up, but, well, Appy's mentioned it and I—well, I thought I should say something, you know?"

Get to the damn point, Gavin. I just need to fucking leave.

"I know you're probably curious about us, that we are new to the neighborhood and all. But Appy's, well, she's going through a tough time right now, so maybe you could give her some space?"

Wait, what?

"I—I'm not sure I know what you're talking about."

He gave me a knowing smile.

"I've seen you, staring through your window at us. Coming down our drive. Look, under normal circumstances it's no big deal, really. I know you guys love to snoop around."

You guys?

"I do *not* snoop!"

Be nice, Paloma. You don't get anywhere being difficult.

I couldn't take this anymore. I kept the smile on my face. I probably looked like a lunatic. But this accusation was preposterous.

Gavin had the decency to look a little embarrassed.

"I'm sorry for bringing it up. Really."

For once in my life, I was lost for words. Completely and utterly defeated.

"Look, I'm sure—whatever your wife said—I'm sure she just got confused."

"I guess it must be that." Though his tone suggested that he didn't agree with me at all.

"If that's all, then I'll get going." I was about to turn around.

"There's just one last thing—" Fuck me, he wasn't done yet? He studied his feet very carefully and then took a breath, like he was determined to say what was coming next.

"Ida's asked us to keep an eye on her place when she's out of town. Now, I'm sure you probably know her already, but I have to ask, does she know that you've been going in there?"

What the fuck?

It's not just your wife, huh, Gavin? You've been spying on me too.

But beneath my anger and irritation and sadness, I felt a small glimmer of hope.

"She told you she was going out of town?"

Gavin frowned.

"She usually tells Appy. She visits her sister in San Diego every month or so."

An ounce of relief. I gave him my sweetest smile even though I felt like exploding.

"I practically grew up at Ida's," I said, hoping the touch of haughtiness I added to my voice was enough to get him to back off. "I've known where she keeps her spare key since I was a child."

"Sure. Um, I wasn't insinuating—I just wanted to check."

He looked like he'd rather be anywhere else in the world, and I felt exactly the same.

"I'll see you around, Gavin."

34

PERERA SIR LIKED TO read at the front of the building, on the verandah. He sat on a *haansi putuwa*, a woven chair with a winged back, probably made exactly for reading. His cup of tea rested on one of the arms, a fly buzzing around it. He didn't even wave the fly away, that's how engrossed he was in his book.

No one disturbed Perera sir when he was reading. Not even a fly. But here I was, knees shaking, hoping to do just that.

I'd thought about it under the ambarella tree. Lihini needed help. She needed to talk to someone. It wasn't good for her to continue like this. Who knew what Lihini would do when I left? She'd probably have a full-on meltdown.

"Paloma, what can I do for you?" His voice jerked me back to reality. I suddenly didn't know what I was supposed to say.

"Sorry to disturb you, Perera sir. M-may I please speak with you?"

"Of course, child. Is anything the matter? Not getting cold feet about moving to America, are you?"

"N-no, sir. It's not that."

"Then what, child?"

I took a deep breath.

"It's Lihini, sir. I'm worried about her."

His eyes changed, just a little.

"Yes, I've been worried about her too."

"Y-you have?"

"Yes, in fact, we all are. Tell me, is she still filling everyone's head with this nonsense?"

"You mean about—" I looked down. I felt bad saying it.

"About this Mohini business." The way he said it, he could have been talking about the weather or some news he saw on TV.

"That's what you girls call it, right?"

I nodded. I still couldn't look directly in his eyes.

"Tell me, Paloma, do you believe in ghosts?"

The question caught me off guard.

"Sir?"

"Ghosts, Paloma. Or ghouls. *Holmang*, as you say."

"N-no, sir."

"The girls, especially the younger ones, they seem to all believe in it."

"That's because Lihini is upsetting them, sir. That's what I came to tell you."

"Still? She promised me that she wouldn't anymore."

"I know, sir, but—but I think she really believes it." I was letting her down, I know. But it was the only way I knew how to help.

"Surely, she's too old to believe in ghosts. Isn't she?" Perera sir looked tired.

"What do you think I should do, Paloma? That is why you came here, isn't it? Because you wanted me to do something?"

He was asking me? How was I supposed to know? I came here to ask for *his* help.

"Sir, I think, well, I think she's doing all of this because she's upset that I'm leaving." I let my words hang. I felt like such a traitor.

"You think she just wants attention, do you?"

"Y-yes, sir." If I could have died, right then and there, I would have done it.

"You know, I told her that I would try my best to find her a family as well, if she'd stop."

"I know, sir, she told me."

"But you're telling me she hasn't stopped, am I right?"

Was I ruining Lihini's chances of being adopted? Oh goodness. This wasn't what I came here for at all.

"No, sir, I mean, I was wondering if you could please keep trying. Maybe ask Mr. and Mrs. Evans if they'd like to take both of us?"

Perera sir rubbed his eyes and sighed.

"No, child, that's not how it works."

My insides felt like they were being squeezed. I couldn't take this anymore.

"I'm sorry, sir."

"What for?"

"It's because of me, isn't it, that all of this is happening?"

He smiled at this, though his eyes remained hard.

"No, no, Paloma, it isn't."

Perera sir took off his reading glasses and started polishing them.

"I know you girls take it badly when an adoption happens. We try so hard here to make it easy for everyone." He suddenly looked very old and tired. "But some of the girls, well . . ."

"I know, sir. It's not just Lihini. Shanika has been pulling the worst pranks as well."

He looked up at me and frowned. "Shanika? I thought she mostly keeps to herself now."

"No, sir." I didn't want the possibility of Lihini's adoption ruined just because I was worried about her. I wanted Perera sir to help her, not be upset with her. If he was going to be upset with someone, let it be Shanika. She deserved it anyway. "She's been really terrible since she heard the news. You saw how she attacked me that day? And that's not all. She ruined the copy of *Wuthering Heights*. She—" I looked down. "She rubbed red paint all over it. To make me think it was blood. It was Mrs. Evans's favourite book, remember?"

Perera sir's forehead creased.

"I see. And is that all?"

"No, sir. She took one of my passport photos and scratched my eyes out in it."

"And you are sure it was her?"

"Of course, sir. She's always wandering around. Scaring the other girls."

Perera sir sighed again. I actually felt very sorry for him. It must be difficult, having to find solutions for so many problems all the time.

"She walks around at night, sir. She's never in the dormitory. I think Miss Chandra has given up trying to keep her inside."

He stopped looking tired and started looking angry instead.

"It's been difficult with Shanika. No matter what we've done for her."

"Yes, sir."

"I'm starting to think it's best we send her to St. Margaret's Home for Girls after all. Maybe some discipline from Sister Cynthia is what she really needs."

My heart started to race. I wanted Shanika to pay for all the terrible things she did to me, but did I really want her to be caned by Sister Cynthia?

It suddenly felt like everything was crashing down on me. First, Lihini getting angry with me, now Shanika being sent away because of what I just said.

The tears were hot and sudden. I didn't even know where they were coming from. Was I feeling guilty or relieved? I couldn't even tell.

Perera sir reached out and stroked my head, his eyes fixed on the darkening evening sky.

"Don't cry, child. Don't cry. Leave it with me now. I'll take care of all this. The Evanses will be here the day after tomorrow. That's what you should be focusing on."

I wish I'd known then how things would change. How I had just ruined everything. How my curse had just started.

Or maybe there was never a curse. That I just brought it about myself, because of what I did to her.

35

I STORMED AWAY FROM Appy and Gavin's house and slammed my front door shut. I couldn't even make it to the sofa. The Burches—I couldn't even imagine that that was their last name. Burch. It seemed way too normal and not nearly sinister enough.

The fucking nerve of Gavin. To suggest that *I* was the creep? That *I* was the one snooping around? I guess he and his batshit-crazy wife deserve each other.

And I was no closer to figuring out anything else.

I rubbed my face and was surprised to find tears streaming down.

Appy and your mom used to hang out all the time.

What a fucking leech.

I guess they didn't waste any time. I wonder how long it took my parents after they stopped speaking to me to befriend Appy. It was such convenient timing for them.

I sat up straight.

Much too convenient.

And the book. Surely, *surely* Appy was trying to send me some sort of message? I wonder if Mom told her.

They got quite close before your parents left on their trip.

I swallowed. There was no way Mom would have told her about my letter, right?

And then my breath got stuck in my throat.

What if Mom and Dad gave Appy a set of keys to the house? Mom was super trusting about things like that. Everyone in the fucking Bay Area was. People left their keys with neighbors and under garden gnomes and secret compartments made to look like rocks or sprinklers all the damn time. It seemed odd now to think my parents hadn't done the same.

Of course, we had a security system installed too. But, I remembered, deflating, I've been pretty lax about turning it on. And what's to say my ignorant, trusting parents didn't just give out the code to everyone? I mean, they hadn't even changed the combination in years.

Could it have been her? Could she have broken in here and left me the photograph? Slept in my parents' bed?

My phone started to ring.

I looked at the name on the screen and then threw it across the room in frustration.

I don't have the time to deal with Mr. Williams right now. Not when I was smack in the middle of—in the middle of what? What the fuck was even going on?

My phone stopped ringing for a moment, and then it started up again.

I groaned, and put my hands over my ears.

But I couldn't block out everything else.

I know. Arun leered from the kitchen table.

Que sera, sera, Mohini whispered in my year. Or was it Appy, cradling her doll?

No.

I took a deep breath.

It didn't work.

I took another deep breath and tried to count backwards from ten.

I got to seven when the ringing started again.

Except it wasn't my ringtone.

And it was coming from the kitchen.

I jumped to my feet and ran over.

The phone screen lit up. Three missed calls, it said.

Fuck. I'd missed them.

My chance to find out something about Ida and I missed it.

What the actual fuck was wrong with me?

I grabbed one of Mom's decorative vases from the windowsill and smashed it on the floor.

Que sera, sera.

The voice was back.

I smashed another vase. It didn't help.

I held the third in my hand when the phone rang again.

I took a breath to calm myself.

The caller ID said Dotty. My thumb shook on the screen when I slid the green arrow to answer.

"Hello?" My voice didn't even sound like my own anymore.

"Ida, it's Dotty. Is that you?" She sounded friendly. And old.

"N-no. This is Paloma, her neighbor."

"Oh, I see." A pause. "Is Ida there?"

"N-no. I'm afraid. I found her phone."

"Oh, could you please tell her to call me back? I've been trying to ring her and I've been getting a little worried."

"Um, sure. I think she's supposed to be visiting her sister in San Diego. Do you have a way of getting in touch with her?"

There was a beat of silence.

"Who is this?" Dotty asked. The warmth from her voice had evaporated.

"I told you, I'm Paloma, her neighbor. Paloma Evans. My parents were close friends of Ida's. Perhaps she's mentioned them?"

"Oh, I see. Well, there's no way she could be visiting her sister in San Diego."

The sense of dread that had been lurking in the shadows from the moment Ida went missing choked down on me.

"W-why's that?"

"Because I am her sister in San Diego, dear."

I felt dizzy.

Oh my god.

I was right. Ida was missing. Something had happened to her.

Urgency crashed over me in waves.

"Look, I tried reporting this yesterday but they wouldn't believe me. It's a long story. Would you please phone the police? And tell them it's urgent?"

"Yes, I'll do that right away." She was all business. It reminded me of Ida in a way that made my heart twist in my chest.

"Um, also—" I had to ask.

"What is it?"

"I know where Ida keeps her spare key. Shall I go over and see if I can find out anything else? Maybe she left something—?" It was a long shot, and I'd already been over there twice, not that Dotty needed to know that. But I had to fucking do something. And if Ida's sister gave me permission to go over, well, then that asshole Gavin couldn't accuse me of anything dodgy, could he? Besides, it would be a good chance to get those documents of mine that I didn't have the foresight to grab the last time. Maybe they had something to do with Ida's disappearance.

"Yes, yes, of course. She might have taken a fall. She might be hurt.

Oh, dear—" The worst thoughts were just starting to enter her mind. But they still weren't as bad as what was racing through mine.

"Give me your number," I asked, keying her details into my phone. "I'll call you if I find anything."

I hit save and then went back outside.

Let Gavin and his insane wife spy on me all they wanted. I didn't have anything to hide.

I walked over, shoulders back and chin high. Let them look if they wanted. Let them judge me all they could.

I shot what I hoped was a withering look towards the Burch house while I retrieved Ida's key and stuck it in the lock. If only my hands weren't shaking so hard, I could've gotten it in on my first try.

I let myself in and triple-checked that I had locked the door behind me. I picked up the mail that had fallen by the door, and set it on the kitchen table. Then I grabbed the bottle of sherry and put it in the cupboard under the sink. Out of sight, out of mind.

A quick scan through the house showed that nothing had been disturbed, so I sat down at the kitchen table and pawed through her mail. Just a bunch of flyers for car washes and dental clinics and god knows what else.

I rubbed my face. It was puffy and swollen and my cold fingers felt nice against my eyes. I pulled them away. I didn't deserve to feel nice. I was pathetic. Hiding from the truth for so long. Letting the world explode around me without caring who would get hurt. My parents, Ida, even that asshole Arun. Who else would be hurt because of me?

I went over to the desk to grab the folder. Maybe there was something else in there that I had missed the last time.

But the folder wasn't there. The drawer was empty. That's strange. Had someone else moved it? I had thought about taking it the last time I was here, and I did leave in a bit of a rush. Did I take it with me? I was pretty out of it on Ida's sherry, but surely I would remember something so significant, wouldn't I?

Ida's asked us to keep an eye on her place when she's out of town. Could Gavin or Appy have taken it?

I couldn't dwell on it for long, however. There was an urgent yapping outside. It sounded like Snowy. And then, out of the blue, a scream.

I went over to the front door and yanked it open, scanning the street.

Appy, Snowy, and Gloria were at the top of my driveway, and it was obvious they were in the middle of something. Appy was gesticulating wildly, her hands flying in the air. She was more alive than I had ever seen her. Gloria said something back, head down, trying her best to back away from her while Snowy tugged at the leash. Then Appy swung her arm towards her, connecting with Gloria's face.

Gloria shouted out as I ran up to them.

"What the hell is going on?" I asked, my voice loud. Let the neighbors hear me. I don't care.

Appy didn't stop to take in anything. She just turned around and started hurrying back to her place.

Snowy continued to yap, pulling away.

"She hit me," Gloria said, clearly shocked.

"What?"

Gloria continued to cradle her cheek in her hand. She reached down with the other and tried to calm the dog down, but the terrier wasn't having any of it.

"Hey, where do you think you're going?" I asked, starting to follow Appy.

"No, Paloma, don't." Gloria grabbed my arm and pulled me back. Appy had made it to her house in record speed.

"Why? She tried to attack you."

"Please. Please don't. I don't want any trouble."

"What do you mean?"

"Please. She's a wealthy woman from a good neighborhood and I'm—" She gestured to herself. "If she complains to the cops, there's no chance they will believe me. I'll lose my job."

I knew a little something about the cops not being on your side, so I relented.

"At least let me get you some ice for your face?" I offered.

Her hand was still on her cheek. Damn, Appy must have hit her quite hard.

"No, no, it's okay. Really."

"I insist. Come on."

I didn't wait for her response but instead started walking up my drive. I knew she'd follow, and I was right.

"So what was all that about, anyway?" I asked, once we got to the kitchen and I'd given her a bag of frozen peas to hold over her face. We'd put Snowy in the backyard and he calmed down after a while.

"I don't know," she said. "She was walking towards your house, I think, and when she saw me coming, she freaked out and started shouting. I couldn't really make out what she was saying."

She was coming towards my house, huh? Guess she'd recovered from her phantom flu, then.

"I don't know what the hell is wrong with her, really. She keeps watching me. Watching the house. It's starting to really freak me out."

"Yeah, she's got issues." Gloria shrugged.

"How does your face feel? Shall I take a look?"

"No, it's fine, I'll just hang on to these peas, if you don't mind. It's helping a lot."

I racked my brain for something else to say. Anything that would ease the tension. This was the type of thing Mom was always so good at. She'd say something that was insightful and sensitive but also lighthearted without being too funny, and anything uncomfortable would be quickly swept away into a corner. But I was having a hard time doing that today.

Gloria stood up to get herself a glass of water.

Say something nice, Paloma. Pay her a compliment.

"I like your hair," I offered. It was random and, truth be told, awkward as fuck. I mean, this was the kind of shit girls told each other, right? How the fuck was I to know anyway? It's not like I really had girlfriends, but my mom said stuff like this all the time and everyone always seemed to eat it right up.

Her back was to me, so I couldn't see her reaction. But thank god she didn't sound weirded out when she spoke next.

"Thanks. I know it's a little much. I just felt like a change, you know."

"A change from what?"

I usually didn't give a shit about people's personal lives, but I felt like I owed it to her. I felt responsible for her attack, somehow. Like she'd gotten caught in the middle of this weird, undefined war between Appy and me.

"A change from everything. Don't you ever feel like you need that?"

Did I ever.

"So, I thought to myself, why not pink? It's my favorite color, after all." She turned and leaned against the kitchen counter, moving the peas up just a fraction so she could bring a glass of water up to her lips.

"That's a good enough reason as any. Pink was my favorite color, too, when I was a child."

"Only when you were a child?"

"Yeah, well, a lot has changed since I was a child."

Gloria smiled at that. "I'm sure it has."

Something in the air slackened. We both started to relax a little.

"You know," she said, pushing her glasses up the bridge of her nose with her free hand. "I used to play this game when I was a child. I would pretend to be someone else. An adult. A teacher. Someone, any-one else who wasn't me. I loved it. I just never thought I would end up playing the same game as an adult."

"What do you mean?"

"I mean, it all feels make-believe sometimes, doesn't it? Like I'm just wearing an adult costume and pretending to be someone else."

"I think we all pretend, don't we? I know I do." Lord knows no truer words had ever been spoken, but thankfully, Gloria wasn't here to judge me. She smiled again, turning back to the sink and setting her glass on the counter.

"I guess at some point, maybe this will all feel natural, and we can take off our masks and find out that it's not quite so bad."

Sage advice from a dog walker with pink hair.

There was a moment of comfortable silence.

"Any news from Ida?" she asked finally.

Ida, fuck. The spell was broken. Back to the real world, where every-thing was a fucking mess.

"Her sister called, from San Diego." Gloria's eyes grew wide. "She's not with her. She's calling the police to file a missing persons report."

"Oh." Gloria's hands flew to her mouth. "Did she say anything else? Do you think the police will come here?"

Damn it, I'd just freaked her out again.

"They might, but look, don't worry. I'll handle it."

She clutched the ice to her face a little harder.

"There's really nothing much we can do right now, and panicking won't get us anywhere." Damn, how the hell was I managing to sound so calm when I was freaking the hell out myself?

I suddenly remembered the missing documents.

"Also, have you been inside Ida's since we realized she's been gone?"

"Me? No. I've kept Snowy with me, but I came by today to get some extra food for him. Why?"

I was suddenly overcome by the urge to check on something. Luckily, Gloria was gathering her things and calling out to Snowy too.

"Let me know if anything comes up," she said, and I made my way to my parents' room.

If I had taken the folder in my drunken state, well, there's only one place I would put it, right?

IT WASN'T THE BEDDING—the decorative pillows were just as they were when I changed the sheets and made the bed yesterday.

It was the smell.

Mom's smell.

I could recognize the fragrance of Anaïs Anaïs anywhere. The jasmine notes were strong and didn't fade easily—reminding me every day of the jasmine vine that grew in the orphanage. Their room shouldn't smell like her. Not now. It should smell of the freshly laundered sheets, or the organic carpet cleaner I'd sprayed before vacuuming, not of Mom's perfume.

My heart hammered in my chest as I opened the closet door and reached up.

My fingers didn't connect with anything.

I tried again. Still nothing.

Fresh bolts of fear shot through me as I pulled the stool from Mom's dresser into the closet, and used the flashlight from my phone to check, but I knew it wasn't there. Just empty space. Dust bunnies and empty space and—

A head.

I almost dropped my phone.

A doll's head. The light from my phone flashed on its cheap plastic eyes. The kind with the wiry, black eyelashes that stuck out like spider legs. Its ruby-red lips were painted into a frozen smile. Synthetic yellow hair matted into tangles. And it was dirty. Smudges of soot on its cheeks. Like it had been rescued from a fire.

I picked it up, waves of panic and nausea pelting down on me. I had seen this doll head before. I wasn't going crazy. She had found me. It might have taken eighteen years, but she had finally found me.

I jumped out of my skin as my phone started ringing.

"H-hello?" I really shouldn't have picked up. I hadn't even looked at the caller ID.

"Paloma, hi! It's Sam. I'm just outside. I tried you a few times but I couldn't get through. I got some amazing Indian for lunch today and thought you'd love it. Can I come in?"

"Now's not a good time."

"Shall I leave it on your porch, then?"

I'll be damned if I ever let anyone anywhere near my house again.

"Now's *not* a good time," I repeated firmly, ending the call.

It felt like she had reached out and wrapped her thin, bony fingers around my neck. I couldn't breathe.

I managed to pull myself out of my parents' room and collapsed on the landing.

Deep breath in. Slow breath out. I'm Paloma.

Deep breath in. Slow breath out. Think, Paloma, there must be an explanation to all of this.

Deep breath in. Slow breath out. Just like Nina said.

Nina. I needed to speak to Nina. She would know what to do.

I pulled up her number on my phone. It took two tries to hit the green button, but it went straight to voice mail. I tried her cell. Voice mail too. What day was it? Tuesday or Wednesday? Fuck, she didn't see clients on Tuesday. Would she even be at the office? I didn't know where she lived. She never told me. What kind of friend was I? I never thought to ask. I just went on and on about myself. And I couldn't find her, now that I really needed her.

Maybe she would be by the office. Maybe she spent her days off just soaking in the pristine whiteness, napping on her couch, having spotless white dreams. I knew it was a stretch, but I had to go. I couldn't stay here.

I struggled to my feet, pulling on a jacket and grabbing my purse. I knew you didn't want to see clients on your days off, Nina. But this was an emergency. I eyed the liquor cabinet as I waited for my Uber. There was a half-empty bottle in there. I opened it up and took a small swig. Just for good measure. Just to relax a little for the ride across the bridge.

36

"PALOMA? PALOMA, SERIOUSLY?" NINA'S voice was distant, but she definitely sounded pissed.

"Paloma, what on earth are you doing here?"

My palm felt like chicken wire across my face when I rubbed it. Hang on. That burn was real. It wasn't a wire, my face was stinging.

What the actual fuck?

My eyes hurt as I opened them. My head hurt. Actually, my whole fucking body hurt.

Nina's face peered down at me.

"Paloma, are you all right? Oh my goodness." And then, to someone behind her: "Call 911."

Call 911? No fucking way.

"Nina." My words felt thick in my mouth. "Nina, I'm fine."

Her eyes flashed angrily at me.

"I hardly think you're fine, Paloma. You need help."

"That's why I came here. To speak to you. Because I need help."

"I think you need a little more than me right now, Paloma." Puh-LOW-ma. Just like Mom said it.

I sat upright. I sat upright on the steps to Nina's office. That meant—fuck. That meant I would have collapsed on the steps to Nina's office.

"I'm so sorry, Nina. I was just having such a bad day. So many weird things keep happening."

"It's a good thing the building security recognized you and called me, not the cops."

I held my head in my hands. Everything was still spinning around.

"I'm honestly so sorry, Nina."

"Paloma, you know I trust you, right? You need to answer me honestly. Have you been drinking?"

I just continued to hold on to my head.

She sat down on the step next to me. Her lips were set in a tight line. There was a brown smudge on her white skirt, and this was somehow more upsetting than the lack of her usual warmth.

Something inside me felt like it was about to explode.

"What happened?"

"Ida's missing. And the neighbors, well, the woman is crazy and she won't leave me alone. And Arun's dead, I just know it. I found a doll's head, Nina. A doll's head. In my parents' room. It was from her. It was definitely from her." Everything just bubbled out. I wasn't making sense, but Nina would understand. She had to.

"A doll's head?" She frowned. See. It wasn't just me.

"I know it's crazy, Nina. That I sound absolutely fucking crazy, but I think she's found me."

"Who?"

"You know who, Nina. She's managed to follow me here. After all these years she's followed me here."

"Paloma, please, you have to calm down." She paused for a moment and took a deep breath, which forced me to do the same.

"You were in your parents' room?" she asked, finally. Her face shifted.

I managed a nod.

"That's good progress, right?"

"If you want to ask, you should just fucking ask without tiptoeing around it, Nina."

To her credit, Nina didn't flinch.

"Paloma, you and I both know that you've refused to talk about your parents since they died." Her voice softened. "It's never healthy to suppress trauma like this. I'm glad you're finally letting me bring this up."

"I'm not crazy, you know, not completely. I know they died, okay? I know my parents fucking died."

She looked at me and smiled sadly.

I had finally said it.

Took me two fucking months and I finally managed to say it out loud.

I begged them not to go. Not to leave me. Not to go back there. Especially after the letter. After we argued. But they wouldn't fucking listen. And then they died. A goddamned car crash on an island so tiny that most Americans don't know it exists. The irony is almost comedic.

What the hell are you supposed to do when your one lifeline, when your sole saviors, when your real-life angels die on you?

It was just easier to push the thought to the back of my mind, where it hardly existed. Their postcards made it easy. The postal system in South Asia is so terrible that they were still being delivered. And so I stuck them on the goddamned fridge and let myself pretend for a little, because it was better than accepting that they would never come back at all. That, once again, I was an orphan.

I started to sob.

"This is a huge step for you, Paloma. I'm so proud of you."

But she wasn't getting it.

"But she was there, Nina. She was in my house. She was leaving me messages."

"Messages?"

"The doll's head, Nina. Weren't you listening? She's been following me for years and now she's found me."

"Paloma." Her voice was too gentle. "We've spent so long talking about Mohini. I thought we agreed that she was just a part of your childhood nightmares?"

Fuck you, Nina.

"This isn't the same, Nina. This is different."

"How, Paloma? How is this different?"

"The woman across the street from me. She's—she must be someone from back home. She has something to do with this. With all of this. I—I just don't know what yet."

"Is she from Sri Lanka?"

"I—I don't know. But that's not the point."

"But if you're not sure where she's from, then how do you know she's from your past?"

Nina might have been my friend, but right now she was the most goddamned patronizing woman on the planet. Fuck her.

"I knew it. I knew you never believed me. Not once. I finally have proof, Nina. Proof that someone or something from Sri Lanka has finally found me."

Her voice was quiet when she asked her next question.

"Paloma, how much have you drunk today?"

"I'm not drunk right now, Nina."

"That wasn't my question."

"Nina, I'm telling you, I'm not making this shit up, and you would see that, too, if you stopped being so fucking judgmental for a minute—" But Nina looked like I had slapped her. I had cussed in front of her before, just never directly at her.

"I'm not judging you, Paloma. I just want you to be safe. You've been living in your parents' house, refusing to acknowledge that they died. Fixating on your past. You're drinking with your meds. You know how that affects your state of mind."

"I've been a bit absentminded lately, Nina. But I'm not being irresponsible."

"And how did you end up passed out on my stairwell, Paloma? Were you being responsible then?"

I rested my head in my hands again. She wasn't even trying to understand.

I felt her put a hand on my shoulder but I couldn't bring myself to look at her. Her scarf was trailing on the stairs next to us.

Only this orange-and-pink monstrosity couldn't be her scarf. Nina never wore anything that wasn't white, or perhaps a very pale beige if she was being really adventurous. The fabric that pooled on the floor was dotted in a paisley print, and there were even, god help me, gold threads running through.

"Your scarf?" I asked, looking up at her.

"My scarf?" She was confused now, but she picked it up and started to fold it on her lap. "Do you like it?"

No. No way. Nina lined the books in her office with the spines facing the back of the shelf. Seeing a bright splash of color on her was just wrong. An abomination. It went against everything she was. And had I seen a scarf like that before?

"It isn't white."

"What? So I can't own anything that isn't white?"

"Well, no. I mean. Of course you can. It's just strange, that's all."

Nina had the kind of smile that was like a light switch that flicked her from Nina the therapist in a white office to Nina who could knock back a few mojitos and let someone feel her up on the dance floor. Maybe if I kept talking about the scarf, she'd forget that I just swore at her.

"Where's it from?"

"It was a gift. From one of my newer clients. She's just moved here. Probably close to your parents', actually, now that I think about it."

I stood up.

Nowhere was safe. I didn't know why, and I didn't even know how, but it was Appy. She'd been the one messing with me. She'd even managed to track me all the way over to Nina. I knew it, deep in my bones.

No wonder Nina didn't believe me.

The door was heavy and I struggled with it a bit.

"Where are you going?" Nina stood up too.

It finally swung open and I didn't bother answering her. I just left.

"Paloma, come back!" I heard her shout as I stumbled away.

The street was busy as I burst outside, and I darted across quickly in case Nina was following me. I didn't stop until I was a few blocks away. I needn't have worried though. There was no one on my trail.

Now what should I do?

I supposed I should go back home, but a part of me really didn't want to. I didn't think I could manage going back to my own apartment yet either. I pulled out my phone. Maybe I could check on Airbnb and see if there's anywhere cheap I could stay the night. It was just too much. I just needed a fucking break.

I sorted by price, lowest to highest. The cheapest was a little over a hundred dollars. Damn, I should let out the spare room at my parents' after things settle down. But then I'd have to deal with making small talk with strangers the whole day. No, thank you. It was far kinder to my sanity to run my other little side business.

There was no chance I could go back home tonight. I was about to book a bed for $120 in the Castro, what a fucking rip-off, when a message lit up on my screen.

It was Sam.

> I'm sorry about this afternoon. I don't want to be the guy who keeps bugging you. I won't keep trying to reach out. If you want to hang out, you know how to find me.

I read the message twice and hit the call button. He answered on the first ring.

"Hey, Sam. Text me your address. I'm coming over."

37

I WONDERED HOW LONG it would take Shanika to notice that
her doll was gone. She usually had it with her all the time except for
meals. Did she think she had lost it, or forgotten where she left it? I
didn't see her at all during the day. She wasn't in the playroom when I
got there after my talk with Perera sir.

I didn't have to wonder too long though. Her wails reached us in
the playroom, shrill and rasping.

By the time we had all abandoned our books and toys and run to
the dormitory, Miss Chandra and Miss Nayana were trying to restrain
Shanika as she flung her pillows and sheets aside searching for it.

"Where is it?" she screamed, over and over again. "Where is it?"

"Where's what?" Maya asked.

"My doll. *Mage bonikka*. My doll." She had started sobbing now.

"Come now, child. You have to calm down," Miss Chandra tried.

"No," she continued to wail. "Where is it? Where is it?"

She started clawing at her face and her arms and tearing at her hair.

"Go get Perera sir. Tell him Shanika is having one of her episodes," Miss Chandra ordered, and Maya ran out.

They kept trying to soothe her but she was screaming, and when she wasn't screaming she was gasping for air like someone was choking her.

"What's this commotion now?" Perera sir strode into the dorm looking irritated with Maya right behind him. He was holding a syringe. Lihini stared at it with her eyes wide, but before any of us could react, he walked over to Shanika and stuck it in her arm.

"There, there now," he said. "This is very mild. Just to help you calm down."

Shanika's eyes got a little glassy, and she quietened a bit.

"Don't worry, girls. This is just to help her relax. She'll be back to normal in no time." Perera sir gave us his usual smile, but a strand of his hair had flicked free of his middle part, and that felt very, very wrong.

"Why don't you help her find it?" he asked, and left us.

We were all quiet for moment, but Miss Chandra said loudly, snapping us out of it, "You heard him, girls. Start searching please."

"It must be here somewhere," Dumila spoke up. "Let's look."

"Yeah, we'll help look," I added, rubbing my palms against my dress. I didn't expect her to be this upset. I just, well, I just wanted her to leave me alone.

I noticed Lihini giving me a look but I ignored her.

We all got together, looking through everyone's bunks, and even under the beds. We searched in the drawers where we kept our clothes, and the shelves where we kept extra sheets. Of course it wasn't there.

"What about downstairs?" someone asked, and a few of them went to check.

Shanika just sat in a corner, on the floor, rocking herself back and forth. She had a faraway look on her face, and listened to Miss Nayana when she promised her a new doll for Christmas.

When it became clear that the doll couldn't be found and Shanika started to look drowsy, the girls left. The sun was setting. It was time for evening washes and dinner and chores.

"Let's give her a little time, shall we, girls?" Miss Chandra said, and we left Shanika there, in the darkening room.

I followed the rest of the group towards the dining hall, but something Maya was saying to Lihini caught my attention.

"So twelve midnight, then? Sharp midnight? That's the time she walks around, right?"

"The time who walks around?" I asked.

"Mohini, of course. We are going to wait for her today."

"What? Are you mad?"

"What?" Lihini spoke up defiantly. "No one believes us, so we are going to wait for her and call Perera sir and Miss Chandra."

"So you've both seen her?"

Maya looked down. Of course she hadn't seen anything. She was just going on a wild-goose chase led by Lihini.

"Why are you doing this, *sudhu*?"

But she just kept walking away from me.

"*Sudhu?*" I called out louder, grabbing her shoulder.

She spun around. I had seen her angry before, but it was never at me.

"Leave me alone!" she hissed.

"No, *sudhu*, you need to stop doing this. You need to—"

She shoved me then. Hard.

I stumbled backwards and fell onto my bum.

I couldn't move. It's not that I was hurt. Not really. Just shocked.

Hot tears stung my eyes, but I jumped to my feet. I wanted to push her back. To hurt her. But I couldn't do it. I couldn't move.

Maya grabbed her arm and pulled her away. "Come on," she said, and Lihini followed her.

I went to dinner but I couldn't swallow anything.

I couldn't believe she would do this to me. And right in front of Maya.

The other girls sat away, like they knew what happened. That my best friend turned against me. They giggled to themselves, shooting looks in my direction.

I made myself be calm. Mr. and Mrs. Evans would be here to get me soon. I just had to get through the next two days. Even though it hurt my heart so much that I wanted to curl up into a ball and stay that way.

I left dinner early and went to bed, though I couldn't fall asleep. I just lay there, imagining Mrs. Evans and how she would smile down at me when she came to pick me up. I wondered what my new room would look like. I hoped it was pink. With a lot of books. Mrs. Evans would have her own copy of *Wuthering Heights*, I was sure of it. I hoped she'd let me borrow it.

I shut my eyes and pretended to be asleep when the other girls came in.

I think I might have drifted off at some point though. The sheet wrapped around my legs as I turned in bed. The night air was too hot and stiff. It felt hard to breathe. I think I was dreaming, because Lihini's words wouldn't stop ringing in my ears.

You were never my friend. You only care about yourself. You might not believe me now, but I'll prove it to you that I'm right. I'll prove it to all of you.

I guessed she wasn't wrong to feel that way. I was leaving her. I was leaving her and I don't believe her. I'm leaving her the way my mother left me. Was this how my mother felt, after she had me? That there was a life, a better life, but she had to leave her old life behind so she could have it?

It wasn't fair. I didn't ask to be picked. If Lihini was chosen instead of me, she would leave too. And I would be happy for her. Right? But I knew I was lying to myself. If Lihini was leaving instead of me, my world would end.

But I still wouldn't be horrible to her the way she was being to me now. I wasn't angry with her. I just didn't want to leave with her feeling this way.

I was dozing again when I heard it. It was soft, at first, and then it grew louder.

Was it scratching?

I didn't move. I didn't even breathe loudly.

There it was again. Definitely scratching. Or a muffled scraping sound.

The yank on my braid was sudden and painful. It pulled me half off the bed. A thin, bony arm was reaching out from under my bunk, my braid wrapped around its wrist.

She pulled herself out, using my hair like a rope. I tried to scream but I couldn't even breathe, I was so afraid. I felt frozen solid.

Shanika's face was ugly and contorted as she pulled me close to her, her hair hanging in greasy strands. Her eyes were glazed over, like she wasn't even really here.

"My doll. Have you seen my doll?"

I finally found my voice and began to scream. It was loud and long and echoed through our dormitory.

It seemed to jolt her back to reality.

She dropped my braid and jumped back to her feet.

"*Mage bonikka*," she whispered, but only halfheartedly, before she turned around and ran off.

But I wasn't letting her get away this time.

I clambered out of bed and chased after her.

"Hey," I called out. I didn't care who I woke up. I didn't care if I was going to be in trouble. "Hey! Stop!" I wasn't wearing my slippers, and my feet pounded against the wooden staircase as my heart hammered in my chest.

One by one the lights in the orphanage were onned. Miss Chandra and even Perera sir would be here soon. She would be caught now, and punished. She wouldn't be able to bother anyone anymore.

I couldn't see her, but I ran towards the garden. That's where she would go. It's where she always went at night.

I didn't expect to crash into someone on my way there.

"What are you doing?" Lihini asked in a fierce whisper. Maya was right next to her, clutching her arm in shock.

"Shanika! She grabbed me. Grabbed my hair. Tried to pull me under the bed." I bent over and panted. My knees were shaking. My whole body heaved.

"Girls!" Perera sir's voice was like a firecracker. He wore a sarong and a *baniyan*. It was the first time I saw him in something other than his creased trousers. And he looked very, very angry.

"What is happening here?" he boomed.

I couldn't find the words to explain it. I was panting hard, and afraid, and I wanted to kill Shanika.

"It was Shanika, sir," Lihini explained. "She attacked Paloma while she was sleeping. We . . . we chased her down here. All of us."

I didn't even care that she lied. I just wanted Shanika gone.

"Why on earth would Shanika attack her?"

"We don't know, sir. But she's been troubling Paloma for some time. She—she's been doing some strange things. She left a photograph with Paloma's eyes scratched out on her pillow. And now she attacked her while she was sleeping. We—we think she's jealous that Paloma is being adopted."

Finally, someone was on my side.

Perera sir's lips disappeared into his mouth. He kept looking around like he expected Shanika to jump out of the shadows at any minute.

"Where is she now?"

"Shanika's probably in the garden. That's where she always goes," I wheezed. I thought I saw Perera sir's eyes widen, but I could have been imagining it.

He led the way into the garden where, sure enough, Shanika sat on the swing as usual. You could even hear her singing again. She really was disturbed.

Que sera, sera
Whatever will be, will be
The future's not ours to see

Shanika didn't seem violent now. Perera sir went up to her and said something to her softly, putting his hand on her shoulder.

She nodded and then stood up.

"Let's get back inside, girls. Right away."

Lihini and Maya hurried in first, and Perera sir practically marched Shanika in behind them, gesturing for me to follow. But I took a moment to catch my breath.

Would this finally be the end of it? The end of her terrorising me like this? I hoped they'd send her straight to Sister Cynthia. Or lock her away in a mental asylum somewhere. She didn't deserve to be here, scaring people, making them feel guilty for things they couldn't control.

The moonlight turned everything silver. There was a light breeze, which felt divine on my face. Everyone else was almost inside when I started towards the door as well.

That's when I felt something. Right behind me. Fingers snaking their way through my hair. A breathing loud and hoarse.

I spun around. A woman, pale and thin, with wicked, black eyes and hair that floated around her like a cloud, stood just inches away from me. I hadn't believed Lihini, but now Mohini bared her teeth, pointy and sharp, at me. I felt a scream rise out of my lips and an aching pain as she bit my face, right on my cheek, over and over again. I tried to push her away but her mouth was stuck to my face. The pain was more than anything I had ever felt in my life. Like my face was being ripped to pieces.

I screamed for what felt like forever, and then everything went dark.

38

SAN FRANCISCO, CA

SAM MET ME ON the curb, hands shoved into his pockets and eyes not quite meeting mine.

"It's not that fancy, okay? My place, I mean."

I snorted.

"Trust me, I'm sure it's fine."

I had been in my share of grungy apartments. Hell, I live in a grungy apartment when I'm not kicking it in the suburbs. But I suppose I hadn't quite anticipated how grungy Sam's apartment would really be. The elevator didn't work, and I swore I saw a roach or two crawling around as we climbed the dank stairs. But I mean, fuck it, I'm from Sri Lanka, I'm used to dealing with creepy-crawlies.

We reached the third floor, and Sam led the way in. The door opened into a tiny kitchen, which smelled strongly of onions and garlic, and two brown guys were eating curry with their hands. Both men stared at me openly and then looked away shyly when I made eye contact.

"Kaavin, Ritesh, this is Paloma."

"Hullo," one of the guys called out, but Sam hurried me to the stamp-sized living room. It was so small because a part of it was flimsily walled off with sheets of cardboard.

"I'm in there." Sam pointed to the curtain that hung in the gap between two boards. This was his room? Really? Cocktails at Heights and this was where he lived? How Sri Lankan could he get?

I must have looked a little confused, because he felt he had to explain.

"This was a two-bedroom apartment, but we thought we could save a bit by walling off a part of the living room and making it three." He stuck his hands back into his pockets. "You know how ridiculous rent can be in the city."

"Looks cozy." I wasn't lying. The smell of the curry reminded me of, well, it felt comfortable, somehow. Familiar.

I pushed the curtain aside and stepped into Sam's room. It was neat, clean, and sparse. Just a small single bed, tiny dresser, and few of those cheap plastic drawer sets you get from Ikea. There was the faintest smell of something else too. Something very different from curry. I couldn't put my finger on it until I saw the small Buddha statue sitting on top of a stool. There was ash next to it.

"You light incense every day?" I asked.

Sam smiled. He hadn't really said much since I got here, which was odd for him.

"I try to. It reminds me, you know."

I guess I did know. I inhaled deeply. None of this was as terrible as I thought it would be.

"I like it." I mean, it's a fire hazard, but I did like it.

"Would you like a drink? We have beer, I think. And soda."

"I'll take a Coke, if you have it." I really didn't want to go back to feeling loopy again. Not so soon, at least.

I sat on the bed and browsed through a Travel Sri Lanka calendar that Sam kept on his bedside table. Waterfalls, coconut trees, elephants—all things I had seen pictures of but never visited. Mom and Dad wanted to take me back around my eighteenth birthday for our family vacation, but I had the worst nightmares for a week until they called it off and we went to Hawaii instead. I did wonder at times what it might be like to visit, but I couldn't risk doing it now anyway.

Thinking about my parents was like reopening an old wound. Or maybe it was an infected wound that never healed. And then there was all this bullshit with Appy next door. Something weird that I just couldn't put my finger on. Something about her that left me off-kilter, and it wasn't just the scarf she had given Nina. And on top of all this I was so fucking worried about Ida that I had trouble breathing every time I thought about it. Fuck, I hoped she was okay. I really couldn't lose someone else right now. It would shatter me. I could feel tears starting to prick my eyes and tried to brush them away before Sam came back.

"My roommates think you are very beautiful." He handed me a can of Coke with a glass of ice.

"Ha." I rolled my eyes.

"What's wrong?"

Fuck, too late. He'd seen the tears, and was now looking over at me like I was a dying kitten.

"Nothing. It's nothing. So, you've been here long?" I tried to change the subject but I was having no such luck.

Sam took my hand and led me over to the bed, where he made me sit down and then pulled a chair over to face me. God, even in the worst of times, he was a perfect fucking gentleman.

"You know, since both my mother and father worked so much, it was my grandmother who looked after me."

Why the hell would I care, Sam?

"And she always said that whatever was in our heart, we must put it out. We have to. Otherwise it will make our hair turn grey." He paused for dramatic effect and touched a strand of my hair that had come loose. "And your hair is really beautiful. You should tell me what's wrong. Let it out. For the sake of your hair, I mean."

It was so fucking ridiculously corny that I snorted.

And then Sam started to laugh.

And I started to laugh.

And before I knew how or why, I started to cry.

I was a goddamned crazy person, laughing and crying and then he was holding me and then his hands were in my hair.

I knew I shouldn't be doing this. But if we were doing this then maybe we didn't have to speak and maybe I didn't have to tell him how my parents were dead and I've been so very, very sad and I didn't know how to cope and it makes me drink too much and hallucinate things from a past I would like very much to forget.

He smelled of Head & Shoulders shampoo and Tide detergent. I let myself lean into him. I hadn't leaned into anyone in a long time.

"Are you sure this is okay, Paloma?" He pulled back a little.

I probably smelled bad. I couldn't remember the last time I shaved, or put on deodorant. I was a disaster in every single way.

But still, this was okay. It was okay because it took my mind off things, for even just a minute. It was okay because no one had asked me if I was okay, not like this, in a long, long time.

I turned my face up and kissed him.

It was awkward and clumsy and my teeth knocked against his.

But it was still okay.

39

THE COVERS FELT WARM and soft as I snuggled into them. They cocooned over me while I rolled onto my side, hugging a fluffy pillow. I hadn't felt this rested in months. I reached over for my phone, but my arm only hit air.

Confused, I cracked open an eye. I was still at Sam's.

I groaned a little as I pulled the covers back over my head and burrowed down, not wanting to think about last night. I could hear Sam snoring, his back to me as he faced the wall. I looked around the room, calculating how much time it would take me to pull on my clothes and be out the front door before he woke up.

Don't get me wrong. It's not like I regretted screwing him. It's just that morning-afters are awkward as fuck. To be honest, the whole thing was pretty awkward. The way he scrunched up his face, the way his moans were clipped and mechanical, like he was embarrassed to make any noise. The way he was more self-conscious about his body than I was about mine.

But it wasn't terrible. What Sam lacked in skill, he certainly made up for in enthusiasm. And he had stroked my hair afterwards, and said all the right things, and I felt a small sense of calm that I hadn't felt in a while settle over my chest.

And his bed wasn't totally uncomfortable. Maybe lying in here a few more minutes wouldn't be the worst thing in the world.

Sam stirred a little and I shut my eyes, hoping he would think I was still asleep. I wasn't ready to have the morning-after conversation about who will call who and whether anyone will even be calling the other person at all. But he didn't wake up, I don't think. He turned over, flinging his arm over my body and moving closer to me.

I opened my eyes just a little bit. His mouth was open slightly and he seemed to be completely knocked out. The sleep of someone who has never done something terrible in his life. His arm was a little heavy and I shifted my weight, hoping it wouldn't wake him. He had a tattoo on his forearm, one I hadn't seen before since he always wore long sleeves. There were scars, too, dotted along his arm and shoulder. Small, circular scars, faded with time.

"Where did you get these?" I murmured, half to myself. I didn't think he heard me, but he opened his eyes just a crack.

"Hmm? These? Remember I told you about the ragging at Colombo university?"

"Hmm." But I was too calm. Too peaceful to think too much about it.

I closed my eyes and let myself drift off again.

I woke up for the second time to my phone ringing.

I groaned and rolled to my side. Sam was gone. I checked the time—fucking eleven a.m. I hadn't slept this late in a while. Sam probably left for work. He did say he had to get in early to help prep for the lunch shift.

My phone kept ringing. I checked the caller ID. It was Officer Keller.

Fuck.

I sat up straight in bed and was wide awake in less than a second.

"Officer Keller?" I asked, answering. No niceties needed here. There was only one reason why he would call. I wished and hoped with everything in my body that it was good news. That they had found Ida. Or that they were at least taking me seriously now and looking into it.

"Miss Evans, good morning. I have some news—"

"Have you found her?" It was all I cared about.

"Her?"

"Y-yes. My neighbor. Ida Mulligan?"

"Oh, your neighbor. Um, no. This isn't about her. It's actually about your roommate. Arun Kumar?"

I froze.

"Y-yes?"

"I'm sorry to be the one to tell you this, but the body of a young Indian man was just picked up. The description matches your roommate. Would you be able to come into the station now and ID the body? We can't seem to track down any other relative."

My hands started shaking.

So I was right.

I knew it.

I knew he was dead.

But the realization didn't bring me any peace. If Arun was dead, that meant that there was a very real killer out there.

And now I had to go and ID a body. Fuck me. I wasn't made to be on an episode of fucking *CSI*.

I stood up and paced the room. Maybe I should call Sam? I mean, it was his friend, too, and I was sure he'd be okay to come with me to the station.

I rang his phone and got his voice mail.

Of course he wouldn't have his phone with him while he was at work.

I paced around the room a little longer.

I had to speak to him. He didn't seem like the kind of guy who would mind if I called his work. Crossing boundaries was one of his favorite pastimes, after all.

Luckily, I already had the number saved.

"Curry Palace," a girl answered. Maybe it was the same girl whose dad owned the place.

"Hi, could I please speak to Sam. It's an emergency."

"Sorry, Sam, was it?"

"Sam, or well, maybe he goes by Saman?"

"Hang on," she said, but I could hear her calling out to someone else.

"Hey, Rinosh, what was that new guy's name again?"

"Prakash," someone else replied.

"We got a Sam here? Or Saman?"

"Nope."

"Sorry." She returned back to the phone. "There's no Sam or Saman here."

"Are you sure? Saman Alwis? I met him there before."

"You guys sure there's no Saman Alwis here?" she called out again.

"Yes!"

"Yep, no one by that name works here."

I hung up, dread starting to hover around me like a swarm of bees. Fuck.

What was happening?

I met Sam at the Curry Palace, didn't I?

No, hang on—

Sam had just fucking walked up to me in the street and introduced himself and I fell for his whole damn story about working with Arun.

The realization smacked me straight in the face.

How could I have been so stupid?

I should have known something wasn't right. The way he kept showing up, the way he couldn't take no for an answer.

The way he convinced me that I imagined Arun was dead.

And if he lied to me about the Curry Palace, what else could he have lied to me about?

Dread settled over me like a cloud of dust. Oh my fucking god, could he have lied to me about where he got his scars from? Could he—?

No way. There was no way he was connected to the orphanage. Right?

I was such a dipshit. All this time I was so focused on Appy that I didn't see what was right in front of my nose.

I grabbed my bag and jacket. I wasn't going to wait around till he came back. I was heading to the police station now anyway. I could fill Officer Keller in then.

40

RATMALANA, SRI LANKA

A GECKO SLITHERED ACROSS the top of the white wall, at the very edge, where the wall meets the ceiling.

Tsk, tsk, tsk, it called out.

Miss Nayana said that the gecko's cry is unlucky.

This gecko was just a baby, no bigger than my little finger. Its tail was just a stub—probably hurt itself somewhere, making it fall off. But it didn't matter to the gecko. Their tails grow back, good as new. It would be like nothing bad ever happened.

It turned back again, moving in short bursts, then holding still to see if it had been spotted.

But there was just me, in bed.

In bed.

In bed at the sickroom.

My face throbbed far, far worse than the time when Shanika slapped me after she found out about the adoption.

I tried to touch it but it was bandaged—the gauze wrapping around from the bottom of my jaw to the top of my head. I started to remember what happened, but it was just bits and pieces that came back to me. Shanika had pulled my hair. I followed her down to the garden. Lihini and Maya were there.

And then—

Fear flooded through every part of me. Mohini. She attacked me. She—she had bitten my face. I started to scream again. I screamed and screamed until Miss Chandra came in and forced me to drink some medicine which made me feel woozy and like I couldn't scream anymore.

I don't know how long I lay in bed. My head didn't feel quite there, like I could only half see the shadows of the tree branches move across the wall, like the gecko was only partly there, like my mind was stuck between two places.

There may have been voices, from time to time, maybe faces, too, appearing just out of my reach. Words spun around in my mind like dried jack leaves blowing in the breeze.

"Her face. There's just no getting around it." Perera sir's voice floated towards me.

"What do you mean no getting around it? We can't send a girl off to America looking like that. It's no small scratch."

"She looks like she's been ravaged by a wild animal."

"It's worse than before. At least with Shanika is was just her arms."

"The adoption has to go through. No matter what. That is final."

I closed my eyes and let the breeze carry me too. People might have come and gone. Checking my eyes, spooning some *kandha* into my mouth. But these were all dreams from another life.

The shadows on the wall were orange when I opened my eyes next. Sunset. How had I been sleeping for the whole day? There were still words, swimming in from outside the door. But my mind was a little clearer now. The ripples in the pond stayed still for a moment.

"You really must be more careful. After she attacked Shanika I thought we'd never get another chance. You know how strict those officers from the NCPA are. The orphanage would get shut down." That was Miss Chandra. Definitely Miss Chandra. And she didn't sound happy.

"I do everything for these girls, do you hear me? Everything. How many men do you know who dedicate their lives to a cause like this? To servants who couldn't keep their legs together in the Middle East. To women who leave their daughters with their abusive fathers on their search for work. This can't get out. It would ruin me. Most people would call me a saint, you know?"

"Most people would."

"Get that judgemental tone out of your voice, do you hear?"

"Sorry, sir."

"Now tell that child that Shanika has been sent off to St. Margaret's, and get everything ready for the Evanses."

So Shanika was sent away? But—but she wasn't even the one who attacked me. I saw her go back inside.

I closed my eyes and drifted off again.

Miss Chandra was sitting next to my bed when I woke up next. She didn't notice me at first. She was staring at a newspaper, her forehead wrinkled into deep furrows. She could have been reading it, but she seemed to be looking at the same place for a very long time.

"M-Miss Chandra?"

My voice jolted her.

"Paloma, *aney*, child. You've been sleeping for a long time."

"What time is it?" It was dark outside.

"It's late. Here, have some tea."

I sat up a little bit and took a sip. My cheek hurt, and the milk powder hadn't been stirred in properly and I could see little white blobs bob around in the cup.

"How long have I been in here?"

"The whole day."

"Why?"

"We had to give you some medicine, Paloma."

"Am I sick?"

"No, child." She stopped talking for a moment and closed her eyes. I could see her throat move as she swallowed, and her double chin quivered a little. She opened her eyes again and looked directly at me, pressing her lips together again.

"Do you remember what happened, Paloma?"

"I was attacked. Miss Chandra, I—I think it was, well, some sort of woman. A monster." My voice trembled as I spoke. Even here, in the sickroom, I could still feel her on me. Breathing down my neck. Biting down on my face.

But Miss Chandra just smiled.

"It's easy to get confused, dear. You've been through so much. Mohini is just a story you girls made up. Shanika was the one who attacked you."

I felt so confused. What was Miss Chandra saying? Everything around me was starting to feel unsteady again. I wanted to cry.

"Now, now, child. Don't be upset."

"I'm so scared, Miss. I don't know what to do."

"I know, Paloma. You just relax. You need to get some rest."

I nodded through my tears. I was starting to feel really, really tired.

"That's a good girl." Miss Chandra started stroking my hair. "Now you sleep a little more. You'll feel better by evening."

My eyelids felt heavy. She must be right.

41

SAN FRANCISCO, CA

OFFICER KELLER MET ME out front and took me into the morgue right away. I couldn't stop shaking, so he asked me if I would like a coffee, as if it made perfect sense to be sipping on a fucking latte when I was surrounded by bodies of murder victims.

The body had been found in the bay, he said, though the blunt-force trauma to the back of the head ruled out drowning as the cause of death. It was most likely the way the murderer tried to dispose of the body. He was so matter-of-fact about the whole thing he might as well have been discussing his taxes.

And then they took me into where the body was being held, and I did everything I could to choke back a scream. It was Arun. An Arun whose face was so contorted and bloated that I had to look at him for a few moments longer than I had hoped. Whose lips that once curled into a sneer as he blackmailed me were now shriveled and grey.

And then I asked to be excused, and hurried to the bathroom and threw up.

Officer Keller was waiting for me with a bottle of water when I came out.

"You all right?" he asked. He wasn't unkind.

"Yes. Sorry. My first time."

"Sure. And let's hope it's the last, huh?"

That was for certain.

I took a deep breath. I should be relieved. My secret was safe. I wasn't hallucinating.

But that meant—what about Ida?

Was Sam behind all of this?

"Officer Keller, I need to speak with you." Maybe now he would take me seriously. "Have you got any information about my neighbor, Ida Mulligan?"

He gave me a small smile. "Her sister called it in. We've put out an alert and are on the lookout, though we don't really have any leads. Do you know who might have seen her last?" I thought back to the white business card I found on her counter. Surely that couldn't have had anything to do with her going missing?

"I'm not sure, Officer."

"Well, I'll keep you posted, then. And, Paloma?"

"Yes?"

"Keep your phone on you. We'll need you to come in for questioning again, now that we have a body."

Need me? Hang on, was I a damn suspect now? I needed to tell them about Sam. I couldn't have them think it was me.

"Th-there's something else."

"Yes?"

"Arun's friend. Sam. I think he might have something to do with— something to do with this." I gestured back in the direction of where we saw the body.

Officer Keller looked serious.

"What makes you say that?"

"Well, h-he kept showing up to speak to me. And he lied, about working at the Curry Palace."

"Anything else?"

"Um, I—I don't know. I just, well, I think he might be involved."

"Okay, I'll have someone take down his details."

He seemed more serious this time, like he actually might believe me. I mean, I was fucking right. Arun was dead. Even though there was a part of me that wished I had been wrong.

"You'll keep me posted?"

Officer Keller narrowed his eyes.

"Just keep your phone on you," he said.

IT WAS LATE AFTERNOON by the time I collapsed into the taxi and buckled my seat belt. We hadn't been driving two minutes when I dozed off, and only woke up again when the car pulled up to my parents' house.

I hadn't left any lights on before I rushed out, obviously, and the darkened windows felt lonely. A call from Mr. Williams popped up on my screen.

Fuck him.

I instinctively looked down the street for a blue Camry, and then across from my house to see if Appy was watching me.

Fuck him. Fuck Nina. Fuck Appy and Gavin and my parents and Arun. Fuck everyone.

If I'd slept with a murderer, then facing Mr. Williams wouldn't be the scariest thing I've done.

I let the call go to voice mail, and opened up my texts.

If you want to meet, then let's meet, I keyed in. *Tomorrow morning, 10 a.m. Come to my parents'. I trust you know the address.*

My dad had bought me a stock of pepper spray when I was sixteen. I wondered if the box was still in my closet.

I let myself in and walked through the house, turning on every light I could find. I made sure the front door was locked, and managed to rummage the pepper spray from my closet. I tucked it into my pocket, plugged in my phone to charge, then poured myself a healthy two fingers of whiskey and sat down on the couch, nestling the cold glass on my head, which throbbed like someone was pounding it with a mallet. You would need a healthy two fingers, too, if you just had sex with the guy who murdered your roommate.

I turned on the Disney Channel. Yes, the fucking Disney Channel because I needed all the goddamned comfort I could get right now. I thought about ordering a pizza but must have dozed off again.

All I knew was that something woke me up a little bit later. My head still hurt. I hit the mute button and looked around the living room. Nothing out of the ordinary. Maybe it was just something on TV? I heard it again, a soft rapping. It was coming from the kitchen. What the actual fuck?

Every hair on my body prickling, I slowly made my way over to the noise, brandishing the pepper spray in front of me.

Rap rap rap.

There it was again.

I took a deep breath and stepped in.

The kitchen was empty. Of course it fucking was.

I looked under the table, just to make sure. Nothing.

I even opened the cabinets under the sink. Nothing.

Rap rap rap.

The window.

I inched my way over, wishing I hadn't had that glass of whiskey. Or maybe I was shaking so much because I was fucking scared out of my mind.

I held my breath and pulled aside the lacy curtain. Nothing.

Exhaling slowly, I peered into the now darkened street. I grabbed a glass and turned on the faucet. I glanced up at the window again, and the glass slipped from my hand, shattering into the sink. There was a face. A woman's face. Pale as death.

Mohini. She was here. She was finally here for me.

But it's wasn't her. Of course it fucking wasn't.

It was the woman across the street. Her hair was wild and her eyes were wide and glassy. She put a finger to her lips, not blinking, not even once.

Holy fuck. I gasped as I stepped away from the window. I'd seriously had enough of this creepy bitch. I burst out through the front door and into the street. She needed to be told to get lost.

"Hey!" I called. It was dark and I couldn't quite see her yet. "Hey, what the hell is wrong with you?" But the small patch of yard we had leading up to the kitchen window was empty. What the hell? I wish I had grabbed my phone so I could use the flashlight.

I saw some movement over from her house. Maybe she managed to run across and get inside. I crossed the street. She was going to get a piece of my mind, and it was going to happen today. I was fed up with her sneaking around, acting like a weirdo, freaking me out. Who the hell behaved like that anyway?

Her lights were turned off, and the inside of the house was dark as well. She was probably hiding, the dumb bitch. Well, she couldn't fool me. I stomped up to her porch and rang the doorbell. No answer, of course. I rang it again, three times. Then I banged on the door.

"I know you're in here, Aparna," I called out. I tried peering through the window but the curtains were drawn. I thought I heard a muffled bang from inside. Maybe she had knocked something over. I rapped on the window. It rattled loudly, but still no answer.

I turned back to try the doorbell again when I crashed into someone. They grabbed my arm, hard.

"Fuck," I cried out, yanking my arm back.

"Hey. Hey, it's just me." It was Gloria.

"What are you doing here?" My voice was rough, but I didn't care too much.

"I didn't mean to scare you. *Lo siento*. Sorry. Sorry." Snowy was cowering behind her. My yell probably freaked him out, but I didn't care.

"Did you see her?"

"Who?"

"Aparna. Appy."

"N-no?"

"Well, I need to talk to her. Right now, I need to talk to her."

"Paloma, what's happening?"

"She's fucking crazy. And she's driving me crazy. That's what's happening."

"Hey, maybe we should go back home, huh?"

"What? Didn't you hear me?"

"Paloma, I asked around about the lady." She dropped her voice to an urgent whisper. "She's not, you know, she's not okay."

"I don't give a rat's ass. She needs to leave me the fuck alone."

"Paloma, please. Let's go back inside. It's not worth it."

"But she's in here. Why the hell isn't she opening the door for me, huh?"

"Paloma, she lost her baby. It was just a few months ago. She hasn't been quite right in the head since. Her husband told me. He apologized to me today. Her medicine, it makes her act strange." Gloria grabbed my arm again, but more gently this time. "Please?"

I didn't want to, but I relented. I was exhausted. I was exhausted from worrying, from pretending, from mourning. I let Gloria lead me back home and into my living room, where I collapsed onto my sofa and held my head in my hands.

"Rough day?"

"You have no idea."

"I spoke to Gavin. The lady's husband. He told me about your parents. I'm so sorry. I had no idea . . ."

"I wasn't trying to hide it, you know."

"I know. I know what it's like. To be alone."

"You do?"

"Growing up, I only had my sister, but then—it was the worst day of my life."

"I'm sorry." I was. I'm such a selfish asshole sometimes. Of course I'm not the first person to have lost their parents.

She smiled sadly. Her pink hair was more muted in the dark. It suited her. "It was a long time ago. I just wanted to let you know that I know how it feels."

"It's just, really hard, you know. I'm not very good at opening up. Nina, that's my therapist, she says I need to try to build better relationships with people. Be more honest. But it's the hardest thing."

"I know exactly what you mean. You know, you remind me a lot of myself."

"I feel bad for you, then. I don't think you realize how fucked up I actually am."

Gloria smiled and stood up. "You got anything to drink in this place? I think we both need it."

Maybe we were more alike than I thought.

"Cabinet to the left of the sink."

I heard her rummaging around in the kitchen.

My phone lit up. I had a voice mail from Sam. He sounded upset—

Paloma, please call me back. It's urgent. There seems to have been some sort of misunderstanding. Please, just, call me.

Did the police have him, then? God, I hoped so. I started to shiver again. If they hadn't taken him in, he could be anywhere. Oh shit, what if he decided to come here tonight? At least Gloria was with me. Maybe I should call Officer Keller again.

My phone beeped just as I was about to pull up his number.

It was from Mr. Williams.

Glad to hear from you, Paloma. I'll see you soon.

Good. That was one thing I could actually deal with.

I needed to stop being a whiny bitch about it. The poor guy was just trying to do his job as my parents' lawyer. The job my parents had hired him to do in the event of their "untimely demise" as they always joked. Except it ended up not being a joke. My chest burned thinking about them. He didn't deserve to be called a stalker, just because I didn't have the stomach to face him and settle my parents' estate. Because to finalize everything would be to accept that they had died.

He must have been in contact with Ida to get through to me. Maybe he even knew more about what happened to her.

I'd speak to Mr. Williams, and then, after we cleared things up, I'd get his signature and the bank would release the hold on my joint account. I'd put my parents' house on the market. Get my own place. One I don't have to share with a roommate. Maybe I'd even move out of the Bay Area. Somewhere I can start fresh and make some new memories. Make some new friends. Real ones. I could even find a boy-friend who's not a psycho murderer. I think it's time for me to move on with my life.

Gloria showed up with two glasses. She'd mixed in some orange juice with the scotch.

I took a deep sip, waiting for the alcohol to course comfortably through me. It was sharp, acidic, and just what I needed.

Everything was starting to swim around. Surely I couldn't have gotten this tired so quickly?

Shadows from the corners of the room were starting to creep up to me. I tried to stand up, but Gloria put a hand on my shoulder and pushed me down. I sank back heavily. The last thing I saw was her, smiling, as the darkness finally washed over me.

42

RATMALANA, SRI LANKA

I'VE READ ALL ABOUT moors. I mean, the moors are basically a character of their own in *Wuthering Heights*. Miss Sarah says that the moors are a symbol. *Relentless, wild, never ending. The moors represent different things to different characters*, she would say.

Of course, you don't get moors in Ratmalana, so I've never seen one. But what the moors were to Catherine, the ocean was to me—something to get lost in. I dreamed of an ocean, or maybe it was a moor. It rose and fell, a magnificent beast, inhaling and exhaling as Heathcliff, or was it Lihini, called out to me. I had to leave it, my never-ending peace, but wading back to shore was hard. I swam as hard as I could, and then, just when I thought my lungs and my heart would burst, I broke the surface and the biggest wave crashed down on me. I had been attacked. Mohini had attacked me.

It was enough to force the last of the fog out of my mind and sit up in bed. I felt weak. Like I hadn't eaten in days. Like the floor was dropping under my feet as I crossed over to the small bathroom that was attached to the sickroom.

I was wrapped up like a mummy—one side of my face completely covered. The bandages felt itchy against my skin. I tugged a small bit aside. I couldn't really see what had happened.

Miss Chandra said it was Shanika who bit me, but that couldn't be true.

I started to unwrap the bandages. I had to see for myself.

My eyes watered as I peeled the gauze off the wounds on my face. It stung so much that it took me a minute to see myself clearly. I immediately wished I hadn't. It didn't look like a girl had bitten me. It looked like a monster tried to have me for dinner.

Two crescents, like inside-out brackets oozing with blood, marked my right cheek, starting from under my eye all the way down to my jaw. The flesh around the wound was jagged and torn. A piece of skin flapped sadly. There were blue and purple and dark red marks around the rest of my face. Some cuts also. I'm pretty sure my whole right side was swollen. And it hurt.

I tried to put the bandages back on but it started to smart, so I just let it be. I looked like a monster myself. I hoped the scars wouldn't show too much. I might scare the Evanses if they saw me like this.

My body went cold.

What if they changed their minds after seeing me? What if they decided not to adopt me after all? What if I got sent to St. Margaret's instead?

I needed to get out of the sickroom. I needed to speak to Lihini. She would know what to do. She would stroke my hair and calm me down and tell me not to worry. It was dark. I could probably make my way to the dormitory and wake her up.

I padded over to the door. I know I wasn't supposed to leave, but I really needed to see her right away.

I pressed my ear against the door and listened. There was no one outside. I tried the handle. It was locked.

The panic that crashed over me was sudden and sharp. The sick-room door was never locked.

"Don't be scared. Don't be scared. Don't be scared." I kept repeating the words, over and over. It was probably just a mistake. Miss Chandra probably did it by mistake. It had to be some kind of mistake.

"Don't be scared. Don't be scared." I was whispering to myself now. I wished the heavy feeling in my head would go away. I kept rattling the doorknob again and again, but the floor felt like water, swirling around my legs as I fell heavily onto my knees.

What is happening? Why are they keeping me here?

I must have been screaming for hours when they finally burst in. Perera sir and Miss Chandra and Upul and, thank god, Lihini.

"Lihini!" I rasped. "Help me, please help me."

But she wouldn't meet my eye. She stood behind everyone else and bit her lip, looking like she was trying not to cry.

"Restrain her," Perera sir ordered, and Upul put his hands in my armpits and pulled me off the floor.

"No! No! Help me, please." I was still calling out to Lihini as he dragged me over to the bed and pushed me down. My dress rode up to my waist as I thrashed around, but I didn't care. What were they doing? Why wasn't Lihini helping me?

He used some nylon rope from the washing line to tie my wrists to the top of the bed. I could smell his body odour as he leaned close to me. He gave me a disgusting smile and stared knowingly at the bottom of my dress.

But Perera sir and Miss Chandra were there. They wouldn't let anything happen to me.

"Help me," I called out to them, but they were looking at Lihini.

"You wanted to see her, here she is. I told you, she's having a bit of trouble after Shanika's attack," Perera sir explained to her.

Lihini still didn't come close. She pressed up against the wall of the room, like she wanted to be as far away from me as possible.

But she was staring at me now. Staring at my face.

Miss Chandra took her arm.

"See, child. See what we meant? You have to do it. It's the only way."

Lihini's hands were shaking a little. They always did that when she was upset.

Perera sir spoke next. "No point feeling bad about this, Lihini. Paloma will understand when she calms down. She won't be angry with you. She'll understand that it's for the good of the home, for all of us."

Lihini swallowed, and gave a small nod.

43

MY HEAD POUNDED AS I peeled open my eyes. This was a giant mother of a hangover. It took me a minute to realize I was in my parents' garage. What on earth was I doing here? The single bulb from the ceiling cast a murky grey glow around me, throwing deep shadows onto the wall.

Everything looked the same, messy and untouched. My bicycle. The broken freezer. Dad's tools. Neatly labeled boxes of extra supplies.

My neck hurt like a bitch. I was seated upright, my chin sinking into my chest. I was about to wonder how on earth I managed that, when I noticed I couldn't move my arms. They were bound behind the chair, holding me straight. My heart started beating fast. What the hell was going on? I tried to stand but my legs were tied also.

I struggled for just a few seconds when I realized that I was not alone.

She sat in front of me, a few feet away, her face grey, like everything else in the garage. Only it wasn't the Gloria I knew. Her hair wasn't pink anymore but black and long, and she had slicked the heavy bangs off her face. Her piercings were gone. So were her glasses. She had wiped off the heavy eyeliner and overpronounced eyebrows. She wore a black sweater and jeans. They were my black sweater and jeans.

She looked different. Different, and yet recognition buzzed through me like electricity. Like seeing your reflection in a mirror when you weren't expecting it. I took me more than a moment to realize it was her, but it was only when she spoke, her Latina accent harshly replaced with a Sri Lankan one, that it felt like a direct punch to my gut.

"Time to wake up, Lihini. Don't you recognize me yet? It's me. Paloma."

44

RATMALANA, SRI LANKA

"LIHINI!" I SCREAMED. I didn't understand what was happening. Why was she here? What was she agreeing to do?

Why wasn't she helping me?

Miss Chandra picked up a screwdriver and a hammer and led Lihini to the bathroom.

"Wait," Lihini said. She held out her hand. "Let me do it myself."

Perera sir and Miss Chandra stood outside the bathroom door as Lihini went inside. She didn't shut the door, so I could see her as she stood in front of the mirror. She pulled her lips back and looked at her teeth.

Finally, she took a deep breath and picked up the screwdriver, bringing it to her front tooth.

"No!" I screamed. My strength had returned and I thrashed in bed, kicking and screaming as loudly as I could.

But Upul clamped his hand down hard on my mouth. I tried to bite him but my jaw was locked. I swung my head from side to side, but it was no use. He pushed on my chest with his elbows, using his body weight to keep me pinned down on the bed. He reached out with his hand and pinched hard on my nipple.

"Shut up or I'll do much worse to you. Really teach you a lesson," he sneered.

The tears that gushed down my face burned my wound. I couldn't breathe. I couldn't scream. I couldn't believe this was happening. That she would do this to me.

But through all my muffled screaming and thrashing, I could hear it. I knew.

The sound of a hammer hitting a screwdriver. Lihini's small scream. The sound of metal clanking against the tile as the tools slid out of her hands, letting everyone in the room know that she was done. That her betrayal was final.

I twisted my head so I could see her. She was looking into the mirror, smiling wide to study her new, chipped tooth.

45

THE GARAGE GOT SMALL. The walls started closing in on me. One inch at a time. It was getting dark. Dark and cramped and small and I could hear my heart beat like a frenzied, feral animal all the way from my chest to my ears.

"Paloma?" My voice was steady, even though my whole body was trembling. It felt strange to call someone else that after so long. It felt even stranger to have her seated across from me.

"You look like you've seen a ghost." Her lips curved into a smile. A faint scar was visible on her cheek now that her cakey makeup was gone.

"They told me you died."

"Oh, they did, did they? I'm curious. Did they say that Paloma died, or Lihini?"

My tooth was throbbing like I was being electrocuted. My hair was stuck to my face. I wished my hands were untied so I could brush it away. Or do something.

"I'm sorry. Look, I really am."

"You're sorry?" She raised an eyebrow.

"Of course I'm sorry. Paloma, you have no idea what it's been like. I—"

"No idea what it's been like?"

Her voice was flat. I was doing this wrong. I spent all my life calculating, measuring the right words to say and now I was doing everything wrong.

Be sweet, Paloma.

"You don't know what it means to me that you're alive. I—I haven't been able to forgive myself for what I did."

"How gracious of you."

"Stop it. It's true. You're alive. This is—oh god, Paloma, you have no idea how much of my life has been spent wishing I could go back. Wishing I could go back and change everything."

"You must be used to your wishes coming true, no?"

"It's not like that."

"But you got what you wanted, right? A family. A life in America. A life that was supposed to be mine."

"I'm so sorry. I really am. But I had to leave. It was—she was—"

"She?" Her lips twisted into a mangled smile. "She?"

"You know who. I thought I was going crazy, but I saw her, Paloma, I swear I did." My voice was shaking. I tried breathing but it felt like I was underwater.

"Who, Lihini? Who did you see?"

She wanted me to say it.

"T-the woman. Mohini. I saw her. No one would believe me. Only Perera sir. And he—and he gave me a chance to escape her. To escape the curse. I'm so sorry. She—she wanted to kill me, Paloma. I know she did."

The ugly smile grew wider, until she threw back her head and laughed.

"So this ghost wanted to kill you, huh? And that made it okay for you to take my place? To pretend to be me? To keep it going for eighteen fucking years?"

"But you said—you said you didn't want to go. That you hated leaving."

That's how I had justified it. I mean, I had to fucking justify it somehow. How else was I supposed to live with myself? She said the words. She said she didn't want to go. So I shut off the little voice in my head that knew it was a lie.

The smile switched to a menacing glare in less than a second.

"You stupid, stupid bitch." Her voice was steel now. Any trace of laughter was gone. "I only said that shit to make you feel better. So you wouldn't feel left out, or jealous. How the fuck was I supposed to know that you would stab me in the back like this?"

"But you couldn't leave! They wouldn't take you like that. After Shanika—after what she did to your face. If my parents had seen, the whole orphanage could have been shut down. Someone had to go in your place." I could hear the desperation in my voice. Was I desperate for her to believe me, or for me to believe myself? It was a simple choice when Perera sir offered it to me.

Paloma can't go, not like that, he had said. *You have to take her place instead. If you don't go, we will lose our funding and they will shut down the orphanage. All the girls will be without homes. You don't want that, do you? Don't you want to go to America?* Of course I did. I would have gone anywhere where I knew for sure I wouldn't be seeing that vile Sister Cynthia again. Where I wouldn't be terrified of a ghost that no one except Perera sir believed I saw. I didn't know the orphanage would burn down. That I was leaving her there to die. Except, well, she didn't die. She was here.

Her slap felt like lightning. Years of hate, bursting out of the palm of her hand.

"You betrayed me. You were my best friend in the whole world, and you betrayed me."

Yes. Yes, I betrayed her. But I didn't think I was. I didn't think much at all except that none of the girls would have a home if the NCPA heard about Paloma's attack. I thought I was helping. That it was for the greater good. I would have tried to help the orphanage even if the reward wasn't me getting everything I had always wanted. At least, I think I would. I was twelve fucking years old, how the hell could I be held accountable for a decision I made when I was a child?

"I was just a kid, Paloma. I'm sorry. I—I didn't think. You have no idea how much I've regretted it ever since. What it's been like. Feeling so guilty all the time."

She snorted.

"What it's been like? You want to tell me what it's been like? You have no idea what I've had to go through. What I've done to survive."

She slapped me again and again.

I don't really know how long it went on for, but when she finally stopped hitting me, she hunched over, breathing hard.

I tried again.

"Paloma, I swear. I swear I thought they would find another home for you. That's what they told me. I promise." I didn't believe it then. Not really. But she had to believe me now. My voice had taken on a whiny, needling quality that I would have hated if I heard it on anyone else. "That's why, when Perera sir offered to help me, I took it."

"He wasn't trying to help you, you stupid bitch. He was trying to save his own ass."

"I was freaked out by this whole Mohini thing. He knew, Paloma, he knew how scared I was. And then when you got hurt they said they needed someone to be adopted. That we would be shut down other-wise. That I had to take your place. I thought it was the only thing to do." I was repeating myself, but I had nothing else to say.

"The only thing to do. The only thing to do." She shook her head in disgust. "So, tell me, after all this fucking time, do you still believe that Mohini was after you?"

She was a figment of my imagination, right? There was no way. It felt real then, what I had seen. True, I was scared out of my mind, in the way a twelve-year-old would be. But it was just something the girls made up at the orphanage. And then when I came here, Nina said it was my way of trying to cope with the guilt of leaving. She didn't know what I had done to get here, of course. Just that I had left my best friend behind, and that she died in a fire.

"You are so much, so much stupider than I thought, you know that?" She stood up abruptly, grabbing the back of my chair and dragging me backwards to the corner of the garage, where she spun the chair around to face the wall.

She stuck up an old piece of newspaper on the peeling paint. It was at my eye level.

"I hope you're not too drunk to read this," she said. I heard her footsteps head out of the garage, but I didn't turn my head to watch her leave. I was transfixed on the paper, on the picture printed on it, smiling at me. It was her. Mohini.

46

HER EYES DRILLED INTO me as they had so many years ago. Except they weren't blank. Her smile wasn't evil, and her hair fell smoothly away from her forehead. She wore a white dress, but this was no shroud. She was a bride on her wedding day, with Perera sir, a much younger Perera sir, somberly standing next to her.

There was another picture, smaller, and lost amid the columns of text, of a few of the girls playing in the orphanage garden.

Tragedy and Scandal for Internationally Funded Orphanage in Ratmalana, the headline read. It looked like more of a tabloid than a legitimate newspaper.

I had to squint and lean forward to read the rest of the article.

> Investigations following a fire at a prestigious girls' home in Ratmalana have led to a surprise discovery regarding the director of the home, Mr. Dudley Perera.
>
> Perera was, as described by many residents of Ratmalana, a kind and well-mannered man, who dedi-

cated his life to raising funds and running the orphanage. His wife, Mrs. Sandamali Perera, was believed by local residents to have succumbed to a grave illness, the details of which were not publicized. However, investigations after the disastrous fire which claimed the lives of three residents at the orphanage brought to light that Mrs. Perera was residing within the very walls of the girls' home.

What the—?

"We thought a ghost stayed with us," a surviving teacher commented. "Many girls reported sightings, and she was named Mohini, after Vana-Mohini, the folktale."

It appears that Mrs. Perera continued to reside within the walls of the home unbeknownst to its residents. Mr. Perera's role in these surprising circumstances is yet to be determined by authorities. Investigators have not determined the cause of the fire but have disclosed that they do suspect foul play.

As both Mr. and Mrs. Perera succumbed to their injuries from the fire before they could be questioned, authorities might never be able to find definite answers to this mystery.

I blinked. Forced myself to inhale.

What the hell did this mean?

She was alive? She never died? But then, what was it I saw? Was it her that I saw? The real, very-much-alive Sandamali Perera, walking around the orphanage when she should be—when she should be what? Hiding? Did he hide her? Did he keep her there?

I don't know how long I sat there, staring at her face. Trying to understand.

"What does this mean?" I asked as soon as Paloma yanked my chair around.

"What the fuck do you think it means? He kept her in the fucking orphanage. I mean, Mrs. Perera was completely batshit crazy herself. They were going to take her away to a mental hospital but Perera sir couldn't deal with the fucking shame of that, so he kept her there instead, all drugged up. He told everyone she'd died, but she was trapped in the cupboard in his office the whole time. You know the one. He was letting her out only at night. His little prisoner."

"But I saw her."

"Exactly. You fucking saw her. You saw her and thought you saw a ghost and you wouldn't shut your damn mouth about it. So he needed to get you out of there. Offered you a deal. He wasn't taking any chances after the close call with Shanika."

"Shanika? What did she have to do with it? Didn't *she* attack *you*? Isn't that why Perera sir wanted me to come here instead? Because Mom and Dad would have alerted the NCPA if they saw your wounds?"

She let out a short, dry laugh.

"Even after all this, don't you get it? Shanika didn't attack me. I knew it, even then. It was a fucked-up, drugged-up Mrs. Perera that all you morons thought was a ghost. Shanika was just a pawn in this whole thing. A liability after Mrs. Perera attacked her the year before, and Perera sir had to cover all that shit up by claiming that Shanika was crazy and tried to hurt herself. It's so fucked up. Miss Chandra knew and helped him keep her medicated enough that she could never really talk about it.

"And then crazy Mrs. Perera attacked me too. Fucking tried to bite my face off. Now that would really have been a disaster with the NCPA. The orphanage would have been shut down for sure. The

Evanses had to adopt someone, it was all settled. And anyone in their right mind would have alerted the authorities if their brand-new child showed up with chunks of her face bitten off. Someone had to be adopted. It just couldn't be me."

No. No. No. This wasn't happening.

"Oh my goodness."

"Oh. My. Fucking. Goodness. Does Perera sir's little angel understand now? How she wasn't saving anyone? How she fucking betrayed me?"

"Fuck, Paloma, I—I don't know what to say. He told me he was helping me, that he was helping all of us." I was pleading again.

"You are so fucking stupid. I can't believe you thought Shanika was capable of attacking me. You just ate up all his bullshit. Guess it was easier to swallow than your own."

But she shrugged. "Whatever. He's dead now. She's dead now."

"The fire. Was it—was it Mrs. Perera? Who did it? Was that real?"

"Of course it was fucking real. I burned that hellhole to the ground myself."

"Y-you burned it yourself?"

"I wasn't going to let any of the other girls suffer the way I had. With psychos locked in closets and evil nuns and a fucking pedophile."

I flinched. She had completely lost it.

"Don't look so surprised. You think Perera sir was your little savior? Or that Miss Chandra actually cared about us? You have no fucking idea what happened after you left. What they allowed others to do to me. They tried to keep me drugged up too. Just like Mrs. Perera. Just like Shanika."

The animal in my chest that had calmed down suddenly started scratching at me again.

"There's no fucking way I would ever let you get away with it."

"I never—" My voice broke. "Paloma, you have to believe me. I never wanted to hurt you."

"You never wanted to hurt me?"

"No. God. I swear."

"Never. Not once?"

Her eyes bored holes into mine.

"Paloma, you were my best friend. Why would I want to hurt you?"

"You know, that's what I thought too. Why would my best friend want to hurt me? Why would she want to scare me?"

"Scare you?"

Oh, fuck.

"The ruined book. The photo with my eyes scratched out. For the longest time, I thought it was Shanika. She was the only one crazy enough, sick enough to do that."

I swallowed.

"I hated her, you know. You let me hate her. I never thought—I mean, why the fuck would you even do that to me?"

I wish it wasn't true. I wish it wasn't fucking true with every bone, no, with every goddamned fiber in my body.

"I didn't—I'm sorry."

"There you go again with the sorries. I don't give a fuck about whether you're sorry."

"Please! I didn't want to scare you. I just—I just wanted you to believe me. About the ghost. About the curse. I swear. That was all." My face stung where she slapped me earlier. I didn't even realize it was from the tears running down my face.

"And you thought destroying my photograph would make me believe you?"

"I was scared. I was scared out of my mind. And no one believed me. Not even you. I thought that if you believed you were cursed

339

too . . ." The tears dripped down my cheeks and trailed onto my neck. Into my hair.

Her face wavered. I had to keep trying.

"Paloma, I'm so sorry. Please. Please let me go and we can figure things out. My parents are dead. It's just me. We can figure things out."

I trembled, but she was composed. My voice shook, but hers was calm.

She was soft when she spoke next. Soothing, almost. Like you would speak to a child.

"Don't you understand, Lihini? You betrayed me. You were like my sister, and you stabbed me in the back the first chance you got. And now I'm here to take back what was supposed to be mine."

That was when I noticed the open scissors she held in her hand. The animal inside me began wailing in fear.

47

RATMALANA, SRI LANKA

I DIDN'T DRIFT AWAKE this time. I was suddenly completely alert and fully aware of what happened. I had been untied, thankfully, but the door to the sickroom was still locked.

No matter how much I hurt, no matter how much I was angry at Lihini, I knew one thing and one thing only—I had to get out of here. I had to somehow make my way over to the Evanses. They had to save me. They had to get me out of here. But how could they do that when I was still locked in here and the real monsters were roaming around outside?

There was a window, but it had a grille, of course. And I was on the first floor. I moved the jug and cup from the small table and pushed it next to the wall. I tried to be quiet, but I didn't think anyone was listening anyway.

Climbing on carefully, I looked outside. It took a moment for my eyes to adjust, but when they did, the garden looked deserted. It would be. If today was the day that Mr. and Mrs. Evans were coming, then today was also the first day of the new term at school. I had no way of checking the time, but the sun didn't look to be that high in the sky.

I stood there for a few minutes, still feeling light-headed and wondering what I should do, when I saw it. The dirty white van that took us to school. It pulled up the drive to park just under the window where I was standing. Upul got down, swinging the keys in his hand.

He was disgusting and repulsive. He was a monster himself. But I knew what he wanted. I knew how I could get him to help me.

"Upul!" I called out.

He scratched his stomach under his T-shirt and yawned. He couldn't hear me.

I reached up and knocked on the glass, hard enough to make it rattle.

"Upul!"

I rapped hard on the window once again. I tried the latch to see if it would open. Miraculously, it did, just a few inches. But that was plenty for me.

"Upul! Up here!"

He broke into his usual disgusting grin when he saw me.

"*Moko meh?*" What are you doing there?

"Upul. Could you please come up here? Please?"

"And why should I do that? You want a little more of last night?" He made a squeezing gesture with his hand and I wanted to die.

"Please, Upul. You have to help me." I swallowed. "I'll owe you."

He stopped and licked his lips slowly. His smile grew as he spoke next.

"Oh, you'll owe me, will you?"

"Y-yes. Please. Just get me out of here."

"You want me to break you out? You must be joking. If Perera uncle catches me, he'll have my neck."

"No, no he won't. I'll make sure of it. *Aney*, please."

"What's in it for me?"

"What?"

"You surely don't expect me to risk everything for nothing in return. What's in it for me?"

"I'll give you anything you want."

"Anything, ah? How to say no to that?"

The disgusting creep. I'd promise him anything he wanted now. Anything for him to get me out of the sickroom. When I was out and the Evanses saved me, I would never see him again.

"I know where Miss Chandra keeps the keys. I'll be up soon."

I exhaled.

"I know you want more of last night. Can't help yourself, can you?"

"Please, just hurry."

I paced around the room for so long that I thought I was going to faint from the anticipation. I barely noticed the pain in my face anymore. Asking Upul to come up here was a risk, but I could push past him as he came into the room and make my way out.

I heard a key rattle in the door. My body shuddered as I heard—I think it knew, even before I did, that my life was going to be very, very different from now on.

But I had a plan.

I would creep out of the sickroom and into the main wing. I would hide in the hallway just outside Perera sir's office. When the Evanses came, I'd find a way to rush to them. Or they would demand to see me. Surely, they would still recognise me? Even though Lihini had chipped her tooth they wouldn't be fooled so easily. They wanted to adopt me, to be my parents; they would still know it was me.

Upul grinned as he slunk into the room and locked the door behind him before I could even think of pushing past.

"W-what are you doing?"

"You said you would do me a favor."

"I didn't mean right now." Oh gosh. This wasn't happening. "I have to get out before Mr. and Mrs. Evans come."

"They won't come for another hour, at least. This won't take that long."

"Please just let me go. I'll come back. I promise."

What had I gotten myself into?

Upul snorted.

"Don't lie, *men*. You'll be long gone to America by this evening. How can you give me what I want then?"

I shivered again.

"W-what *do* you want?"

Upul took his time answering. He walked over to the bed and sat down, leaning back on his elbows. He smiled at me again.

"No need to be such an angel, okay. We both know you're being a tease."

"A tease?"

"Yes, a tease. Asking me to come up here. After last night. I knew, even then, even though you screamed, that it was just an act. That you actually liked it. Now come over here and sit down."

He patted the mattress next to him. I continued to stand, my knees knocking together. The corners of my eyes were starting to feel cloudy and dark.

"No need to be so shy. I don't want *that*."

"Th-that?"

"I don't want to do the sex, you know. I'm not a bad guy. But you do owe me big-time if you want me to let you out."

I exhaled a little.

"Then what do you want?"

He undid the button on his trousers and pushed his hand inside. The scars on his arms were more noticeable up close.

"Take off your T-shirt."

"What? No!"

Upul looked annoyed, but he didn't take his hand out.

"Do you want to get out of here or not?"

"Please, anything else."

"I didn't think you'd want to do anything else," he said, licking his lips and smiling.

I would get out of here and find Mr. and Mrs. Evans and everything would be all right. They would be able to save me. This is just a dream. My head was swimming around enough anyway. I just had to do this one thing.

I closed my eyes tightly. The last thing I wanted was to see his disgusting smile.

It was like pulling off a plaster. I had to do it quickly. Then it would be over and I could leave.

I yanked off the dirty pink T-shirt I had on. It had the word *Barbie* printed on it in sparkling silver letters. I remember when I got it—a box of donations from last Christmas, and Lihini and I promised we would share it. I tried to remember our agreement, the way we touched the glitter, the way the other girls looked at me jealously when I wore it. I tried to remember anything that distracted me from thinking about how cold the breeze from the fan felt hitting my bare chest. But Upul wouldn't have it that way.

"Not bad," he said. "Now move your arms away. And turn your face to the side. Your wounds are disgusting."

I opened my eyes for just a second and immediately wished I hadn't. His gaze smothered me like a thick oil, covering every exposed bit of skin, trying to soak itself all the way inside me.

"Not like Rose in *Titanic*. Now, that was a real woman. You look, well, you're nothing compared to her."

Shame clung to me like smoke. I squeezed my eyes shut again. The Evanses, I told myself. I'm doing this for them.

"Come over here," he said, gesturing to the bed again.

I stood where I was.

"Don't make me ask again."

I still didn't move.

"I'll tell Miss Chandra what you've done. How you let me in and asked me to sex you. Then you'll never get to go live in America."

It was a dream. It was a terrible, terrible dream.

I sat on the edge of the bed. I could feel his breath on my cheek. He smelled of betel leaves and cigarettes and coconut oil.

"Do you want to see?"

His breathing was heavier now, and I shook my head, my eyes still firmly closed.

"You don't want to see? This is all for you."

He grabbed my hand suddenly and pushed it into his trousers, too, locking his fingers around mine. At least, that was what it felt like. My eyelids pressed together so hard my forehead hurt.

"You like how that feels?"

I couldn't answer. I couldn't breathe. It felt . . . softer than I would have thought. And it moved easily, up and down with my hand that Upul moved with his own. I let the fog that followed me around from morning swoop over me now, pushing myself into the darkness. But the darkness wouldn't come. Not completely. It was punctured by Upul's grunts and moans. It was chased away completely when he pawed at my bare chest with his other hand. Vomit rose to my mouth when his dirty, yellow-stained fingers squeezed at my nipples. It hurt, but I didn't make a sound. I kept trying to sink deeper and deeper into the fog, trying to let go. It was like in *Wuthering Heights*. The fog clouded the moors at night, hiding everything evil and rotten and ugly. And then morning would come and bring the light with it. And everything would be over. I just had to wait until this was all over.

Upul moved my hand faster, and breathed harder, until finally he grunted loudly and I felt a sticky wetness envelop my hand.

He gave my breasts a final squeeze and went over to the bathroom.

I pulled on my T-shirt and was waiting by the door when he stepped out.

The screwdriver and hammer were long gone, of course, but there was the jug on the side table that was slippery in my hands as I held on to it now.

I swung it at his head with all my strength before he even noticed me standing there.

It connected with a hollow crack.

"You fucking bitch," Upul mumbled, but he was on his way down.

Thank goodness.

The fog was lifting. I was about to find my way back.

48

SHE STOOD UP AND started walking around me in a circle. She was slow. Deliberate. Like she had all the time in the world.

She did.

No one would miss me. No one would even notice I was gone.

"Look at you," she said. Her voice had more life in it now. "It's unreal, seeing you all grown up. I thought about you every day. It was the only thing, you know? The only thing that kept me going. I thought about what you'd look like. How did you manage it, anyway? Convincing the Evanses that I was you."

It hurt me to say it.

"They didn't . . ."

"They didn't even notice it wasn't me, did they?"

I couldn't meet her eyes.

"What kind of pathetic excuse for parents wouldn't even notice that they had the wrong child?"

Was it such an easy mistake to make? We were still close to the same height, though it was hard to tell now that I was sitting down.

We were certainly the same build. Same skin tone. Our hair would be the same if we both left it alone.

Was I seriously comparing myself to the girl who I stabbed in the back so many years ago? Was this really even happening?

She came and stood behind me, pulling the tie off my ponytail and stroking my hair. It felt soft. Caring.

"I've really enjoyed watching you these past few weeks, you know. You're such a fucking mess. It was such a waste, you coming here."

"Th-these past few weeks? But I only met you a few days ago."

She yanked on a bit of my hair and held it taut.

"Sure. Of course you wouldn't notice. You're so wrapped up in yourself and your sorry, pathetic excuse for a life."

My mind felt blank. Like I was running repeatedly into a brick wall.

"Don't believe me. Let me show you."

She went over to a stool where she had left something. A shawl. Orange and pink, with a paisley print. I'd seen it before. My body went cold.

"Nina! Is she okay?"

"Oh, relax, will you. Your precious little shrink is fine. I couldn't get to her without ruffling any feathers anyway. She's too high-profile."

She smiled, picking up the shawl. She'd brought it here just for this. For her little show. For the moment when she would show me everything I'd missed.

Pulling the shawl over her head, she cast her eyes down and smiled shyly.

"It's funny, for all your ranting and raving about white people not being able to tell us apart, you couldn't get your head out of your own ass long enough to notice." She was almost laughing now. "All you need is pink hair, or brown skin, and suddenly, that's all people see. I couldn't believe how easy it was. How easy you were."

She went back to where she was standing behind me, and this time when she pulled on my hair, it was hard. I heard the snip of the scissors before I realized what she was doing.

"What the hell?" I pulled forward and tried to turn around, but she held my head in a death grip as she started snipping faster.

"Of course, so much of it was your own fucking stupidity. The drinking, of course. You never even noticed that I let myself in here. Wandered around the house while you were sleeping. Finally getting the chance to be close to them."

Snip. Snip. Snip.

I could see chunks of my hair fall on the floor around me.

"It was really fun fucking with you, just like you fucked with me. Moving your shoes to Ida's back door, just to watch you squirm. Scratching out the eyes in your photograph. Hiding the TV remote. Leaving that doll head for you to find. It was fucking hysterical. Though, sleeping in your parents' bed, that bit was just for me."

I let out something that sounded like a whimper. I still couldn't understand. Couldn't put everything together.

I had to ask.

"And Arun?"

She moved in front of me, to get to that part of my hair, I assumed. Her scissors never stopped.

"Arun, well, that was a fun little caveat, wasn't it? I needed him to get close to you. To find out more about you. To get access to, well, everything I needed. So I took the job upstairs, caring for Mrs. Jenson. She was disgusting, but it was so very, very worth it. I befriended Arun. Made him fall in love with me, even. I'd climb in through your window from the fire escape upstairs. It was too easy."

A shudder ripped through my entire body. Mrs. Jenson's hydrangea petals would float into my room whenever the window was left open.

The pile of hair on the floor was growing.

"Of course that greedy shit found your letter. What an asshole.

Trying to blackmail you like that. Ruining my plans. Can you believe that he was going to speak to the cops?"

That was probably the arguing that everyone heard.

"S-so you got Sam to—?" I suddenly felt afraid of her answer.

She gave a little laugh.

"Sam? Now that was another pain in my ass, but you insult me by thinking I would ever use him. I did everything myself, Lihini. Just me. The way it's always been." She was enjoying this. Taking credit for all her planning. An artist, finally unveiling her masterpiece. If I kept her talking, would I be able to figure out a way to escape?

"How did you make Arun disappear?"

She was pleased with my question. Like she had been waiting for me to ask it.

"Simple." She grinned. "You even saw me wheel him away. Don't you remember?"

My mind spun. Mrs. Jenson from the apartment upstairs had been wheeled off somewhere early that morning. At least, I'd assumed it was her. She had been swaddled in her large coat and I hadn't seen her face. Her hydrangea petals were in my bedroom the next day, which meant that someone could have easily climbed through her fire escape and into my room, or out of it. Maybe even carried a body upstairs. Maybe I would have realized something was off if I wasn't so freaked out.

"It was really fun to let you think you'd imagined the whole thing. I thought for sure I was a goner when you saw me in the apartment, but you're more fucked in the head than I thought. Had a panic attack, right there in the stairwell. I just slipped you a little something to keep you out of the way until I cleaned up. Your super keeps his bleach in stock, so that was a relief. Luckily for me Arun kept me posted on how to avoid most of the cameras. Hey, you taught him that, didn't you?"

But it wasn't a question, and something else struck me like a punch in the gut.

If she killed Arun, then, oh my god—

"And Ida?"

She frowned at this, and put the scissors down. Grabbing a small tub of what looked like a pink paste, she started rubbing bits of it into my hair.

"I didn't want to kill her, really. She was a sweet old dear. But she knew you. And then she went and set up a meeting with Mr. Williams, and I couldn't have that. I couldn't have him seeing you. Being able to recognize you. It would ruin my entire plan. I had to make Mr. Williams think she wasn't home that morning, before you went over. That's who she wanted you to meet, in case you were curious. I'd just knocked her out when Mr. Williams rang the doorbell. Thank god you were late, or you'd have walked in on the whole fucking mess."

But I could only focus on one thing.

"Ida's dead?" I thought my chest would burst.

She shrugged.

"You almost found her, you know, locked in the downstairs bathroom. Thank god you didn't break your way in until after I had gotten rid of her body. I'd gotten sloppy, though, and forgotten her phone. All this would have been a lot cleaner if everyone simply believed she'd gone to San Diego."

No. No. No. This couldn't be happening.

I choked down a sob. I had to keep going. I had to keep her talking, at least.

"But why? Miss Chandra sends a letter and now you find me. How?"

She grinned. It was sudden and cruel.

"I was hoping you'd bring up my letter. It was my first stroke of brilliance. You see, I spent years searching for you. We didn't have the internet back then, of course, but the moment I could get online, I was hooked. There were too many damn Evanses and I thought it might be impossible, at first. I had no other information to go by. No first names.

Didn't even know if you still lived in California. But I waited. I bided my time. And I was rewarded. Elizabeth Evans finally made it to the news. The Angel in the Bay. It's funny, I used to think she was my angel once. Little did I know . . . Anyways, all the press made it easier to find her. To find you.

"After that, it was easy. Two letters—one from a guilt-ridden Miss Chandra to Mr. and Mrs. Evans, finally looking to make peace with herself for the crime she committed all those years ago. They had no way of knowing Miss Chandra was already dead."

I swallowed.

"You sent the letter?" I couldn't believe it.

"The other letter," she continued, ignoring me. She stepped back and surveyed what I looked like now. She was loving this. Loving how she was tormenting me. "The other letter invited them to participate in some ridiculous charity event in Sri Lanka. Once they were there, a cut brake line on their rental car was all it took."

She didn't slap me, but I recoiled like she had.

"M-my parents?"

I could barely breathe.

She smiled.

"You're so much stupider than I thought. It's like you didn't even care what was real and what wasn't. You never even realized that the last postcard wasn't from them. That I sent it to you myself. That message was from me. I couldn't wait to see you, *my sweet girl*."

Oh my fucking god. She was crazy. She was absolutely nuts.

Fear and desperation crashed over me in waves.

"W-why?" I managed. "Why would you go through all of this?"

She stepped behind me again and started undoing the rope that bound my hands.

"That's a really good question, Lihini. Why. Why not? I suppose is the better question, no? Why not? Why shouldn't I have found you?

Why shouldn't I have left you alone? Why shouldn't I have, when you took away from me the only chance of hope that I ever had? Why not?"

She yanked me up to my feet and pulled my hands in front of me, retying the length of nylon. I didn't try to twist away. Not just yet. I had to pick the right moment. I had to keep her talking.

"S-so, all this was revenge?"

Paloma's smile wavered. "Don't get me wrong. It was fucking hilarious watching you go crazy. But there's something more important that I wanted."

What? What more did she want? She'd already taken my parents away from me. What else was there?

"Access to your life, you dumb bitch."

What?

"I needed all the documentation, of course. Ida had some, which was great. Your parents had entrusted her with most of it, and she kept it labeled in a handy folder, right there for me to find. But I still needed your social security and adoption certificates and all that. And I only just managed to get them. To think that dumb bitch next door almost fucked everything up when she caught me leaving this house. I only just managed to hide the box when you came out to *save* me."

The missing box from my parents' closet.

"It's a good thing she's freaky as hell, because it was so easy to get you to believe that *she* attacked *me*." Paloma snorted. "But I have everything I need now, finally."

I had to get out of my binds. To get out of this garage, and out of this house. Now. I had to get out now. But I also had to ask—

"E-everything you n-need for what?"

Her smile grew wide. The Cheshire cat.

"To get my life back, of course." She was tying the rope into something. "Don't get me wrong. It was fun watching you unravel. But now it's time for me to finally take back what's mine."

She held a kitchen knife between my shoulder blades and started to lead me out of the garage back inside the house. Oh fuck, where was she taking me? Maybe I could distract her.

"It's money you want? Oh god, you can take it. Take it all. I'll meet Mr. Williams and get the paperwork signed. Then this house and whatever is left in their bank account is mine. You can have it all."

Her smile slipped.

"You think that's all this takes? You think I went through hell all these years for the money? God, you really are fucking stupid. No, Lihini. I don't just want your money. I want your life." She raised an eyebrow. "There's not much left of it anyways. No one left to recognize you. No friends, no boyfriend, no family. No Ida. Definitely no roommate. It'll be easy for us to swap places again. Simple, in fact."

She led me to the kitchen and straight over to the stove. The hot plate was already turned on.

"A-are you going to kill me?" It was a stupid fucking cliché. I sounded like an absolute moron.

"No, Lihini. I'm not going to kill you."

The little animal inside me took a gulp of air. She wasn't going to kill me. She wasn't going to kill me. She wasn't going to kill me. But then why was she still smiling?

"But Gloria is about to die."

And with that she grabbed the rope off my wrists and pressed my hands down onto the piping hot stove.

49

RATMALANA, SRI LANKA

THE GROUND FELT SOFT, like I was sinking into it. But that didn't stop me. I finally saw the heavy, old clock that hung at the top of the main corridor. Ten twenty.

Mr. and Mrs. Evans were supposed to arrive at ten thirty. I had to think fast. The corridor leading to Perera sir's office was deserted, thank goodness. I tiptoed the best I could to a small cupboard I could hide inside and was just opening it when someone grabbed my shoulder, hard, spinning me around.

"You never learn, do you, child?" Miss Chandra's face was red. I had never seen her this angry. She raised her arm up high and slapped me across the good side of my face, but I couldn't even feel it.

"Please, just let me go with them. I won't tell anyone anything. Just let me go with them."

"Too late, child. Too late. I kept you locked up for your own good but now you've ruined it. Looks like no amount of Piriton can keep you down."

Just then, we heard the grating metal sound of the gate being opened.

"Good lord, they are here. What are we to do with you?"

I thought she would drag me back to the sickroom. I got ready to scream well and good. But to my surprise, she pushed me roughly into Perera sir's office.

"I promise," I spluttered. "I promise I won't tell."

"Sit down."

"Thank you. Oh, thank you."

I collapsed into a chair and held my head in my hands. My face was wet. That's funny, I didn't even remember starting to cry.

"There, there now. It'll all be okay." Miss Chandra was rubbing my hair. I didn't see the needle in her hand until it was too late.

"No!" I tried to shout. Tried to push her off. But it was like I was moving in slow motion.

"Stay calm now, child." She hugged me to her wide chest and lifted me to my feet.

I could hear cheerful American voices coming down the corridor. Just in time! They would find me. There was no way Miss Chandra could drag me to the sickroom now.

But she pulled me towards the door behind Perera sir's desk instead. Everything started swimming around me. The injection was working. I fought it as hard as I could, but it wasn't long before I felt my body go limp like a doll.

I slipped between the real and unreal. I could feel my body being pushed into the small room. I knew when Miss Chandra tied my hands together, and when she pushed a rag into my mouth to muffle my voice.

The room was barely more than a cupboard. The mirrored panels on the door only reflected one way, I supposed, because I could see right into Perera sir's office. It was hazy, of course, but then again, everything was hazy.

Mrs. Evans! She wouldn't be fooled by Lihini and Perera sir and Miss Chandra. She would know right away that it wasn't me. She would find me here, and take me home. She would rescue me. She would protect me. She had to. I escaped and got to America. That's the way my story ended. I moved to America and lived happily ever after. It had to be this way.

Mrs. Evans fanned herself with a small booklet as she entered the room. Mr. Evans and Mr. Whittaker followed as Perera sir asked them all to sit down.

I'm here, I screamed, but no sound left my body. *I'm here. Come and find me.*

"They told me she didn't have any special dietary requirements, but I just want to double-check . . ."

Mrs. Evans! I'm right behind him!

"Of course, we know the first few months will be an adjustment, but we are hoping that . . ."

Please! Help me!

"What's the Sinhala word for hello? Do you know if . . ."

I need you! I need you! Please help!

Maybe a weak sound left me then, because they all stopped talking.

"Did you hear that?" she asked. I couldn't see it, but I could just imagine her perfect forehead wrinkling as she spoke.

She started to get up.

Yes! Yes! I'm right here! Please help me!

The door to Perera sir's office swung open. It was Miss Chandra and she was leading in—

Oh my goodness, she was leading Lihini inside. Her hair was in one braid instead of two, and she was wearing my new pink dress from House of Fashions.

She smiled, and I saw her tooth, and it made my stomach hurt—Lihini wasn't my friend anymore. She betrayed me. She was trying to take what was supposed to be mine.

But Mrs. Evans would know. She would know right away that it wasn't me. That it wasn't the same girl who was reading *Wuthering Heights* and who loved pink as much as she did.

"Good morning, Mr. and Mrs. Evans," Lihini said in the same practiced voice that Miss Chandra makes us use when we memorize something. "It's so lovely to see you both again. I can't wait to be your new daughter."

Any moment now.

Any moment and Mrs. Evans will figure it out. She'd realise it was an imposter and demand to see me. Me. I was Mrs. Evans's sweet girl, not Lihini. Perera sir would have no choice but to let me go to them.

"Paloma!" Mrs. Evans cried out, leaping from her chair and wrapping her arms around Lihini. "Welcome to our family!"

I wanted to scream, I wanted to bash my head against the wall, I wanted to kill her.

But it was no use.

Whatever part of my soul that was left withered and died. They were gone. They were supposed to be my family, but they didn't even know it wasn't me.

50

IT TOOK A FEW moments for my brain to register the heat. For a second there, it just felt like my hand was freezing. Then smarting. Then white-hot, agonizing pain.

She shoved a kitchen towel in my mouth as I screamed, until I finally dropped to my knees.

I could barely think through it. Never before had my mind worked so slowly. What the fuck was I supposed to do? I had to buy some time.

"The police!"

"What?"

"Th-they'll call me about Arun. They said they would."

Paloma rolled her eyes. "Oh please, they all could see what a train wreck you were. I doubt they'll come looking for you anytime soon. And even if they did, I'll be long gone by then."

She had tied up all my loose ends. There was no one else. No one who would come for me.

The doorbell rang. Her head snapped back and she glared at me.

"Expecting anyone?"

Maybe it was Sam. Maybe his persistence would pay off after all. But my heart sank. Fuck, the police probably had him in custody. My one shot and I fucked that up too.

"People know I'm here, Paloma." I was crying. My hands throbbed and my head was spinning. "People know who I am. Let me help you. I'll give you the money. Help you set up a life here. I'll make it all up to you, I swear."

Fuck, I just needed a way out of this. One final goddamned lifeline. *Please*, I pleaded silently. I didn't even know who I was pleading to. It's not like I ever prayed. *Please, let me get out of this. If I get out of this, I swear I'll come clean. I know what I did was wrong. I really am sorry. I'll fix it. I'm not lying when I say I'll fix it. I'll explain to everyone what happened. Help Paloma get the life she deserved.*

The doorbell rang again. Maybe if there was a higher power, they'd actually heard me. I had no clue who it was, but Paloma was distracted. Her eyes darted around the kitchen, calculating what she would do next.

"Hello, Paloma? You there?" It was Gavin from next door. Thank god. "Paloma? Look, I know it's the middle of the night. Appy said she heard screaming. Wanted me to check in on you."

"They know where my parents have hidden the spare key. It's only a matter of time till they come inside." It was a full-on lie, but she didn't have a way of knowing that, right?

I could see her weighing this out in her head when the doorbell rang again.

"Paloma?" It was a woman's voice this time—thin and frail. "I'm sorry about earlier. Are you okay?" Appy was here too.

The doorbell again.

And again.

And again.

"Calm down," we heard Gavin say. "Maybe she's not home."

"I'm telling you, something's wrong. I saw that dog walker lady come in here. We have to call the police."

That caught Paloma's attention.

"If you so much as breathe differently," she warned, pulling me back onto my feet and pressing the knife against my back again. My hands were untied but she held my wrists in her left hand, making me yelp.

We shuffled out of the kitchen and into the living room.

"Tell them to go away," she hissed in my ear. "They know you're upset with her. Tell them to fuck off."

The doorstep was quiet. Maybe they'd already gone. I felt like I was going to faint.

"Paloma?"

Appy had crossed over from the front door and rapped on the kitchen window, peering directly at us. It took all three of us by surprise. This was my chance. I stamped down hard on Paloma's foot, driving my shoulder into her neck. It was clumsy, but it bought me the few seconds I needed.

"Appy!" I screamed. "Call the police."

I pushed my way to the front door, screaming in agony from the burns on my palms as I tried to undo the lock.

That was when I felt the knife, hot and red, swipe at my side. It was a heavy throb. More like a punch than a cut. I turned around, leaning back against the door, and kicked her chest, my fingers searching for the doorknob. I heard the knife fall with a clatter. I found the brass handle just as she reached for me again, my forward motion as I swung open the door throwing her off balance.

Served that bitch right.

I didn't wait to see if she recovered. I turned around and tried to flee. "Help!" I screamed. Everything was swimming around me. I could feel my pulse where she had stabbed me.

She yanked my shoulder back as I collapsed onto the porch, forcing myself to roll down the stairs. But she was on top of me without missing a beat.

Her punches and scratches rained down on me. I couldn't breathe. I could barely see. I tried rolling onto my side but she grabbed a fistful of my hair.

Anger pumped through me, almost dulling the pain. I couldn't let her get the better of me now. I reached up and bit her shoulder, as hard as I could.

"You bitch," she snarled as my fist finally connected with her jaw. White-hot pain zapped up my arm, but I felt a snap and used that moment to roll on top of her, anchoring my knees on either side of her body.

It was the first time I really saw her. Her face contorted now in pain and anger. The life that might have been mine.

"You never should have come here," I spat. "You should have spoken to me. I would have helped."

"Yeah, right. So you could screw me over a second time?"

My fingers found their way around her neck. The pain from my burns was blinding, the throb in my side wouldn't recede, but I was determined to hold on.

"I never screwed you over. It was supposed to be me, all along."

"What the fuck do you mean?" Her voice was softer. My thumbs were pressing down hard on her windpipe. I could feel her pulse as well as mine. Black spots danced in front of me.

But I still needed her to know. Eighteen damn years and the selfish bitch still didn't get it.

"The book, Paloma," I spat as I struggled to stay conscious. I could feel something warm ooze down my side. "*Wuthering Heights* was my book. You took it from me and never gave it a second thought. It was always about you. Always so entitled. If anyone was meant to be adopted that day, it was me."

Her eyes widened a little. I couldn't tell if it was because she was finally learning the truth or that she was about to pass out. Probably both.

I was panting now, but I kept on going.

"Tell me, did it even cross your mind that the book belonged to me? That it should have been me instead of you? That you just went ahead and took something that wasn't yours?"

Her face was starting to go slack.

"I didn't want to hurt you, Paloma. I didn't. I was just doing the same thing you were. I was just trying to make things better for myself. How could I have not? You would have done the same. You almost did. It wasn't my fault you got attacked."

I could do it. I could end everything right here. All the guilt and the suffering and lying.

Each breath I took felt like a new stab in my side.

"Paloma!" Gavin was running towards me with a baseball bat.

"Paloma, hang on!"

Finally, some backup. It was over now. I was safe. It was all over.

I could hear the sirens in the distance. I guess Gavin or Appy had called the cops. The cool Bay Area breeze fanned at my face. The sky was inky blue and bright with stars. The prettiest sky I had ever seen, even though it was all dimming around me.

Everything felt like it was moving in slow motion. I could see Gavin run up my drive. At least, I thought it was him. It was all a blur.

He raised the bat high above his head.

"I'm here, Paloma. It's over now."

The last thing I heard was a crack.

51

THE GIRL SITTING ACROSS from me on the BART gave me a once-over before she sat down. It was a quick, summarizing glance. Not one I'm unused to. Just a brief measure of my level of attractiveness, likelihood of mugging her, of stinking up the place with body odor. But there I was, the model minority—well dressed, clean, attractive enough not to be a visual pollutant, but not so attractive that I would be a threat to the date she was no doubt meeting, in a blouse cut so low that she was just one ill-fated jolt away from nip-slip territory.

She gave me a little smile. No need to find another seat this evening. Sure, everyone's nice enough when you're hitting all the right checkboxes.

I ran a hand through my now chin-length hair. The change in style did nothing to stop the frizz from coming on strong as the rain spat down outside. I'd spent a good twenty minutes trying to iron it into submission. What a waste of time and energy. Still, it was a nice reminder that things were different now. I think it was one of those bougie designers who once said that a woman who changes her hair changes her life. And nothing has characterized my life more than constant, evolving change.

I had three more stops to go and it was hard to keep myself from fidgeting. I pulled out my phone and read the email I sent for the millionth time. The reason I was coming out to the city in the first place.

Dear Sam,

I'm sorry I've been quiet. I've read your emails. I got your messages. I understand that you're angry, and upset, and I can't say I blame you. I'm sorry for so many things that I know an email would probably never make up for. But we've both had to make do with so much already, so here goes—

I'm sure by now you've gathered the truth about what happened, or some version of it anyways. It turns out that our past always has a way of catching up to us, or we catch up to our past, I guess. Either way, it's been a rough few months.

That's why I thought it would be best for me to stay away from you, at least for a little while. I needed time to, well, to wrap my head around everything, as cheesy as that sounds. To come to terms with who I really am. To be honest with myself and carve out some semblance of the life I've always wanted. A life without lies. Without masks.

But I do have one last thing to take care of, and that's how I left things with you.

I was right—an email will never cut it. You know I'm terrible with words and I think you deserve to hear an

apology from me directly. Could we meet? Maybe we
could start over? Heights on Friday, at 7:30?

x Paloma

His reply came minutes later—a clipped *Sure, see you then.* He was
wounded, and rightfully so. It's not every day that the woman you're
seeing accuses you of being a murderer and then refuses to speak to
you for six months.

But he'll be there. That was who he was. He'd never stand up someone he loved. And I know he did—why else would he not give up?
Calling, emailing, going by the house and speaking to the neighbors,
even though I was long gone by then.

The city ebbed and flowed as I made my way out of the station. It
was damp and perhaps a little dirtier than usual tonight, but I loved it
anyways. I was finally free to float along as I liked. To swim away to my
new life, leaving my past behind me, just a black dot on the horizon.

I was so lost in my own world that I almost bumped into a white
man holding hands with a brown woman. I froze for a second, my
heart jackhammering in my chest while I fought off the instinct to
duck into a dark corner. But I had nothing to be worried about, of
course. Of course it wasn't Gavin and Appy. The woman smiled politely at me and stepped aside, making way for me to get around her. I
exhaled as I passed through. I'd done a really good job of avoiding
them since the attack, and I'd hate to ruin my streak. I still wake up in
a panic every night, with dreams that he killed me instead of her. I
know that he'd pretty much saved my life. That they both did, in their
own way, even though she was too hopped up on antidepressants and
edibles to function half the time. Understandable, I suppose, when
you're drowning in grief. I've never lost a child, of course, but I know

a little bit about being overwhelmed by the unfairness of it all. To look for different ways of escape.

I never thought I'd say it, but thank god for Mr. Williams, who took care of everything I didn't want to deal with—which included the police, the finances, and all the space I needed from the couple across the street. Everything except convincing an overzealous Sri Lankan boy to leave me alone, not that he didn't politely try. But even he finally shrugged and told me that I should think about making my peace with Sam. That Sam said he would report me missing or something ridiculous like that if I didn't return his calls.

A homeless woman sat on the sidewalk wearing an oversized green jacket, her hood pulled all the way over her forehead. I stopped to drop some change in the bowl she had set down by a cardboard sign—GOD IS A WOMAN, AND SHE'S DEFINITELY MENOPAUSAL. I hear you, sister.

She grabbed my ankle as I started to move away.

"I know," she sneered.

"Excuse me?"

"I know what you did," she said, baring her yellow teeth. Bits of spittle flew at me.

"Get off me," I barked, pulling my foot away.

"Excuse me, miss, is this woman troubling you?" A clean-cut Boy Scout type stepped in, ready to save me. But I didn't need saving. Not anymore.

"I'm fine." My tone was rough as I pushed past them both and kept walking. I made sure to kick over her bowl of change as I left. I was never a sweet girl.

I took a deep breath as I climbed the stairs to the bar. I wanted Sam to be there, seated, when I arrived. If he was seated, then he was committed. He couldn't leave as easily. Every little bit helps.

The air was chilly up on the rooftop, and it was early enough that the place wasn't too busy yet. I spotted Sam right away, at a corner table, away from the bar.

He was staring at his phone, scrolling the way you do when you don't really care what's going on but still want something to do. Killing time, I guess.

His lips pressed together tightly, and his shoulders were pulled in like he still held on to every molecule of tension from the last months. The police must have really grilled him, because his many, many emails to me explained everything in unnecessary detail. That he never said he worked at the Curry Palace, that the Taj Masala was just across the street and the uniforms looked similar enough for anyone to just assume. That he never, ever claimed that Arun was a friend from work, just a friend. That he never lied. That he never had a reason to. His desperation to be believed grew stronger with each message, even though I knew beyond a doubt that he was innocent.

But still, he was here, wasn't he? Angry or not, he had showed. Not trying as hard with his outfit as when he was here the last time, though he did have product in his hair and his sneakers were so white they were practically glowing. He looked thinner than I remembered, and he'd grown a short, neatly clipped beard. I didn't hate it.

I tried not to let that distract me. I couldn't afford to get distracted now.

He looked up as I approached his table, smiling, though it melted away into disappointed confusion when he locked eyes with me.

"Sorry, for a second there I thought you were someone else."

I didn't let his deflation affect me.

"I usually have that effect on people." I smiled just the right amount. Enough to be amiable but not wide enough to be overly friendly. The balance had to be just right. There was too much riding on this. "I guess I just have one of those faces. This seat taken?"

His smile this time around was polite, and didn't really reach his eyes. The smile of someone who still didn't know he was my very last loose end.

"Actually, yes. I'm waiting for someone."

He instinctively checked his watch while I stuck my hand in my purse just long enough to make sure the knife was still there. Good. You should have left it alone, Sam. You shouldn't have kept poking, asking to see me, threatening to go to the police.

"Looks like they're running late," I laughed, helping myself to the stool across from him. He had been waiting for at least an hour, after all. Even he wouldn't wait forever. "I'll make you a deal. If your date doesn't show up in the next ten minutes, why don't we get out of here and go for a walk?"

He hesitated a moment. I could feel my heart beat harder in my chest. Could hear it in my ears.

But then he gave me a little smile and shrugged.

"Sure, why not?"

I smiled back.

"Whatever will be, will be."

Acknowledgments

When you are a sappy, gushy softie who expends a considerable amount of energy in order to appear composed, writing acknowledgments is a dangerously slippery slope. I've reached for the box of tissues far too many times since starting this, but here we are, my dream has come true, and I am so very grateful. Words on a page will never be enough, but here goes . . .

To my wonderful, amazing agent/therapist/reassurer/idea-soundboard/friend, Melissa Danaczko. Thank you for always having my back, and working with me to make this story what it is today. It would take a book far longer than this one to realistically convey how lucky I am to have you in my life.

To my brilliant, inimitable editor, Jen Monroe. I knew from the moment we spoke that you *got* me and the story I was trying to tell. Your enthusiasm and excitement have made such a difference to (typically anxious) me. I absolutely love working with you and can't wait to write more dark, twisty stories with you in the years to come.

ACKNOWLEDGMENTS

To Jessica Mangicaro and Elisha Katz for being so proactive, de-lightful, and so very good at navigating a terrain which I am absolutely petrified of—marketing. To Loren Jaggers and Stephanie Felty, who handled publicity. To the fantastic production and copyediting team, Jennifer Myers and Angelina Krahn, I am indebted and awed by your attention to detail. To Candice Coote for all your hard work. To Tawanna Sullivan for handling my sub rights.

To Emily Osborne for my absolutely stunning cover that I can't stop staring at.

To everyone else at Berkley who has done such an amazing job of getting this book on the shelf. I am so privileged to have such a wonderful team.

To my terrific UK & Commonwealth editor, Eve Hall, and the wonderful team at Hodder and Stoughton, especially Sorcha Rose. I am so glad my book found its home across the pond with you!

To everyone at Stuart Krichevsky Literary Agency, and especially to Hannah Schwartz, who helped me navigate the tricky waters of international agreements and (my worst nightmare) taxes.

To Hannah Vaughn, my film agent, whose love for the book early on really bolstered my confidence in this story.

To Janet Reid, aka the Query Shark, who calmed me down, helped my revise my query, and continues to inspire a multitude of writers through her blog.

To Tory Hunter for being an early reader of my book and whose positivity and helpful feedback gave me the confidence to finally start pursuing representation for my writing.

A huge thanks to DvPit and its organiser, Beth Phelan, for giving writers from minority backgrounds a platform to connect with agents. The work you do is truly life changing—I should know.

Any writer will tell you that stringing words together comes with mountains of self-doubt. I don't know how I could have ever gotten by without the constant stream of support from my cheerleaders.

To my 2021 Berkley Debut Group—fondly known as the Berkletes. The road to publishing might be bumpy, but we've held one another's hands through the good times and the bad. Meeting you talented, inspirational writers has been my favorite part of this journey.

To Sisters in Crime, and especially my chapter, the Guppies. To Karin Fitz Sanford, who swapped manuscripts with me and gave me such fantastic feedback. And to the phenomenal Hank Phillippi Ryan, whose support and encouragement means the world to me.

To Crime Writers of Color, with a huge shout-out to Kellye Garrett.

To the Sri Lankan writers and creatives who have always supported and encouraged me—Yudhanjaya Wijeratne, Navin Weeraratne, Thilani Samarasinghe, Thushanthi Ponweera, and of course, the multi-talented Sandun Seneviratne.

To the strong, amazing women I am proud to call my friends. Who always go out to bat for me, who are always excited for me, who always keep it real—Hanni, Mondi, Tashi-wawa, Raai, and Mariya.

To my incredible, supportive family— To Amma & Thaththa, who have always been more excited for my successes than I am. To Malli and Ashi Nangi, for their unwavering love. To Aunty Shehani, and of course, to Thaththi, who told me stories on the way to school every single day.

To Granna, who taught me, through her own example, what it meant to be fearless and independent. Who encouraged me to unapologetically chase my dreams.

To my huskies, Hector and Harley, who never let me write in peace but fill our lives with so much love.

To my little brother, Gavin (who can finally leave me alone now that he has a character named after him), for his fierce, unquestionable support, even when I'm being a demanding princess.

To my mother, Kanisha, without whom this book would never have been written. Without whom I wouldn't be half the woman I am today.

To CJ for being my first reader, idea generator, ruthless analyzer, head cheerleader, and, most importantly, best friend. Every day is a happy day because I have you next to me.